THEN COME LIES

SILVER SPOON SERIES
BOOK 2

NICOLE FRENCH

raglan

To mothers out there of all sorts.
You are queens to me.

PART 1

THE CHEF

PROLOGUE

SIXTEEN YEARS AGO

Xavier

A finch chirped somewhere nearby. It was a proud chirp, loud enough to channel through the crisp February breeze and announce the bird's presence over the polluted noise of buses, vagrants, and pedestrians hurrying their way down South End. Right in the middle of Croydon, on the roof of my mother's flat and above our restaurant on the street, a bloody bird was the loudest thing around.

I took a pull on the cigarette I'd pinched from Emmanuel, the dishwasher, then turned to glare at the bird. It hopped toward me along the rooftop ledge, looking for crumbs, maybe, or seeds like Mrs. Abbott sometimes left on her window next door. Its beak opened again, and out came a song audacious enough to match its orange plumage, the only bright thing in this godforsaken corner of London with its crumbling bricks, deserted storefronts, and tagged signs.

How fucking dare that bird, today of all days?

"Fuck off," I ordered it, and then, as if to emphasize the point, I stubbed out the cigarette a few inches from the finch and rose to my feet, pinched in the too-tight shoes Mum had bought me last year for a school performance. My feet were so big then she'd had to order them special, save up a month's wages from selling bentos to the Japanese school downtown. Now my feet were almost a size fourteen.

But who would find me shoes now?

The finch chirped again, took another daring hop, then chirped once more, proud as can be. Cheeky bugger. Couldn't it recognize a brush-off when it saw one?

"I said, fuck off," I told it. "No one wants to hear your silly song this morning. We're busy."

"Well, I hope you've got better manners for the rest of us."

The bird flew off, and I turned to find Elsie Crew standing at the rooftop entrance, tapping her black patent leather shoe and beckoning me with a gloved hand. She looked as prim as ever in her typical skirt and buttoned jumper. Only this time, everything was in black. And Elsie never wore black.

But we all were today.

"Your relatives are asking for you, boy. I can't understand a word they say, but I think the one who's your granddad wants to talk."

I sighed but obediently rose. Not my style, I know, but I owed her respect, at least. Elsie was Mum's best friend. Her only friend, really, since it's hard to make many when you're dividing your time between raising a kid and running a restaurant. They'd met when Mum first started the izakaya, just after I was born. Elsie was volunteering at the library, and Mum needed to work on her English after she had to drop out of university to have me. She took Elsie's class, and then Elsie started coming round the restaurant until she eventually started working there too, managing the books when Mum didn't have the time.

Now we were both out of a job. And out of one Masumi Sato.

Elsie had been taking care of things over the past week. Okay, she'd been taking care of me. Not hovering the way the rest of them did, but really useful things like Mum used to do. Changing bedding or Hoovering the floors. Things I never learned because I was too lazy or stubborn. A bad son.

I'd learn them all now, though. I'd learn every fucking one and wear an apron to boot if it would bring Mum back.

"I'm coming," I told Elsie, suddenly unable to contemplate what that meant to either of us. A world without Mum. Fuck. It hurt so fucking much.

"Wait, boy."

I turned to find Elsie extracting a mint and a can of air freshener from her bag. She offered the mint, which I took without argument, and then proceeded to douse me with the spray.

"Elsie!" I protested, waving my hand through the scent. "Christ, I didn't ask to smell like a fucking rose garden."

"Watch your mouth," she said, as always, without a pause. "And it's better than smelling like a pub, I daresay. You've still got relatives to care for down there, and they'll want answers without thinking Masumi's son is no better than a common street urchin."

"Maybe I am a street urchin." I waved away the spray, though some of it did land on me. Great. I smelled like a bloody flower shop.

"You're too tall for that," she countered with another stealthy spray. "You can't pickpocket when you stand a foot above most people on the street. No way to blend in. Especially with those eyes and that smile."

I just scowled.

Elsie's face softened, and it was then I noticed the small lines around her gray eyes and pursed lips had deepened over the last week. "I know it's hard today, but don't forget to smile," she said and reached up to tuck a bit of my black hair out of my face. "Your mother did love it so."

She turned and dabbed a finger in the corner of her shining eyes. I sighed. I wasn't the only one struggling in the wake of Mum's death.

"What about you, Els?" I asked her. "What will you do now?"

She turned back to me and straightened her shoulders. "Take

care of you, that's what. I told Masumi I would, and I plan to keep my word. Don't you worry."

I snorted. "When would you have told her that? Before or after the car hit her?"

A jerk on my tie forced me to look down again. Elsie was a little thing, but she was strong.

"Xavier Sato Parker," Elsie enunciated clearly, using all three of my given names, even the last one I hated. "If you think there is any chance your blessed mother would leave you in this world alone and penniless without a single person to care for you, my boy, you've got another thing coming. You will absolutely finish your studies, and you will do your very best. You were the center of your dear mum's world, and the only thing she ever wanted was for you to make something of yourself, more than she could. So I am not going anywhere."

I opened my mouth, then snapped it shut, feeling a bit like an awkward crocodile. "W-what—how?"

Elsie sighed, looking a bit resigned. "I didn't want you to worry about it all just yet. When I started helping Masumi with the accounting, she insisted we set up a separate trust for you. It's not very big, but it's enough to give you something, my love. Enough to hold off a disaster."

She told me how much was in the account, and not for the first time, I thanked my ancestors that Elsie had taught Mum English all those years ago. It wasn't a fortune by any means, but it was enough to pay Emmanuel and keep the lights on until I took my A-levels and figured out what to do with the place. It was enough to keep my home.

"Ch-Christ on a bike, Els," I croaked. It was all I could manage. "I didn't know."

The hand on my tie reached up to stroke my face again. It was hard not to cry. That's exactly what Mum did the last time I saw her. Right before she went out for groceries and never came back.

"You weren't meant to, sweetheart," Elsie said kindly. "Now

come on. Time to return to reality. Can't sit up here squawking at the birds forever."

As if in agreement, the finch gave a loud chirp from the other end of the roof, then flew off into the gray.

I followed Elsie down the flight of stairs and through the landing into the living room with its secondhand furniture and cracked tile. I tried to get it as neat as I could without Mum's help, but of course, Elsie came in with a cart of cleaning sprays to finish the job. I was glad she did. This morning, the place had been packed with neighbors. Now, though, only a few well-wishers remained.

Emmanuel was busy cleaning the kitchen, despite the fact that he wasn't getting paid for it today. He nodded with a wink, as if to say, *Don't worry, I got this.*

I turned to the small sitting room with the old, flowered sofa Mum and I had dragged up here from the curb when I was ten and the furniture she thrifted from the local Oxfam when I was a baby. The only people left were my grandfather, Kiyoshi, and my uncle Ichiro, both of whom had flown all the way from Japan. They stood together near the table I'd used as a buffet, eyeing what was left of the food like they thought it might be poisoned.

As I approached, I offered a slight bow, palms pressed together, just like Mum taught me.

"*Gomen-nasai*, Ojiisan, Oji," I said in my limited Japanese. "Just needed a bit of air. Elsie said you needed something?"

My grandfather nodded with the same tired, bewildered expression he'd worn since walking into his estranged daughter's home for the first time two days ago. I'd only met the man once before, during a week-long trip to Okazaki three years earlier. To say it was disappointing would be a massive understatement. After being branded a foreigner and a bastard here in England my entire life, I'd hoped for a bit more of a homecoming. But at thirteen, I was lanky and overgrown, already topping six feet with a face full of acne and teeth we couldn't afford to straighten yet. My height and blue eyes already made me different—then I opened my mouth, and my stunted

Japanese, learned from my mother in her few off hours and the Saturday school I practically slept through, earned only snickers and disgust.

Kiyoshi muttered something to my uncle, his default interpreter, once he realized my Japanese wasn't great. Ichiro turned to me with a mild scowl, which seemed to be his permanent expression.

"My father, he want to know when we will go..." He frowned harder, waving his hand around like he was batting away a fly. "Put the ashes."

"Put the..." After a second, his meaning occurred to me. "Oh, you mean spread them?"

"No, put," Ichiro snapped. "In the temple. Where it is?"

I swallowed. "Ah...the temple?"

It wasn't the first time I'd gotten grief for cocking things up. Both my grandfather and my uncle had been horrified when they'd discovered I'd had Mum cremated days before they arrived instead of waiting for them. Well, it wasn't like it had ever occurred to Masumi to educate her son about the intricacies of a Japanese funeral. Ojiisan was still a relatively young man, and Mum wasn't exactly planning to die at thirty-six, was she? How was I supposed to know they wanted to sit in the crematorium while she turned to ash, then pass her bones around with chopsticks? At sixteen, how was I supposed to know how to do any of this?

Especially without her?

My grandfather laid a hand on Ichiro's arm and murmured something in his ear.

Ichiro turned back to me impatiently. "My father wants to know if you have a box for the ashes for us to take. Yes?"

I swallowed. Shit. "Ah, no."

"No?" Ichiro repeated like he was parroting an idiot bird.

"Mum didn't want that," I said. "In her will, that's what she said." At least she had that. "She does want to go home. But she asked that I bring her back to Okazaki so she could rest in the river."

With every word, a fist seemed to close itself around my heart. I didn't want to talk about this. Fuck, I didn't even want to be here. I was just a sixteen-year-old kid, for fuck's sake. I should have been at the park kicking the shit out of a football. Maybe getting stoned in Jagger's attic or trying to score with the girls at Croydon High. Literally anywhere but in this room, talking about this subject with these people who so clearly hated me.

My uncle's face turned red, and he looked like he wanted to punch me, but he dutifully turned to his father and translated. Instead of mirroring his son's rage, though, Kiyoshi, a slight man with hunched shoulders bent by years of work, appeared thoughtful and eventually nodded.

"*Hai*," he agreed before making a fluid response I couldn't for the life of me understand.

Ichiro looked like he wanted to argue, but he turned back to me. "My father says this is acceptable. We will take my sister's remains with us tomorrow when we return."

The fist around my heart tightened. "What? No."

Ichiro's eyes narrowed. "No?"

I shook my head. Why was it so hard to talk at moments like these? "I—no." I cleared my throat. "I want to bring her."

Immediately, my uncle shook his head. "We are her family, and we go home. You—who knows if you can—"

"No," I interrupted, clearly shocking him with my rudeness. I knew enough to understand that in Japan, my insolence would have never been tolerated. Well, too bad, Oji. You're just going to have to deal. "Mum wanted me to finish school, and I know she would want me to be the one to bring her home. I can come at the end of term, to have some time to save for the trip, but not before. That's all."

With another sharp scowl, my uncle translated my reply. Kiyoshi just looked at me for a long time while Ichiro muttered something to himself that I would have bet was the equivalent of "this sodding idiot."

Unable to help myself, I rose to the challenge. "What's that, Oji?"

"I say," Ichiro snapped, "this food is wrong. We should have fish."

I glanced at the table, with its picked-over menu I'd prepared that morning with Emmanuel. All Mum's favorites, ones that had earned us a fair number of regular customers and reviews in the local papers over the years. They were her legacy, really. The only thing she left behind other than my sorry self. I wasn't going to let this arsehole shame that.

"I made them in her honor," I told him. "I know it's not fish, but perhaps you'd like to try the inari? That's the closest to sushi we've got."

I picked up a tray of rice-filled tofu skins off the table and offered it to my relatives. I was a lousy waiter, but I could hold a damn tray. My uncle scowled at the platter and shook his head. My grandfather, however, removed one from the platter and took a small bite.

His features were transformed with surprise, and his dark eyes popped open. "Not inari."

I closed my eyes with dread. "No, technically, it's not. I'm sorry, Ojiisan. It was Mum's favorite, though."

I turned to replace the platter, not wanting to see the look of disapproval I knew would be there. This time, I couldn't quite bear it.

I was maybe ten when I combined the traditional tofu skin with the risotto I made from Mum's secret dashi, shitake, lion's mane mushrooms, and the best black garlic in her kitchen. It was an expensive mistake that forced her to remove her black garlic miso soup from the menu for a week. But she was so happy with the new recipe that she served it instead. And once a week, I'd make it just for her so that, for once, she didn't have to cook for anyone else and could be the guest.

I turned back to take my seat only to find my grandfather watching me while he finished the inari.

"Who make?" Indelicately, he polished off the final bit and reached around me for another.

I watched warily. Did he actually like them? "Uh, I make. I mean, I made them."

Kiyoshi's surprise deepened. "You make?"

I nodded. "Yeah. I thought—"

"Ichiro," my grandfather interrupted, then rattled off something I roughly translated as "eat this *now*." That I knew. I'd heard it enough from Mum growing up.

My uncle frowned and shook his head, not even sparing a glance at me. But Kiyoshi snatched the tray and jabbed the inari at him until Ichiro had to take one.

"Mmmph," he grunted. But then he took another bite. And another.

Kiyoshi smiled, then broke into another string of exuberant Japanese. Begrudgingly, my uncle nodded back. And then, almost as if he didn't want to, he popped the last bit of the inari into his mouth and swallowed.

I frowned at both of them, wondering what the hell had just happened. Kiyoshi caught my bewildered glances, and his worn face softened.

"I say," he offered in stilted English. "Best inari I eat."

I blinked, unsure if I'd heard him correctly. "Thank you," I stammered. "*Arigato*, Ojiisan."

"Now. When you come?" He snatched the last inari, took a bite, and waited.

Watching him eat my food relaxed me enough to respond. I never understood it, but there was something satisfying about watching someone enjoy dishes I'd cooked. I wasn't worth much, but I could make things taste all right. It was the one thing I could actually add to this world that was any good.

"Well, term ends in June," I told him. "But I've got a break mid-April. If I can save up enough, I could probably bring Mum then, if Emmanuel and Elsie can run the restaurant without me. So long as I'm back before the twenty-fifth of April, I think it will work."

I waited for Ichiro to interpret, but before my grandfather could reply, another voice interrupted.

"It will need to be a bit after that, unfortunately."

The three of us swung around toward the unfamiliar voice. Well, unfamiliar to them. Though I'd only heard it a few times in my sixteen years, I would have known it anywhere.

A boulder-sized pit grew in my stomach as I turned. "Dad?"

My voice emerged about an octave higher than its normal level, like I was again that scrappy thirteen-year-old skulking after his mother, trying to be a man before he could quite get there.

Rupert Parker stood in the doorway of the flat, gazing over the scene before him like he was surveying newly conquered territory. At the six feet, five inches that matched my own, he was one of the few people I'd ever met who could look me in the eye. That and his blue eyes were the only things I'd inherited from him.

His skin was fair, his hair an ashy, graying blond, his clothes designer and tailored—a far cry from my own lightly tanned skin, black hair, and the badly fitting suit Elsie had forced me into this morning. Nothing about him belonged in this flat. This scrappy little life that had belonged to Mum and me. He'd never wanted anything to do with us at all.

My father's steely eyes hopscotched over each remaining person in the room—Emmanuel, Jagger, Elsie, my erstwhile relatives—before landing on me.

"Hello, Xavier," he said in a voice that was low but still channeled around us. He turned to my grandfather and uncle and nodded politely the way certain men do to the help. "Gentlemen. You must be Masumi's relatives. Rupert Parker, at your service."

Behind him, someone cleared his throat, and my father stepped into the flat, revealing my other uncle, Henry Parker. My uncle was maybe an inch shorter but shared the same pale features and long nose as the rest of the Parker dynasty. His eyes, however, were slightly kinder than my father's steely blues.

He nodded at me. "Hello, boy."

I just nodded back.

"I'm afraid my son's trip to the Far East will have to wait," Rupert reiterated as he eyed the refreshment table skeptically. "He is due to start Eton next week."

My mouth fell open.

"What?" I demanded, finding my voice at last.

"Oh," Elsie gasped from the sofa. "My...goodness? Eton *College*?"

"No, Eton primary," Rupert answered sarcastically. "What other Eton is there?"

"Don't talk to Elsie like that." I stood up a little straighter. "And I have a school. I don't need to change now. I've only a year left after this."

"Orchard Park is hardly an acceptable institution for a Parker," my father stated while he studied the room.

"Well, I'm not the bloody Prince of Wales," I argued back. "I'm not going to any Eton fucking College."

My father's blue eyes, as unfazed as the sky, glanced at his brother, who only shrugged, before turning back to me.

"I'm afraid you're mistaken," he said. "Now, I regret very much the unfortunate circumstances in which we find ourselves. As I regret we have not had time to become properly acquainted before now. But that is not your choice to make. You are my son, Xavier. And you are my responsibility now."

ONE

Francesca

"Ces. Ces, baby, are you all right?"

I blinked ferociously, trying to get the flashes out of my eyes, along with the sudden sting of tears. My ears rang with strangers calling my name, capped with the roar of engines and constant clicks.

Or not my name, exactly. Only one person called me that. Ces, pronounced "Chess." A shortened version of my full, formal name. Francesca Zola. Which seemed to roll off only one man's tongue. Someone with a deep voice. And blue eyes. And an English accent.

That exact voice pulled me from an oblivion laced with too many other voices to distinguish. This one, though, had a deliciously deep accent born in South London. This one growled through my dreams and beyond.

That's right, I was with Xavier Parker. All six feet, five inches of gorgeous, brooding man who took my virginity and gave me the greatest piece of my life: my daughter.

To some, it would have been a fairy tale. And in some ways, it did feel that way. What else would you call it if you'd run into your child's father not quite six months ago on a wintry night and close to five years since you'd seen him last?

And then held him at arm's length for months afterward, trying to determine whether this seemingly cold, brazen man was, in fact, fit to be a father?

And then discovered that said man wasn't simply a chef and restauranteur but, in fact, a member of the British peerage, something of a prodigal duke?

And then fell completely in love with him anyway, secrets and all?

Xavier's harsh exterior had melted into a more loving and kind man than I'd thought possible—especially when it came to Sofia, our daughter. And then, by some miracle, he'd fallen in love with me too, despite the secret I'd kept, thinking it in my own best interest.

Fate intervened, so they say. And after four years of life as a single mom, I'd not only found my child's father but also the love of my life.

Talk about luck.

Now I was here. In England, a land I'd visited through countless novels, seen through the eyes of too many heroines. I'd pretended to be Elinor Dashwood or Elizabeth Bennett in my dreams since I was a kid. But here I was, in the arms of my love like a real-life British romance heroine.

Or not quite.

We were outside Heathrow Airport, where, just as Sofia and I had found Xavier, the three of us had been absolutely swarmed by cameras, reporters, and throngs of people interested in...me?

"*Mamaaaaa!*"

A loud wail further yanked me out of my daze, and I turned toward Sofia, who was flailing from Xavier's arms toward me like a baby octopus, crying and rubbing her eyes as the flashes continued to go off around us.

"Baby, don't rub," I said, taking her from him and balancing her on my hip despite being half-blinded myself.

"Do you mind?" Xavier snapped at the crowd. "She's four."

"Your Grace, who is that?"

"Is that your daughter, Xavier?"

"Is this the American you've been seeing?"

"Fuck off," Xavier growled.

Without waiting for a reply, he shepherded Sofia and me through the crowd, out to the curb, and into the back of a large black car with tinted windows. The doors shut, and though the questions continued through the windows, they were much easier to ignore.

"Here, darling," Xavier murmured as he stroked Sofia's hair back from her face, which was currently buried in the collar of my fleece. She turned sideways and rubbed her nose into his Arsenal jacket, which left an impressive trail of snot leftover from her cryfest.

Xavier, to his credit, didn't seem to care. That would have told me he was an actual parent if nothing else did.

"I've got you, Sof," he told her as he petted her black curls, mussed from the flight. "They're gone now."

"Xavi, our bags—" I started.

"It's fine. Jagger'll get them."

A few seconds later, the back of the car opened, and I turned to find the rakish, goateed face of Jagger Harrington, Xavier's best friend, grinning at me over the seats as he tossed my suitcase, backpack, and Sofia's various paraphernalia into the trunk. Elsie, Xavier's assistant, had already taken her seat up front with the driver. After he finished, Jagger elbowed his way through the reporters and climbed into the middle row, and turned around to greet us.

"All right?" he asked.

"Did you know it was going to be like that?" I wondered to Xavier over Sofia's head. Her whimpers were softer now, but her eyes were still scrunched closed while she clutched her favorite stuffy, a unicorn named Tyrone.

Xavier looked over my shoulder, toward where I assumed the

paparazzi were still in view, and shook his head. "Not like that. It's never been like that."

"Well, except after your mum passed."

Jagger turned from the front and flashed what could only be called a cheeky grin. Other than the Wayfarers perched atop his head, he looked like he had marched right out of a Regency novel, ready to duel over the honor of a fair maiden or maybe just a gambling debt. My baby sister Joni, an equally shameless flirt, would have been all over him.

"Crowded their way down South End, didn't they? Once your dad came through, anyway," he continued. "And then, after you found out you were the heir. That was pretty bad. And again when Rupert died. And when you expanded the Parker Group, and you brought that model to the opening—"

"That's enough, Jag," Xavier cut him off. His tone was sharp, though his touch on Sofia's neck and the hand that sought out mine were gentle. "Jagger, Els. You've already met Ces. When she's ready to say hello to the world again, this is our daughter, Sofia."

Sofia just buried her face deeper into my neck, clearly unwilling to meet anyone just yet.

I offered a grim smile to Jagger and Elsie. "Hi, guys."

Elsie offered a sympathetic nod. "Hello, darlings."

I stroked Sofia's back, as I had since she was a baby, while she shifted herself back and forth on my lap in a move I recognized as a search for movement, just like when she was a baby. My little girl was growing, but she wasn't too big for rocking hugs yet. And truth be told, I could have used a little rocking too.

Lord, we hadn't even left the airport, and we were already overwhelmed. Six weeks ago, I'd taken the biggest leap of my life since becoming a single mother at twenty-three by agreeing to spend the summer with Xavier. Eight hours ago, I'd still been sleeping on my brother's landing. Two days ago, I was still an elementary school teacher struggling to make ends meet while raising her four-year-old daughter.

It was supposed to be the start of a fairy-tale ending. But right now, I was feeling less like a princess and more like Alice toppling down the rabbit hole. Agreeing to spend the summer in London with Xavier was just the next crazy stop in Wonderland.

Because I wasn't anything special. Just plain old Frankie Zola. Bookworm, wallflower, messy bun-wearer. Fourth child of six, daughter of a deceased mechanic and a recovering alcoholic, raised in the most average house in the Bronx. The idea that someone like Xavier could love someone like me was still, well, unbelievable.

Even now, on a casual Sunday afternoon, we didn't match. Xavier's dark jeans, red and white Arsenal jacket, and flashy blue sneakers all looked like they had been purchased at the mall on the way here. His shiny black hair, cut close at the neck, slightly longer up top, was casually mussed in a *British Vogue* sort of way that paired delectably with the trimmed stubble around his jaw and the tattoo that snaked up his neck from beneath his jacket collar.

I, on the other hand, looked exactly like I had just gotten off a six-hour flight with a four-year-old, complete with a wrinkled T-shirt from Target, my favorite grandpa sweater that was pilled under the arms, and leggings stained with the remnants of chocolate milk Sofia had spilled on the plane.

Hot, I know. They call me Princess Pajama Party back home.

And yet, when I looked up from comforting our daughter, there was Xavier, hovering over us both like we were the most precious things in the world to him. His clenched jaw cut in the car's dark interior, full bottom lip pulled apprehensively between his teeth. Those dark blue eyes sparkled with concern, yes, but also joy. Especially when they met mine.

Men like Xavier Parker didn't fall for women like me. But he had. Twice.

"'I wonder which way I ought to go,'" I murmured, quoting Lewis Carroll's classic.

The hand on my lap squeezed, and I looked up to find Xavier watching me with a knowing look. Our eyes met, and for a moment, I couldn't breathe. Gone were the phantom flashes and echoed shouts as everything about him came into focus.

"Who are you now?" he asked quietly over Sofia's whimpers.

I smiled shyly. He always knew, somehow. "Alice. In Wonderland, of course."

I was rewarded with his own smile, which somehow warmed the car and quieted the chaos outside even more. "Welcome to London, gorgeous."

I couldn't help but grin as that warmth extended into my chest and made me hum with happiness. I knew how rare Xavier's smiles really were. I could have basked in the glow of it for hours.

"All right?" he asked.

Tentatively, I nodded. "We are now."

Even so, the knot of anxiety in my belly remained, particularly as I recalled Jagger's comments. Was this what his life was like here? Hounded by cameras and crowds? Cornered into luxury cars that were no better than moving cages?

Why had he never mentioned it before?

What had Sofia and I just stepped into?

"Daddy?"

As if she could hear me thinking, Sofia stopped sniffling and sat up to face Xavier.

My heart thrilled. It never stopped, that feeling when Sofia used the D-word to address Xavier. For all four years of her life, I'd never told her who he was, believing at the time that he had abandoned me for another woman. I hadn't known the whole story, of course. That his former fiancée was only a friend, Lucy. That she had had cancer and never really wanted to marry him in the first place. And that she'd died shortly after he'd gone back to help her.

How could I have known? I'd never tried to contact him, either.

When he'd returned to New York last winter, I'd been terrified all over again, not just of being hurt myself, but that he would hurt Sofia too. My own heartbreak—I could handle that. But hers? Never. But despite the fact that he was definitely still learning the ropes of parenthood, Xavier had turned into a surprisingly gentle and devoted father. And once Sofia had learned who he really was to her, she hadn't looked back either.

Daddy, he was now. Daddy, he would always be.

"Hello, darling."

Xavier grinned at her too, the blinding brightness of his smile making her squeal. She wriggled out of my arms and climbed into his lap, still clutching Tyrone by the horn. Yeah, the last weeks apart hadn't done much to quell her enthusiasm for her dad.

As for us...well, it wasn't quite as clear.

On the last night I'd seen him, Xavier had told me in no uncertain terms that he loved me. It had been the night of his restaurant opening in New York. Chie was an homage to his love for his daughter...and, as he confessed that night, for me.

They didn't work without me, he said. He needed me. Loved me, even.

And then he promptly had to return to London, though not without inviting us to join him when we could.

At the time, it felt like all my dreams were coming true. Since then, however, despite daily phone calls for Sofia, check-ins, and text messages, he hadn't said the words again. Apparently, we were at the "I love you" pronouncement stage but not at the generic type before the end of a phone call. Definitely not at the phone sex stage—not when we hadn't even had a real date yet.

And so there was this odd tension. It was a strange feeling to be sitting next to a man I had slept with exactly twice since he had walked back into my life, fantasized about nearly every night since (and, let's be honest, a whole lot of nights prior), who had told me once he loved and adored me...without knowing at all how to act around him.

Xavier extracted one of his hands and squeezed mine, almost as if to say, "me too, babe." I offered a slight smile in return, but the discomfort remained. Was it selfish of me to want a hug too? I also could have used a kiss hello. Hell, I wanted a lot more than that.

I just had no idea how to ask for any of it.

That's one thing they never tell you about motherhood. It becomes almost impossible to ask for things for yourself when you spend almost all your time anticipating the needs of others.

"'If I loved you less, I might be able to talk about it more,'" I murmured to myself as I gazed toward the blocked traffic.

Over Sofia's head, Xavier quirked a black brow. "Another quote?"

I blushed. "How did you know?"

"You had that dreamy look on your face," he replied. "Who were you pretending to be now, then?"

I reddened even more. I had forgotten about his annoying habit of reading even my daydreams so easily. No one else in my life had ever figured out my tendency to pretend I was the heroine of my own romance novel.

"*Emma*," I admitted.

"Is she hot?"

I rolled my eyes. "She's a book character. Although that particular quote was spoken by her true love, Knightley."

Xavier rolled his eyes. "Wanker."

Sofia chuckled and whispered "wanker" into his shoulder.

"Oh my God," I said. "Don't be jealous of a fictional character."

Xavier just leered. "Ben, let's go," he called to the driver, though he made no move to release Sofia.

Obediently, Ben started the engine and flipped on the blinker as he looked to move into the outgoing traffic. Still, Sofia lay in Xavier's arms, happily singing a song under her breath that sounded a lot like the arrivals jingle in the airport crossed with "Twinkle, Twinkle, Little Star."

"Xavi, um..." I gestured at the two of them as the car began to move.

Xavier looked up sweetly. "What's that, babe?"

I felt like I was a penguin living in the Twilight Zone, the way I was flapping my hands around. Did he really not know what I was thinking here?

"Xavi, she needs to be in her own seat."

He glanced toward the traffic, which was hardly moving, then back at Sofia before pulling his hand from mine so he could wrap both arms around her. "No worries. I'll keep her safe. Can't stop a girl from hugging her daddy, can we?"

I frowned. This was legitimately sweet and all, but was he being serious?

The car moved again, then came to a lurching stop. Ben slammed on the horn. Sofia jerked forward with the movements.

"Xavi, seriously," I said. "Her booster is in the back. She can't sit in your lap like that. It's dangerous."

Xavier opened his mouth like he wanted to argue, but before he could, Elsie turned from the seat up front.

"I'd do what she says, boy," she said. "It's a thousand-pound fine if you're not wearing a seat belt. And they might call social services if the girl's not in a proper car seat. You don't want to end up looking like that pop star in the papers, do you?".

"I remember that," Jagger concurred. "They practically crucified that Katie Derek for driving around with a baby in her lap. You don't want to be called an unfit mum, do you, Xav?"

Despite the jokes, Xavier scowled at all three of us. Reluctantly, he unwound his arms from Sofia, reached a long arm to grab her booster from the back, then placed the seat between us and took a few extra moments to buckle her in safely.

"There we are," he said. "Snug as a bug in a rug."

Sofia giggled and gripped Tyrone harder. "That's for sleep, Daddy, not the booster."

"Ah, well. How about...sweet as a beet in your seat, eh?"

Sofia tipped her little head and wrinkled her nose. "Are beets sweet?"

Xavier winked. "They are when I make them." Then over her head to me, with considerably less sparkle: "Happy, now?"

It was slight, but the resentment in his voice surprised me. Xavier wasn't typically passive-aggressive—no, he was the type to come banging on your door in the middle of the night, shout profanities at prospective suitors, and growl at anyone who looked at him wrong. Or maybe that was just Xavier in America. Was Xavier in London the type who cared more about what the damn papers thought than his own daughter's safety? I didn't like to think it, but apparently so.

"I am," I told him cautiously. I didn't want to fight. Not within minutes of seeing each other. "So, where are we headed?"

He pulled out his phone. "There's a bit of a fire I've got to put out at one of the restaurants." He smirked. "Chef's acting up again. Got to put him in his place."

In front, Elsie tittered to herself. I could only imagine what Xavier "putting him in his place" looked like.

"Then I thought maybe we could take a walk down to the river. Maybe see London Bridge, and later we could all get dinner. There's this new place in Camden I'd like to try out. They've got a black cod that's getting raves, and I want to know if it's better than mine."

"Like the song?" Sofia immediately started singing "London Bridge is falling down," though without the ability to pronounce the letters *r* or *l* fully. She was working on it, poor kid, but they weren't quite there.

"That's right, babe," Xavier said. He looked at me. "What do you say, Mum? Feel like a codfish?"

I made a face. "Mum? Codfish?"

His grin turned a bit more mischievous. "Babe?"

I shook my head, suddenly annoyed. "Why don't you try something that isn't what you call hundreds of other people? Frankie's fine."

Instantly, his grin disappeared. For a moment, I thought he might give in to the urge to argue too.

Instead, Xavier leaned over Sofia, who was still singing her song, and whispered into my ear, "How about my perfect, luscious, inexplicably delicious Francesca?"

He ended with a nip on my earlobe that no one else in the car seemed to notice before sitting back in his seat, clearly satisfied. No wonder, since my heated face had once again turned the color of a scarlet rose.

How could he do that with just a few words? And in a car full of people, no less?

I bit my lip. His eyes lasered onto the movement.

"That works," I murmured.

The grin returned.

Between us, Sofia gave a massive yawn that was big enough to interrupt her rendition of "London Bridge."

I looked up at Xavier. "I think the restaurant and the rest will have to wait, though. Can we start with a nap? She didn't sleep well on the way here."

Xavier's hard edges softened a bit more. "Of course. I should have thought of it in the first place."

His guilt was palpable. He was getting much better at anticipating Sofia's needs, but I could tell he still felt horrible when he missed something so basic. Things like car seats and naptimes weren't quite on his radar yet.

"Ben," he called up front. "Back to Mayfair."

TWO

"Why all the press?" I asked while we waited for an elevator inside the lobby of a gorgeous Georgian building. In other words, relatively modern as London design went, but still practically ancient to my American eyes.

Mayfair was full of this type of architecture, white stone facades and curling millwork that decorated the outsides of otherwise modernized flats or, if the residents were wealthy enough, three and four-story houses that lined curving streets sandwiched between Hyde Park, Buckingham Palace, and the lively Soho district. Xavier's building was the tallest of them all, high enough that its top floors had a solid view down to the Thames—or so he said.

Jagger had taken the car to attend to whatever restaurant issues needed fixing so that Xavier could accompany me, Sofia, and Elsie up to his apartment.

Beside me, Elsie arched one gray-flecked brow at my question but said nothing.

"Er—" Xavier looked somewhat ashamed. "Sort of bad luck, really. *The Guardian* ran a profile on me and the Parker Group last week. Part of the new push for Chez Miso and also Chie's opening in

New York. But then the tabloids sort of picked it up alongside my uncle's disappearance. And then someone tipped them off that you were coming. Then about Sof. And here we are?"

I frowned. "Someone 'tipped them off' about Sofia and me? Who would do that?"

He blinked. Elsie looked distinctly uncomfortable.

"To be honest, it doesn't matter," he said.

"It doesn't matter who's gossiping about us? You and I literally just got back together. Only a few people really even know I exist."

Xavier just huffed and stared at the ceiling. "Honestly, Ces, if I worried about every cook or hostess who passed on some bit of conversation they overheard in the restaurant, I'd have to fire every person who works for me. It's not worth our time or energy to figure it out."

I glanced at Elsie, who was only watching Xavier with an expression that looked almost like regret.

The elevator doors opened, and we stepped inside.

"But why is your uncle still such a story?" I pressed as the doors closed. "You found him, didn't you?"

Xavier had only shared the bare minimum over the last six weeks, generally preferring to keep our daily phone calls to matters concerning Sofia and our impending move to London. Our conversations had been friendly, but to my disappointment, not particularly deep or emotive. He just wasn't a phone person.

Although he did like sending suggestive texts. Those were fun.

His uncle, however, was the reason we were in London at all. Henry Parker's sudden disappearance last spring forced Xavier to cancel his plans to expand his restaurant empire to other cities in the US. Parker wasn't lost anymore, but not, so far as I had gathered, in a state to continue running the family's portfolio of holdings.

There my knowledge on the matter ended.

"Well, someone found him, yeah," Xavier said. "The old man had a stroke when he was hunting in Scotland. Don't know why he was up there alone in the first place. First rule of stalking—go with someone or tell them where you've gone. It's too easy to get lost in the Highlands." He shook his head. "Bloody Georgina."

"That's your stepmother, right?" I asked, trying to remember our earlier conversations.

Xavier nodded. "Narcissistic bit—of a disaster," he recovered with a sharp look at Sofia, who was watching him expectantly for profanity. She earned more off her dad than her uncle—and that was saying something, given my brother's penchant for cursing.

"She's quite the treat," Elsie added dryly.

"She's probably the one who put him up to it," Xavier added. "All she wants is the place to herself. Can't stand the way he curbs her spending and the like." He shook his head with obvious disgust. "Anyway, a sheep farmer found him and brought him to the hospital. Took nearly three weeks for him to get enough speech back to say who he was. That's why we didn't find him right away."

Xavier's eyes darkened. More than a little guilt was obvious there. As if he could have prevented any of this from happening.

"The papers just like a good story," Elsie said. "Nothing you could have done about it, boy."

"Yeah, well, now I have to—" Xavier started before the elevator doors opened, effectively cutting him off.

Sofia bounded out in front of us, eager to move and explore her new surroundings after hours on a plane. Family politics forgotten, Xavier grabbed our suitcases and led us into the biggest apartment I'd ever seen. A landscape full of shine and polish, gleaming chrome, and bright light.

And completely devoid of color.

"Ooh! Comfy!" Sofia's sneakered feet screeched across a white marble floor that covered nearly the entirety of an enormous loft space and at least thirty feet between the entrance and a giant white couch she had spotted. Under which was a very white and expensive-looking rug.

"Sof," I called out. "Shoes off, baby girl. Be careful—"

"Let her be, Ces," Xavier said. "Well, except for the shoes off. We don't wear shoes inside, babe," he told her.

I obediently slipped off my beat-up New Balance and set them beside his bright Nikes, then straightened the sparkly slip-ons Sofia had thrown toward us.

There. Three in a row, nice and neat.

At least they seemed to make sense together.

Then I turned, and everything else seemed surreal.

I wasn't sure what I'd been expecting. Given the old-fashioned nature of the neighborhood, I'd rather thought the inside would be equally traditional, if anything. But despite being in a neighborhood that looked like it was sketched straight out of an Austen novel, Xavier's apartment was clean and utterly modern, firmly grounded in the twenty-first century.

It took what seemed like an hour just to tour the cavernous space. The living room alone was bigger than the entire house I'd grown up in, including two seating areas situated around a house-sized gas fireplace that flickered despite the fact that it was the beginning of July. One contained the couch into which Sofia had dived like a swan on vacation, plus two oversized white leather chairs. On the other side of the fireplace stood a white baby grand piano bookended by two light gray Chesterfields for listening. Beyond that, framed by floor-to-ceiling windows through which a panoramic view of London twinkled, was a Lucite dining table that could seat at least twelve with a crystal chandelier bearing at least as many lights.

"I didn't know you played," I said, gesturing toward the piano.

"Hmm?" Xavier looked up from his phone. "Oh, I don't. The designer chose that to fill the space."

Ignoring the fact that he even lived in a place and had the money to spend on an extremely expensive musical instrument *to fill space*, I continued to look around.

Xavier headed toward the kitchen, which somehow managed to be the biggest space on the floor. That at least made sense, considering Xavier's profession. Even so, it was also the most intimidating, set back against the same view of London as the rest of the place, with luxe marble counters that matched the floors. Bright white cabinets shone with the light, surrounding two sets of double ovens, two six-burner AGA ranges, the biggest fridge I'd ever seen, and three separate prep sinks arranged on an island that went on for miles.

Everything was immaculate. Nary a sponge left in any of the sinks, not a smudge on the chrome fixtures, nor a single crumb lingering on the marble. Like everything else in this apartment, it was bright, white, and showroom perfect.

Cue my entrance in stained leggings and a messy topknot, with a four-year-old version of Pigpen in tow.

This was all very pretty to look at, but how in the world were Sofia and I supposed to *live* here?

"My office is just there," Xavier said, pointing toward a desk the size of the Mayflower ensconced in a room entirely made of glass. "And then down the landing are the bedrooms and the other bathrooms."

"Who are they all for?" I asked, wondering why I actually hoped there would be only two. "You, Sofia, me..."

"For all of us. We need our own space."

He seemed to think he was giving me something. And he was, I supposed, though I didn't know why the idea of living separately made my heart sink. Then again, we'd known each other—really known each other—for only six months or so. Why should I expect to move into his bedroom in that short a period? He'd invited me to spend the summer with him, not marry him, for Pete's sake.

Right?

Elsie cleared her throat loudly but appeared to be inspecting the counters in the kitchen.

"Er—and for the rest of your family, should they ever want to visit," Xavier amended.

The rest? I had five siblings, two of them with spouses and kids, plus a grandmother and an errant mother. Xavier was perfectly aware of this. Just how many other rooms were there?

I found I didn't want to know. Not yet.

"Why do you always get the penthouse?" I wondered as I tiptoed into the kitchen. "I'm assuming that's what this is. We're too high up for it not to be."

I shouldn't have been surprised. Xavier had a thing for the top floors, even springing for the Plaza penthouse in New York as his primary residence for the last several months, despite the fact that it must have cost more than Ivy League tuition.

"Because he wants everything to be as tall as he is." Elsie chuckled before crossing the room to sit with Sofia.

Xavier only offered a crooked smirk while he shoved his phone into his jacket pocket.

"Why?" I found myself pressing. "Considering how much you travel, it seems like you're barely here to enjoy it."

"I spent long enough at the bottom of things," Xavier said quietly. "Now I prefer to be above it all. Is that so wrong?"

I frowned at the defensiveness again in his tone. We were the ones with jet lag, but that was the second time I'd heard that kind of fatigue. "I was just wondering."

Xavier cast a sort of shy glance my way before striding to where I stood, picking up my hand, and pressing a quiet kiss to my knuckles. "Take a look around. It's your home now, too."

Home?

Nothing had been more uncertain than that concept was at this moment. Now that my brother was getting married, home wasn't necessarily the red brick house in Red Hook anymore. Nor was it my grandmother's place in the Bronx, where I hadn't lived for over four years.

But it wasn't this place either, cold and white and sterile. I was already imagining spending the next two months hovering around Sofia to make sure she didn't inadvertently turn something pink with a broken marker or leave footprints across the marble. Could anyone really come back here and feel as comfortable and safe as one needed for a place to be considered home?

"'Home is the place where, when you have to go there, they have to take you in,'" I murmured as I continued to look around.

Well, if that was the case, was Xavier taking us in here because he felt like he had to? Or was there an expiration on this invitation?

I guess we were here to find out.

A set of fingers slipped under my chin, and I looked up to find Xavier watching me with another crooked smile.

"Another quote?" he wondered.

"Robert Frost," I replied with a low exhale. "One of my favorites."

Xavier tipped his head. "You know, Ces, I wonder sometimes if you use other people's words to avoid saying what you really think."

One black brow rose, as if to dare me to admit the truth. But before I could, we were interrupted by Sofia's loud squeal.

"Mama, watch me!"

I turned to find Sofia running all out from the dining room into the living room, then stopping suddenly to slide several yards in her socked feet across the marble. Right toward the edge of another plush carpet and a coffee table with a very expensive-looking planter in the center of it.

"Sofia!" I cried. "Oh, honey, wait!"

But before I could stop her, her feet caught on the rug, sending her head-first into the plush white expanse. She somersaulted across, knocked into the bottom of the coffee table, and sent the planter with the biggest white orchid I'd ever seen—and its collection of soil —flying.

"It's okay, Mama," Sofia said, sitting up proudly as if she'd just completed an impressive stunt on the jungle gym. "I'm all right, see?"

"I'm glad, Sof," I said, hurrying over to squat next to her. "But I'm not sure Daddy's carpet is."

Sofia looked to where I was trying to gather the remains of the orchid into its glass container. Unfortunately, the more I dug for the bits of soil, the more they seemed to sink into the strands, which were far too soft to be made from something as pedestrian as polyester or even wool.

"Relax," Xavier said, coming to stand next to us. He bent down to pick Sofia up. "It's just a stuffy white rug. I don't care about it, anyway."

Behind him, Elsie's brows practically touched the roof, and I thought I heard her mutter, "Since when?"

"Xavi, oh, I'm so sorry." I wagged my hands around, unsure of what I should do.

I'd never stopped to wonder what his home might be like before we agreed to come here. For some reason, I'd pictured him in a flat like the one he'd described from his childhood, but of course, he wouldn't be content with a one-bedroom apartment over a restaurant. This was Xavier, who liked things big and luxe and wasn't afraid to foot the bill. Of course, he would own a penthouse in one of the most expensive neighborhoods in London. And, of course, it would be almost exclusively decorated in things that could be stained in a half second.

Perfect for a rich bachelor who was hardly here.

Less than perfect for a spill-prone daughter and her mommy.

"Elsie," Xavier called to his assistant. "Can you—"

"Already on it." She squatted next to me with a miniature vacuum, a spray bottle, and a rag. "It's a good job, too. Otherwise, we'd never get this mess out. Ruin a twenty-five-thousand-pound rug."

My jaw dropped. The rug alone cost more than half my entire salary.

"I think we need to make a few changes in the decor, Els," Xavier said, still holding Sofia's hand. "Not quite appropriate for Little Miss here, and I'm sorry I never thought of it. Can you get Rose to redo it?"

Elsie nodded. "I'll see what her schedule looks like."

Xavier turned to Sofia. "I do have one more thing to show you. Would you like to see your room?"

"I have my own room here, Daddy?" Sofia wondered. "Just like at home?"

Xavier winced slightly at the mention of home. "Of course you do, babe. What kind of dad would I be if I didn't at least give you that?"

Sofia giggled. "Show me!"

To the tune of Elsie's vacuum saving the day, I followed them down a long hallway, counting at least seven doors before we reached the end, where two opened into a large bedroom that I guessed was the primary suite, and another that appeared to be for Sofia.

"I seem to remember someone loves a certain Disney movie," Xavier said as he led us into the smaller of the two. "I hope you're all right with a *Moana*-themed bedroom, babe. Because that's what I told the designer."

It was every little girl's dream—especially Sofia, who immediately catapulted onto the bed in the center of the room. The walls were painted with a tropical mural of palm trees and water with decals of the Disney characters from the movie integrated into the scene. The bed itself was shaped like one of the Polynesian ships the characters took and draped with blue and green veils of silk to recall the sea, while the rest of the furniture similarly evoked the aesthetics of life in the South Pacific. There was even a replica of Maui's hook on one wall, an array of Disney princess costumes hanging on the other side of the room, and every single character in stuffy form lay waiting for Sofia to explore on the bedspread.

"I hope it's not too much," Xavier murmured as I came to stand beside him.

"Oh, it's definitely too much," I replied. "But look at her. She's so happy."

"Well, I've got some years to make up for. Figured I'd start here."

"I think you've filled your quota."

But Xavier just shook his head while he watched Sofia discover a dollhouse in the shape of a Polynesian hut. "Not even close. Come on."

He took my hand, and we left Sofia introducing herself and Tyrone to a new collection of dolls while he guided me into the room next door. Well, sort of room. Suite. Apartment. Mansion-sized wing. Airplane hangar.

"This is my room," he said.

Technically, it was a bedroom, if you could call something that might shelter a small jet a bedroom. It was covered wall-to-wall with the same plush carpet that made up the rug in the living room, with a four-poster bed swathed in near-transparent white fabric that matched the linens. A couch faced another fireplace near a window overlooking Hyde Park and a sliding glass door opening onto a terrace. One of two other doors opened into a bathroom the size of the Taj Mahal, continuing the same gorgeous marble as in the rest of the apartment, with a tub that could fit four Xaviers, a shower for as many, and a double sink lit with mini-crystal chandeliers that sparkled light all around.

I wandered back out to the bedroom, where I found Xavier leaning casually against a long bureau, thumb to his lip while he watched me pensively.

"Well," he asked. "Like it?"

I couldn't quite read his face.

"It's beautiful," I agreed, somewhat nervously. This felt like a test.

"But?"

I sighed. "Why do you think there's a 'but'?"

He folded his hands over his belt. "Because I know that look on your face, Ces. It's your 'good mum' look, when you're checking for danger."

I grimaced. "That obvious, huh?"

Sometimes I could be a good mom or a good girlfriend, but certainly not both.

Xavier just shrugged and waited for a reply.

"I am a bit afraid to touch anything," I admitted as I looked around again. "Especially after what happened out there with the planter. But you've already called your designer. It's fine." I took a deep breath. I didn't want to spoil things with criticism before they'd already started. "Do you want to show me my room now?"

"Your room?"

I turned. Xavier's tone was even sharper than before, and he stood tall now, on alert.

"*Your* room?" he asked again. "The fuck do you mean, your room?"

I looked around, feeling even more like I was messing things up. "Out there. All the bedrooms. You said...we...we all needed our own space. I figured one would be mine. I just assumed—wha!"

Before I could finish, I was literally swept off my feet, then tossed onto the cloud-like bed with a distinctly ungraceful thump. The duvet floated up around me, then back down as Xavier crawled up my body and pinned me to the mattress while he framed my face with his hands.

For the first time since I'd arrived, our differences faded away. Here, I couldn't see the contract between our clothes, housing, or anything else that made me feel so utterly inadequate compared to Xavier and all his glory.

Here, it was just his beautiful face, with its full lips, angular jaw, and penetrating blue eyes peering down at mine.

"Francesca."

The formal use of my full, given name sent ripples up my spine. Xavier slipped a hand down to my waist to hold me still. As if I could move at all, caged under his big body.

"I thought you were smarter than that," he said as he peered down at me, dark eyes fathomless, unmoving.

"I—I am smart," I stuttered, though I'd never felt more like a fool.

"Then how in bloody hell could you think I'd ever let you sleep alone under my roof?"

Oh.

Realization and relief flooded me all at once. And finally, that tightness in my chest started to unravel.

I tried to move, to get out from under that penetrating gaze, but he was stone, holding me in place.

"Woman," he pronounced, keeping my chin firmly in place. "I thought I made it clear. You belong to me. Just like I belong to you. You're not sleeping less than two feet from me anymore, much less in another fucking bedroom. Is that clear?"

We gazed at each other for a few seconds until it became obvious he wasn't joking. Or looking away until I answered.

"Yes," I said, feeling a bit like a chastised schoolgirl, albeit a very turned-on chastised schoolgirl. "That's clear."

His grip on my jaw softened, and Xavier closed his eyes. When they opened again, the anger was gone, replaced by something gentler and yet somehow more potent.

"I missed you," he admitted as his thumb stroked my right cheekbone.

The tension in my chest loosened a bit more. "I'm glad. But you could have said so once in a while, you know. It was a long six weeks of five-minute phone calls."

Xavier shook his head, causing a lock of black hair to fall forward and tickle my brow. "Honest? I think I was afraid to say it. If I admitted how much I really missed you and Sof, I'd have flown right back across the ocean to find you again. And I had to wait. I had to be here." His forehead met mine again. "But I promise, I hated every fucking second without you."

Trying to encourage his timorous touch, I nuzzled him back. "Well, I missed you too, Mr. Parker. A lot."

Those full lips smiled against mine. "Yeah?"

"So much."

He kissed me, sweet and slow, as he cradled my face between his broad palms and worshiped my mouth for several minutes. But just as I was about to slip a foot around his calf and tug him close by the belt loops, he rolled to one side, freeing me from my Xavier-shaped cage so we could look at each other.

"I want you to be comfortable here," he told me. "Both of you. I know it's not right yet. The furniture, the colors, everything. But we'll make it right for all of us. Whatever you want. The cost is no matter."

I stayed quiet, unwilling to admit, either to myself or to him, that I wasn't sure I could ever be comfortable in such grandeur. Back home, I hadn't even graduated from a landing at the top of a stairwell to a full bedroom of my own yet. And Xavier wanted me to accept a palace?

I couldn't help wondering how Elizabeth Bennett might have felt on her first day at Pemberley. It seems all happiness and sunshine in romance novels. No one ever writes about what happens after you say "I love you."

"Earth to Ces," Xavier murmured, taking me by the chin again to pull me back to the present. "Stay with me, babe. Don't go daydreaming too far just yet."

"I—let's just take one step at a time," I said. "Like getting to know each other again. Maybe go on a date first, before you let me redecorate your house."

He examined me for a moment or two before apparently making a decision and pulling me back against his body, tucking me into the crook of his arm so he could curl around me there on the bed.

The effect was immediate. From the moment I'd left New York, it had been nothing but chaos. But here, cocooned against Xavier's warm body, I started to truly relax for the first time since getting on the plane. I had a feeling it was less to do with the sumptuous bed and more with the iron-strong arm draped over my waist and the solid heartbeat under my cheek.

Maybe Robert Frost was wrong. Maybe home isn't where they have to take you in, but where they'll always want to.

Would that ever be the case with Xavier?

I found I hoped it could be true.

Xavier's lips touched my brow. "Better?"

I hadn't said anything, but he had still sensed my discomfort.

I inhaled his clean, strong scent and sighed. "Better."

"Good." He shifted, moving as if he was going to get up.

"*No*," I said, burrowing further into his chest. "I don't want to get up. I'm finally comfy. Six hours in coach with Sofia sleeping on my lap isn't comfort."

"I said you should have let me pay for first class," Xavier chided. "Anyway, this was just a preview. Elsie is on duty for the night, Ces. If I leave you here, you're going to fall asleep too. Up you get."

And then he was gone, bounding off the bed and through a door that apparently led to a walk-in closet the size of his kitchen.

I pushed up from the pillow, my limbs heavy. Lord, I was tired. And it was only four o'clock.

"You up?"

I rolled over as Xavier appeared from the closet dressed in only his jeans, putting his impressive physique on display. I sat up with appreciation, taking in the stacks of lean, sinuous muscle that paved its way down his stomach and past the denim waistband, including a winding tattoo that covered most of his left shoulder and arm and curved just up his neck. For such a large man, he was really quite graceful.

"Mmm," I hummed at the view.

He turned from the dresser. "Like what you see?"

"I do. I'd like to see the rest of it, too, if you're willing."

Suddenly, I did not want to get out of bed at all. But I didn't want to go to sleep either.

"Oh, no," he said with a grin I mentally noted as his "cheeky one." "Remember, you're the one who said you wanted me to pretend to be a gentleman. So we're going out before that jet lag sets in for good, lady. Pop an espresso and let's go."

THREE

Two hours later, after a long shower, unpacking, and enjoying the best espresso I'd ever had from an enormous Italian-made contraption in the kitchen, I was ready for my first night out in London.

Just the idea banished all sense of jet lag and had me dancing in my sensible black pumps while I swiped on the last of my mascara.

Here I was, getting ready to explore a city I'd dreamed of visiting since I read my first Jane Austen novel at the tender age of ten. I stood in front of the floor-to-ceiling mirror in Xavier's walk-in closet. It was hard to call it my closet too when the things I'd brought from New York occupied approximately one-sixteenth of the space. The rest was filled with rails of designer suits, stacks of bright new denim and impossibly soft T-shirts, and an entire wall of limited edition sneakers that had probably been worn all of once, if at all. It was a far cry from my thin collection of thrifted sweaters and out-of-fashion jeans.

And so I stood in a new-to-me silk frock, borrowed from my sister Kate's vintage collection, which fluttered around my shoulders and knees as I tried to determine whether I was ready for my first actual date with a restauranteur-cum-duke.

I'd been waiting years for this. Maybe my whole life. How many romances had I devoured on my little landing in Brooklyn? How many times had I watched *Bridget Jones* or *Four Weddings and a Funeral*? How many times had I pretended that I was one of the women picked from obscurity, seen by a gentleman of standing when no one else could?

Maybe I wasn't exactly getting a happy ending here. Not yet. After all, this was just a date, not a wedding. And yeah, my duke was the filthy-mouthed Arsenal fan, not a genteel Byronic hero.

But my little Anglophile heart was brimming with excitement, anyway. Excitement and nerves.

"We're going to have a lovely time, aren't we, Little Miss?" Elsie was saying as I found her sitting with Sofia at the Australia-sized kitchen island. "We've made good friends already, you and I."

"Mm-hmm," Sofia replied, mouth full of a crumbly treat. "Best friends."

"That's a compliment right there," I said, joining them at the counter. "Not just anyone gets to be best friends with this one. She's picky."

My heart skipped a bit, taken back to similar moments I'd had sitting at the bar in my grandmother's kitchen, helping her make manicotti or roll out cookie dough. Elsie, Xavier had told me, was much more than an assistant. His mother's best friend, she had been in his life since he was a child himself and had been the only stead-fast part of it since Masumi passed when Xavier was just sixteen. Considering my own mother's less-than-stellar presence in my life, and Nonna's age, this lovely woman might be the closest Sofia was ever going to get to a grandmother of her own.

"Well, don't you look nice," Elsie said, clearly approving of the swishy blue dress. "That color looks just like Miss Sofia's eyes, doesn't it?"

"Just like them!" Sofia agreed. "And Daddy's too!"

She gave me a crumb-wreathed little grin, as if she'd been planning it the whole time.

I tried not to flush. Okay, maybe I had been thinking of Xavier's bright blues when I'd picked the dress out of Kate's collection.

"Don't eat any more of those, baby girl," I told her. "You don't want to spoil your dinner with cookies. And Elsie, please try to keep her awake until at least six thirty to get on London time. Otherwise, she'll be up at four, I'm guessing."

"Of course, dear. No problem at all. That's what the sugar's for, you know."

"They're not cookies, Mama. They're biscuits. Elsie said."

"She sounds English already."

I jumped at the sound of Xavier's deep voice, and we all turned to find him lounging on the sofa across the room, one long arm spread across the back, the other hand busy texting. He had changed too and looked more duke-like than I ever remembered. The sporty clothes and Arsenal paraphernalia had been replaced by a sleek, black three-piece suit that made his shoulders look impossibly broad and his hair shine black as night.

"Look, you match!" Sofia announced with glee, pointing at Xavier's blue shirt and tie and my dress. "Like a prince and princess!"

I grinned. But Xavier did not, suddenly scowling when his phone buzzed with another message.

"Everything all right?" I wondered, approaching cautiously.

"Fine, yeah. Someone's...misbehaving."

My spine tingled. I knew exactly what Xavier was capable of when I "misbehaved." In the past, we had a tendency to fight that generally evolved into toe-curling kisses and being taken on kitchen counters like this one.

But I didn't think he was referring to that sort of transgression.

Lord, it had been a long six weeks, I thought as I watched him scowl at his phone. For a second, I had a mind to let Sofia go to bed as early as she wanted, drag Xavier back to the bedroom, and let him take out his frustrations on my hungry body for as long as he needed.

Xavier continued to look at his phone, oblivious to my thoughts. But eventually, he seemed to feel the intensity of my stare and looked up.

"Sorry," I murmured. "You, um, ready to go?"

He shoved his phone into his jacket pocket with a huff and then stood up and faced me as I slid off the stool. The scowl fell away, replaced by something equally wild yet deliciously wicked as his eyes scanned up my body, taking in my black heels, bared legs, short skirt, tailored bodice, and the hair I'd washed and curled around my shoulders.

The tingle in my spine returned. I bit my lip.

"Damn," he said quietly. "You look like a fucking treat."

"Daddy! Swear jar!"

"What's a swear jar, love?" Elsie asked.

I grinned at Xavier. "At home, we keep a jar in the house to help my brother with his, er, speech. He has to put a dollar in every time he swears. Sofia thinks Xavi has the same problem. She's earned a pretty penny off him."

"Well, I can't help it, can I?"

Xavier got up and crossed the room in four quick strides. Sofia watched expectantly as he plucked a twenty-pound note from his jacket pocket and dropped it in an empty vase at the end of the counter.

"There's twenty in there, babe," he told her. "Mummy's just too beautiful. She makes me forget my language."

Sofia just scoffed. "Daddy, that's ridonk-u-lous. Mommy's just Mommy. Have some self-control."

As prim as she sounded, I had to laugh a little when she pronounced "control" without the *r* or the *l*, yet managed to sound as imperious as the Queen of England herself.

"Mommy's a princess." Xavier slipped a hand around my waist and landed a kiss atop my head, making me glow. "And princesses make men like me act like animals."

"When the jar fills up at home, we go to Coney Island to ride the

Ferris wheel," Sofia said as she played with a doll on the counter, apparently done with the cookies. Then she frowned, a spitting image of her father's own scowl. "Dad, do you have a Coney Island in London?"

"No, can't say we do," he admitted. For a moment, Xavier looked like he wanted to whip out his phone to have his designer build one right here in the living room.

Sofia's frown intensified. "Then what the heck are we going to do with all that money? I'm going to earn a lot from you."

Xavier released me, swept Sofia up from her seat, and carried her to the window in an avalanche of giggles.

"Ah! Daddy! Ahh!" she squealed through her tinkling laughter.

He held her tight, turning her toward the glass. "I don't have Coney Island, but did you see the Ferris wheel there?"

"Oooh. That's a big one."

"That's the London Eye, my love," he told her. "Tallest wheel in all of Europe. One of the biggest in the world. You can see everything from up there. You'll forget all about Coney Island, I promise."

Sofia's bright blue eyes blinked furiously, and her mouth quivered. Lord, she was as mercurial as her father, going from laughter to tears in the space of a few seconds. I shook my head. How was I supposed to deal with them both?

"But I like Coney Island," she was telling him. "I don't want to forget it."

Xavier slumped, obviously sensing he'd said the wrong thing. A glance at me told me I was right. I just shrugged, as if to say, *your mess, your clean-up.*

He turned back. "Well, no. You don't have to forget it. All I'm saying is that we're going to have fun. Maybe more than you've ever had. What do you think about that?"

Sofia examined him for a long minute, then, as if she planned it, cracked another smile. I shook my head. She knew how to milk those moods, too.

"Let's go!" Sofia cried, flinging her arms around her father's neck.

The tip of his long nose pinked with pleasure. Xavier smacked a kiss on her cheek, making her giggle again before releasing her to the floor. "Be good, you little terror. Els, thank you. We'll be back late."

"Don't you worry about a thing, boy. She's in good hands here. Enjoy yourselves!"

———

THE STREETLAMPS WERE on now as twilight fell over London, but the city was still crackling with a different kind of life. This wasn't the hurried crowds of working folks or bumbling tourists making their way through the sites. Instead, it was a mix of those, like us, who came out at night. Women in clothes made to be stared at, men with their chests puffed out like pigeons.

With the windows down, I caught the occasional peals of laughter from pubs or bits of live music dancing out of windows as we made our way through the city. It was a lot like New York that way. Always alert. Always on the move. Always singing with life, in a way.

The ride alone would have been enough for me as the car toured alongside red double-decker buses and hackney carriages. Ben took several detours so that Xavier could point out sites I was eager to find. There was the Tower Bridge. Big Ben. The Houses of Parliament. And so forth.

Soon, I had a list on my phone of too many places to see in a lifetime, much less a few months in one summer. I was jittery and babbling with plans to get to them all when the car finally stopped.

"Come on, you," Xavier said as he helped me out and onto the sidewalk at the corner of Euston Road and what a street sign said was St. Pancras. "Text you later, Ben."

"Right around the corner, sir."

"I think it would take at least a full morning to tour the Tower of London, don't you think?" I asked as he guided me down the pavement. "Then we can walk the Tower Bridge too, and maybe go across the river to explore Maltby Market. Or is that too much in one day?"

Xavier tucked my hand into the crook of his elbow, then escorted me to a crosswalk. "I think," he said, "you'll have time enough to see everything you want."

"Easy for you to say," I told him. "You've lived here your whole life. I only have a single summer. There's too much!"

"Well, right now, there's just this. Look."

He turned me to face the opposite side of the busy street, and it was then I finally stopped jabbering when I realized just where we were.

King's Cross was famous. Anyone who had watched any kind of modern movie about London would know its arched windows and the clock tower, not to mention the gothic spires and romantic arches of the St. Pancras Station alongside it. Down the street, I saw a sign waving for Platform 9 ¾; people shuffled by us, many carrying luggage on their way to catch a train, others finishing their commutes home via the Tube.

There was only one reason Xavier would have taken me to a train station. We were going somewhere—or at least he wanted to.

My heart deflated. Yet again, I was going to have to play the wet rag. But did he really think I would fly six hours to a strange country only to get on a train and leave Sofia? Elsie was nice, but she was still a relative stranger. There was no way I could go anywhere outside the city.

It was like the mishap with the car seat—meant in good faith, but horribly, disappointingly, wrong. And I had to be the one to spoil all the fun.

"No, Ces." Xavier took my shoulder and rotated me gently away from the station. "This way."

After we crossed Euston, he pulled me to the left, then turned briskly down a different, slightly quieter street curving north, lined with brick row houses on one side and an enormous building on the other that extended down the entire block.

My breath caught in my chest.

No. It couldn't be.

Compared to the winding towers of St. Pancras or the relative grandeur of some of the other sites we'd seen on our way here, the building in front of me was staid and dull—a colossal box of red brick that extended for what seemed like miles. No fuss. No beauty. No decorations but the bright flag bearing its name, waving above us like a standard calling me to arms.

I couldn't have been more impressed.

"You didn't," I breathed.

Xavier grinned down at me, the dimple on his left cheek making a rare appearance. "Didn't what?"

I couldn't stop staring. Not because anything I was looking at through the black iron gates was particularly interesting. The utterly normal set of steel-bound double doors wouldn't have impressed anyone, nor would the basic steps or the blasé sidewalk out front.

But none of that mattered. It was the promise of what was inside that already had me spellbound.

"I thought a lot about where I'd want to take you on your first night in London," Xavier said, standing behind me and placing his hands gently on my shoulders. "Buckingham Palace. Victoria and Albert. Maybe just dinner and a walk down St. Martin's. But then it occurred to me there really isn't anywhere else you'd rather see than this."

"The British Library," I whispered.

Xavier looked like he'd just won an Olympic medal. "The one and only."

I turned, and without thinking, flung myself at him with utter joy. Xavier caught me with a laugh, his deep voice echoing off the brick as he lifted me by the waist and spun me in a circle on the cooling summer night. Several passersby looked at us curiously, but we only had eyes for each other.

"Like it?" he asked, lips just an inch from mine.

I clasped his face between my palms. "I love it. You couldn't have done better."

"Is that a challenge, then?"

His mouth found mine, daring me to resist a thorough, breath-stealing, mouth-plundering kiss, right there on one of the busiest streets of London. We had no real audience—yet. No press, no cameras, no intrusive questions. But it was clear that Xavier couldn't have cared less if we had.

Seconds passed. Maybe minutes. But oh, I had missed this over the past several weeks. I spent most of my time hyper-aware of every-thing, tracking the children in my classroom, whether or not Sofia had forgotten her jacket, thinking about bills or work or family, or any of the other minutia I'd carried my whole life.

This man's magic kiss, though, had always managed to make everything fade away.

Xavier kissed me until my breath was gone, and I barely remem-bered where we were. Only that I was in his arms, carried and desired. Wanted beyond measure.

"Welcome to London, my little bookworm," Xavier whispered, brushing my cheeks with his broad thumbs as he gently deposited me back on the ground.

For no apparent reason at all, tears pricked my eyes. I was here, in the city that had beckoned my entire life, in the arms of the man I'd only dared hope could love me. The world was still big and scary, and the future was unknown. But it had him in it.

And right now, that was all I could ask for.

FOUR

"It's very...empty."

A few minutes later, I found myself standing in the lobby of the British Library. Otherwise known as Mecca.

And there wasn't a soul here.

I turned, trying not to notice the way my heels echoed in the great hall. "Xavi, where is everyone? They aren't closed, are they?"

It didn't make sense. The main doors had been open, after all.

Xavier shrugged, even as he stared up at the ceilings, taking in the sheer enormity of the place. I had a feeling he hadn't ever been here either, despite growing up in this city.

"Today's a bank holiday," he said. "I simply requested they open a few rooms for us instead of closing completely."

I blinked. "Open a few rooms."

Meaning, what, the entire block-spanning complex? I didn't even want to think about how much essentially renting out one of the largest libraries in the world must have cost him. Or what kinds of favors he'd have to repay.

"Good evening."

We turned to find an approaching woman in a tweed skirt, hair in a bun, glasses perched on her nose, and a pair of oxford shoes that clipped noisily as she walked across the stone floors. She looked like she had stepped out of a BBC series where she was playing a bookish extra in the background.

"Welcome, Your Grace," she said, nodding in Xavier's direction.

"Xavier, please," he replied, tensing slightly at the address as he reached out to shake her hand. "Or, Mr. Parker, if you must."

"Mmm." The woman did not seem to approve. "I am Edith Willoughby, Chief Librarian of the British Library. And this is your wife, I take it?"

"Girlfriend," Xavier said shortly.

"I—yes," I confirmed, too gobsmacked by the woman addressing us to notice Xavier's quickness to correct her.

This wasn't just someone who spent her days reshelving books or creating Dewey Decimal labels. Edith Willoughby was in charge of some of the greatest treasures of the English language at one of the largest caches in the world. Her being here was like having the President of the United States substitute for a tour guide at the White House.

"Very nice to meet you," I told her.

Ms. Willoughby nodded primly, though she did not return the compliment. "Our collections are entirely at your disposal for the next three hours. However, per His Grace's instruction, we have prepared the requested materials in the Manuscripts Reading Room. Come with me, please."

She turned on her heel, leaving us no choice but to follow her up the steps of the entrance hall.

"Bit stuffy, isn't she?" Xavier whispered.

"Shh," I reprimanded. "You're going to get us in trouble."

For that, I received a cheeky smirk. "Wouldn't be the first time."

So this was what it felt like to be with the bad boy in high school, I thought with a thrill. I'd always been the girl too busy reading to get mixed up with the wrong crowd.

"You sound like a naughty schoolboy," I told him.

"Well, I'm always naughty with you, aren't I?"

As if to demonstrate, Xavier reached behind me to pinch my backside, causing me to emit a squeak that echoed off the tall ceilings. I stifled a giggle when Ms. Willoughby looked over her shoulder at us and quickened her pace.

We were led to a room on the vast second floor of the library, our footsteps immediately quieted on a layer of thick green carpet, atop which rows of reading of carrels lay waiting under high boxed ceilings.

In the center of the room, a number of desks had been laid with a variety of materials, including what looked like several letters, at least three manuscripts, some kind of transcribed music, a box with a flower drawn on the top, and a portable wooden desk opened with a pair of glasses inside.

"If you wouldn't mind," said the librarian, holding out two pairs of white gloves—a smaller set for me and a large set for Xavier.

I took them eagerly, curious to explore the treasures laid out. Then I peeked up at Xavier, who was frowning while he tugged on the gloves. "What have you done?"

He bit his bottom lip and offered a mischievous half-smile. "Can't you tell yet?"

"Please keep the manuscripts on their cradles at all times," Ms. Willoughby instructed. "I shall wait at the desk if you have any questions. These are national treasures. So...do be careful." She opened her mouth like she wanted to say more. It was clear she was very hesitant about allowing either of us to touch the things she'd set out. "Please," she finished, then left us to explore.

"How did you do this?" I wondered, approaching the tables. "You need a pass to access these rooms. My friend did research for her dissertation here, and she said there's an interview and everything."

I tread carefully, feeling like I was disturbing someone's grave or something equally taboo.

Xavier just shoved his hands deep into his pockets and smirked, watching me look around. "One thing I've learned: there's no door you can't open for the right price. In London or anywhere else."

I nodded, though I wasn't sure how I felt about that, honestly. Some things were sacred, in my opinion. I didn't think access to Shakespeare's folios or the Magna Carta should be granted based on the size of one's wallet.

But that didn't mean I wasn't going to take advantage of the opportunity while I had it. It wasn't until I read one of the letters between a sister and her brother, detailing news from home and hopes for a novel meant to meet the success of P. and P. , that I realized what I was looking at.

I jerked up when I saw the familiar signature at the end. "Xavi."

Hands clasped behind his back, his gaze was firmly on me, not the manuscripts. "Hmm?"

"Did you—is this—this is the Jane Austen collection, isn't it?"

Xavier blinked, cheeks ruddy. "Just might be."

"Xavi!"

Finally, his full grin emerged. "Like it?"

"Like it?" I mimicked back.

In response, I received a laugh of pure joy before he pulled me close to deliver a brief but forceful kiss.

"Oh my God," I murmured. "Not in front of the letters!"

He laughed again, then kissed me once more before releasing me.

"I just like to see you happy," he said. "Now try on those specs. If I'm a naughty schoolboy, I want to see what you look like as a naughty librarian."

I shook my head; all jokes evaporated as I looked at the glasses sitting on the desk my favorite author *of all time* may have used to write some of her novels. The idea that such greatness had even touched it—that she might have even worn those exact spectacles while dreaming of Mansfield Park made me shiver, like I'd seen a ghost. "No. I couldn't."

"Scaredy cat."

I turned. "I am not."

"Are too. It's a pair of glasses, Ces. What do you think would happen—the police appear and arrest you for sitting? Break a rule for once."

"I—but she's—but they belong to—"

"Do it for me." Xavier delivered another quick smack to my backside. "Otherwise no supper for you."

I glanced between him and the glasses, torn between seeing that smile on his face once more and obeying my desire to follow the rules.

To absolutely no one's surprise—not even mine—Xavier won.

WE PERUSED the collection for nearly an hour. Well, I perused the collection. Xavier just perused me, apparently content to watch me read, listen to me yammer on about Austen trivia, and noodle on his phone while he waited.

For once, I didn't care about any inconvenience I might have caused. After all, this was a gift, a once-in-a-lifetime experience, and I wanted to soak it up for as long as I could. I was utterly fascinated by the curves of the wordsmith's writing, the little notes she left in the margins of the alternate chapters of *Persuasion*, and the care she took with detail even when corresponding with family. For a few moments, I even sat at the portable writing desk famously gifted to her by her father when she was only twenty. Even at that age, Austen had at least had the belief of her family. He wanted her to continue her passion wherever she went.

I swallowed as I drifted gloved fingers over the fine wood edges. I'd only been four or so when my father died. The same age as Sofia. I had nothing he'd given me—none of us did. And though my mother was still alive, she'd left her children to be raised by their grandmother in what was a warm and loving household but ultimately was still missing the two people who should have been there for us no matter what.

Not like this, I thought, imagining I could *feel* George Austen's adoration of his daughter's talents through the burnished wood—amazing now, even more so from a time when most women were expected to marry rather than work. Certainly not to become professional writers. George Austen supported his daughter in every way he could.

I snuck a glance at Xavier, who was busy answering an email.

Would he have done this for Sofia back then if she were in the same position? Would he have supported her no matter what, loved her even when she didn't do exactly as he thought?

Would he do that now? For either of us?

When, at last, I had read through the final manuscript, I removed the white gloves and set them next to Xavier's discarded ones, then decided to do a bit of exploring around the rest of the rare books room before the librarian returned to fetch us. Xavier immediately got up and followed.

"What's back here, then?" he asked when he caught me examining a full printed version of the *Oxford English Dictionary*. "Christ, twenty books just listing words? How many are there?"

"I think the last count was somewhere around six hundred thousand," I said, then found myself humming lightly as I watched him stare at the books with a deeply furrowed brow.

"Mmm?" he wondered when he caught the song.

I chuckled. "Sorry, it's from a movie."

Xavier turned, looking adorably confused. "Er—do I want to know?"

"I just feel like Belle right now," I said as I ran my fingertips over the spines of the books.

"Belle? As in beautiful? Well, you are fucking gorgeous."

I turned with a smile, unable to contain my blush. "No, I meant the character from *Beauty and the Beast*."

Xavier frowned. "As in the fairy tale?"

"The Disney version, yeah. Sofia loves it. Especially the part where they dance in the ballroom."

"Ah. So it's one of those movies."

I nodded, feeling a little sheepish. But I loved it too. After all, what woman didn't dream of the beast in her life turning into her prince after all?

"There's this scene," I said. "Where she really falls in love with him. What she loves more than anything in the world is books, and then he opens these doors, and he gives her an entire library." I waved my hand around us, as if to demonstrate. "It's a meme. I don't know. Maybe you need to see it."

Xavier didn't say anything for a few minutes, leaving me to focus on the gold lettering of the dictionary spines as I wandered further into the stacks.

He must have thought I was an idiot, quoting Disney princess movies at him. Simple and childlike.

"So, does that make me the beast?"

When I found the courage to turn back, I found Xavier watching me with a particularly feral expression. The blue of his eyes had disappeared into a deep black. His shoulders seemed even larger than normal.

"I—no—um—"

With a quickness that belied his size, he strode down the aisle until he stood directly in front of me, caging me against the shelves and forcing me to look up at him. Carefully, he took my chin in his hand and brushed his thumb over my lips, watching its progression like a panther tracking its prey.

"I am a beast," he said without a trace of humor. It was practically a growl.

"Are—are you?"

I couldn't really argue. Xavier was anything but tame.

A slight smile cracked, though his focus on my lips didn't waver. "So, what did the beast do next?"

"I—I don't remember." I was having a hard time recalling my own name, much less the plot of a children's movie.

He tugged my lip, then slid his thumb between my teeth and pulled down slightly, urging me to bite.

I obeyed, slipping my tongue around the salty end of his finger.

His smile was full of teeth.

"I think he ravishes the young girl," Xavier said as he ran the pad of his finger over the edges of my incisors. "I think he rips off her clothes to examine his prey. Has her right there. Marks her as his own."

My breath shook. Everything around me was fading away. The books. The art. Everything but this larger-than-life creature and the shadow he cast.

The hand at my mouth dropped down, briefly gripping my neck, then continued a path downward, toying with my neckline, then the buttons just below.

"I reckon he takes whatever the fuck he wants." His eyes sparked like embers as he watched his hand progress down my chest, pausing to pull lightly at one of my nipples through the thin silk.

I sucked in a harsh breath. "Is—is that so?"

"I don't think she has a choice."

Xavier rubbed his stubbled chin over my neck, grazing his teeth over my thumping pulse. His other hand traveled up my leg, slipping under my skirt to find a solid handful of my backside and slip between my thighs, teasing for more.

He squeezed. Hard.

I grabbed his jacket with a gasp as his fingers touched the dampness forming just under the lace that separated me from him. "Xavi." My voice was a breath.

"Your Grace?"

"Fucking hell," Xavier growled into my ear.

Forehead against the bookshelf, Xavier swore again under his breath, then pushed away hard enough to make the wood creak and turned his head toward the voice that beckoned. I thanked God his frame was large enough to block me from Edith Willoughby's shrewd gaze. For some reason, getting the stink eye from the top librarian in the entire UK seemed worse than receiving punishment from the queen herself.

"Dinner is served," she called across the room.

I relaxed at the sound of her retreating footsteps and took a moment to put myself back together. There would be no helping the rosy flush that was no doubt all over my skin, but at least I could smooth my hair and fix my dress.

When I finished, Xavier was watching me once more with a curious expression.

"What?" I asked. "Is my dress straight? Is my hair sticking out?"

"Is it fucked that I sort of want you to walk out there a mess?" he wondered with a sheepish expression. "I'd mark you all over too if I could. Maybe I am a beast after all."

He reached out to brush my hair off my neck, his fingers lingering over the spot on my neck where his mouth had been. No doubt there was already a bruise forming in the shape of his mouth.

He looked so guilty, but I couldn't help but smile as I finished patting things into place. Then I popped up on my toes to give him a quick kiss, which he immediately turned into something a bit more.

"Maybe you are," I said against his lips when he finally let me go. "But you're my beast, aren't you?"

God, I wanted it to be true.

That rare grin reemerged, lighting up the dim room. "Damn right, I am. Now let's go. This beast needs to feed his girl and get her into bed, pronto."

FIVE

"This wasn't necessary," I told Xavier for probably the fourth time that night.

And for the fourth time that night, he just snorted and ignored my comment.

It was quite the little game we were playing. One where I tried to tell him that I didn't expect anything like this evening ever again, and where he treated my comments like clay pigeons he could shoot out of the sky.

I'd done it while we wandered through the stacks (and kissed behind several) on our way to dinner.

I'd done it again when Xavier had led me to the library's terrace, where a chef from one of his restaurants had prepared a four-course dinner.

I'd done it again when he took me on a walk through Hyde Park at night to walk off the four-course meal.

And now we were here, standing outside his beautiful building under the twinkling lights of the summer-lit city. I was loving every moment of it. But I wanted him to know too—I didn't *need* it.

Xavier joined me on the curb as Ben drove away. Though the

street was far from empty, there was still no sign of the press. I expected it was difficult for someone of Xavier's size to avoid them, but maybe it wasn't as bad as Jagger had led me to believe.

"One day," he said as he pulled me to face him, "I'm going to teach you to think far beyond 'necessary,' Ces. I'm going to teach you to dream."

I blinked. I wanted to tell him that everything I had ever dreamed of was right here in this city. Delicious food. Every treasure in the English language. A man who seemed to love me. Our daughter asleep in a glass palace in the sky.

Xavier crouched down, and for a moment, I lost my breath. Was he? No, he wasn't. Down on one knee, though.

He looked up at me, blue eyes winking in the night air, and for a moment, I saw a dream I didn't even know I had playing out right in front of me. His mouth was going to open, and he would smile, and then he was going to ask the question I'd unconsciously dreamed of since I'd met him that night in a bar all those years ago.

Four simple words.

Will. You. Marry. Me?

Oh, God.

I—

"Just have to tie my shoe," he said, then made quick work and stood back up.

I shook my head and shook the heady vision away. Lord, what was wrong with me? Wasn't this night enough? Weren't those dreams of books and love and family enough?

Why couldn't I accept them, then?

And did I even deserve them at all?

Xavier watched, as if he could see the conflict written on my face. Then his gaze drifted to my lips. And stayed there.

Kiss me, I thought. *Do it now.*

Instead, he took my hand and led me through the lobby to the elevator with a gruff nod at the concierge. It wasn't until it started moving that I spoke again.

"Why didn't you kiss me?"

He frowned. "What?"

"Outside, just now. I thought you might—" I took a deep breath. I almost said "propose." Lord, what was wrong with me? "I thought you might kiss me. But you didn't. You didn't at the airport, either."

"Why didn't I..." The surprise on Xavier's face had me mentally kicking myself by the time the question exited my lips, loosened as they were by a bottle of excellent French wine.

I didn't retract it, though. Hadn't even realized it had been bothering me all day, like sleeping on a tiny rock—it seemed insignificant at first but bothered me more and more as time went on.

"You hugged Sofia. But I—"

I dropped my head, unable to continue. I could hear myself. I felt foolish, being jealous of my own daughter. I didn't ever want Xavier to feel like he had to choose between us—no parent should. But regardless, despite those lovely things he had said to me nearly two months ago now, I still wasn't sure if he loved me because I was her mother...or if he loved me for myself, this beautiful evening notwithstanding.

Sometimes actions *don't* actually speak louder than words.

Sometimes you need to hear the words themselves.

"Ces."

I looked up, expecting to see shame or disgust. Maybe a bit of pity.

Instead, I met a wall of blue fire.

"Is that what you want?" he asked.

I couldn't look away. Really, he wouldn't let me look away. "I—"

"For me to take you, right there on the street? In front of cars or cameras or anyone else who wants to watch like fucking vultures?"

"It didn't matter before at the library. Or outside it, for that matter."

"Well, it matters here. They know where I live, Ces."

The vitriol in his voice had me back against the wall. Suddenly,

Xavier seemed to fill the entire car. I wasn't riding up with my boyfriend. I was trapped in a box with a feral animal.

"I—I didn't mean—"

In a few short movements, my arm was pinned to the small of my back, and I was snapped back into Xavier's arms, lifted off my feet, and shoved against the elevator wall.

"Your kisses are for me," he growled. "Not the fucking papers."

Then his mouth crashed into mine, daring me to resist a thorough, breath-stealing, mouth-plundering kiss that I swore shook the car itself. It certainly erased every doubt I had.

When at last, he released me back to my feet, I was gasping. Xavier just coolly adjusted his collar and offered that characteristically sharkish grin of his.

"Next time, just ask," he said as the elevator door opened. "Come on, then. I want to show you one last thing."

So focused was I on the way my mouth was tingling, I didn't realize until we were totally outside that we hadn't returned to the apartment, but instead were walking into one of the most beautiful places I'd ever seen.

I gasped. "Oh...wow."

It was the last thing I expected to be atop a restaurant mogul's bachelor pad. In theory, I'd known it existed—he had mentioned a rooftop garden when giving me the tour earlier. But I'd imagined the sort of place that would host glamorous parties. A collage of chrome furniture to match the interior, a garish barbecue area, perhaps. Maybe an infinity pool or a jacuzzi.

This was a sanctuary.

The entire roof was sheltered by carefully organized greenery. Full-grown trees in car-sized clay pots lined the periphery, more than a few already heavy with fruit. Apples, some of them. Cherries, maybe. Others looked like some kind of nuts. Across carefully raked pea gravel, multiple trellises held the remnants of summer blooms, wisteria and hydrangea among them, waving in the breeze as if to say hello. Smaller plots held a variety of flowers and edible plants.

Of course, I thought. What world-famous chef wouldn't cultivate his own food, London be damned?

"This is my favorite spot in the whole city." Xavier released my hand, allowing me to explore on my own. "It's where I come to think."

As I floated my fingers over a planter of fragrant mint, I could certainly see why.

It was a Zen garden in the middle of one of the busiest cities in the world. Tranquility permeated the entire space, seeping into my pores, my mind, my heart.

"Camellias," I murmured, as I found another familiar flower. I touched their light pink petals, velvet soft under my fingertips, as I was transported back to our walk last December.

"You remember?" Xavier asked.

I smiled, thinking of our snowy walk after he chased me out of that party. It seemed like kismet now, running into each other like that after five years. The odds of it happening were so infinitesimal.

And along the way, of course, we'd encountered a few camellias, just like these, and he'd told me about their connection to his mother. And their meaning.

"Of course I remember," I said. "Red for passion. White for waiting. Pink for...longing, you said."

"I had them put in after New York," Xavier replied quietly. "They seemed to fit."

The levity in his voice was gone as I turned back to him somewhat shyly. "Are you longing for anything now?"

He watched me carefully, sapphire blue eyes shining, as deep as an ocean and twice as opaque. "I think I'll always long for you, Ces. Even when you're right here."

I opened my mouth, taken aback by the statement. I found I understood it, though. Maybe it was because, like me, Xavier understood the phrase that always rang through me like a bell, no matter how good things might be. That one single fear.

Not enough.

"It's so...peaceful here." I turned away from the camellia bush and his woeful expression, desperate to get away from that feeling. I'd been running from it my entire life—why confront it now and ruin such a beautiful night?

Instead, I focused on the rest of the garden, on the serenity laid out before me. But before I could take any more steps, a pair of hands encircled my waist, and I was tugged back against Xavier's broad chest as he set his chin atop my head.

"Like it?" he asked for the second time that night. This time, however, the words were threaded with more than a bit of vulnerability.

I twisted to look up at him. "You are full of surprises, you know that?"

The shy, crooked smile that was quickly becoming my favorite version of Xavier's rare grin made another appearance. "Got one more for you, if you're willing."

He led me through the garden to the very edge of the building, where eventually, I noticed steam rising into the night, directly from the leaves of a lush set of—or no, not from leaves at all. As we approached, I found, to my shock, that there was a pool out here after all. Of a sort.

"One of my favorite parts of Japan was the onsen," he said. "The hot springs. There is something like twenty-five thousand of them, with bathhouses built around them where people can just...relax. When I came back and bought this place, I missed them. So I built one for myself."

I blinked, taking it all in. It wasn't a typical pool—smaller but looked more like it was built into the side of a mountain than an apartment building. The garden extended up the sides, which was framed by a variety of river rocks, complete with ferns and other sorts of greenery growing between cracks and crevices.

"You must have loved having that to escape to," I said. "This is so beautiful."

"They're not all like this. And I wasn't allowed to go to a lot of them, you know. Because of the tattoos."

"Oh?"

My face heated at just the thought of Xavier's tattoos, elegant and sharp, curving over his shoulder and neck.

"Tattoos aren't very popular in Japan," he told me. "For a long time, people assumed they were marks of the Yakuza, so a lot of the onsen don't permit them at all, hoping to avoid that sort."

"When did you get yours?" I wondered.

He'd had some when we met, though not nearly so many as he had now.

"Actually, I got my first, just these characters here on my shoulder, when I visited with my mum and we stayed with my grandfather. I was thirteen, I think?"

"You got your first tattoo at *thirteen*?"

I'd heard of kids doing that back home, but they were usually the kinds who were involved with a gang of some sort. Or maybe I was just too much of a prude to have known anything more.

Xavier just smirked. "Yeah. Far too young to be inked, but everyone thought I was older. Anyway, my grandfather and I got into some sort of fight. He said I was rude, disrespectful, no better than the criminals. So I decided to go out and mark myself like one just to spite him. It's the characters for Sato, the family name." He chuckled. "God, he was so mad. Said I'd dishonored the family by marking my skin. Mum was not pleased either."

At the mention of his mother, all levity vanished.

"And the rest?" I wondered, hoping to pull him out of that sudden sadness.

"The rest I had done in America when I was at Dartmouth for a bit." He gestured to his left arm, where I knew there was some kind of serpent ringing his biceps, attached to a much larger tattoo that crawled over his left collarbone and moved down his side. "The ones on my arm and wrist after I opened my first restaurant." He shrugged. "Ojiisan was right, you know. I'm not a particularly nice man now, and at twenty, I was a right shit. I fought with everyone. Never stopped, really. I'm just as difficult at thirty-two as I was at twenty, wouldn't you say?"

He seemed to find it funny. I had to be honest, I did not.

"You do fight a lot," I observed.

Xavier looked up, humor gone once more. It wasn't an opinion. He couldn't really argue with it.

"Yeah, well. That's what you do. I had a choice. Accept what everyone said I was and what I had to be—a bastard, right? Or else fight to be what I wanted and make my own way." He shook his head. "Some things just become habit."

"It sounds...difficult."

I reached out and touched his hand, which didn't move. He was lost in some sort of memory.

"Sometimes I wonder if I can stop," he admitted as he stared at the pool of water. "I want to. For Sof, especially."

Something else he said was bothering me, though. "You keep calling yourself that. A bastard."

His brow crinkled. "Yeah, so? It's what I am."

"I'm not saying I like it. But if it's true, then how could you inherit your father's title? I thought titles and things like that only pass to legitimate offspring in England."

He peered at me with more than a little suspicion. "You looked that up? Everything about peerage inheritance laws?"

I nodded, feeling a little embarrassed. "Well...yeah. I wasn't snooping or anything. It's just that...I was thinking that our kid could be, what, a duchess one day, too, right?"

"Er," Xavier said, almost amused. "I hadn't really thought about it."

I blinked. He hadn't thought about it? Not in the six months since we'd run into each other and he'd discovered he had a daughter? He hadn't even considered the fact, as the holder of one of the oldest titles in England (yes, I'd looked that up too).

"But then," I rattled on, "I found that she wouldn't inherit anyway since you and I were never married."

Xavier's amusement immediately morphed into a scowl. "Sofia is *not* a bastard. And I'll rip out the tongue of anyone who says so."

It was clearly a sensitive topic.

"Well, technically, she is," I pushed, though I didn't particularly care for that designation myself. "That's sort of my point."

The scowl deepened. "What do you mean?"

I huffed. He was playing dumb. He had to know what I was getting at.

"Xavi, UK law is pretty clear, if I was researching correctly. Only legitimate offspring can inherit a title. Since Sofia can't become a duchess, how could you become a duke if you were also a—" I cut myself off, trying to move past the word that clearly triggered Xavier so much.

"A bastard?" he supplied anyway, quite testily at that.

I heaved a great sigh but didn't reply. Instead, I just waited him out.

It took a while. But eventually, Xavier huffed, like he had to admit something horrible.

"Technically, I suppose I'm not a bastard after all," he said.

I frowned. "What do you mean, technically?"

His long nose wrinkled. "It's a bit muddy, to be honest. After my mum died, and I got kicked out of uni for maybe the second time? I'm not really sure. Anyway, my uncle Henry found a marriage certificate. Apparently, my parents were married at one point. In Japan, at a Buddhist temple. Just by the time they came back, the Parkers made it clear they wouldn't accept Mum, so they split up and never registered the marriage in the UK." He shrugged. "So I became a duke, after all. Despite what everyone said my entire life, I was in fact the legitimate offspring of Rupert Parker, Fourteenth Duke of Kendal." He cast me a narrow glance. "Disappointed?"

I blinked, confused. "I mean...no."

"Well, I was." That tenacious scowl reappeared. "I never wanted that. Any of it. Certainly don't now. No one wanted a tattooed half-Japanese giant to hold one of the oldest titles in England, and I certainly wasn't interested in fitting the mold for it either. It's why I let Henry take over the estate, the family's portfolio, all of it. He cared. Not me."

Henry. The uncle who had hovered in the background of Xavier's life since he was sixteen or so. I had gotten the impression that he was sort of the second fiddle of the Parker family. The spare, so to speak, both to his brother and then to his nephew.

Yeah, I knew the feeling.

"But he needs you now, doesn't he?" I asked quietly.

Something passed through Xavier's expression that I had never seen before. A different kind of vulnerability mixed with fear. That's why he had come home, of course. I just wasn't sure what he planned to do with it. Or how Sofia and I fit into the grand scheme of things.

"Trust me," he said. "It's better for Sof anyway if she doesn't inherit. No one needs that kind of pressure. Not me. Definitely not my little girl."

I nodded, but I wasn't so sure. Not that I cared whether Sofia became a duchess, but more the question of whether or not she would want the choice.

After all, who wouldn't?

Or was there a different reason he didn't want her—or me—to be a part of that world?

I turned to the pool, unwilling to entertain that question for now. We'd opened up enough baggage for the evening. This was supposed to be a reunion, not a therapy session.

I sighed, my muscles suddenly aching for release. "Well, your onsen looks divine. I can't imagine anything but total tranquility in there. Bliss."

"Ces."

I turned to find the crooked smile I loved so much had reappeared. Like a direct call to my heart, it made me sing from within.

"I'm really fucking happy you're here." Xavier's deep voice

carried over the breeze, like he himself was a part of the lush surroundings. "I might forget to say it sometimes. I'm not very good at saying how I feel. But I am."

I swallowed, heart so full it felt stuck in my throat. "I—thank you. That makes me happy to hear. Really happy."

The smile widened, and Xavier reached out to take my hand. His thumb drifted over my knuckles, then he pulled me to him and pressed a kiss to the top of my head. "Good. Now, about this pool..." He stood back; one black brow rose impishly. "Want to relax with me?"

SIX

Steam rose from the hot water like the lace of a bride's veil, clouding the blue of the night. For the first time, I realized just how stressed I'd been.

All day, since leaving for the airport in New York. For the last several days, getting Sofia and myself ready to leave our home for an entire summer.

For the last six months, since reconnecting with Xavi.

Since having a daughter at twenty-three.

Lord, maybe I'd been wound tighter than a guitar string my whole life.

Relax, yes. That was definitely what I needed.

I moved to unzip my dress, but the sight of Xavier removing his clothes, casually unaware of the way his muscles flexed and simmered in the moonlight, stopped me.

He looked up, catching me gawking, and smirked. "All right?"

"Oh, um. Yeah." I blinked but didn't stop staring. Because I could. He was all mine, wasn't he? And he really was a work of art.

He slowed his movements, peeling off one layer at a time until he stood before me, shirtless and utterly comfortable in his skin.

I tipped my head, peering. "Did that always go so far down, or has it been too long since I saw you last?"

I gestured toward his tattoo, its amalgam of designs twisted and turned around his left wrist up to his neck. Now it slid down his chest as well, past his ribs, dipping even beyond his jeans.

Xavier looked shyly down his chiseled body and back to me. "I—er—added to it last month."

I approached but didn't touch him. Not yet. Instead, I leaned close and examined the black ink that decorated the otherwise smooth, golden skin.

"A camellia," I said, charmed by a collage of blooms over his ribs and the foliage that played down his oblique and hip bone.

"Among other things."

There was snow. And fire. Vines and foliage, both full and withered. Sofia's name—in both English and as Chie, its Japanese equivalent—in multiple places. Delicate botanical designs mixed with slashing whorls, not a few weapons, and unidentifiable art that evoked beauty and savagery.

Just like him.

"I missed her. And you." Xavier shrugged under my gaze. "Some nights it got too much, so I called Gav, my artist. He did my other work too, except for the one I got in Japan."

I frowned, trying to imagine what, exactly, was too much for Xavier to bear, that he would rather be stuck with needles for hours at a time than lie alone in his bed.

"No kanji?" I wondered. I'd seen plenty of people with Japanese tattoos who weren't actually Japanese. "Other than your name, I mean."

Xavier just snorted. "Think I should get the characters for 'peace' on my arse?"

I chuckled. "Definitely not." My fingers touched a serpentine tail that writhed below his belt. "Just how far does it go?"

"Why don't you find out?"

When I looked up at him, those deep eyes flickered with a familiar blue fire. The hottest part of a flame.

Without breaking our gaze, I reached down and unfastened his belt, then his pants. Xavier hissed as I slid my hands over the curve of his backside, pushing his pants and boxer briefs over the smooth muscle and then down his legs, where he helpfully kicked off the rest, along with his shoes and socks.

When I stood back up, it wasn't a man before me. It was a god.

"Oh, Xavi," I murmured again, at a loss for words. "You're beautiful."

Something in those hard features softened at my admission. He wasn't used to being called that. Most men weren't. But there was no other word for this carved perfection. He was strong, yes, scarred here and there either from the hazards of his profession or from remnants of his past. But every nick and imperfection created something so perfect, it nearly broke my heart.

"Your turn."

I reached behind me again, looking for the zipper, but instead, Xavier turned me gently to face the pool, away from him.

"Let me do that."

Obediently, I waited while he unzipped my dress and dragged the thin straps over my shoulders, then allowed the silk to drop to the decking like a fallen parachute. He slipped off my underwear, then knelt to unfasten the straps of my shoes, allowing me to step out of one, then the other, until I was just as naked as he was. Gentle hands drifted over my shoulders and slowly rotated me around so I was facing him again.

"Shouldn't we—what if your neighbors see?" I asked, fighting the urge to cover myself under his heated gaze.

Yes, I'd been staring at him, but he'd shown no modesty out here on the deck. Xavier never slumped, as proud and tall as a warrior. And, um, as hard as one too.

Unable to look away from the very distinct part of him that wasn't exactly small either, I blushed.

But hadn't he said my kisses were only for him? And what about the very sizable rest of him?

"We're the tallest building for miles," he said, gesturing toward the open air around us. "There's privacy at the top of the world, Ces. I intend to make use of it."

I relaxed again. Of course.

"And what would the queen say?" I teased, stepping backward toward the onsen. "If she knew a duke of the realm was doing such naughty things on his rooftop?"

That smile turned dark. "The queen can kiss my arse."

"I doubt very much she would mind that," I said as he pulled me close.

Xavier's smile moved against my forehead. "Dirty, dirty."

I shuddered as his large hands drifted over my skin, feeling every bend and sweep of my shape.

"God," he breathed, chin in my hair. "This body. These curves. Delicious, you know that? Like a croissant."

I looked up. "Did you just compare me to puff pastry?"

"Might have."

"I'm not sure what I think about that."

The canine grin I loved so much gleamed in the night. "It's a compliment." Xavier leaned down, and his lips grazed the place where my neck and shoulder met. "You're buttery." Kiss. "Sweet." Kiss. "Perfectly shaped." Kiss. "Utterly devourable."

This time his teeth found my skin, as if to demonstrate just how much he wanted to devour me whole.

I shuddered. "Xavi."

"Hush."

Without waiting for me to answer, he grasped the backs of my legs and lifted me suddenly, encouraging my legs around his waist so that now we were face-to-face.

His lips touched mine gently, tentatively. So different from the kiss in the library, different still from the one in the elevator. This wasn't just the fervor of nearly two months of pent-up sexual frustration. This was something more. Longing, he'd said. Each kiss was a question.

Did I feel the same way?

I wrapped my arms around his neck, pulling him closer, opening more to each one.

Yes, I wanted him to know. I felt exactly the same, down to the very depths of my soul.

He walked us up the steps to the edge of the pool, then down a few more into the water, still kissing me all the way. Heat crowded me inside and out. The kiss deepened, tongues tangled in dewy sweat. Water splashed.

I broke away when a few drops slid down my cheek and landed on my tongue. "It's salty."

I released my hold on him, allowing the water to carry me away.

"It's a saltwater pool," he said, watching me float. Or rather, watching my breasts, mostly. They were small but bobbing pleasantly enough that he seemed entranced. "Better for the skin. It's therapeutic."

Xavier did not seem interested at all in therapy, though. Instead, he moved like the serpent on his arm through the water, eventually caging me against one side again. He dipped his head and traced his tongue over my collarbone, sucking every salty drop of water from my skin until it was clean and bright.

"Delectable," he growled, then ducked down and pulled my nipple into his mouth.

I stared up at the bright sky, marveling at the few glimpses of stars. London was like New York in that, here too, most of the stars were hidden under the corona of the city's light.

But in Xavier's clutches, I felt like a star myself, set ablaze by his fiery touch.

"Up," he muttered. "I want to taste more of you."

I found myself lifted from the water to balance on the edge of the pool. Gently, pushing my knees apart, Xavier stared at the dark space between my thighs like a starving man.

"Well?" I wriggled impatiently.

One black brow quirked at me before he turned back to examine his quarry.

"Patience," he murmured, sinking into the water. He slipped one knee, then the other over his broad shoulder then pressed his face between them and licked. Again. And again. Slow, maddeningly long licks.

"You don't have to do that," I said as I combed my fingers through his damp, dark hair. "You can just—oh!—get to the good part if you want."

I was so used to hurrying things like this. Not that I'd had any partners besides him. None, actually. And only the few times over the last six months. Since he'd left New York, we'd tried to maintain some sort of intimacy...over the phone. But it was always in hushed tones, flirting messages—never anything explicit. Usually, I'd be left with unspoken fantasies I had to use in the dead of night when I couldn't help but touch myself and wish to God it was this man instead.

"No," Xavier grumbled as he licked up the tender skin of my inner thigh. "I want to take my fucking time with you, baby. I want to savor every inch."

Closer, closer, he moved until his nose grazed the slick, sensitive nub that was already quivering in anticipation.

I gasped, grasping for purchase on the decking, finding none. "Xavi, please."

His finger dug into my flesh as he yanked me toward him and licked me straight up the center.

"So fucking sweet," he pronounced and did it again, eliciting another hoarse cry.

"Xavi." I gasped. "Just do it."

I shoved both hands into his thick locks and yanked. With a grunt, he obeyed. And fucking feasted on me.

My entire body writhed against his face, aching for that tongue to slip deeper. His fingers followed, one, then two, maybe three. I could barely tell, lost as I was in the ecstasy of his touch.

"I—oh, God—I'm so c-close." Every word was a struggle, a stammer against the onslaught of his talented tongue and fingers. But just as my orgasm was about to hit, he stopped and stood, water streaming from his body like a monster from the deep.

No, not a monster. A god.

His hands grabbed my hips, and he yanked me forward, entering me with a swift, harsh shout.

"Xavi!" I yelped.

He paused a moment, allowing me to adjust. He was big, and I was so small, but somehow, we always fit. Always.

"All right?" he muttered as his hips rocked forward.

Breathlessly, I nodded.

Another hip rock. "You feel fucking amazing. My God, Ces. Six weeks is too fucking long."

His hands slid over my body, silky under his damp touch. Drops of water followed his fingers, lit gold and silver under the moon.

"You're the real royalty," he murmured, watching the water's progress. Then he leaned down to lick some from my breast, fixed his teeth around my nipple, and sucked. Hard.

I shivered as he thrust again, even deeper this time. "Am—am I?" Right now, I could barely remember my name.

"You're a princess to me, you gorgeous thing." Another thrust. Another pull. Another grunt as he palmed my breasts, kneading them lightly in time with his movements. "Perhaps I shall make you my queen."

I swallowed hard. What did he—was he saying what I—did he really want to—

"Ces."

His deep voice pulled me out of my wonderings. "I—hmm?"

One hand pulled my chin to face him. "Focus."

His blue eyes held mine, and everything else faded away as Xavier really began to move. His other hand slipped between our bodies, finding my clit as he pummeled forward, finding that unique, punishing rhythm guaranteed to split me apart. Teeth found my shoulder again. And bit.

I split into a thousand pieces.

"Xavi!" My voice bounced around the rooftop, joining the chaos of the city below.

"Just—fuck—hold on, Ces. Hold the fuck on!"

He shoved my thighs apart, hands gripping my thighs with complete and utter abandon. I shook violently beneath him, my orgasm wracking my body with every merciless movement.

"Fucking—oh, God, Xavi, I'm *coming*!"

One final thrust and Xavi fell over me, his big body quivering and spasming under my touch as I moaned beneath him. The stars, obscured as they were by the clouds, twinkled somehow brighter than before while the city roared right along with us.

"Xavi," I whimpered again and again.

"Francesca," he murmured into my shoulder, more breath than voice. "I love you."

His voice was so low it was barely a vibration on my skin. I threaded one hand into his soft, wet hair and massaged the back of his neck, enjoying the way his body sagged into mine with relief.

"I love you too," I whispered, hoping he heard me. Hoping he felt the truth.

Then there were no other words for either of us for a very long time.

A few or maybe a hundred breaths later, we returned to earth at last, cheek to cheek, skin to slippery skin, breaths and heartbeats mingling as one. With a tender kiss, Xavier pulled me up from the deck and into the water, bodies still united. Together, we melted into a pool of light and love.

PART 2

THE DUKE

INTERLUDE I

THIRTEEN YEARS EARLIER

Xavier

"Have you figured out what you'll say to your dad?"

The train chugged away from Oxenholme. It was a connector, but not taking it meant I'd have had to tell them I was coming. And I hated telling Rupert Parker I was coming. I hated everything about the man.

Fine, so maybe he tried a little. After Mum died and he chucked me into Eton, he took me to the estate that summer, had the shop closed up, and the flat rented out. I didn't remember much about that summer except for the horses. Rupert liked horses, and he liked polo, and it was the only thing he could ever convince me to try for myself.

But off the pitch, his attempts at being a real "father" after sixteen years of absence were about as transparent as the last bits of hair he combed over his bald spot. Everything I did was a disappointment. Polo was all right, though I'd never love horses the way he did. I didn't mind the fresh air, but stalking for deer was probably the most boring thing in the world when I'd have preferred playing football with the lads back home. And having a son who cooked? Please. I might as well have been panhandling every time he saw me in the kitchen.

I turned to where my neighbor Lucy was sitting beside me in the train car. She was a good sport, Luce. Had volunteered to ride up to Kendal with me a week early instead of staying in London for the start of the Season with the rest of her family.

It wasn't really a surprise. Imogene, her sister, was all for the garden parties and horse shows, all the excuses for the rich and powerful of England to act like anything they did really mattered, but Lucy was never one for that scene. They tired her out too much, and there were too many potential allergens that could set off a reaction. Imagine going through life knowing you could experience spontaneous anaphylaxis for no apparent reason. All I knew was that it made her really sick sometimes and miss out on a lot.

I should have gone. I was supposed to go. But I'd have rather drowned myself in the Thames than wear tails and grin with all the other peacocks, especially since it was always the same bloody faces at every one of those things. Lucy and I had that in common too. I'd had enough of their pompous faces at Eton, then the American sort at Dartmouth, and back to England again at Christ Church.

Well, I was done with all that now. They'd have to lock me in a cage to get me back to university.

"I don't really think it matters," I told Lucy. "He's going to go berserk no matter what I say anyway. Can't think of a single duke who'd be happy his son got expelled for fighting for the fourth time. Unless it was fencing anyway."

We both snorted, as if the idea of me dressed like a cotton swab with a rapier was equally ridiculous to both of us.

"I can't imagine it was only the fight that got you expelled," Lucy put in wryly. "More the punch you landed on the nose of an actual prince. And the fact that it got you the front page of the *Mail*. Again."

"I didn't mean to hit the prince of Denmark. I was going for his mate. The royal idiot just got in the way."

Right. So I was full of it. And yeah, it probably wasn't the greatest thing to give a future king a black eye. Even worse, to do it outdoors, where plenty of students had iPhones and social accounts. And maybe I shouldn't have shouted right after, "Who's a prince now, bitch?"

Yeah. Not my finest hour.

I rubbed the bruise forming on my jaw. I had to give it to the prince—his punches were soft, but he'd managed to get in a few. Not enough to save himself a walloping, but enough to command a bit of respect.

"You're lucky expulsion is all you got, you know," Lucy pointed out.

"True. He could have had his great auntie lock me in the tower. He's related to the queen, right? All the royals are related somehow."

"Don't be an ass, Xavi. No one gets locked in the Tower of London anymore. She might have had you thrown into Broadmoor, though. You could argue insanity."

I snorted.

"Here, I brought some ice from the club car. You really do look dreadful."

Begrudgingly, I accepted the offered bag of ice and pressed it to my jaw, which was admittedly throbbing after yesterday's scuffle.

"Are they still giving you problems, then?" Lucy asked after about ten minutes.

"Different school, same jokes. Half-breed bastards are easy pickings, don't you know?"

"Even at uni? I'd have thought it would have stopped after Eton."

I grunted and dropped the pack on the tray in front of us. "Schools change. People don't. I thought it would be different in the US, but it wasn't. Come back here, same old rubbish. I shouldn't have even tried."

You'd think in the twenty-first century, things would be a bit more modern, but not with this lot. Not when the names and titles they used were created centuries ago. Not when half the laws governing their precious inheritances were nearly as old.

"I don't know why he even bothers," I said. "It's not like any number of posh schools are going to change the fact that I'm the brat he got on the cook. Honestly, things were better for me in Croydon with—"

I bit off my words and swallowed back the tears that pricked whenever I thought of Mum, even three years after her death. It was only late at night that I'd let myself think of her sometimes. When I was back from school, and could creep down to the kitchens of Corbray Hall after the staff had gone for the day. There, I'd nose around and make a bento for myself out of whatever I could find. Cut the rice into shapes like Mum used to. Shave a bit of carrot like hair and make faces with sesame seeds.

She always did want me to eat healthy.

And sure, maybe sometimes I'd cry a little. At first.

But not anymore.

"At least they are still trying to help you fit in." Lucy sighed and kicked her feet out in front of her. She was short, so they barely grazed the floor. "Imogene came out this year, you know. Mummy took her to London and everything. She was so excited. Told Papa, 'Finally, one of them can actually be a real Viscount's daughter.'"

I scowled. Maybe this was why Luce and I had always gotten on from the moment Rupert had dragged my stubborn arse up to Cumbria and plopped me on the estate adjoining hers. We both knew what it was like to fall short in our relative positions—me because of the circumstances of my birth and Luce because of her health.

"Your dad gives my dad a run for his money in the arse department." I looked her over curiously. "I thought they took care of the cancer, though. What did the doctors tell you this time?"

Something in my chest squeezed. Over the years, Lucy had been in and out of the hospital more times than I'd visited the headmaster's office. Every time she went to London, it was to see another specialist at a different hospital to get another scary diagnosis. There were a few times they weren't sure she'd make it.

She shrugged. "They say it's still in remission, but now there are the adrenal insufficiencies to worry about from all the steroids. Not to mention spontaneous anaphylaxis, of course." She sighed. "I can't seem to get it right."

I swallowed, unsure of what to say. I didn't really understand Lucy's condition—something called mast cell activation syndrome. From what she said, it was like having extreme allergic reactions all the fucking time, and in her case, actually caused a type of leukemia. That was scary. I spent most of my free weekends that year keeping her company during chemo. It was the only reason I ever studied for A-Levels—I read to her while she lay there feeling sick. If I believed in God, I'd have thanked him when they said she'd recover.

"Well, you look great to me," I told her, patting her hand. "Ready to join the Premier League, eh? I hear the Arsenal Scouts are having a tryout next week."

She rolled her eyes. "You never change. Single track mind."

I grinned. "You can take the boy out of Croydon..."

She sighed and looked out the window as the countryside zoomed by. "Do you ever think about what things could be like away from here? If we didn't have to come back to Kendal?"

"Are you kidding?" I asked. "Only all the bloody time. I'm counting the days, you know. Taking you with me, too."

Lucy turned in genuine surprise. "You are not."

"I am." I held up my hand like I was framing a painting. "Picture this. You. Me. My mum's flat in South End. You can have the bedroom, I'll take the sofa. You'll go to LSE like you always wanted, and I'll do culinary school. We'll get out of fucking Kendal and live our lives the way we actually want. It'll be perfect, Luce. Just us."

Lucy seemed enraptured with the dream, looking through my fingers like she could actually see the picture I was describing.

Then, suddenly, she made a face. "I don't know if I'd want to live with you, Xav. You're kind of disgusting."

I scowled. "Disgusting? What's that supposed to mean?"

"It's just that I don't really fancy living in a sea of condoms and girls' knickers," she said. "Especially the kind you go after. Chelsea Nobbs in the stables? Really? She's shagged half the village, you know."

I snickered. I wasn't going to lie. Girls had never been the problem when it came to fitting in around here. It was their brothers who usually hated me. And mothers. And, of course, the fathers.

I nudged Lucy's arm. "You don't have to worry about that. I'd never bring any of them around you. Not to our home."

Lucy snorted. "Just wait until you fall in love with one of them, Xav. Then we'll see how much I really matter."

"Nah, that'll never happen," I told her. "What've we been discussing this whole time, eh? I'm a heartless bastard, Luce, through and through."

It didn't seem to make her feel better.

"But, hey." I pulled at her jumper, making her turn back to me from the window. "I'm also your best friend. You and Jagger and Elsie —you're the only ones who matter to me. Nothing could ever get in the way of that."

The train pulled to a stop at the Kendal station, and both of us peered out the window to where a few people were waiting for the arrivals. In the center of the platform stood Lucy's mother's personal assistant, whom we both affectionately called Mrs. Poppins for her tendency to carry an umbrella with her, rain or shine.

Beside her, to my surprise, loomed my uncle, Henry Parker.

"Looks like the dean called ahead and told the duke anyway," Lucy remarked, then looked at me sympathetically.

"Sent his right-hand man, too."

"He does look a bit peeved," Lucy agreed.

"Secondhand irritation. I know the duke means business when he sends Uncle Henry to fetch me instead of the driver."

"That's because he knows Barney will let you knock off to the pub for a few hours. And possibly end up in Chelsea Nobbs's bed, which means you won't get to the estate until, oh, Tuesday."

"Bah. We never make it to a bed. I can't fit through the window anymore when her dad gets home."

We gathered our things and exited the train, Lucy taking my hand as she stepped carefully onto the platform. She was a bit shaky on her feet but not as skinny as she used to be. That was something. Mrs. Poppins rushed to meet us, cane in hand, which Lucy shooed away.

"I can walk," she said smartly, then clapped a hat on her head full of fine, newly grown curls and waved at me. "Xav!"

I turned back. "Yeah?"

"Tea on Sunday?"

"Tea" was Lucy's code for "my parents will be at church, so come over and cook." Unlike everyone else living in this mausoleum, Lucy actually liked it when I experimented in the kitchen. Especially when I made Mum's old recipes and told her stories about Croydon.

I grinned. "You got it."

"I'm afraid you'll have to make other plans."

I turned to where my uncle stood a few feet away, watching Lucy leave while we waited for the porters to unload my luggage.

Uncle Henry was one of the many "family" members I'd gained three years earlier, the day when Rupert Parker showed up at my mother's wake. While the rest of the Parker clan—including Rupert's wife and her son—tended to treat me like an old shoe they'd prefer was left in a mudroom, Henry was one of the few who attempted legitimate conversation. I wouldn't have called him friendly. But he actually asked me questions about myself and seemed to be interested in the answers.

Low bar, maybe. But it was something in a world where most everyone's standard response was, "Mmm, well."

When I'd first arrived at Kendal, Henry had been the one to show me to my room, tour the grounds, and basically get me acquainted with the ins and outs of life on a large country estate. It made sense, of course, since, as the second son, he was the estate's steward. He managed everything about my father's life, from bank accounts to tenants, to investments and staff. Why not an illegitimate son too?

"Looking good, Hal," I teased him.

Henry just blinked, as implacable as his older brother was testy but otherwise looking almost like his twin, right down to the Barbour jacket and wool cap that covered graying hair. I'd inherited the family eyes and height, but that was it for our resemblance. The rest of the Parkers were as fair as I was dark, with the long noses and hunched backs of aristocrats who had spent too many centuries counting their money.

At least Uncle Henry was reasonably nice. Well, maybe nice wasn't the right word. Respectful? Didn't treat me like gum on his shoe?

"Xavier," he said with a brusque nod. "You're wanted in time for tea."

I rolled my eyes at the dour tone. My uncle sounded like he dreaded going back to Corbray Hall as much as I did. "I suppose His Grace received the news of my expulsion."

"From the dean himself, as it were." Uncle Henry shook his head. "What were you thinking, fighting a royal? What could you have possibly thought you'd accomplish other than making the papers yet again?"

I shrugged. "He got in the way."

"That cannot possibly be all." Henry directed the porters to the exit, and we walked together behind them.

"And I didn't like his face." I grimaced. "Or what was coming out of it."

I wasn't about to explain myself to my uncle or anyone. It never mattered what my reasons were—reasons like them calling my mum a whore or Lucy a cripple. The rich pricks caught on quick that while I never cared what they called me, I couldn't shake off what they called the few people in this world I did care about. But whenever I explained why I punched out the Viscount of Arsholebyshire or broke the Marquess of Cuntythwack's nephew's nose, the answer was always the same: gentlemen don't brawl. Or at least they don't get caught throwing the first punch.

Which, of course, only taught me one thing: I was never going to be no gentleman.

Henry only sighed. He knew when to press and when not to, and the older I got, the less he seemed to try.

I believe that's why they call me incorrigible.

"So, what's my punishment this time? No polo? Please, don't take away my ponies. Or, let me guess, cut off the allowance I don't use? Stop tuition at the next school I get kicked out of?" I chuckled at the ridiculousness. It was like tempting a bee with honey they had already made themselves.

Henry just shook his head as we stopped at the Rolls, where he opened up the boot for the porters to put my bags. "I'm afraid not. This time you're staying here. For good."

I snorted. Fat chance, that. "That is a real punishment. Honestly, Henry, why doesn't he just disown me and get it over with? Throw me back to the South End. I don't belong here, just like everyone keeps telling me."

"That's where you're wrong, boy."

Henry gave the porters a tip, then waited until they were fully out of earshot to turn and speak again. "There's been some records found. In Japan. Your mother's...people...sent them."

I frowned. I'd barely heard from my grandfather or my uncle in Okazaki since the funeral. My uncle apparently took it personally when I'd, you know, obeyed the law and gone with the man who now had legal custody. There was no way he would have voluntarily communicated with the family who had shamed his sister.

Henry was solemn, however. He never joked, and certainly not about something like this.

"What did they send?" I asked, hoping it might be good. Some really good salt, maybe. Or some packaged mochi. Once, they sent Mum a bottle of aged soy sauce, which she prized like the crown jewels.

But they were likely letters from Mum, I guessed. Or some old pictures of me when I was young. Maybe my birth certificate, which had been lost a while ago. Deep down, I'd always hoped I'd actually been more in Japan, not England, despite the fact that Mum insisted, again and again, I'd been delivered right there at Croydon Hospital.

I perked up. "Don't tell me—I'm not Rupert Parker's son after all. My dad's in fact a samurai lord who's been searching for me and his long-lost wife for the last nineteen years. He's heard of my fighting prowess and wants to bring me home to learn the family trade. Have I got it?"

Even Henry couldn't help rolling his eyes. I laughed. I might not have had the same coloring as my dad, but even I had to admit, there was no denying that I was half Parker.

"It is a marriage certificate," he told me. "Between your father and Masumi Sato—your mother, of course. Dated the year before your birth at a Buddhist temple in Okazaki. Rather heathen, of course, but legitimate just the same. It seems that your parents were secretly married in your mother's hometown just before she ended the relationship. She left Kendal for London just before their divorce went through. But not before you were conceived."

He looked almost ill as he said it, but to his credit, Henry didn't show the disgust most people had when they imagined the Duke of Kendal knocking up—or in this case, marrying—a local student who worked part time as his family's cook. It was more like he was shocked.

I honestly thought I might puke as I reached for the top of the Rolls to steady myself. "I—who—what? They—you mean—I'm not a—"

"Bastard," Henry finished, like the word physically hurt. "No, boy, it appears not. Which means you will be the next Duke of Kendal, not some distant cousin. And so, my lord, since you are so determined not to succeed at university, it has been decided that you will continue your education here. You will learn what it means to be a duke. And you'd better get used to it."

SEVEN

Francesca

"Daddy! We're home!"

Sofia flew into the apartment like a jet, even to the point of letting her arms fly out behind her like a tiny kite racing through the sky. Xavier always laughed when she did that, calling it her anime run. According to him, all kids in Japan flew around the playgrounds that way, imitating their favorite cartoon characters. Hilariously, it seemed to demonstrate her pedigree to him more than anything else —especially when he zoomed after her with the force of a B-52.

"Bean!" I called from the elevator. "Shoes off, babe."

"Oh, right."

Obediently, Sofia trotted back to the front door and toed off her sneakers—new ones that Xavier had bought her last week, which had unicorns on the sides. She tipped them onto the pile of other shoes that buried the sleek rack by the door. The rack itself was only good for propping up umbrellas and the occasional grocery bag. But that didn't stop it from becoming the catch-all for coats, shoes, bags, and the other debris of a family coming and going.

It was a mess, but it was our mess.

After a month in London, Sofia had truly made herself at home in her father's apartment, and it showed. Multiple parts of the penthouse had been completely refurnished—some because they simply could not withstand the wear and tear of a four-year-old (read: pink glitter paint spilled all over a white angora rug), and some simply because Xavier decided at one point that he wanted the place to feel more "homey." The white and chrome furniture had largely disappeared within the first week, supplanted by worn antiques, overstuffed furniture, and more than a few pieces with a faintly East Asian feel to them. It was no less luxurious, even now, when the living room was scattered with the remains of a Lego set and the contents of a fake kitchen in the corner. Even the piano no one played had been replaced with an enormous indoor playset that essentially designated that part of the floor as Sofia's private jungle gym.

The place all but belonged to her.

We'd also settled into something of a routine. Although Xavier frequently took an afternoon or two off each week to join us, Sofia and I were generally on our own during the days. We were left with Ben, Xavier's driver, to explore London and the surrounding areas while Xavier worked at one of too many restaurants to count. On top of managing his properties in London, he and Jagger were retrofitting one of the original izakayas he'd started with his mother's recipes, alongside taking a day trip to Paris here and there to plan another international opening. Sofia and I had tagged along there too, and those trips had been fun. She particularly loved Disneyland Paris, the Eiffel Tower, and pains au chocolat.

Playing tourists, though, had its downside. It was already August, and I was running out of things to do with my daughter each day. She only had so much patience for museums and shopping. We'd visited the Tower of London and Big Ben at least three times, had explored every nook and cranny of Buckingham Palace, enjoyed Hyde Park several times per week, and had ridden the London Eye to the point I was ready to jump off the top into the Thames for a reprieve. I was still dying to explore the British Library more, not to mention visit Cambridge and Oxford. But I hadn't had the guts to ask for a day to myself when Xavier was working so hard. More than that, though, I was simply ready for a break from the city. London was a lot.

Sofia was feeling fatigued as well and getting more than a little homesick. She missed her friends. Her preschool teacher, Ms. Talia. And her family most of all. We FaceTimed each evening with at least one of her aunts, her uncle, or Nonna, but it wasn't enough. We needed more to do. Or at least a deeper purpose for being here.

As if on cue, my phone blared to life as I dropped my bags on the kitchen counter, which, like the rest of the apartment, was covered in Sofia's debris of half-finished drawings and art supplies.

Okay, maybe we didn't need purpose so much as the housekeeper to come more than twice a week.

"No, no, no screens!"

Sofia skittered away to her room at the familiar FaceTime ring. She particularly disliked talking to her family members through a camera. What was a novelty at first had turned into a chore, and now she ended each conversation asking when they were going to visit, only to burst into tears when they admitted they were not anytime soon.

"Hey, Lea," I answered the phone, propping it against a stack of books on the kitchen counter so I could set down my purse and get myself a glass of water. "Just me today. Bug isn't in the mood to talk."

"No worries," she said. "How's the palace?"

I rolled my eyes. Lea had a habit of making everything about Xavier's money. I knew it was because she and her husband were basically scraping by off his garage salary and the bits she made helping with the books.

"Cluttered," I joked. "Sofia has made every room her playroom now. Yesterday she constructed a fort in Xavier's office and he won't let her take it down. It was the last frontier."

"Sounds about right. And good for her. Xavier got to skip the first four years of child mess, so it's only fair she catches him up. So, has he popped the question yet?"

I scowled at the screen, then checked that Sofia was really and truly out of earshot. "You could at least ask if Sofia is around before you do that, you know."

"Please. Like that little girl isn't secretly hoping to high heaven that her parents have a big white wedding where she can be the flower girl. And be honest. You telling me you don't want to be a real life duchess either?"

My stomach twisted. I had to admit, the thought had occurred to me more than once. Yesterday, we'd passed a boutique on Bond Street with the most beautiful lace wedding dress I'd ever seen. Long sleeves, V-neck, full skirt. It would have overwhelmed a short person like me, but that didn't stop me from imagining what it would be like to walk down the aisle of an old Gothic church with a forty-foot train. Especially if the man waiting for me at the other end had blue eyes, black hair, and a penchant for cursing when he was really excited.

I shook my head. "Still. Don't you think it's a little soon to be asking that question? Especially every time I talk to you?"

"No," Lea replied immediately as she started yanking out some bread and peanut butter from the fridge. She slapped them on the counter and began making sandwiches with the crisp, no-nonsense movements of a mess hall cook.

"No," parroted Tommy. Or maybe it was Petey. The screen was blurry. One of my nephews had jumped across the screen so fast I couldn't really tell who it was.

"Pete, did I not tell you to get your shoes on? If I don't see those laces tied in five minutes, I'll make you wish you'd chosen the Velcro in ways you don't want to imagine, sir." Lea turned back to me placidly, as if she hadn't just threatened her seven-year-old. "I swear to God, summer camps are gonna be the death of me. Every day, a new time, new things. If it's not one kid who gets kicked out, it's the other. I should send one to London with you just to give Xavier a taste of his own medicine."

I could only laugh. Parenting was a language Lea and I spoke fluently outside of our other siblings, and she seemed to appreciate an outlet, as she was inundated with the stressors of four children to my one. I didn't envy her that. Just Sofia overwhelmed me most of the time.

"Besides," I said, continuing the conversation from before. "It hasn't even been eight months since we ran into each other at that party. And not even two since we officially got back together. Not everyone is you and Mike, you know. Running off to Atlantic City isn't really my jam, and it's definitely not Xavier's."

Lea applied jelly to the sandwiches with an audible slap. "Under normal circumstances, I'd agree with you, babe—Tommy, I said get your shoes on now. But this is different. You've already been involved, the two of you were pining for each other for five years, and you have a freaking child together already. You moved there. So, what's he waiting for? A divine sign from God?"

"I was never pining for Xavier," I protested weakly. I couldn't exactly argue the other two points.

"Frankie."

"Fine, but there was no way you knew."

"Frankie."

"Shut up, Lea. You don't know everything."

My sister just chuckled, clearly thinking otherwise. In her high-chair next to Lea, where she was playing with some mashed peas, baby Lupe gave a squawk as if to agree with her mother.

"Oh, I meant to ask—I have a bunch of baby clothes this one just grew out of. Since we are officially done with the child-rearing over here, do you want me to set them aside? They're the only cute girl's clothes I ever bought."

I frowned. "What? Why would I want baby clothes? Sofia is four."

Lea gave me her patented "what are you, stupid?" expression through the camera. "For your next one, obviously."

I cocked my head. "As far as I know, there is no next one. Getting a little ahead of ourselves, aren't we?"

Lea huffed, then turned to baby Lupe and tapped her nose. "Aunt Frankie is clueless, isn't she, sweet girl?" Then she turned back to me. "Frankie, don't be dense. I assume the Kitchen Duke over there wants you to stay in London permanently. Inviting you there this summer was obviously a trial run."

"A trial run for what? Being the world's greatest tourist?"

Nervously, I glanced over my shoulder to check that Sofia wasn't eavesdropping. There was no sign of her, which likely meant she was still playing with dolls and avoiding the camera.

"No, you dummy. For living together. For marriage. Now it's been a month. That's long enough to know whether it's going to work."

"Lea, there's a lot more that goes into it. Sofia would have to be enrolled in school. We'd have to bring the rest of my things here. He hasn't said a word about us staying past August."

"Exactly," she said. "So, what's taking him so long?"

I opened my mouth to protest some more but found I couldn't. Not quite. Because the truth is, my brain had led me down the same strange path.

There had been a few more moments, too, when I'd almost thought he was going to do it. A few nights when we were out to dinner or after Sofia had gone to bed and we were enjoying a glass of wine together in the onsen. He'd given me this look, and the blue of his eyes had positively sparkled. And I could have sworn he was going to say something. Ask me something.

But he never did.

"Nothing," I lied in the end. "It's probably not something he is thinking about any more than I am."

Lies. All dirty, rotten lies.

"Anyway, tell me what's new with you?" I pressed. "Did Tommy win his baseball game last weekend?"

At that, Lea launched into a play-by-play of her eldest's game, leaving me to zone out while I sipped water. It was only when we had finally signed off sometime past six o'clock, and Sofia wandered in looking for food, that I wondered where in the heck Xavier was.

So, apparently, did she.

"Mama? Where's Daddy?"

Before I could answer, the elevator doors opened, and Elsie walked into the apartment, sensible shoes squeaking on the marble floor.

"There you are!" she exclaimed. "We've been trying to reach you for the last hour, loves."

I glanced at my phone, which now bore a raft of messages and missed calls from both Xavier and Elsie.

> Xavier: running late at Chez Miso. Swing by for dinner with Sof? I'll have the chef make her something off-menu.
>
> Xavier: You home yet? Or stuck in the tube? What have you been up to today?
>
> Xavier: Ces, where are you? Getting worried.

I cringed guiltily and sent a quick message letting him know I was all right and with Elsie. "Sorry, I was on the phone with my sister. Everything okay?"

Elsie nodded. "Everything's fine. The boy just wanted you to know he had to put out some fires at Chez Miso tonight. The chef there is being a real pill and walked out for the fourth time, if you can believe that, so Xavier had to step in and cover. Again. Between you and me, I'm not sure he'll take him back this time."

I frowned. "Oh dear."

At this point, I'd been around long enough to hear more than one rant about the various chefs in Xavier's employ. They seemed like a moody type, and while Xavier dearly loved to cook, I was certain he didn't like being taken advantage of. Especially when it came to his time.

"Is there anything I can do?" I wondered.

"No, dear. That's why I'm here, checking to see if there is anything you need. Groceries or dinner, maybe? The boy won't be home until very late, I'm afraid, and if I know him, that fridge is empty."

I looked at my phone. "He did ask us to come to the restaurant. But now it's almost six, and Sofia's bedtime is seven thirty. I think it's a bit late for her to be going out again."

"Of course," Elsie agreed. "Little Miss needs her beauty sleep, doesn't she?"

"And dinner."

I checked the fridge. Though I'd been keeping it full of snacks, Xavier generally took care of evening meals. And it was, unfortunately, bereft of anything I could manage. Down the hall, I could hear the clear sounds of Sofia singing one of the *Moana* songs in her bedroom.

"Actually, Elsie, I know it's outside of your job description, but would you be interested in—"

"Babysitting? I thought you'd never ask!"

Elsie, I'd discovered, had a very bad case of granny lust—which was unfortunate, since she had no children to provide her with said grandkids. Xavier was the closest thing she had to a son, and so she was always offering to take care of Sofia, who equally adored her.

"If you don't mind," I replied gratefully. "Sofia can't go, but I'd like to check in on Xavi, especially if he's had a hard day. Maybe if he can bear giving up some power to one of the sous-chefs, I can pry him away from the stove, too."

Elsie looked doubtful at the idea but nodded anyway. "I wouldn't get your hopes up, my dear, but certainly, the boy would be glad to see you." A crease formed between her brows as she considered. "Just be careful."

I frowned. "Careful with what?"

Elsie grimaced. "With him. He's in one of his moods tonight. Best to be quick, in and out."

What exactly did she mean by that? Xavier was mercurial, yes, but it had never been something I couldn't handle. Generally, when he had had a long day, all it took was a glass of wine and one of Sofia's impromptu "plays" to make him smile again. His temper was actually becoming a thing of the past.

"Anyway, you've got to get yourself ready." Elsie dropped her own purse on the counter next to mine and immediately started off in the direction of Sofia's bedroom, where I heard her proclaim loudly, "Sofia, my dear, it's a date for you and me! Shall we dine on fish and chips, lovey, or would you prefer a nice curry?"

EIGHT

Chez Miso occupied a corner in one of the trendiest neighborhoods in London, less than half a mile from Xavier's Mayfair apartment. The weather was nice, so I chose to walk through the city, taking the rare moment to enjoy the bustle of the early evening without a four-year-old in tow. After a quick shower, I'd changed into a short black skirt, a flirty green top that matched my eyes, and a pair of espadrilles that lent me about five inches—always helpful when your boyfriend had you by more than a foot. I also happened to know that Xavier liked this skirt a lot. At least, it seemed like it, since every time I wore it, he copped a feel as much as he could get away with.

The menu was, like most of Xavier's restaurants, a fusion of east and western cuisine—this one specifically a mix of French and Japanese comfort food, but elevated to something truly spectacular, if the reviews were to be trusted. My mouth watered as I entered the restaurant. Scents of what must have been the miso French onion soup (one of the restaurant's signatures, Xavier had said) wafted from a few tables. I caught glimpses of a few other dishes I wasn't familiar with. One looked something like deconstructed ramen plated around duck confit. Another seemed to be some form of sushi but was topped with a variety of fish I couldn't place.

The whole place hummed, full of people eating at one of the thirty or so tables, and a few patrons crunched into the foyer and bar while they waited for another to open up. This wasn't a surprise—all of Xavier's restaurants I'd seen were busy. Whatever my duke was cooking, people wanted. Including me.

"Hi, Mal," I greeted the hostess, whom I'd met the week before when Xavier had taken me here for dinner. "I'm—"

"Francesca!" She looked slightly terrified when she recognized me. "Oh—I mean, Ms. Zola—bloody—are you supposed to be—he didn't tell me you needed a table—"

Okay, so more than slightly terrified. As the girl spoke, I could practically see her blood pressure rising. She looked like she needed to breathe into a paper bag.

"No, no, no," I said, reaching out to touch her arm. "He's not expecting me. Elsie said he was working late, and he had asked earlier if I'd meet him here. I thought I'd surprise him. He's in the kitchen, right?"

"I—er—" The girl glanced behind her toward the kitchen doors. "Perhaps you'd better wait. I'll clear a seat at the bar for you."

I glanced at the bar, which was completely jammed. I didn't particularly want to aggravate hungry, inebriated people by kicking one of them off their stool.

"Oh, it's all right," I said. "I won't stay long if he's occupied, but he'll be happy to see me."

I gave Mal what I hoped was a reassuring grin, then skipped around her, ignoring her clear distress as well as the irritation of the other waiting diners.

"Miss—Francesca—it's not really a good time—"

"Thank you!" I called, giddy at the prospect of finally sneaking up on Xavier for once. He always laughed at how easy it was to sneak up on me, often making it into a game with Sofia. This time, I'd be the one to surprise him.

After a rather exhausted-looking waiter emerged from the kitchen, I slipped through the swinging door. I expected chaos—by this point, I knew that restaurant kitchens during dinner hour were a flurry of activity. Instead, every person in the place was stock-still.

No one turned to look. No one even noticed my intrusion. They were all watching Xavier, who was towering over a shriveled, miserable-looking man whose hunched, sallow body and wide-set mouth strongly resembled a toad's.

It was the first time I'd ever seen Xavier in kitchen clothes. Usually, when he was working, he wore the suits of a businessman, looking more like an owner or investor than the people who actually made the food. Tonight, however, he was dressed as a chef in simple black pants and a white double-breasted jacket with a mandarin collar, sleeves rolled up to his elbows, revealing the tattoo twisting around his left arm.

He'd clearly been working hard, if the light sheen of sweat on his brow and rumpled black hair was any indication. He also looked as edible as anything they were making.

And angry. Very, very angry.

"What does this menu say, Le Fray?" Xavier demanded. "Tell me, what does this fucking menu say?"

The toadish man muttered something unintelligible under his breath, but it sounded as though it were in a French accent.

"Speak the fuck up," Xavier ordered. "My patience already walked out the door, along with your next reference. What does it say?"

"It says *soupe l'oignon gratinée avec* miso," repeated the chef through his teeth.

"And is that what you made?" Xavier demanded.

"*Oui*, I made the soup. But it tastes like food for the pigs."

As quick as a lunging snake, Xavier's hand darted out to take a handful of the chef's white collar and yanked him close. Given the difference in their heights, this required the man to step onto his tiptoes as his nose quivered next to Xavier's.

"Whose restaurant is this, Le Fray?"

Xavier's voice was low. Dangerous.

I took a step back. I knew that tone, though I hadn't heard it in a while. Not since the day Xavier had seen Sofia for the first time. We'd walked to the river, where he'd yelled at first upon discovering he had a little girl and I hadn't told him. But it was the end of the conversation that had scared me the most. The one where his temper had burned hot into embers and turned into threats of legal action that had haunted me for months.

That was the sound of Xavier's real fuse being lit. Right before the explosions were detonated.

"Get your hands off me!" snapped the chef, who then proceeded to rattle off what I would have wagered were some choice insults in French. "You are lucky I come back at all, *espèce de brute*! This restaurant will fail without me. I *am* Chez Miso."

"A beast, am I?" Xavier snapped.

I frowned. Xavi spoke French?

"Well, you're not wrong, you stubborn, insubordinate piece of shit," he continued, using Le Fray's collar to march him over to a stove, where a large stock pot full of something that smelled absolutely delicious was bubbling.

Several other cooks skittered out of their way, causing multiple empty pots and pans to clang as they fell to the floor.

Xavier dragged Le Fray's face down to the pot and spoke in a low growl close to his ear. "I am a beast. But I'm also the owner of this restaurant and your boss—a fact you seem to forget every time you throw these fucking tantrums. You make the recipes we design. You prepare the menu as it's written. You cook like I want you to cook, or you don't cook for me or anyone else in London at all." Xavier grabbed a ladle, then yanked Le Fray up to standing and held it out to him. "Is that clear?"

"Is that clear?" Le Fray mimicked over his shoulder, clearly refusing to pick up the ladle. Then he mumbled something else in French.

Whatever it was, it must have been bad.

Xavier flipped him around to face him, grabbed him fully by the fabric of his chef's jacket, and lifted him completely off the floor. "Say that again to my face, monsieur! I dare you. You'll find out what happened to the others before you. They were unrecognizable after they left the fucking hospital!"

Shit. I had a feeling dinner wasn't happening. Nor anything else pleasant that Xavier might have planned. My man was angry—maybe more than I'd ever seen him—and wild in a way I knew very well. Several of my family members had this exact kind of temper—a long fuse that, when it went off, blew a fire so hot nothing could put it out. It simply had to burn. Nothing was safe from this particular brand of rage. Maybe not even me.

Xavier dropped Le Fray into a crumpled heap on the floor, looking over him with his hands balled at his hips.

"Get out," he told him.

The chef scrambled up, eyes bugged, but no longer muttering. Fear had replaced contempt. I wasn't sure it would be better for him.

Xavier took a step forward and, this time bellowed his order. "Get. The fuck. OUT! AND DON'T COME BACK!"

The few pots and pans hanging from the ceiling shook, as if even they were terrified. Everyone else in the kitchen looked like they wanted to sink into the walls and disappear.

At that, Le Fray swiped the chef's hat off his head, hurled it to the floor, and bounded out of the kitchen, shoving into me as he did. I backed away, intending to make my escape behind him as silently as I'd entered.

And promptly sent a rack of pans clattering to the floor like a cascade of cymbals.

Everyone in the room jumped and turned. Xavier looked up, still holding the ladle as his chest rose and fell like he'd run a marathon. And when he caught sight of me, the fire in his eyes turned a deep, dangerous blue. Frozen and blistering all at once. A flame that could burn through anyone and anything in a moment.

"Ces?"

"I..." I flapped a hand weakly. "Surprise?"

He shoved the ladle at another cook standing next to him and shoved him toward the simmering pot.

"Fix it," he barked. Then, to everyone else, "Back to work."

The kitchen sprang into action.

Xavier crossed the room to where I stood, his footsteps masked by the sudden clamor. I watched him come, reminded of Moses in the Red Sea, the way the activity around him seemed to part with each step.

"What are you doing here?" he asked when he reached me.

"I—er—Elsie told me you were here, and I saw your texts. I thought I'd surprise you." By the time I was finished, I sounded like a mouse squeaking for a bite of cheese.

"Thought you'd surprise me..."

He looked me over, only then taking in what I was wearing. My shirt wasn't particularly tight, but Xavier's gaze made it feel like a second skin—particularly since my nipples were making it more than obvious how nervous I was. When he caught sight of my skirt, he chewed on his lips for several long seconds before he grabbed my hand, apparently deciding to offer a proper greeting.

"Come with me," he ordered.

Maybe not.

He dragged me through the kitchen to a propped-open back door, which he kicked shut as soon as we exited the restaurant. I found myself in an alley off the main street, locked in by a building at the far end and the racket of Charing Cross on the other. Cars zoomed by, pedestrians crowded the sidewalk, and I could hear the tinkle of silverware and music from countless restaurants and bars from here. Still, where we stood was relatively quiet. Or maybe the noise was just swallowed by Xavier's intensity.

"Is everything all right?" I asked as he yanked me farther into the alley, well past the set of dumpsters used by the restaurant and a shipping container that stored supplies. "Xavi, wait. What was going on back there? Was that really just about soup? Babe, are you okay?"

Suddenly, I was jerked around, then found myself shoved against the brick wall of the building, barely hidden behind the shipping container. Xavier's big body trapped me against the brick.

"No," he said flatly. "But I will be."

Before I could reply, his mouth crashed into mine, sucking, biting, drinking from my lips like he was an alcoholic falling off the wagon. It was a far cry from Xavier's usually sensuous kisses. This bruised just as deeply as anything he had wanted to do to the man inside. I was completely at his mercy as he raided my mouth, as merciless as a marauder, ruthless as a fiend.

"Xavi," I gasped when he finally released me minutes later. My lips were so swollen, I could barely speak. "What—"

"This day," he muttered as his hands roved down my body, seeking contact through the thin fabrics of my clothes. "This skirt. You had to wear this *fucking* skirt, didn't you?"

Without another word, said skirt was suddenly wrenched over my hips, and the hand that slipped between my thighs ripped through my lace underwear with a single tug. Xavier tossed the fabric aside, where it fluttered to the cobblestones, a scrap of pink against the dirty grays and browns. Then he lifted me bodily against the wall, bringing me face-to-face so he could crush his lips to mine all over again. Frequently, he said he wanted to devour me whole. But this was the first time I felt truly consumed.

"You," he snarled between punishing kisses. "Should not. Be here."

"But you said—I—oh!"

His long, unforgiving length pressed against my core, the fabric of his pants literally the only thing separating us. The bricks at my back and the traffic at the end of the street all seemed to fade away as he ground his hips into me, hard and brutal.

"I don't want you seeing me like that." His teeth grazed my neck, sharp as any animal's. "Ever."

"Xavi," I panted in between more ruthless kisses, his tongue twisting with mine that robbed me of every breath. "Please. Just tell me what's wrong."

I wanted to know. I really did. But another part of me, a completely debauched part that had zero shame, wanted much, much more.

"No." Xavier wrested one hand from my backside only long enough to undo his own pants. His stiff erection fell against my thigh, a heavy, smooth weight that already had my mouth watering.

"Like that, do you?"

Before I could answer, he spread my thighs and shoved inside me in one sudden, harsh thrust that filled me completely and stole every word I had.

"Would you get down on your knees for it?" he asked as he pummeled into me. "Would you suck my cock with that sweet, succulent mouth of yours?"

My head knocked back against the wall as my entire body clenched around him. I shouldn't like what he was saying. I should have felt completely demeaned.

Instead, my treasonous body was that much closer to climax.

"Yessss," he hissed for me as he continued his savage thrusts. "You. Fucking. Would."

"Ah!" I moaned as he took my bottom lip between his teeth and sucked ruthlessly. His mouth slid to my neck, then to my ear, biting as he went, hard enough to leave marks. "Xavi!"

"Shut up!" he barked before he covered my mouth again with his, tongue twisting with mine while pounding into me, robbing me of words beyond a low moan deep from my belly.

My head thumped against the bricks with each rough movement, but I hardly noticed. He was huge—that in itself was nothing new. But generally, he took so much more...time...to prepare me. This was Xavier everywhere all at once, primal and pure instinct. Conquering my body more than making love to it. I couldn't deny my response, but where was it coming from?

I squirmed under him, struggling to adjust to his size and power. But he was driving harder now, creating a slightly painful friction that quickly gave way to pleasure the longer he worked.

"Francesca," he huffed, breath hot and heavy in my ear. "Fuck me, you're so..."

His words faded as his teeth found my earlobe, eliciting a screech from deep within me.

"Hush," he snapped. "I'm going to tear this body in two, d o you hear me? And you're not going to argue. You're not going to fight me. You're just going to take it, do you understand? You're Just. Going. To. Take. It. Aren't you, you dirty girl? Fuck!"

"Xavi—oh!—Xavi, someone could see us!" I could barely string together a full sentence against the force of his movements.

He groaned, as if just the idea made him that much more animal. "Do you really think I fucking care about that?"

He clearly did not, thrusting as relentlessly as he had begun, as if his movements could also drive away the rest of the world, even as my orgasm approached from only the connection of our bodies and the singular fullness of him.

"Take it," he ordered. "Fucking take me, Ces."

"Oh my God, Xavi, yesssssss."

The final word came out as a ragged hiss while my head banged against the wall particularly hard. The slight pain combined with his punishing pleasure proved to be my undoing. My entire body clenched around him as I came, right there in the alley, completely at his mercy while he pumped again and again, giving no quarter as he released every last bit of his aggression.

"That's it," he snarled. "My God, squeeze me, Francesca. Fucking milk me, baby."

I obeyed, unable to do anything else. As I shook in his arms, the hands holding me up suddenly shoved me harder against the brick. Xavier came with a shout, slapping one hand against the wall behind my head while the other gripped my ass hard enough to leave black and blue fingerprints behind. The moan into my neck was a pained howl, like a wild wolf. His hips jerked while the rest of him tensed, pouring into me with every tiny movement.

And I took it all. I wrapped my legs around his waist, arms around his neck, and squeezed, throbbing with him until our heart-beats were finally one.

Eventually, though, the rest of the world returned. I inhaled deeply, relishing his clean scent along with the salty musk of sex and sweat. Gradually, I recognized the way the bricks at my back were prodding uncomfortably. The traffic at the end of the block grew louder. My sense of propriety emerged from its hiding place like a scared kid in a fort. Meanwhile, the clink of Xavier's belt buckle sounded far too much like the click of a camera.

"Xavi—" I gasped, wriggling weakly against him. "Oh my God, please."

The press had largely left us alone over the past few weeks, having moved on to other stories, but that didn't mean they wouldn't find us again. I was fully aware of how I must look should anyone stumble upon us. Loose. Easy. Utterly wanton.

Xavier's breath was warm against my collar. He was still gasping in recovery, but eventually, the rhythm of his heart slowed to some-thing approximating normal.

"I have to finish work," he muttered behind my ear, clearly unaf-fected by our compromising position. "I'll have one of the cooks wrap something up for you if you like."

That was...it? That was all he had to say after what had just happened?

Gently, the hands gripping my ass squeezed, and then he allowed my feet to drop back down to the ground. I swallowed thickly. Lord, I was still tingling.

"Sure you can't get away?" I ventured shyly as I put myself back in order. "I'm no chef, but you seemed to have a lot of them in there."

One hand still braced on the wall next to my head, his eyes raked over my body, and for a second, I thought he might take me all over again, right there. I had never felt so torn in my life. For one, it was like I was his prey, resisting the urge to flee a dangerous predator looking for its next kill. But another part of me wanted to be captured all over again. Maybe more than I'd ever wanted anything in my life.

In the end, Xavier made the choice for me. He brushed an absent kiss atop my head, then pushed off the wall. With a long sigh and an expression resembling something like regret, he straightened his jacket collar and walked back to the door to the restaurant, leaving me to follow on my own.

"I'll see you at home," he said vacantly, without looking at me again as he opened the door.

Sounds of clinking pans and chopping knives filled the space between us.

Then the door closed, and he was gone, leaving me in the alley to find my way back to Mayfair without him.

NINE

The apartment was deadly quiet when Xavier came home sometime past two in the morning. I wasn't in bed—I couldn't have hoped to rest there, or anywhere. Not after what happened in the alley. After arriving home just in time to wish Sofia good night, I'd retreated first to the TV room for my four hundred and ninety-eighth viewing of *Sense and Sensibility* (the Ang Lee adaptation) before adjourning to the living room for a cup of tea and *Wuthering Heights* to calm my nerves.

It didn't work. Hours later, Nelly had barely started telling her story at all, and I was still swimming in mine, trying to find some kind of reorientation.

Over the last month, I'd thought we'd found a sort of comfortable rhythm together, the three of us. It wasn't a forever kind of thing—vacations never were—but it worked. We'd had the time and space at last to learn each other's rhythms and moods. I'd thought I'd seen most of Xavier's.

Until tonight.

With a gentle *bing*, the elevator doors opened. Xavier stepped into the apartment, looking more than a little worse for wear. His jeans and the chef's coat he had worn at the restaurant were smudged with soot and other inscrutable substances, his hair was mussed on one side and flattened at the back, and his red sneakers were now scuffed beyond repair, laces half undone and filthy from being dragged on the ground. Even from fifteen feet away, I could smell the alcohol coming off him in waves. Bourbon, apparently. Maybe with a bit of wine laced through it. Whatever it was, it was a potent combination, and not one that suggested any more self-control than he had demonstrated earlier.

I tucked myself into the corner of the couch.

"Rough night?" I asked as he kicked off his shoes.

Xavier started, then swayed in place like he might fall over. Instead, he grabbed a prong of the coat rack and pushed himself upright. "Er—yeah. You could say that. We managed in the end."

He rubbed his face wearily, like just recalling the rest of the night caused him a hangover on top of whatever he had consumed.

For a moment, I blinked and was brought right back to my childhood. Right back to the days after my father had died, when my mother would still at least *try* to show up for her children, albeit usually wasted and during the wee hours in the mornings. She'd wake us up from our slumbers—usually it was Matthew and me who slept the lightest and would creep down the stairs to find her arguing with Nonna at the front door.

Sometimes she'd look up through an alcohol haze and smile to where we peered through the rungs of the banister.

I never smiled back. I barely felt like I knew her at all.

But I wanted to. What child wouldn't.

"Where the hell have you been?" I snapped before I could help myself. "The restaurant closes at eleven."

I hated how I sounded. Harping and unforgiving. The very definition of a ball and chain, and we weren't even married.

Xavier's gaze held mine for an extra few seconds before he grunted and dropped his messenger bag next to his shoes. "The restaurant closes, but no one goes home until late. And then that bloody frog—"

"You mean the French chef you were in the process of throttling when I got there?"

Another grunt. "He came back begging for his job. Then quit again when he wouldn't cook the duck the way I like." Xavier shook his head as he unbuttoned the chef's jacket, revealing a tight white undershirt that put his muscled chest and biceps on display. "I don't like babysitting my staff. And I *really* don't like people playing games with me. He learned that the hard way."

I curled farther into the couch. I wasn't sure I wanted to know what that meant.

Xavier looked up finally and found me sitting on the couch. At once, he stilled, that dark blue gaze tracking over all of me, taking in my bare legs, the short hem of my nightdress, the thin strap falling over one shoulder, the tousled hair I hadn't yet braided back. By the time he reached my face, that blue flame was back. And I could see exactly what he wanted to do.

For the second time.

"Oh, no you don't," I said, plastering myself into the couch's corner. "Not again."

"No?" He padded his way across the carpet like a big cat tracking through the forest. "I'm not so sure about that, babe. If you don't want to be chased, you shouldn't look like you want to be caught so bad."

By the time he reached me, I was shivering—out of fear or anticipation, I wasn't sure. Xavier licked his full lips, eyes gleaming.

For a moment, I was back in that alley. Caught in the throes of pleasure, yes. But then in a wave of utter disappointment.

"Xavi, no," I said fiercely, forcing myself to meet his gaze despite the fact that a part of me very much wanted to give him what he hunted. I loved him. I loved what he could do. But at moments like these, I had to love myself more. "You will not use me again like that."

He paused, hovering over me, then blinked. The feral look disappeared. "I—yeah. No, I won't."

He sighed and collapsed on the couch next to me with such utter despondency, I couldn't help wanting to crawl into his lap and hug him, even with the anger I was harboring. I'd never felt so torn between what was right for me and what was right for someone I loved.

"You going to tell me what happened this time?" I asked carefully.

"What do you mean?"

I sighed. "Xavi you were about to kill someone when I walked into that kitchen. And I know your chef pissed you off and every-thing, but it was a bit much, don't you think? And then you dragged me outside, fuc—screwed me in the alley like some girl you picked up at a bar and proceeded to leave me there. Next to a dumpster. Like I was t-t-trash."

By the time I was finished, my lip was trembling, and more than one fat tear had welled in my eyes. Viciously, I swiped at them. I didn't want to be weak right now. But saying it out loud like that really drove it home. I'd felt a lot of things with Xavier in the past, but never like this. Never like I meant nothing to him.

He watched me for a long moment, seemingly waiting until I had gotten myself together. Then, all at once, he yanked me into his lap, cradling my shivering form against his big body while he stroked my hand and wrapped his other arm firmly about my waist.

"You," he said, "are *not* trash. *Never*, Ces. Do you hear me?"

I swallowed thickly, but I was reminded of one of the bits of pop psychology I'd learned in teacher training—that telling a kid what *not* to do only reinforced the negative actions more.

He said "not." He said "never." But all I heard was "trash." And it was a difficult word to unhear, even if I was the one to say it first.

"God, I'm so sorry." He gathered me into him, guiding my head to his shoulder while stroking my hair. "So fucking sorry. I didn't—fuck, I didn't really think. I was just so upset when you walked in, Ces. And then I saw you, and I felt like a bull seeing red, you know? Rage was everywhere, and you were the one thing that could solve it for me. And then after..." He shook his head. "Fuck, I was so ashamed. I couldn't face you. What a fucking coward."

"And this was all because of the chef?"

I frowned. I'd heard more than one story by this point of Xavier's tempestuous cooking staff. He employed artists—it was one of the reasons for his success. But they gave him more than his share of trouble, too. Still, manhandling an employee seemed like the definition of unprofessional. It sounded dangerous.

"Le Fray was just the cream atop a very sticky pudding."

Xavier loosened his hold around me, though I kept my cheek to his shoulder, enjoying the warmth of his body. I was finally starting to relax. I spent so much time holding my child that I often forgot the comfort of someone else holding me.

"My uncle," he said in a voice so low I almost couldn't hear him. "I got news earlier today. He had another stroke. They don't think he has long."

I sat up to look at him, and involuntarily, my hand rose to cover my mouth in shock. "Oh, God. Xavi, I'm so sorry." Sorry, yes. But also, why didn't he tell me?

He heaved another sigh that ballooned his broad chest, then shoved a hand into his disheveled black hair. The movement made the muscles in his forearm flex, causing its tattoos to dance in the low lighting.

"To make matters worse, the estate's temporary steward quit today, too. So there's no one to manage things, and it'll all fall apart if I don't step in."

"Is it a lot to manage?" I asked. I imagined a country manor, perhaps with some animals, probably a garden, and a few staff members paid to guide tours or something like that.

Xavier offered a dry expression. "It's nearly twelve hundred years of accumulated assets, Ces. Makes the Parker Group look like child's play."

I gulped. I didn't know much about how the business of the gentry worked in the UK. They didn't really cover that in Austen adaptations. This sounded like a lot more than some topiaries and barnyard animals. If Xavier, CEO of an international restaurant group, was intimidated, then it was more than I could possibly imagine.

Still, I sensed he was upset about more than just taking over his family's affairs.

"He means a lot to you, doesn't he?" I asked, reaching out to stroke Xavier's hair. "Your uncle."

With closed eyes, he leaned into my touch, and his sigh told me I was right. We hadn't really talked a lot about the role Xavier's uncle Henry had played in his life, but I gathered he'd always been around, particularly after Xavier's mother died and he was finally welcomed into his father's life. He said he wasn't needed in Kendal, but when he thought I wasn't listening, Xavier would call the estate a few times a week to check on the man.

It was clear Henry Parker was more than just a distant relative and someone to manage accounts.

"He was always nice to me," he admitted. "Well, as nice as the Parkers get. Now I think he knew something was wrong with him. He started pestering me to come back to Kendal last year. Take my rightful place at the family's head. Learn everything he does." He nodded at a particularly ornate clock that had been mounted on the wall behind us. "Sent me that as a token a few months ago. Said I had to bring it back, ready to work. Just like me."

I watched as a multitude of expressions crossed his beautiful face. Grief, yes. Maybe a bit of resentment. And a lot of guilty.

My heart twisted on his behalf. Family was complicated. I knew that better than most.

"But now..." I urged him on.

"Now I don't really have a choice, do I?" he replied. "*Now* I have to go. Or else I'm the fuckup bastard they always thought I was, title or not."

"But...you're not a bastard," I said. "You keep saying that, but you're not."

There was a loud snort. "Christ, Ces, you think because someone corrected a mistake that the first twenty years of my life don't exist? You don't forget two decades of being called the Parker bastard just because someone finds a piece of paper." He groaned. "It was Henry who found it, you know. After my father's accident— the one that kept him from having more children. Georgina, my step-mum, she left him for a bit, threatened divorce unless he passed the estate to Frederick—that's my stepbrother, see. But then Henry discovered my parents' marriage certificate and dissolution papers. He's the reason why the people in this life were forced to accept me. He's the reason I became a duke. The only one who ever believed I could."

A few more pieces of the puzzle began to click together. The first time Xavier had told me the story of how he reunited with his father, it had sounded like Rupert Parker had had a sudden change of heart regarding his long-lost son. But now it was apparent that relationship was engineered more by his uncle Henry. A person who probably cared for Xavier more than he let on. And someone who, despite his attempts at distance, Xavier cared for too.

A man who, at this point, was the last remnant of family Xavier had.

I turned fully toward him so that I was straddling his waist. His hands rested comfortably on my bare thighs, though without any lascivious intent as his hands stroked my skin. The flame was gone. Now it was just bright blue sadness. The color of new tears.

"Come here," I told him, wrapping my arms around Xavier's neck and guiding his head to my shoulder this time. To my surprise, he allowed me to comfort him. He buried his nose in my neck and inhaled deeply.

"God, you smell good," he said. "Like fresh milk. And that soap you bought at the Portobello Market last week. What was it?"

"Sweet milk," I admitted. "Good nose."

His lips found my shoulder. "You smell a fuck lot better than me."

I chuckled while I massaged the back of his neck. "You do have the air of a distillery about you."

He inhaled and exhaled several more times until his shoulders started to relax. "I don't like who I am in Kendal. And the people there don't like me either, Ces. I'm an intruder. I always have been."

"That might have been true when you were younger," I said, despite not really knowing who "these people" were. "But you're the duke. They have to respect that, don't they?"

Another grunt, which told me he was nearly done talking. That and the heaviness of his palms on my legs indicated my man was relaxing at least, and with that, perilously close to sleep. Well, it was beyond late. At this rate, we'd have maybe three hours of sleep before Sofia crawled into bed with us, intent on telling us all about her dreams.

"I have to go up there," Xavier mumbled into my skin. "Tomorrow."

My heart sank as I threaded my fingers through his soft, shiny hair. "Well, then. I suppose that's how it has to be. Don't worry. We'll manage without you."

I waited for him to correct me. To tell me that obviously he meant all of us together. That he wouldn't let this event stop us from doing what we had come here to do—keep our tenuous little family together.

But Xavier didn't answer. He was already asleep.

"I STILL DON'T UNDERSTAND why you have to leave this early."

The sky was barely starting to change colors when I sat at the enormous kitchen counter the next morning, watching Xavier go through a smart, efficient routine. We had probably gotten all of two hours of sleep before he woke me just before four to make up "properly," he said. I wasn't about to argue. But after that, there was really no point in going back to sleep, knowing that a certain black-haired sprite would be up anyway within minutes.

Now the sky was just starting to glimmer with a suggestion of dawn while I stirred a cup of coffee and Xavier prepared the strangest breakfast I'd ever seen.

"You don't understand," he said as he scooped a double serving of rice out of the cooker on the counter and into a large cereal bowl. "The stroke was quite severe. I have to get up there and see to things today."

I knew it was selfish to resent a man who had just had a stroke, but I couldn't help it. We'd been here a month, but Xavier had been working like crazy. Sofia was still desperate to spend time with her dad. And so was I.

"You won't enjoy it in Kendal," Xavier said before I could even suggest it.

He plucked an egg from the basket stored in a sleek box next to the fridge. With the brisk, practiced movements of a professional, he cracked it with one hand into the rice, added some soy sauce, and started mixing it all together vigorously with a pair of chopsticks. I loved watching him cook. It was a bit like watching an artist paint.

"Stay in London," he continued. "See the sights. Take Sof to Big Ben and London Bridge and another palace and enjoy yourselves. I'll be back as soon as I can."

By the time he was finished stirring, the egg, rice, and soy concoction had taken on a slightly frothy texture. He sprinkled a mixture of sesame, salt, and seaweed crumbles called furikake on top. It still looked like something that had been washed up from the sea, but the garnish was a bit more appetizing.

I shrank around my latte, which had been thoughtfully prepared from a surgical-looking contraption at the end of the counter. Xavier had made do with a double espresso, already consumed. I had a few moments to dredge up the guts to say what I really wanted. I didn't want to put any more pressure on him, given the circumstances, but I also knew that if I didn't say what I really wanted, I'd regret it.

"Sofia and I have already seen those things a million times at this point," I pointed out. "If your driver can come with us, we can explore Cumbria while you work, can't we? Isn't it a major tourist area too?"

"It's not as great as everyone says. Just a lot of water and hills, really."

I frowned. I had seen enough pictures of the famous Lake District to know that was a total lie. "Do you—you really want us to stay away, don't you?"

The idea made my stomach drop. There was a part of me that thought back to Lea's question: what was he waiting for? His family relations were obviously a much more important part of his life than he had led me to believe, but even after a month, there had been no mention of meeting any of them. Nothing about visiting any of his family's properties or engaging with them in any way.

Was it them he wanted to keep from us? Or I wondered as I picked at a thread from the faded black robe I'd brought from home, the other way around?

Xavier turned from the fridge, set several glass containers on the counter, and frowned. "I don't understand the question."

I sighed and stared into my coffee, imagining it would be more articulate than I was right now. Why was this so hard to say? "Never mind." I wasn't going to beg.

But he was done examining his food. Now his piercing blue attention was fully on me. "Are you telling me you want to come to the estate? Deal with these stuffy people who hate me and likely will not be particularly welcoming to you or Sof? Just for me?"

I worried my jaw for a moment. I wasn't used to telling someone what I wanted or how I felt. I was used to teaching children how to do it, waiting for my siblings to take what they wanted, making do with whatever was left over for me. And yet, here was Xavier, asking me point blank for the opposite.

Well. Why not?

I stuck my chin out. "We didn't come here for Big Ben or Buckingham Palace, Xavi. We came here for you. We came here to be a family. And the way I learned it, you're supposed to be there for each other when it's hard too, not just when it's easy." I swallowed. "Not every day can be summer and sunshine. Winter has to come eventually. But that won't make us love you any less."

His dark blue eyes skipped over me as if looking for something else. A joke, maybe. Or some kind of tell that I was lying.

I wasn't.

Then he was moving suddenly around the counter until he had picked me clear off my stool and set me on the marble so he could step between my legs and capture my face with both hands. His kiss was brief but thorough, a quick swirl of tongue and promise for much more.

"I love you for that," he told me when he pulled away. "More than you could possibly know."

I gazed up at him, basking in his open adoration as I waited for an answer to my question. He opened his mouth, then let his hands drop so he could take my left hand and look at it for a long time. His mouth opened, like he wanted to say something.

I swallowed. This...he wasn't...was he going to ask what I thought, maybe even *hoped* he would? Right here in his kitchen, with no warning, no pomp or circumstance of any kind?

"Francesca," he said softly. "I...will you..."

I stiffened, practically slipping off the counter in my agitation. In a way, it would be the most perfect way to declare his intentions, in the space he loved the best.

Ask me, Xavi, I begged internally. *Please, just ask.*

But Xavier just offered a lopsided smile, then stamped another kiss to my forehead and left me on the counter. He returned to the other side, back to his bowl of rice and egg, which he topped with a variety of vegetables, something pickled, and another egg yolk cracked into the middle before he covered the bowl with a plastic lid and set a pair of disposable chopsticks on the top.

"*Tamago gohan*," he said before I could ask. "My favorite breakfast, in case you were wondering. I'll eat it on the way."

I twisted around, unsure of what to do here. Was that whole interaction a figment of my imagination? Or had he really just been about to ask me to marry him?

I got no indication either way.

"Should I get Sof up?" I prodded, returning to my original request. He still hadn't answered one way or another. Were we going with him? Did he want us to stay?

"Don't bother." My heart fell as Xavier swept toward the door. "I'll have Elsie arrange everything. Go back to bed and get some more rest, babe. I'll see you in Kendal."

Kendal? We were going after all?

But before I could ask exactly when that would be, he was gone, leaving me with the inexorable feeling that despite very little happening at this moment, everything was once again about to change.

TEN

"Mama, sheep!" Sofia shrieked for what had to be the fifteenth time in two hours.

"Yep, sweet pea. There they are again."

I smiled down at her, then offered an apologetic glance to the elderly couple sitting across a plastic tabletop from us. They had gotten on the train in Manchester and were no doubt weary of hearing about passing livestock. Ten-minute updates about every cow, horse, sheep, and duck in the country was probably not how they intended to spend their trip this afternoon.

But these things were extremely interesting for a little girl who had grown up in a concrete jungle, and I wasn't about to spoil her fun. The most green Sofia had ever seen was Central Park in the summer, and while the Green Meadows Farm in Brooklyn was a fun place for city kids to see a goat, this kind of spread was beyond her comprehension.

For the last several hours, Sofia and I had been chugging along fast enough that the hedges bordering the tracks blurred into long green snakes. Beyond that, though, the English countryside had been yawning in front of us as industrial suburbs and suburban villages gradually gave way to the rolling green hills and tiny hamlets that appeared in countless films. Sometimes, when the train turned, I spotted the shadows of sharper peaks in the distance, informing me that we were approaching our final destination, nearly three hours north of London.

True to his word, Xavier had contacted Elsie, who had arranged for transport from King's Cross to Kendal. It wasn't until I'd risen fully, alone in our sprawling bedroom, and spotted the first-class tickets on the nightstand that I understood exactly what was happening. Which only became clearer when Ben showed up to take us to the station.

So much for London.

Well, I supposed I'd asked for it.

Sofia turned back to a show she was watching on my tablet, allowing me to sink back into the novel on my Kindle. *North and South* was a classic and seemed to fit given where we were going, even if the industrial town of Milton wasn't exactly these lushly rolling hills. But before I could get too far into the scene where Margaret Hale finally realizes that cotton baron John Thornton isn't quite the heartless man she thought he was, I was interrupted by the buzz of my phone.

Finally, Xavier checking in.

But it wasn't Xavier.

> Kate: How's merry old England?

I sighed. I'd spoken with Kate last night, in need of someone to process the events at the restaurant before Xavier had come home. Since Kate had been at a family dinner at the time, however, our conversation had only led to near-continuous texts from all my siblings since.

Matthew had threatened to teach the duke his own lesson in civility if he didn't get his act together. Kate had wanted to know what the dress code was for a real-life English manor. Lea said if

Xavier didn't pop the question before Monday, I should just leave him to his terrible family and come home. Nonna suggested I make everyone her manicotti and was appalled they would actually hire a cook to feed everyone rather than making it themselves. And my younger sisters, of course, mostly just wanted to know if there were any other available young gentry in the area they could meet if they wanted to visit.

The truth was, they were all worried about me. No one had actually thought spending the summer in England was a good idea in the first place—except Joni, the youngest. And if Joni thought it was a good idea, it probably wasn't.

> Me: Merry enough, but very old, as usual.
> And now it's very green.

I snapped a picture of the passing countryside, which currently included a lot of picturesquely crumbling cottages in the distance and sent it to her.

> Kate: Looks cold. Those places can't have very good insulation. I bet they get moth holes like crazy too.

I rolled my eyes. My fashion hound sister would think first of the moth holes.

> Me: I honestly wouldn't know. All my knits are acrylic, not wool. Only the cheap stuff for me, you know.

> Kate: So where's the duke taking you tonight? He better have a fantastic date night planned since he's dragging you all the way up there.

Since discovering that Xavier was actually a member of the peerage, my siblings no longer used his name, only his title. As if, despite the fact that they never saw him, they knew it would get under his skin. I supposed it was better than "cheating douchecanoe."

> Me: We're getting to Kendal late afternoon. I doubt there will be much time for a date. He's pretty busy, especially with what's going on with his uncle.

> Kate: He's not with you?! Why the heck not?

I sighed, already anticipating where this was going.

> Me: He left early this morning. But he got us train tickets. It's fine.

> Kate: Wait, wait, wait. First the guy makes you cry last night, then leaves you for his castle, and once he finally lets you tag along, he's abandoning you to the train?

> Me: omg he is not abandoning us! He has a lot of stuff with family he has to deal with.

> Kate: YOU are his family.

I paused. Was I, though? Sofia, yes. And I'd be lying if I said I wasn't the slightest bit peeved he hadn't waited at least for her. Or at least volunteered to send the helicopter he'd apparently taken back for us. She would have liked that a lot.

Yeah. When Elsie mentioned that one this morning, I wasn't pleased.

But me? I wasn't sure I qualified. Girlfriend, yes. Mother of his child, yes. But family? That was still a work in progress, wasn't it?

> Me: It's fine. We're fine. I'm going to stop texting now.

> Kate: If you say fine one more time, I'm going to smack you across the ocean.

> Me: FINE, I'll stop.

> Kate: Brat. My love to Sof. We miss her.
> And you too, you stubborn fool.

I sighed, brushing my thumb over the text. Love was such a small word, but these days I seemed hungrier for it than ever. It's odd. Sometimes you don't realize how starving you've been for something until you've had your first real taste.

> Kate: Just don't let him push you around.
> You're MY sister. You deserve the best.

"I know you."

I looked up from typing a response to find the elderly woman across the table eyeing me with something approximating glee. "Excuse me?"

"Been trying to figure it out all afternoon," she said in a thick Northern accent, nodding to herself. "Ralphie, don't you recognize her?" She prodded her husband, who awoke briefly at his name, then fell immediately back to sleep. "Yes, you were in the paper yesterday. You and your little girl."

She smiled kindly at Sofia, who gave the woman a suspicious look identical to her father's imperious expression before clutching Tyrone and turned back at the show she was watching.

"Er—are you sure?" I tucked my phone in my bag. "I can't think of why we would be in the newspaper. We don't even live here."

Even as I said it, dread lodged itself in my gut. Maybe the papers had renewed their interest of Xavier's personal life. Maybe Sofia and I had been followed on one of our sightseeing trips over the last several weeks. Or maybe even worse, Xavier and I had been seen in the alley the other night.

Oh God, what if my nonna saw her granddaughter with her skirt around her waist in a freaking news article?

"Americans, yes," said the woman. "Oh, I'm very sure. In the local paper this morning. Adorable picture, the duke kissing his daughter and all at the airport last month." She nodded at Sofia. "Looks just like him, doesn't she?"

I glanced back at Sofia, who was happily entranced with her screen, headphones on, without a clue what the woman and I were discussing.

"I—well—"

"Ralphie, you still have the paper from this morning?" The woman shoved the man next to her, who started out of sleep again with a grumble.

"Hmm? What d'ye want, Evie?"

"The paper, Ralphie. I want to read the paper!"

Ralphie was apparently hard of hearing, based on the way Evie was talking to him. Nonetheless, he managed to procure a rolled-up newspaper from his coat pocket and thrust it at her before folding his arms across a barrel chest and sinking back into his slumber.

"See?" The woman opened the paper and turned it around toward me on the table.

I blinked. It was a local paper, barely the size of a pamphlet, the kind that was probably only circulated within a small area to a population with a mean age of maybe seventy.

But still. There I was at Heathrow arrivals, excruciatingly bedraggled in my *Flashdance* sweatshirt after a long flight, while Xavier beamed at Sofia in his arms like they were a Gap billboard. It was true—they did look alike. I, however, looked like a gremlin.

To my relief, however, it was also an old photo. Which meant none of my fears were true. Yet.

"Lovely," I murmured.

"But she's out of wedlock, isn't she? Too bad, that."

I felt as if I'd been smacked in the face as I passed the paper back to the woman. "Excuse me? My daughter is not 'out of wedlock.' She's four."

The woman just blinked, as if she'd only asked what color Sofia's hair was. "Oh, I didn't mean it in the bad way. Just that you and the duke. You're not married, are you?" A quick glance at my hand apparently told her what she needed to know. "Don't worry, love. I know the truth. She's his daughter, no matter what the papers might say."

I glanced back at the newsprint, wishing now I'd kept it, but too proud to ask for it back to see exactly what it said. I wanted to tell her she was wrong, point out exactly what was wrong with the piece, explicate the damn thing until she and every other person in this train knew exactly what was wrong with that logic and why.

But instead, we just chugged alone as I read the same sentence in my book again and again.

Because the truth was, no matter what I wanted to find, Xavier and I weren't married, of course. And so, instead of arguing with the woman more, I could say very little at all.

WE FOLLOWED a man in a stiff black jacket holding a sign bearing my name, who introduced himself simply as Gibson, out of the Lancaster train station. From there, Sofia and I were driven another hour and change into Cumbria, skirting the actual town of Kendal until we were at the edges of the Lake District, where the farms and paddocks gave way to mountains yawning above glass-blue slivers of water.

"Do you think mermaids live there?" Sofia said as we drove around one particularly large lake, then turned onto a private road that switch backed up a large hill.

"I bet so," I told her. "What other creatures do you think live in those depths? Fairies, maybe? Or maybe they have their own version of the Loch Ness monster."

I held up my hands to mime a monster, making Sofia giggle and squeal.

"There are several species of pike, perch, bream, and eels in Windermere Lake," interrupted Gibson. "There have also been reports of catfish, carp, and chub. Certainly no mermaids."

Sofia frowned. "No, there are definitely mermaids in that lake.

My mommy said so. And you can tell by the rainbow at the end. That's where mermaids live."

"There are none," Gibson argued firmly as he steered around another curve. "The rainbow is caused by the combination of light and rain. It is an illusion, nothing more."

I shook my head, hiding a smile when he caught my glance in the rearview mirror. The man had no idea what he was getting into.

But before Sofia could argue back with him about mermaid mythology, rainbows, or anything else the landscape indicated, Gibson swung the car down another drive and approached a large gate of swirling black iron.

"Welcome to Corbray Hall, miss," he droned as the gate swung open.

I didn't answer. I couldn't with my mouth hanging wide open.

A pea gravel drive approximately the length of Fifth Avenue stretched in front of us, lined with tall beech trees. On either side lay the grounds of an expansive blooming garden containing topiaries, winding paths, vine-wrapped arches, and too many mysterious entrances to potentially secret passageways to count. The drive gradually climbed to the top of a hill where an enormous manor towered over the garden scape on the entrance side and overlooked a view of the entire countryside on the other. I could see three lakes just from the car, and we weren't even at the top of the property yet.

Majestic didn't even cover it.

"Mama," Sofia whispered, clearly no longer interested in mermaids. "It's a castle." Her eyes bugged. "Daddy's a *prince*."

"It's Corbray Hall." Gibson's tone was utterly uncompromising. "And your father is certainly *not* a prince. Castles are fortified against a common enemy. There is a ruin of Norland Castle on the other side of the estate, but Corbray Hall was built well after Cumbria was settled. It is a civilized place."

"Not Camelot," I murmured with a smile, remembering *Monty Python*. "A silly place."

"What's that, miss?" Gibson's tone was clearly irked.

I cleared my throat. "Er, nothing. Go on, please."

"As I was saying, there once was a castle here, as this land has been the seat of the Duke of Kendal since the time of William the Conqueror."

I swallowed. "The seat? So...there is more than one...er...place at the table?"

"Residences?" Gibson sniffed with his large nose. "Of course. His Grace owned four others, including Parkvale House in London, a hunting lodge in Scotland, a second country estate in York, and the house in Bath to winter. Corbray Hall, however, is the jewel of the dukedom and has been since it was built in the late eighteenth century. People come from all around to tour it on Friday afternoons. It is a Georgian masterpiece."

I swallowed. That was...a lot. Xavier and his family owned at least five priceless pieces of property and some of the oldest holdings in England.

I barely owned my handbag.

Wait. Lived. Owned. Past tense. Gibson clearly wasn't talking about Xavier but about his father.

"And the current, er, His Grace?" I stumbled. "Where does he, ah, winter?" I couldn't quite get my mouth around using seasons like verbs.

"The current duke," Gibson said in a tone that practically spat derision, "does not privy the staff with his whereabouts. He has not been seen in Kendal since the passing of the last duke."

"What the heck does that mean?" Sofia demanded. "My daddy is the duke. How can there be a past one?"

Gibson's beady eyes landed on Sofia through the rearview. "Yes," he said in a tone that really sounded like "no."

Gibson pulled around a circular driveway of the same pea gravel up to the manor's front entrance, where a pair of double doors carved with lion heads opened to reveal Elsie, holding her ever-present clipboard and wearing her faithful penny loafers. I grinned. In the midst of all this grandeur and Gibson's tour, Elsie's no-nonsense person was a welcome sight.

"Elsie!" Sofia squealed, not waiting for Gibson to walk around to open the door. She catapulted herself out of the car and sprinted across the gravel into Elsie's waiting arms.

"Thank you for the ride, Gibson," I told him as he opened my door for me to exit. "Er..."

He looked at me with beady eyes. "Yes, miss?"

I glanced at Elsie and back to him. It was common to tip porters and drivers in London, but I wasn't sure about what to do with my boyfriend's estranged staff. What was the protocol for that?

"I'm sorry, here," I said, taking out a five-pound-note from my wallet and handing it to him. Better safe than sorry, I supposed.

Gibson just stared at it, eyes suddenly afire. "Certainly not, miss," he declared, then abruptly moved to the trunk to unload our two small suitcases.

Crap. I guess I was sorry after all, although something told me either way, I couldn't have avoided it.

"Hello, loves," Elsie greeted me while she stroked Sofia's hair from where she was wrapped around Elsie's hips. "Sorry I couldn't be the one to meet you at the station. Gibson here doesn't like to drive, but Ben had a cold this morning. He's feeling better, though."

Gibson just sniffed. "Please request that Benjamin move the car to the garage, Mrs. Crew. I have things to attend to." He turned to me with a stiff tip of his head. "Miss."

Without waiting for an answer, he angled around us with our weekend bags and strode off into the manor. Sofia and I turned back to Elsie.

"Why does he call you 'miss'?" Sofia asked once Gibson had left us. "You're not a little girl. That's what Elsie calls me."

I smiled. As ever, my girl was possessive of her family.

"I think because I'm not married, peanut," I told her. "Although I'm not sure I'd want to be ma'am either. That just sounds like what the butcher calls Nonna back home."

"Yeah, that won't work. Nonna's *grandma*." Sofia's button nose wrinkled. "Why can't he just call you Frankie, like everyone else?"

I shrugged. "That's not how they do things here, bug." I grinned at Elsie. "Right, 'Mrs. Crew?'"

Elsie just snorted and patted her gray bob as we all started to walk toward the house. "Don't mind Gibson. He's a terrible snob. He's just mad I made him pick you up since Ben couldn't do it. Thinks it's beneath him to drive a car."

I frowned. "Why?"

"Because he's the butler. Very few houses have them anymore, but Gibson has been for, what, thirty years now? Since Xavier was a boy. His Grace, I mean," she corrected herself when another staff member passed by. "They like things formal up here," she whispered conspiratorially.

I looked around the imposing entry hall as we walked inside the manor. "I can understand why."

Elsie followed my gaze while Sofia returned to my side, as if she too had suddenly become aware of the grandeur of our surroundings.

It felt more like a museum than a house—which, I realized, was probably accurate. A huge staircase crisscrossed up at least three floors, with enormous wood banisters carved with what looked like the history of the estate. The stairs were padded with a sumptuous carpet that appeared to continue down arched corridors in nearly every direction from where we stood. Each was lined with richly polished doors and a variety of priceless antiques, along with gilt-framed portraits of people who looked like royalty from nearly every major era of English history over the last several hundred years. I looked up at a particularly large portrait that hung probably ten full feet above a grandfather clock in the entry hall. It was of one of the previous dukes, I assumed, based on his pose and stature. Xavier might have inherited a lot of his mother's features, but it was very clear where he got his imperious blue eyes, prodigious height, and long nose that his ancestors enjoyed looking down.

Xavier's family, I realized, was Sofia's family too.

"I'll give you a proper tour this evening if you like," Elsie said. "But for now, I'm here to take you to Xavier. Poor boy, he's just swimming in papers."

"What exactly has been going on?" I wondered, taking Sofia's hand so she wouldn't accidentally "explore" something along the way into pieces.

"It's his uncle Henry," Elsie said as she led us up the main staircase.

"Yes, Xavi said he'd had another stroke. Is he able to speak?"

"In a manner," Elsie said, veering to the right at the top of the stairs, where we passed another parade of painted relatives. "He woke up screaming, apparently, about some sort of deal that had to be signed today. The boy can tell you more if he wants, but the short of it is that Henry invested a great amount of the estate's money into something that will ruin everything if it's not taken care of this week." She gave a few disapproving tsks. "Likely tip of the iceberg, if you ask me. Where there's one, there's a whole mountain below."

"That sounds...stressful." I wasn't sure what else to say. I didn't exactly have a head for business, nor did I understand in the slightest what went into maintaining a place like this.

"It is," Elsie said shortly. "He's in here."

With a sharp knock, she pushed open a heavy-looking wood door the color of almost-burned caramel. It opened into a room with windows that looked out onto the gardens, sunlight streaming over a collection of leather furniture built to last, and a fireplace that stood empty in the summer afternoon. The walls were covered with tartan wallpaper and more imperious paintings than I could count, with a wall of priceless books on the other side begging to be read.

But I barely noticed any of it. Because there, sitting in the middle of the room, looking more like the duke he was than ever I'd seen him, was Xavier.

ELEVEN

Xavier was hunched over an enormous antique desk bearing two computers, a pile of papers, and several empty teacups. He looked a bit worse for wear in a rumpled button-down, sleeves rolled up to reveal his tattoo, and one hand shoved through his hair as he perused documents. Dark circles marred his lovely pale skin, and his eyes, still blue as the sky, seemed slightly overcast and dulled. I knew I was responsible for some of that fatigue, but not all of it. He was a far cry from the restaurant tycoon who had left me in London and even further from my lighthearted chef.

But everything about him spoke of ownership. This room had clearly been constructed for people his size, and he fit into it like a piece of a jigsaw puzzle. His shoulders were arched as he shuffled through a few more papers, more focused now that I'd seen him even in the kitchen.

His eyes, however, brightened considerably when they caught sight of Sofia and me entering the room. "There you are," he pronounced.

"Dad!" Sofia wrested her hand from mine and scampered around the desk to hop in Xavier's lap. He welcomed her with a kiss, which made her squeal. "Ah, Daddy, your face is scratchy!"

"That's because Daddy has had a very long day and never had time to shave."

He shoved back from his seat and, even carrying Sofia, took less than a few seconds to cross the room completely and wrap another arm around me while delivering a quick, yet deep kiss that set my lips tingling.

"We made it," I murmured with a smile, all resentment about helicopters and failed proposals vanquished.

I was rewarded with another kiss—this one slightly more thorough than the last, though neither of them carried any remnants of the passion of last night.

"Took you long enough." Xavier released us, setting Sofia back on the ground so he could return to his desk.

"Can I get you anything, boy?" Elsie asked, still standing in the doorway. "Shall I have the cook send up another pot of tea?"

"No, thanks, Els. I'll be fine."

She nodded and winked at Sofia before leaving us alone with him.

"Sure you don't want that tea?" I asked doubtfully. "You look like you could use it."

"I've just had my head in these accounts all bloody day," Xavier replied with a grunt. "It's a fucking mess."

"It certainly is, you poor thing."

At the sound of a voice I didn't recognize, Sofia and I turned. In the corner near the far window stood a woman I hadn't seen when I'd first walked in, considering I had eyes for only Xavier. Now, however, I definitely noticed her. As would anyone, man or woman, when faced with that kind of perfection.

Tall and blond, she looked like she had walked off a fashion spread, dressed simply and chicly in loose cream trousers and a crisp white blouse that perfectly complemented her golden hair, pink lips, and polished nails. Tasteful diamonds sparkled from her ears and around her wrist. Standing by the window, the summer sunlight shone through her hair, casting a golden halo all around her while she smiled.

She didn't just look like money. She looked like very old money. The kind that announces itself just by existing.

"Oh," I said, reaching out a hand. "Hello. I'm Frankie Zola."

"Fran*cesca*," the woman corrected me. On my own name. Kindly, of course, but still a correction. "I've heard so much about you."

"You...have?" I glanced between her and Xavier, who was back to fumbling through papers at his desk.

"Yes, yes. Kip's told me all about you." She strode across the room and accepted my hand at last with a quick squeeze instead of a full handshake. "Imogene Douglas."

"Lady Imogene Douglas," Xavier added wryly with a wink her way. "Gibson won't stand for informality around here, remember?"

They both tittered at some inside joke before Xavier looked back at me.

"Imogene is Lucy's sister, Ces. Their father is the Viscount of Ortham. They own the estate next to ours."

"Oh..." I nodded, half-wondering if I was supposed to curtsy or something else. Or was that only something you did for royalty? After the fiasco with Gibson's tip, I didn't want to embarrass myself any more, so I contented myself with a nod in acknowledgment.

"If you can even call it that anymore," Imogene put in. "Papa sold the last of the paddocks last year, so we're just down to the house, if you can even call it that. Really, it's more of a cottage."

I blinked. I had a feeling that what I called a cottage and what this woman called a cottage were not the same thing.

But another name was niggling at me. Lucy Douglas. Xavier's once best friend and fiancée, the woman he had originally left me for before she passed away from cancer. This was her sister? Xavier had described Lucy as homely and weak. I couldn't imagine anyone with that description being related to someone who was a dead ringer for Gigi Hadid.

"I'm so sorry for your loss," I told her. "Your sister, I mean. Lucy."

Was it me, or did Imogene's lip curl slightly at the mention of Lucy? Either way, it was clear she was surprised to hear I knew who she was.

"Yes, Lucy was...a great tragedy for all of us," she agreed. "Darling girl. We all grew up together, didn't we, Kip?"

I frowned at the nickname. She'd used it twice now. "Kip?"

Xavier had the decency to blush. "As in kipper. Like the fish. Ah, herring, in the US. They used to make fun of me because I hated it so much."

"But you love fish, Dad," Sofia piped up as she climbed onto the window seat with her stuffed unicorn. "Sake, uni, hotate..."

She continued to list the Japanese names for various types of fish that Xavier had taught her at the market, more to Tyrone than the rest of us. I smiled. Xavier had taken her to the London fish market a few weeks ago, early one Sunday morning, so I could sleep in. I'd been hearing about it ever since.

Imogene just looked slightly appalled.

"Oh, isn't she a darling?" she cooed. "Kip, she looks just like you. She really does, no matter what the papers say." She bent down so that she was face-to-face with Sofia. "Are you your papa's princess, sweet girl?"

Sofia just set Tyrone in her lap and frowned. "I'm not a princess."

"No, that's right." Imogene nodded. "You're the daughter of a duke. So that makes you a lady, doesn't it? Just like me." She stood and tapped her finger on her mouth. "Although I'm not sure that's appropriate either, given your mummy never married him."

I tensed and darted a glance at Xavier. He just chuckled and clicked through an account ledger on his computer screen.

"Well," Imogene continued. "Perhaps we can make an exception, just this once. What do you think, Lady Sofia?"

Sofia's frown flattened her features, and she shook her head hard enough to toss a feather of black hair into her face. I hid a smile. She had the exact same errant lock over her forehead that Xavier did, and it flopped forward in exactly the same way when she was annoyed.

"No?" Imogene was not deterred. "Well, give it time. I'm sure your papa would buy you some lovely new dresses if you asked him. Then you'll really look the part."

For a moment, Sofia looked tempted by the idea. Her eyes darted around the room again, landing on all the clearly fancy things that, even at four, she would know not to touch without asking. But stubbornly, she shook her head and clutched her doll to her chest. "No. I like pants now. No dresses."

My eyebrows rose. That was new. Especially since there were no less than three sparkly princess costumes shoved into her overnight bag right this moment.

"Well, then, he'd better get you a pony instead."

Lady Imogene straightened while chuckling, as if she'd made an excellent joke. She smoothed nonexistent wrinkles out of her trousers and turned.

"It really is a mess, though," she told me as she strode over to stand next to Xavier. "When I heard about it, I came straight over—I helped Papa manage the sale of the paddocks, you know."

I didn't answer. My eyes were glued to the place where her hand now rested on Xavier's broad shoulder. It was just a touch, but it annoyed me. And Xavier didn't seem to care at all.

"I still don't understand why Henry would have invested in a mine, of all things," she was saying. "And slate, too. All of them have been shut down in Cumbria. The red tape alone will be a nightmare. If he really wanted to get into mining, he should have invested in the new coal mine like Papa. First one in thirty years, they're saying. Now that will mean some real money."

She looked at me as if for backup. I just shrugged. I hated that I had absolutely nothing to add to this conversation. Part of me wanted to be snarky and ask exactly what the sale of a few paddocks had to do with an entire estate's finances, but I knew it was only my insecurities talking. After all, Imogene grew up here. The only thing I could offer was third grade arithmetic lessons.

To my satisfaction, Xavier patted the top of Imogene's hand like she was Sofia offering Tyrone's expertise on cutlery.

"Maybe if it were the beginning of the twentieth century, not the twenty-first," he said. "It's a dead industry either way unless we're investing in the past, not the future. If Henry really wanted to do something useful, it should have been silica."

"Well, maybe it's not too late to change the deal." Imogene hovered her hand over Xavier's head. Then, with a glance at me, stroked it lightly before striding around me toward the door.

This time, I rather wanted to rip her hand off her body and smack her with it. But again, Xavier didn't react.

"If you want help changing the terms, let me know," Imogene told him.

"We have our own lawyers, thanks," Xavier said distantly.

"Nevertheless, a second opinion is never unwarranted. I'll call Humphrey and have him on the next flight to Kendal. Just say the word." She glanced at me. "Did you take the four o'clock? Was the airport crowded?"

"Er, no," I said. "We took the train this morning to Lancaster."

"Oh, you poor dear. What a slog that is. Kip, why didn't you book her a flight instead? I thought you took the helicopter."

Xavier just shrugged. I tried to pretend it didn't mean anything, but I was starting to wonder the same thing. Given our discussion, I still wasn't sure he really wanted us here, to begin with, and this interaction wasn't helping things.

"I'd better be off," she said. "I promised Papa I'd be back for tea, but we'll dine with you this evening. Speaking of horses, I promised Tommy we'd go riding tomorrow. Would you and Francine like to come?"

This time, I couldn't stop my scowl. "It's Francesca."

Imogene didn't answer.

"Er, Ces doesn't ride," Xavier said. Then he finally looked up from his computer at me. "Do you?"

He was so hopeful; I wanted to say yes. Unfortunately, I could not.

"No, stables aren't particularly available in the Bronx," I admitted. "Or Brooklyn, for that matter."

"I'll teach you one day, babe," Xavier assured me, and I enjoyed the way Imogene almost winced at the endearment. "Probably not tomorrow, though."

Imogene just laughed. "That'll be the day. Better let me teach her. I showed this one how to get his foot in the stirrup without kicking the horse."

With a dry cackle, she crossed the room once more to deliver a quick kiss to Xavier's cheek. At the window, Sofia tensed, but shockingly kept quiet, though I now saw her blue eyes hadn't missed a thing.

"Tonight, then," Imogene said to both of us.

I just nodded politely as she left.

Xavier relaxed back into his chair and started flipping through papers again. I waited for him to say something to Sofia and me, but when he didn't, I wondered if he thought we had left, too.

"I'm sorry you have to deal with all of this," I offered awkwardly. "Is there anything I can do to help? I'm pretty good with numbers. And organizing stuff."

He sighed and dropped the paper he was holding. "No, not really. It's not exactly what I wanted to be doing when I invited you two to spend the summer with me. I knew I'd have to pop up occasionally, but I was hoping to put it off until September."

I frowned. September. Of course. Because that's when we were going to leave.

It was the first time he'd stated that was his overt expectation, though, and though it had always been my plan, it hurt.

Sofia had left the window and started venturing around the room, exploring as quietly as a four-year-old could. This apparently consisted of her mimicking Gibson's quick history of the property to Tyrone, only this time involving as many magical creatures as she could think of. Especially mermaids.

I took the opportunity to join Xavier on his side of the desk, comforted when he wrapped his arm around my waist and pulled me close while he continued perusing the mess in front of him.

"It's making me wonder how long Henry's been this way," he said quietly. "He sent me some odd letters this year—I thought it was just because he wanted me back. But now..." He shook his head. "Something is really wrong here in how he's been managing things. It's good I came. The tenants, for one, need more from the steward."

"Tenants?" I frowned. "You actually have tenants? Like in *Downton Abbey*? I didn't think estates like that still existed."

Xavier looked up from his desk, brow arched wryly. "It's not really like that. Large rural estates suffered for a long time and many collapsed, although some did come out ahead. People like the Parkers—"

"Like you," I interrupted.

"Like them," Xavier insisted with a scowl. "Gentry, I mean. They still own about thirty percent of all the land in the UK." He shrugged. "The Duke of Kendal was the eighth largest landowner in England, owing mostly to lands granted over a thousand years ago. There are more than a few other peers on that list alongside the Crown. So yes, we have tenants, though they tend to be commercial farmers rather than individuals. Not to mention leases on other parts of the land for things like this. Bloody mines and what. And then there are all the other investments that sustain things." He tossed the papers around on the desk like he was fluffing a pillow. "It's a lot to manage. Clearly too much for one old man who has been struggling for who knows how long."

I balked. This was on a scale that was completely baffling. "There isn't a...team of people?" I asked. "It's like running a corporation, isn't it?"

"There is," Xavier said. "We have a financial firm that manages the portfolio. But the temporary steward was apparently quite the tyrant with the others. Most of the people Henry hired over the years to oversee the other sides of the family holdings have left at this point. Now there's no one."

Xavier was clearly in over his head with it all. Maybe that was what was most shocking of all. My man always seemed to be perfectly in control of things. There wasn't anything he couldn't conquer, along with his trusted team. Except, apparently, his own family's legacy.

"Look," he said with a sigh as he pushed back from the desk and pulled me between his knees. I leaned back to sit on the edge of the wood. "I'm bored to tears looking at this rubbish, and I'm in charge of it all until I can find someone better to do it. But there's no way I'll be able to leave after the weekend. There's too much to do. I wouldn't blame you at all if you'd rather go back to London. It's a lot more fun there."

I peeked over my shoulder and found Sofia sitting on the floor, quietly paging through an old atlas she'd found. I turned back to Xavier and set my hands on his broad shoulders.

"Do you want us to go?" I asked. "Would it be easier if we weren't here?"

A thin line formed between his dark brows. "What? How can you ask that?"

I shrugged. "This is the third time today you've suggested we stay in London. I can't help feeling like maybe that's what you really want."

"Well, it's absolutely fucking not."

"Swear jar, Dad!" Sofia called.

We both smiled in her direction, then turned back to each other after Xavier had taken a bill from his wallet and tossed it into an ornate vase at the end of the desk.

"Will you be able to make at least some time for us?" I asked, hating that I even had to wonder.

Xavier's hands came to rest just below my waist, thumbs stroking lightly over my hip bones through the leggings I'd worn to travel. I shivered, knowing full well what those thumbs were capable of. Along with all the other fingers on each hand.

"Of course," he said solemnly. "That's not even a question."

I pushed that errant lock of black from his forehead, enjoying the way he nuzzled into my hand. "Then it's not a question for us either. Where you go, we go."

His hands slipped behind my knees and pulled me toward him, tipping his chin upward for a kiss.

I obliged. Xavier purred like a cat under my lips, tongue just barely slipping out to touch mine. But just before things got a bit more interesting, he pulled away.

"That's that, then," he said as he stood, reaching toward the ceiling with a back-cracking stretch. "Why don't you two find Elsie to give you a tour of the grounds? There's actually loads to see. Library, of course—you'll love that. Gardens are worth a walk or two, and there's swimming in the pond. Horses, stables, all sorts to explore. Mrs. Niles—that's the housekeeper—gives tours to the general public at four on Fridays, so you could join them tomorrow if you want to know a bit more of the history."

"You don't know it?" I wondered. "I was hoping to get the tour from the duke himself."

For that, I received a wry smirk and an arched black brow before he caught me in his arms and lifted me up so we were nose to nose.

"If I'm giving a tour, it will only be for you, Ces," he growled. "Show you all the secret, forbidden places in this pile of stones. Spots where a girl can be taken advantage of. Believe me, you will be getting that one."

I smiled into his lips. "I can't wait."

TWELVE

Ten minutes later, Xavier declared that he needed a break.

"Come on, Sof," he said as he turned off the computer. "There's someone I'd like you to meet. Let's find Elsie, and Mummy and I can go for a walk."

After dropping Sofia off with Elsie in one of the sitting rooms, it took nearly fifteen minutes for Xavier and me to cross from one end of Corbray Hall to the other, and in that time, I got the tour I wanted, if a bit abrupt and truncated. It was clear from his bleak gestures that Xavier didn't care much for the place. He obviously knew a lot about it, but his curt answers made me think he resented the knowledge more than he wanted to share it.

"What's that painting?" I asked as he steered me down another long corridor filled with priceless (and enormous) portraits.

"What? Oh, that's Sir Roderick Parker."

"Another relative?"

"They're all relatives, babe."

"Yes, but which one is that?"

"Brother to my fifth great-grandfather, I believe."

"He looks like a soldier."

"Colonel, yeah. Fought in the Napoleonic Wars. Come on."

And so it went—him giving the shortest answer possible, me trying to drag more information out of him until he cut me off in pursuit of another direction.

"I'm not doing a very good job of hosting you, am I?" he said as he tugged me down another corridor. "First the paparazzi, then getting buried in paper, now this lousy tour."

"The paparazzi are no matter," I said, getting temporarily sidetracked by what looked like a Monet painting. "They haven't bothered us for weeks. Although—a woman on the train today made the strangest comment to me. And then Imogene too. Supposedly, there are articles circulating somewhere saying Sofia isn't yours. Did you know that?"

To my surprise, he just shrugged as he turned up a staircase. "It's just stupid gossip, Ces. The locals up here always found things to say about the Parkers. Don't pay them any attention."

That was it? No indignation? No shouting? Oddly, I was a bit annoyed. The Xavier I knew had a temper, yes, but he cared deeply about Sofia and me. Why wasn't he more put out?

"Well, I don't like the insinuation," I said.

Xavier's big shoulders moved up and down again as he strode. "Honestly, they've always been more interested in printing lies about me than is good for them. Nothing sells like scandal, even if it's one they make up."

"I realize our relationship didn't exactly progress in the normal fashion," I said, "but I don't appreciate being called a liar, no matter who says it. Or her"—I glanced down at Sofia before leaning down to whisper in Xavier's ear—"any less your daughter."

He stopped at the top of the stairs, almost as if he were annoyed more with the conversation than the rumor. "I don't care what anyone else thinks about this family other than the three of us who are in it, babe. And neither should you. All right?"

It wasn't really a question, but an end to the discussion. A duke's end to the discussion, no less.

I didn't mind Xavier bossing me around in some places. The bedroom, for instance. Or back alleys, apparently. But I didn't care for it right now.

Still, I nodded as we walked on, but only because I knew there was no point in continuing this as a debate in front of Sofia.

But are we a family? I wanted to ask. No one else seemed to think so. We weren't married. I wasn't even sure I'd call the last few whirlwind weeks cohabitation. Random reporters were basically calling me a con artist, faking my daughter's parentage to, what, get to Xavier's money?

We were...something else. I didn't know what.

"Who's that?" I asked when he finally slowed at the end of yet another mile-long hallway.

We were at the opposite side of Corbray Hall, so far as I could tell, though there had been so many twists and turns that I honestly wasn't sure which direction the enormous windows were facing.

Xavier glanced irritably at yet another portrait—this one of a lovely young woman from the Regency era with blond hair and the blue eyes he shared with many of the other sitters. "Ah, that'd be the Countess of Letham. My seventh great aunt, before you ask. But listen, Ces, there's someone I want you to meet. Someone real, this time, not a stuffy portrait."

Immediately, my interest was piqued as he turned to the door next to the countess's plump pose and led me into the room.

In the center of what had to be the nicest bedroom I'd ever seen lay an elderly man in a four-poster bed approximately the size of Heathrow Airport. With the gilt millwork, cream walls, and countless pieces of art and tapestries surrounding us, it looked like the set of a period drama—even an Austen adaptation—were it not for the fact that the man in the bed was hooked up to a few machines beside the bed, with an IV and several sensors connected to wires slipping under his sheets.

"Oh," I whispered, as the man's eyes were closed. "Xavi, is he—"

But Xavier was already leaving my side, approaching the bed with light footsteps.

Even so, the man awoke with eyes a bright shade of blue to match Xavier's.

"Hello, Uncle," Xavier greeted him as he dragged a Queen Anne chair across the carpet like it was no more than a folding camp chair. He propped it next to the bed and sat beside the man. "How are we feeling today, eh?"

The man blinked but said nothing. His eyes, however, were bright and alert, lasered right on Xavier with an emotion I couldn't quite place. Was he happy to see him? Sad too? Nervous?

It was intense, whatever it was.

"I know you're not saying much these days," Xavier said as he clasped his uncle's hand between his two big ones. "But I've brought someone to meet you. Ces, come over here."

Slowly, I made my way to stand next to him and placed a hand on his shoulder. Xavier patted it but returned his attention to the man in the bed.

"Well, that's her," he said. "Francesca. My girlfriend, before you ask, and more importantly, Sofia's mum. I'll bring Sof up later, when she's had a bit to eat. Anyway, I know you wanted to meet her, but you didn't have to throw yourself down the stairs to get me here, you know."

There was a wheeze from the bed, which approximated laughter. Xavier chuckled with him, and I watched as the hand clasped between his squeezed his wrist tightly.

"Francesca, this is my uncle, Henry Parker. Now you know why I've been so busy the last six months, Uncle. You can't fault my taste, at least. Look at her."

From the bed, there was another noise, this one even more chuckle-like than the last.

"It's lovely to meet you," I said, bending down to offer my hand.

Xavier released his uncle's, which rose with some difficulty to touch mine, fingers grazing the tops of my knuckles before falling back to the bed. It clearly took a great deal of effort, but instead of letting him struggle, Xavier captured Henry's hand again and set it on his knee.

"Don't even think about it, you old geezer," he chided him. "She's mine, got it?"

Another spurting chuckle. I couldn't help but smile myself.

"I don't know," I said. "This one has a lot of charm, Xavi, and all you've got is a bad temper. I might be won away if you're not careful."

We were rewarded with another difficult laugh, though this one seemed to take a lot out of the old man. When I glanced at Xavier, he was still trying to look cheerful, but worry was furrowed into his brow.

"Ces," Xavier said quietly. "Wait for me outside, will you?"

I nodded. "Of course. It was nice to meet you, Mr. Parker. I hope to see you again soon when you're feeling up to it."

I WANDERED up and down the hall for nearly thirty minutes, taking closer looks at the portraits and art that we'd flown by with nary a word. At last, Xavier emerged, eyes somewhat bloodshot, like he'd either been laughing or crying.

"Sorry about that," he said. "I, ah, had some things to say to him." He shook his head. "He looks so different since his last fall. Can't even talk."

"I didn't realize you were so close," I said as he retook my hand.

"We weren't, really. But there are things between us, you know? History. He helped me catch up to life here after Mum died. Was really angry when I left for good, though. I didn't realize how much I depended on him for that until, well..."

He trailed off. But he didn't need to finish. It struck me then that Xavier wasn't just struggling with the finances of the estate, but a fair amount of grief.

"Sometimes, we don't realize what we've really lost until they're gone," I said, thinking of my grandfather.

I was only ten when he died, but that was ten years of having him around, raising me as my own father should have. He favored Matthew, the only boy in the family, much more than any of the girls. But we were still always his *tesorinas*, his sweethearts, his baby dolls. He was a rock, and at ten, I didn't realize what I'd had. Now I knew I'd always have a *Nonno*-shaped hole in my heart.

I could only imagine what that would feel like now, at Xavier's age.

"Ah, well," Xavier said. "He'll get better. Whatever it takes."

There was sadness in his voice, though. We both knew that even if the man in that room did improve, it wouldn't be enough. He'd never be what he was.

"I'm honored I got to meet him, however he is," I said honestly. "Thank you for having us join you. And thank you for introducing me."

It was sad, but I felt better for it. Like finally, Xavier was giving me access to a part of his life that truly mattered. I didn't want to be a tourist in England, I was coming to realize. I was done with sightseeing. I was ready for real life with Xavier Parker, whatever that might entail.

Xavier peeked down at me with one of his rare, shy smiles. But before he could reply, we were interrupted by the sharp clip of footsteps on marble. By the sound of it, a pair of them.

"Xavier? Is that you, dear boy?"

Xavier froze.

"Who is that?" I asked, tugging lightly on his arm.

His eyes shuttered with an expression of what could only be termed dread. "Fuck."

"Xavi?" I squeezed his hand harder. "Xavi, what's wrong? Who is that?"

"Xavier! We are trying to say hello. Wherever are your manners?"

Xavier exhaled heavily before turning to face our new company. A woman in a pastel suit, with expertly coiffed light brown hair and a set of pearls around her neck and at her ears, strode toward us on tasteful pumps. She looked to be perhaps in her late fifties or early sixties and was followed by a young man who looked a lot like her and was perhaps ten years younger than Xavier.

"Hello, Georgina. Freddy," Xavier said when they reached us, leaning down with a very Eeyore-like expression while the woman delivered air kisses to his cheeks. "Ces, may I introduce Georgina Parker, my stepmother."

"And duchess," she added with a smirk at me.

"Dowager Duchess of Kendal," Xavier corrected himself.

I wasn't really sure what the difference was, but I did enjoy the way the comment appeared to knock her down a peg or two.

"Dear boy, we didn't know you were returning to Kendal," said the duchess. "Frederick and I were in town enjoying the Season, but when we heard from Imogene that you'd popped in, we immediately came back, didn't we, darling?"

"Darling" appeared to be Frederick, the man standing next to her who was currently looking at Xavier like he was a bug he wanted to squash. Until, of course, Xavier caught him staring. Then the expression turned to mild terror.

"So I gathered," Xavier snapped. "Left Henry to rot for the last four weeks. Or didn't you know he'd been found?"

"Of course we knew," Georgina said. "Who do you think rearranged his bedroom for him? But there wasn't anything else to be done about his condition—the doctors said so. And he wouldn't have wanted Frederick to miss out on the Season. The queen herself invited us to the garden party this year, I'll have you know."

"Oh, the queen's garden party," Xavier muttered. "Meanwhile, Henry has been here dealing with second and third strokes. And would it have really killed you to help with the estate while he was missing? I know it's not your bloody son's, but you do live here, don't you?"

The duchess didn't blink an eye at Xavier's coarse language. It seemed to be something she was accustomed to. "Of course I do, darling. It's my home."

She was still speaking kindly, but the last word had an edge to it that I didn't like. It reminded me of the way my own mother talked about her children. Like they were possessions she could come back to whenever she liked, not when they actually needed her.

And yeah, I knew exactly what that felt like, too.

"And who might we have here?" she asked, turning to me as if she sensed my instant disdain. Her steely gray eyes drifted over me like the knife edge of a blade, cutting through the simple leggings and T-shirt, snipping through the casual sneakers I'd worn for walking about the gardens.

"This is Francesca Zola." Xavier snaked an arm around my shoulders, pulling me securely to his side. "My girlfriend. Up from London."

"Oh, how lovely." The duchess smarted. "We'd heard you'd brought that American and her daughter with you. Horrible rumors. So glad to see you've met someone new."

"Er—" I started.

"Not that there's anything wrong with Americans, of course, but Corbray isn't really the sort of place for, er, that sort, don't you think, Frederick?" she continued.

"There you are, Mama!"

If it weren't for the sounds of Sofia's feet pattering their way down the corridor, I was sure you could have heard a pin drop in the awkward silence. I grinned, then caught her as she jumped into my arms, followed by Elsie struggling to keep up behind her.

"All right?" Xavier asked the older woman.

"Goodness, yes. She's fast, that one," Elsie put in.

She said something to Xavier I couldn't understand, then left with a quick farewell to Sofia and a daggered expression at Georgina. Apparently, I wasn't the only one who didn't care for the duchess.

"As I was saying," Xavier said, accepting Sofia from my arms.

"This is Francesca Zola. My girlfriend, and also the mother of my daughter, Sofia. They're spending the summer with us. From New York."

Georgina did an excellent impression of a painted owl as she blinked between us. "I—see. Just the summer, then?"

"Not if I can help it," Xavier murmured. His blue eyes sparkled down at me.

Excitement bubbling inside me, I opened my mouth to ask him exactly what he meant by that, but was interrupted by the appearance of Mrs. Niles, the housekeeper.

"Mr. Larsen is here from Brooks and Weston, sir," she said to Xavier. "And I believe Gibson has already directed a Mr. Rhodes to your office as well."

He grunted, squeezed my shoulder, then released me. "Lawyers and accountants," he said. "Must go."

"Can I come with you, Daddy?" Sofia asked, reaching across me to pull on his tie.

To my surprise, Xavier grinned. "Only if you promise not to make Elsie chase you anymore, babe," he told her. He delivered a quick kiss to my cheek. "I'll catch up with you later, yeah?"

But there was no more time for a response. He strode away, Sofia in his arms, and I found myself alone with the Dowager Duchess of Kendal and her son, both of them now eyeing me like I was bait on a hook.

"So, you're the American."

I blinked, resisting the urge to fidget with my shirt. "Uh, yes. I suppose that would be me. I'll, um, promise not to take advantage of your stepson. Or anyone else, for that matter."

I tried to sound haughty, but it was hard when this woman was an actual aristocrat, and I was dressed with less propriety than a member of the cleaning staff.

Georgina continued to peruse me up and down.

"It's a very important time for us, you know," she said. "A very important time. Frederick has finally caught the eye of the royal family. Even been invited to some of the events at the palace. Kensington, not Buckingham. The smaller ones, you know, not the ones everyone makes a fuss about in the papers. At least not at first." She crooked a delicately plucked brow. "He's got it in mind to run for his father's old place in parliament, haven't you, darling?"

Frederick peered at her, then back at me with hooded eyes. "It would appear that way."

She turned back to me. "I'm sure you understand. We need all the spotlight on him. Not on a...distraction. Especially one the tabloids seem to adore."

She pulled a rolled-up paper from under her arm and waved it in front of me. I recognized the same article I'd seen earlier with pictures of Xavier and me at the airport.

I looked up. "Xavier says to pay those no mind. And what does it matter to you if the tabloids like Xavi? He can't help it, can he?"

"There're only so many spaces one can occupy in the minds of those in power. We can't have them taken up by things"—she looked disdainfully at the picture of Sofia—"that in the end, don't matter. And if they think association with us includes a scandal..."

My mouth dropped. "She's his daughter, not a scandal."

One of Georgina's brows arched again. "So you say."

"Mother." Frederick's voice, for the first time, sounded less than bored. "Shouldn't we..."

Georgina blinked. "Yes, of course. We are hosting Lord Ortham and his family for dinner tonight," she informed me with another searing drag up and down my body. "If you must attend, see that you are dressed...appropriately. And be quiet, if you can manage that."

And before I could say another word, she turned on her heel and left, Frederick in tow.

THIRTEEN

I t took another twenty minutes of wandering around Corbray Hall like a lost mouse, but eventually, I did find Xavier again when he rushed out of another double-doored room.

"There you are," he proclaimed, spotting me. "Sorry about that. Been waiting all day for those two. It'll take a lot of money, but they can get us out of that mine. And then Jagger called with another fire at one of the restaurants." He sighed wistfully, clearly wishing to be doing that work in London, rather than being stuck here.

"It's all right," I said. "I just chatted with your stepmother. She was a..." I tipped my head back and forth, trying tactfully to explain my impressions. "Snooty bitch" didn't seem appropriate.

"Nightmare," Xavier supplied to my relief, taking my hand in his and pulling me down another corridor. "Ignore her, always. Before she showed up, I meant to show you your room, anyway."

"Good." I confirmed. "I need to get changed for dinner. Duchess's orders."

"What do you mean?" He looked down at my clothes, which still consisted of the black leggings and T-shirt I'd worn on the train. "I think you look fine. It's a dinner, not a ball."

"But aren't you hosting the Douglases?" I asked. "Or is it Ortham? Orthams? That's Imogene's family, correct? Are they the same people?"

Xavier nodded. "Yes. Their last name is Douglas. The title is Ortham, so that only applies to Imogene's parents. It's confusing, and frankly, I think they all do it on purpose."

I tried not to make a face, though it wasn't because of the naming conventions. The idea of sitting at a fancy table on my first night here, across from someone who basically looked like Elsa from *Frozen*, sounded less than appealing. Imogene's entire outfit today had probably been worth more than every item in my closet back home.

Xavier's wry expression told me exactly what he thought of that. "I suppose we should. Lady Ortham likes to wear her furs whenever she dines here. Even in August." He pulled me farther down the corridor with renewed urgency. "At any rate, it's just down here. I imagine you'd like to rest a bit before I wear you out later."

"Xavi..." I warned, though I loved the mirth in his eyes. It was so much better than sadness.

Xavier ignored me, turning the knobs on a pair of tall double doors which were inlaid with irises. And opened onto what could have only been called a paradise.

I'd thought I understood luxury. After all, Xavier liked nice things. He'd stayed at the nicest hotels in New York, paid for the best food, and lived in a penthouse fit for a king.

Or it would be if this room didn't exist.

My jaw dropped. This wasn't a bedroom. It was an entire apartment. Or rather, it was a museum in every sense of the word, filled to the brim with priceless antiques, gilt millwork curling toward twenty-foot ceilings, gaping windows draped with priceless tapestries, and the biggest bed I'd ever seen dressed in sumptuous blue linens so thin they were practically one with the breeze that occasionally floated in from the balcony.

A glance told me the room itself split into a separate sitting room on the other side, along with an en suite bath fit for a queen, a walk-in closet, and some other private sitting area that looked like it was once someone's office.

"This is—ours?" I stammered as I took it all in.

"Yours. Yeah."

I looked back at him, unsure of what to make of that, but found I was too distracted by the grandeur to ask. Yet.

Xavier shifted from foot to foot as he watched me explore the space. "It's a bit gaudy, I know. But what can you do? Heirlooms."

He shrugged, like he was talking about a nice, crocheted doily inherited from a grandmother, not a castle full of art.

I crossed the room to peer at an oil painting hanging between two of the windows. "Is this—oh my God, Xavi, is this an actual Renoir?"

He followed me, leaned over my shoulder, and examined the painting along with the tiny signature in the lower right corner. "Looks like it, yeah. I'll ask Gibson if it's been cataloged. We've been talking about auctioning a few pieces to fund some of the updates for the smaller farms."

I continued to stare at the painting, a still life of vivid pink flowers. "It's beautiful."

Xavier looked up from his phone. "Like it?"

I turned. "Well, yes. It's stunning." I didn't know what else to say.

A shy half-smile appeared, almost as if I'd complimented him, not a lost masterpiece. "I'll make sure that one stays, then."

I wandered around the rest of the room, taking in the glossy furnishings, the gilt fixtures, and the warm yellow walls covered in art. "I feel like I'm going to break something in here. These things have been in your family for who knows how long. Hundreds of years, I suppose?"

Xavier followed me to the doors leading out to a balcony, then pulled me into his arms so we could take in the view together. "They're just things, Ces. I don't care about any of it. Just you and Sofia. If you want me to yank it all out and have a bunch of Scandinavian garbage hauled in to replace it, we can do that too."

I rolled my eyes. "I didn't say I didn't like it. Just that I didn't want to break anything."

"Sleep on the bed. Jump on it if you want. It's lasted this long—it can handle a tiny bird from the Bronx, you know."

I made to punch him in the gut, but he captured my fist and brought it to his lips for a fleeting kiss. It was uncharacteristically gallant of him. But I didn't mind that either.

"No Ikea needed," I confirmed. "Although maybe some things that Sofia can get dirty. A table where she can do some art, maybe. Or a rug where she can play dolls that's not worth roughly a million dollars. We don't want another stained angora on our hands."

Xavier chuckled at the memory. "Your wish is my command. Any time, too. My doors are always open, and just next door."

I frowned. There it was again. The yours versus mine thing.

"Your doors?" I asked. "So this really isn't your room too?"

"Oh, I'll be in here with you. But in the old days, it was always customary for the duke and duchess to have their own chambers. I thought maybe you and Sof would need your own space while you're here. And to be honest, there will be a lot of late nights for me. That door opens up to the nursery. You might just want to be on your own instead of having me wake you at two in the morning."

I frowned. It made sense. But what had happened to always sleeping in the same bed? Given his work, it wasn't like he hadn't had plenty of other late nights at the restaurants, though until this week, he'd mostly kept that to a minimum. Still, I truly believed he'd invited me to share his life, and on our first night, hadn't he promised just that?

That was when you were alone, my conscience reminded me.

Now we were going to have walls between us. Relatives watching. Servants noticing. Neighbors checking in.

"Don't worry," Xavier rumbled as he pulled me closer. "I'll be sneaking into your bed every night I can." He smirked. "I'm pretty good at it too. Quiet as a cat."

He turned me around and began steering me toward the four-poster as if to demonstrate exactly how he planned to do the sneaking.

"Don't you run away now," he said as his hands found their way under my shirt, sliding along my skin in a way that made me forget my initial doubts. "This tour's just getting started."

WE FOUND our way down to dinner a bit later than planned, mostly because Xavier enjoyed watching me fret more than normal about my wardrobe. He vetoed at least two outfits I'd brought with me from London—none, apparently, were sexy enough for his liking.

"Xavi!" I'd squealed when he tackled me back to the bed after taking off a green sundress. "I can't meet your neighbors looking like a showgirl!"

"Just wear jeans, then. Or that tracksuit I like. They both make your arse look fantastic, and who cares what they think, anyway?"

I cared, though. And even if he didn't admit it, so did he. For better or worse, Xavier at least needed to command some respect from these people, even if they were loath to give it. I wasn't going to give them a reason by dressing like the uncouth American they obviously thought I was.

And so, approximately thirty minutes past the time we were supposed to join them, Xavier and I entered the second drawing room, him dressed casually but elegantly in a pair of black pants and a blue shirt that matched his eyes. Unlike the rest of the guests, he had foregone a jacket but kept a loosely knotted tie and rolled up the sleeves of his shirt so that the tattoos twisting around his collar and sneaking down his forearm were his only other accessory.

I was shooting for elegant in a knee-length purple shift dress impulse-bought on Amazon, a pearl pendant on a silver chain that used to belong to Nonna, and my favorite silver hoops. But the moment I laid eyes on Georgina, Frederick, Imogene, and the other two guests I assumed were her parents, I knew I'd far undershot. I looked like I should have been serving them dinner—probably at a local pub rather than a place as grand as this.

It wasn't exactly dressing for dinner at *Downton Abbey*, but it wasn't far from it. Dinner with the duke was clearly an occasion, even if the duke himself didn't think so. The other two men—Frederick and someone else I took to be Lord Ortham—wore full suits, down to the ties and matching pocket squares. All three women wore floaty silk frocks and delicate heels, with subtle jewelry that was obviously very expensive without being overly gaudy.

Georgina's lips drew into a tight line as she took in the purple dress and the slightly scuffed black pumps I wore with just about every "fancy" outfit I owned. With my simple jewelry and simply made-up face, I felt bare. And as common as ever.

Crap.

"Drink, sir?"

We turned to find Gibson, the butler, standing before us, holding a silver tray bearing a glass of brown liquor.

"Macallan?" Xavier wondered, looking at the glass.

"The forty, sir, just as you like."

"Good man." Xavier took a satisfied sip. "It's the best."

I watched him savor the drink. "I didn't know you like whisky."

"I don't usually drink it, but Henry always kept the good stuff here. Do you want anything?"

I noticed it was he who had to ask me, not the butler. "Ah, sure. A glass of wine, please."

"We only serve wine with dinner, miss," Gibson informed me haughtily.

"Do I get a cocktail?" Imogene called from one of the sofas. She wasn't, I noticed, looking at me, but at Xavier—specifically his tattoos—with the same expression of a dog about to go in heat.

Xavier frowned. "Just open the damn wine, Gibson. We're having drinks, not signing a state accord."

"But it's not—"

"Do it," Xavier ordered.

The butler sniffed but turned to do as he was told, leaving us in an awkward silence. Despite the fact that I'd barely said a word, I had a feeling that I had already spoiled the evening.

"You'll have to ignore him too," Xavier said as he took my hand and led me to join the others. "Gibson really is a horrible snob."

"So I was told," I murmured, thinking of Elsie. Where was she, anyway?

"Kip," Imogene called, voice crisp like a bird's, even swallowed by the tapestries that hung from the windows of the elegant room. "Good of you to join us finally," she joked. "You too, Felicity."

"It's Francesca," I reminded her, staying close to Xavier, who squeezed my hand sympathetically.

Then he dropped it to greet the other two people I didn't recognize.

"Lord Ortham," he said as he shook the hand of an older gentleman in a brown suit. "Lady Ortham."

The other woman, who looked very much like Imogene, right down to the slender frame and elegant height, bobbed slightly to Xavier and accepted his hand.

Xavier looked like he didn't really know what to do with that but turned away, nonetheless, to take a long sip of his drink. I was glad, at least, that he seemed as uncomfortable with all the formalities as I was.

"Where's Sofia?" I asked Gibson, who had returned with my wine.

He looked troubled by the question. "Miss Sofia is in the nursery, of course, enjoying her dinner with Mrs. Crew."

I frowned. "Shouldn't she be here with us? We always eat as a family. I'm sure Elsie would like to join us too, don't you think, Xavi?" I didn't like the idea that the two of them had been shuttled away.

"All together?" Imogene asked. "Oh, that's so lovely. So very quaint. Can you imagine, Mummy, if Lucy and I had joined you and Papa every night for dinner. Frederick, would you have done so?"

Frederick snorted from his seat in the far corner but didn't reply.

"So very American," Georgina added from her place on a sapphire-blue chaise lounge.

"It's fine, Ces," Xavier said, blue eyes begging me not to argue. "I reckon they'll be all right together, happy as clams. Sof wanted to bake cookies with Els, so they're probably up to their elbows in flower."

Maybe he was fine with that, but I wasn't. This was our own little pattern we'd started weeks ago. I'd grown up in a house where family dinner was sacred every night, and it was something I had always wanted to pass on to Sofia. Over the last month, I'd come to believe Xavier shared that goal.

"I don't really—" I started.

"Just for tonight." Xavier's eyes silently begged me to stop. "We'll eat together tomorrow. I promise."

"Are you making your assistant take care of that little girl?" Imogene put in. "Xavier, you can't be so cruel. She's got far more important things to do."

"Why would it be cruel?" I wondered. "Elsie seems to like it. She's always volunteering to take her. And God knows Sofia loves her to death."

"Volunteering? Or looking for a raise?" Lord Ortham remarked with a tap to his nose.

Everyone laughed. I just frowned.

"Elsie's not like that," I said.

They acted like I hadn't spoken at all.

"Xavier, how long has the girl been in England?" Georgina wondered, standing up to sway across the room and join our little circle. "One week? Two?"

"Four," I said. "We're staying the summer." *In case you were hoping otherwise, lady.*

Georgina stared at me like an ant she'd like to crush.

"Well, then," she said to Xavier. "It's high time you got proper help, is it not?"

"Elsie has a few candidates arriving tomorrow," Xavier put in, as if to reassure them. The people who didn't know our family at all. "We'll have someone straight away so she can get back to London."

"Candidates for what?"

Georgina's laugh practically tinkled over the crystal glasses everyone held. Imogene looked like she wanted to join her. Her parents looked embarrassed for me, while Frederick just looked bored in his corner.

"Candidates for a nanny, Ces," Xavier said gently, though he didn't look at me while he said it.

Wait, what?

"I—I don't understand," I said. "Why do we need a nanny when I'm right here? And when Elsie doesn't mind watching her."

It wasn't as though I didn't want a babysitter every so often, but I was a bit taken aback. Sofia wasn't in school, and I wasn't working. I was more than happy to take her around the English countryside on the days Xavier had to work, then leave her with a sitter—often Elsie, whom she adored—on the nights we went out. It was the routine we'd fallen into. What had changed?

"It's true, Xavier," Georgina put in. "It's not as if she'll be in charge. Better let her take care of her own child. After all, you'll be busy, and what else is she to do? Fish in the pond?"

I couldn't hold back my glare. It was one thing for me to suggest I was the best person to take care of my daughter. Another thing completely to come from a stranger who was basically saying I had no other talents anyway.

I opened my mouth to say as much, but Xavier's hand on my shoulder stopped me.

"We're getting a nanny," he said in a tone that brooked no argument from anyone. "And Francesca is busy enough." Then, to me, "We'll talk about this later, all right?"

I wanted to talk about it now. Just like I wanted to talk about why in the hell we had to have dinner with people who clearly did not want me there. Why he felt it was more important to put on whatever this show was for his neighbors than be true to his own family.

"Excuse me, sir," interrupted Gibson before I could say as much. "Dinner is served."

Xavier didn't look away from me, but something flickered in his blue eyes that begged me to wait.

So, as everyone stood to adjourn to the dining room, I did.

I just didn't think I would regret it so soon.

FOURTEEN

Dinner was the quietest disaster I'd ever lived through.

It started with a savory carrot soup decorated with digs at my dress. Next was a succulent roast with a side of "When is Francesca going home?" Third, was the salad course, dressed with a game of Pretend Frankie Isn't in the Room, even when I asked direct questions. By the time we took up our solid silver spoons for dessert, a raspberry cream confection, I wanted to throw mine in the faces of every person at the table, including Xavier, whose primary response to every passive-aggressive insult was to blink and squeeze my knee as if to say, *Just deal with it.*

"I'd love to take you shopping, Felina," Imogene had told me as our dessert plates were being cleared.

"That's very kind," I lied through my teeth. "And it's Francesca."

I would have rather jumped in the lake with all my clothes on. And dragged her with me if she purposefully called me by the wrong name one more *freaking* time.

Of course, it didn't help that Imogene probably looked like a supermodel in literally everything she put on, while the wrong outfit made my curves strongly resemble the body of a Cabbage Patch Kid.

I had watched her eat exactly two bites of each dish she was served before setting her utensils primly at the eight and two positions, fork below the knife. I had thoroughly enjoyed all the courses, but if the Douglases' faces were any indication, I more closely resembled one of the estate's pigs chowing down on their nightly slop.

Imogene looked over my outfit somewhat pityingly. "Of course, I wouldn't want to embarrass you. The shops I prefer might be a bit beyond your pocket money." She winced, like it was physically hurting her to think about it. "Kip, you really might increase her allowance. What else shall the poor girl to wear to dinner?"

Xavier chuffed, as if the idea was preposterous, but his hand landed on my knee and squeezed again, silently bidding me to hold my temper.

I didn't understand it. Normally, *he* was the one ready to fly off the handle at any sign of insult to his person. But throughout the dinner, he'd been as placid as a dove, making pleasant, if dull conversation with the viscount about the latest weather patterns.

Before I could declare heartily that as a grown woman, I could buy my own clothes and did not need or want an allowance from any man, thank you, Imogene turned to Georgina to discuss the hat trends at this year's Ascot. And for the fourteenth time that evening, it was like I did not exist.

By the time Gibson and a footman (I still couldn't believe Corbray Hall had one) arrived to clear the table and usher everyone to a different sitting room for after-dinner drinks and petit fours, I was done. I claimed a headache and escaped to my rooms, eager to kiss my daughter good night, only to find that Sofia had already been put to bed.

And I hadn't even been told.

So I stomped around the room, yanking off my earrings like I was preparing for a street fight, throwing my clothes into the laundry basket like they were hand grenades. I tried a hot shower, three different books, and even made myself some tea with the room's kettle. Nothing calmed me down.

It was my own fault for not standing up for myself. I knew that. But I didn't know how to respond to these people the right way. At home, my family was direct, a table full of filterless Italian Puerto Ricans who said exactly what they thought, when they thought it. It was crude sometimes, and hurtful, but at least you knew where everyone stood. I could deal with brutal honesty.

But these games—insults masked as complimentary advice, disdain that played like courtesy—I didn't know how to do that. Every glance was coded, every comment an inside joke. I was completely outmatched.

And so, by the time Xavier came back to the room sometime past ten, I had been seething at the end of the bed in my nightgown and robe for nearly two hours, imagining all the ways I could pin my boyfriend to the wall without actually killing him. I had come to the unreasonable conclusion that it was entirely his fault. Even if I couldn't play the game, he certainly could. And he should have played it for me, dammit.

He opened the door quietly, trying to slip in like a cat, but stopped halfway when he realized the light was still on. "Oh, you're awake."

I looked up from where I was tying and untying the two ends of my robe. A copy of *Persuasion* lay next to me, unopened. I pushed it to the floor. "Oh, you're speaking to me."

Xavier frowned and closed the door behind him. "What is that supposed to mean?" He slipped off his shoes and set them by the door. I only then realized how odd it was to see him wearing shoes inside. The Xavier I knew took them off as soon as he entered any house. Not here, apparently, where there were maids cleaning every room daily.

"Well, to start with, I'm shocked you even noticed I was gone," I said. "You barely said anything to me when I bid everyone good night. I realize none of them could have cared less, but I thought you might a little."

Xavier worried his jaw for a moment, clearly trying to figure out how to navigate this situation. I honestly wasn't sure how to navigate it myself. I wasn't used to this feeling of being indebted to someone by virtue of their generosity while at the same time being furious with them. I was lucky to be here, in this grand house, on an actual estate like the ones I'd read about for years. But I also felt cast out, like I absolutely did not belong.

"I'm sorry," he said finally, though it was wooden and rehearsed. "To be honest, I was relieved." He continued upon seeing my expression, "Not because I wanted you to leave. Just because you were so clearly having a terrible time. I didn't want you to suffer."

That should have made me feel better.

It did not.

"It's not just that," I admitted. "I should have listened to you, Xavi. You are different here. I don't want to go, but I'm not sure what to do about it."

He gave a great sigh. "Ces, it's only been one day—"

"I know," I interrupted. "I know it's only been one day. Not even, really. And I know I need to be patient. But something happened the second you got that phone call."

I wanted to tell him I could feel it in the air. For the last month, we'd been making something of a life together in London. It wasn't perfect, and yes, Sofia and I were still something like tourists, but even when Xavier had to work or deal with something in his real life, I always knew that we came first to him. He was protective of us to a fault and talked us up to everyone he met. I felt like we were the jewels of his life.

But here, we just faded away, hidden in the rest of the grandeur.

I opened my mouth to tell him all of it but found I couldn't.

"There is something about this place that totally changes you," was all I could manage. "You're just...it's not the same as in London." I sank down onto the bed, trying to understand where I was going with this. "For one, those people. Your stepmother, your neighbors. You're so quiet around them. More distant. I think that's the first time

I've ever heard you sit through a dinner you didn't cook without swearing."

"I have to get along with them, Ces."

I nodded. "Okay. But why?"

I couldn't help asking. The Xavier I knew was more stubborn than a rock wall. He told people to fuck off quicker than he could smile. I'd just seen him practically throw his own chef out of his restaurant for messing up soup, but here, he was a tamed tiger. You knew he was dying to break free of the cage, but instead, he was prowling the house, waiting to be let out.

I didn't like it.

He didn't seem to either, as he tugged on his collar.

"Well, for one, as horrible as they are, Georgina, Frederick, and Henry are the only family I really have left," he said. "And honestly, I consider the Douglases a part of that as well. I was going to marry their daughter, after all."

"I—oh," I said. I hadn't really thought about it like that. I supposed family was family, even if you didn't really like them.

"For another," he continued. "I was hoping Lord Ortham might be able to help manage the estate so I don't have to stay here. Frederick is too young to take it over—he's still in school—and God knows Georgina has done enough damage over the past two months. I need help, Ces, like I told you. I don't think I can trust anyone else. I've known Imogene and her parents a long time. They wouldn't do anything to screw things up."

I considered this point. It never occurred to me that he had an ulterior motive when it came to inviting the Douglases to dinner. I'd been too busy fuming to think it through.

"Okay," I said. "That makes sense. But Xavi, please tell me you didn't hire a nanny without consulting me first. Like, what the hell was that?"

Xavier seemed to make a decision, walking further into the room while he undid his tie. "Well, no. I haven't hired anyone. Yet." Then he just looked confused. "Honestly, I thought you'd be happy about it."

"You thought I'd be happy about someone making a unilateral choice regarding the care of my own kid?"

"Well, technically, she's not just your kid anymore, is she?" The statement was only slightly cut with resentment, but it was present.

I wondered if he'd ever forgive me for that.

Xavier sighed as if he knew that line of reasoning wouldn't end in anything good. "My point is, I was trying to do you a favor."

I held back a few choice remarks, still slighted by his earlier comment. "Regardless, it's not a decision you make without me. Ever."

He worried his jaw a moment, then came to stand in front of me and shoved his hands in his pockets. From my vantage point, his legs looked impossibly long, and the undone tie and disheveled collar only added to his general appeal. Damn. It was really hard to stay mad at him when he looked like that, and the spark in his eye when he caught me noticing told me he knew it.

"I don't understand why you're upset," he said. "You've been happy to let Elsie babysit whenever she wanted this summer. I don't expect you to be Sofia's babysitter one hundred percent of the time."

"I'm her mother," I countered, staring up at him. "I'd never be her babysitter."

He sighed. "Ces, I know that. I also know—because you've told me—that you've given all of your time to her over the last four years. If you want to keep chasing after her all hours of the day, fine. I won't stand in your way."

"You say that as if I wanted to give up my entire future to raise our kid on my own." I was reaching now, but I was annoyed. "I had dreams too at one point. I wanted to be a professor. I wanted to study great works of literature and teach them to a crowd full of willing adults, not do glitter art and times tables. I wanted to go places that I chose, not just by the grace and mercy of another."

"Well, you don't have to wait anymore, do you? You can do whatever you want, if that's what this is about. You want me to sack the nanny, fine, I'll do it. You want me to hire one, that's fine too."

I opened my mouth to argue more. I wanted to tell him that he was missing the point—that it wasn't about whether I wanted child-care, it was about whether he asked me in the first place. I felt like another piece of ornamental furniture with the rest of the things in this museum. Aimless, maybe pretty to look at, but generally something that could be moved around at will and didn't have much purpose.

"Even if you did hire someone," I said quietly. "What am I supposed to do with that time? I've been playing tourist for the last month, Xavi. And while it's been lovely, I need more."

"More what?" His brow furrowed adorably. "More money? More places to go? If you're bored, you could go to Scotland for a few days, or Ireland if you'd prefer. Shit, I'll fly you to the continent if you want—"

"No, I don't mean more to see," I said. "I mean, more to do." I shrugged helplessly. "Maybe that's why we wanted to come with you. I know it's not much, but at least being here, being that support gives me more to do than leech off you, like everyone seems to think I'm doing."

I reached out and pulled his hand from his pocket, then tugged him to sit next to me. I was tired of goggling up at him while he leered over me like a gargoyle.

"Every person at that dinner tonight had one question on the tips of their tongues: what is she doing here?" I told him. "It was in their eyes when they looked at my clothes, in their comments when they talked about literally any kind of future. And you know there was a reason they weren't the slightest bit interested in anything I had to say either. To them, I don't matter. Not one bit."

"That's because they're all wankers," Xavier agreed. "I told you, don't pay them any mind, babe. They don't know you—"

"No, they don't," I agreed. "But they don't have to, either. Because I don't mean anything to them. I have no purpose here, Xavi.

I need something to do besides sightsee and look pretty. I need to be a person of value."

I honestly hadn't realized that was the truth until he'd pulled it out of me. The last month had been lovely, but I wasn't cut out to be a lady of leisure. It wasn't in my DNA.

"I thought..." Xavier seemed truly confused. "I thought you'd want the time off. You've been working so hard for so long. You don't have to worry about that now. I can take care of you and Sof, and you can do...whatever you like. Just relax, right?"

He'd told me variations of that over and over for the last four weeks. I was supposed to relax this summer and take an extended vacation on him. But that wasn't what I wanted. I wasn't looking to be someone's kept lady. I wanted to be someone's partner.

"Would that make you happy?" I asked, reaching out for one of his large hands. "You are one of the most motivated people I've ever met. Could you honestly tell me you'd be happy being a man of leisure?"

He opened his mouth to argue with me but seemed to quickly realize he couldn't. "Point taken." He clapped a hand on my knee. "I won't hire anyone without talking to you first. As for support..." The hand on my knee moved up my thigh a little, then paused, as if waiting for my green light.

I smiled. "I'll keep that in mind."

"I can't tell you what to do with your time, babe. You've got to figure that one out on your own."

I leaned on his shoulder. That was the hard part, wasn't it? I'd traveled all the way to England only to feel as lost as ever.

"I'll figure it out," I said. "But I don't want to do it in a different bedroom."

A deep chuckle vibrated under my temple.

I sat up to look at him. "Or is a duke not allowed to sleep with someone who isn't his wife?"

Xavier stilled for a second, and I wondered if I'd gone too far. After all, we hadn't ever discussed marriage, even if my sisters constantly wondered about it. It didn't help that since Matthew had gotten engaged, the entire Zola family had wedding fever.

Too soon, a voice inside my head reminded me. It's far too soon.

But we had a child together. We were a family. And just yesterday, hadn't he almost...

I mean, couldn't we at least talk about these things?

"The duke," Xavier said finally, "is allowed to do whatever he fucking wants. And that includes taking his girl to bed and sleeping where he pleases. And right now he pleases to have you. Come here."

On instinct, I edged away, biting back a grin as I did. We had more to talk about, but as always, I couldn't resist his charm. Especially when it turned demanding in the best possible way.

Xavier tipped his head, causing the mischievous lock of black hair to fall over his forehead. "You know how I feel about that lip, Ces." He turned onto his knees and prowled down the bed toward me.

Giggling, I scrambled backward and pressed myself against the gilt headboard. "Careful," I warned him. "You're bigger than me."

For that, I was rewarded with a wolfish grin. "Bloody right I am. Makes it easier to put you where I want."

Swiftly, he grabbed me under the knees and yanked me forward, forcing me onto my back where he could cage me against the down pillows.

"Francesca."

As always, it was the sound of my formal, given name purred in that delicious low timbre, rumbling against the delicate skin under my ear, that was my undoing.

I melted into the pillows and against the big body that felt more like a homecoming than a cage. The sky's deep blue faded away, as did the lights of Kendal, far below. All I could feel was Xavier's lean, muscled arms winding around my waist and neck, wrapping me with his strength, blocking out everything but him.

His tongue licked a trail behind my ear and down my neck. When he reached my collarbone, he bit. I arched into his touch and moaned.

"The only thing that's changed now is this," he said as he ground his hips into me, making the steel length very clear within his trousers.

I slipped my hands into his silky dark hair and pulled, egging him on.

"You want this?" he asked, both hands dropping to my hips, pulling me back toward him so I could feel his erection straining through his pants at my back. "Or something else first?"

One hand dropped lower to flirt with the hem of my nightgown. Fingers slid between my thighs, tickling the sensitive skin. I jerked and gasped when he dragged one across the damp fabric of my panties.

"I think she wants it all," he rumbled, turning me in his arms so he could capture my mouth with his.

There were more arguments to have. More words to be said. But subsumed by his kiss, I couldn't think of any of them. Xavier's tongue twisted around mine as he shoved my robe down my arms, then reached down and pulled my dress over my head, leaving me, little Frankie Zola, naked in a duke's country estate.

"You know I kind of hate you right now, right?" I murmured against his sweet, sweet lips. "You just distract me from it."

Xavier only smiled before kissing me again. "Well, let's just see if I can't make you forget that completely, eh?"

I grabbed the open sides of his shirt, pulling him away slightly. "I'm still mad at you."

Another kiss. "Fine."

"This discussion isn't over."

Kiss. "I never said it was."

"Xavi—oh—"

"Perfect," he murmured as he cupped my face, bringing me back for yet another kiss. "Fucking delectable."

"Xavi—"

"Hush," he said as he trailed down my body. "We can fight more in the morning. Let's just make up first."

To my surprise, I was all right with that.

"MAMA! NOOOOOOO!"

Like an automaton, I sprang from sleep only to find I wasn't at home on the landing but in an opulent bedroom.

"Mama?"

Sofia's voice was softened by the doors separating my bedroom from hers, but it was still there. I pushed back the covers and swung my feet to the floor.

"Where are you going?" Xavier asked, voice muddled with sleep. He stretched out a long arm and clapped a broad palm on my thigh to still me.

"It's Sofia," I told him as I pulled my robe over my naked body and tied it quickly around my waist. "She's having a nightmare."

That perked him up. "Eh?"

"She'll be fine," I told him.

"Mmmph. Come back to bed, then. She'll fall back asleep."

"Mama..."

"She needs someone," I told him in a harsh whisper.

I paused, wondering, maybe even hoping that Xavier might get up instead. *Hush, babe,* he'd say. *You've been doing this for four years. Let me have a go.*

But he just turned over onto his side and continued sleeping, blissfully unaware of the choices that needed to be made. The child who needed to be comforted.

I crept into her room to find Sofia awake and drying her teary eyes on her covers. She looked impossibly small on one of the twin beds set up for the children of the past, blinking blearily into the night in her new surroundings.

"Hush, baby," I told her, and I crawled into the bed and pulled her into my arms. "Mama's here. You're safe."

She whimpered unintelligibly but nuzzled into my chest,

allowing me to bury my nose in her hair and inhale that soft scent she'd carried since she was born. Something deep within me relaxed. No matter my insecurities about this place and Xavier's life, this was a place I would always belong. This was a place I knew, holding my daughter, comforting her in the night.

I fell asleep in the bed next to hers that had been put in for countless nannies, maybe even governesses over the years who had to spend nights with little ones just like this.

When I awoke just after sunrise, Sofia was still snoozing behind the four-poster curtains. I returned to my room, careful to close the door behind me as quietly as I could to not wake the slumbering giant waiting for me.

I needn't have done so.

The bed was empty. It took a long time, but eventually, I fell back asleep alone.

FIFTEEN

S ofia got up sometime past six and scampered off to find Xavier, but I found it hard to sleep in on my own, despite knowing I could. Sometime over the past month, I'd gotten used to the big, warm body lying next to me, so when he wasn't there to snuggle into as the rays peeked through the curtains, something felt off.

Eventually, I did get up to find the view of the countryside glowing out the window as the new sun danced off the lake below the manor and off the tops of hills rising in the distance. Corbray Hall might have been stuffy, but Cumbria really was magic.

I found something to wear and ventured downstairs in search of sustenance and my family, only to find Sofia and Elsie, but not Xavier, sitting in the dining room at a table dressed with just about every breakfast food I could want.

Sofia looked up at the end, where she had discarded a plate still half full of pancakes and strawberries in favor of watching Elsie draw something on a napkin.

"This is England," Elsie said as she moved the pencil. "That's where London is. That's where we are. And all the way across the big blue ocean, love, that's New York."

"Where I'm from," Sofia added. She grinned at me. "Hi, Mama. You better have some breakfast. It's important for your muscles. Elsie says."

I smiled as I poured myself a cup of tea, then took a seat next to her. "She's right about that. I don't know about all this, though."

"May I assist, miss?" I looked up to where Gibson had brought a plate for me.

"I got it," I told him. "Thanks." He sniffed and walked back to the other side of the room, where he was busy doing...something. Watching us? It was kind of weird.

"Where's Xavi?" I asked Elsie as I spooned some fruit and a flaky croissant onto my plate. "It's only eight. Is he already in his office?"

"Oh, the boy had to tour the alfalfa farms south of town," Elsie told me. "Up at the crack of dawn, poor child. But he said he'll be back at lunch and left this for you."

She passed me a note from Xavier and went back to drawing something else for Sofia.

> Ces—
>
> I meant what I said last night. It's up to you to decide what you want to do. But since I can't give you the British library, maybe ours will help. I'm told it's got a few treasures.
>
> First floor, through the second drawing room. Don't lose the key.
>
> Xavi

I picked up the key, which, rusted and nearly as big as my palm, looked about as ancient as Britain itself. That man. Just like the beast, he'd gone and given me a library. Again. Suddenly, I couldn't wait to see it.

"Elsie," I said. "Er, would you mind—"

"Go, go," Elsie interrupted with a smile. "He'll want to know you explored it first thing. I thought Little Miss and I might visit the sheep down by the pond."

"We have sheepies?" Sofia's blue eyes were suddenly as big as the sky outside.

"Yes, and if you like, you can feed them." Elsie waved a hand. "Gibson, we'll need some feed for the sheep, all right?"

And with that, I was effectively dismissed for the morning. I smiled, stuffed the remainder of my croissant in my mouth, then picked up my tea to take with me to the library. But before I left, I stopped, another thought in mind.

Xavier had offered an olive branch. I could do the same.

"Er, Elsie?"

"Yes, love?"

"Perhaps we should arrange for some nannies to interview," I said. "I know you've got a job to do, and this one isn't helping."

Elsie smiled again, this time gratefully. So Xavier wasn't wrong about that.

"I'll have inquires sent out this afternoon," she said. "Go on."

PART of what made Corbray Hall so fascinating was the way multiple generations of building melded into each other. I'd done some cursory research on the place on the train ride here, discovering that the original Corbray Hall was built as a small manor during the fifteenth century, but most of it had been deconstructed and replaced with newer, more modern sections in the eighteenth and nineteenth centuries as the estate grew.

The library was located in the part of the house that I would have guessed was built during the late seventeen hundreds, when it was fashionable for one large room to lead directly into another without even a hallway to join them. I strode through a drawing room, a sitting room, and what looked like a music room with a very beautiful old piano in the corner, then found myself confronted with yet another pair of twenty-foot doors fastened with an extremely old lock. I procured the key out of my dress pocket and tried it. Open sesame.

The British Library it was not, but it was no less magical. A quick look out the French doors on the far side told me the library was almost directly under the bedroom I'd been assigned, as it opened onto the gardens, with a distant view of the lake beyond them.

I might have been entranced by the view alone if it hadn't been for the books. The room had to be at least forty feet long with twenty-five-foot ceilings, all of them completely stacked with floor-to-ceiling built-in shelves chock-a-block with books accessible by rolling ladders. With a fireplace at one end suggesting endless nights of reading in the cozy club chairs and the enormous wooden table at the other side providing studying capacity for at least ten, it was too easy to imagine myself hibernating here for however long we were staying in Cumbria and never seeing an inch of the surrounding countryside, beautiful as it might be.

Forget the family. Forget needing a purpose.

Everything I'd ever want was right here, so long as the books were good.

And good they were. A brief perusal of the shelves revealed this wasn't a collection of one particular duke in one lifetime, but of many, many people who had lived within these walls. A walk around the room revealed a sampling of some of the most famous works in the English language, from John Donne to Mary Shelley, and too many first editions to count. There was an entire shelf of several Victorian photo albums bound in leather still bearing the original prints scrapbooked between newspaper clippings and postcards, and another held a collection of seventeenth-century cookbooks. A row of children's books and schoolbooks sat close to the study table. One entire wall bore a book recording the Duke of Kendal's entire genealogical records going back to before the Norman Conquest.

This wasn't just a library. It was a family's intellectual history. A bona fide treasure trove.

And Xavier had given it to me.

I pulled out a selection of books to look over and set them on a side table next to one of the club chairs. Before I sat down to read, however, I noticed another shelf near a writing desk where the books were made of what looked like worn black leather but bore no titles embossed on the spines.

"Hmm," I said, ambling over to where they stood. "What do we have over here, Your Grace?"

I plucked the first small book off the shelf and recognized it immediately as a journal of some sort—the kind I'd learned about in one of my classes years ago. I'd done a bit of archival research in graduate school for a class on Early American Literature. I wrote a research paper on the differences between American and British correspondence that had me plucking through similar books in the basement of the New York Public Library for a week.

When the first page noted the date as 14 July 1744, I immediately looked around for kid gloves to wear so I wouldn't damage the book. Finding none, I put it back and made a mental note to request some from Xavier or Gibson. And maybe some boxes to store the more valuable manuscripts and treasures here. And climate control, if the library didn't already have it. I wasn't an archives librarian, but even I knew these things were basically decomposing by the second with this kind of air exposure.

The diaries weren't terribly organized, but it was quickly evident that they were generally kept by whoever was acting as steward of the estate. Some were more typical, noting only a daily sentence or two about things like weather, crops, tenants, and things like that. Others, however, clearly correlated with the taste for literature that ran through Xavier's family tree. I opened up one to find the author—the eleventh Duke of Kendal—was something of a poet.

"Oh!" I gasped, leafing through the book.

The former duke wrote not only the daily business reports, but also full narratives of his interactions in the house. He was, apparently, a bit of a gossip too. And definitely suspected all sorts of things of his family members.

I set the book aside, fully intending to go over it some more, but was quickly waylaid by several more books just like it—all of them written by many other dukes or their brothers. The Parker family had been storytellers, many of them writing what could only be termed nonfiction "novels" about their own lives. And they had been doing it for centuries.

This wasn't just a little family discovery. It was a research coup.

I needed something to do, I'd told Xavier only just last night. And right here, right now, I could see exactly what that was. I'd yearned to get back into research for years, wanted to put my brain to more use than figuring out the best way to teach multiplication tables to third graders and reading Sofia *Cat in the Hat* for the five hundredth time. Leafing through these books, I could see the paper title now. Maybe even a dissertation. *Early Narrative Building of the English Gentry.*

Okay, not the most exciting title. But I was excited. More than I'd been in a while.

Maybe staying at Corbray Hall wouldn't be so bad. Maybe I had a potential future here after all.

I PORED over the journals for what must have been hours, settling myself at the study table after locating some paper and pens to take notes as I read. Really, though, I was just enjoying myself, lost in the process of discovering a text—many texts—for the first time. So much that I barely looked at the time and was completely startled by a voice suddenly in the room with me.

"Oh, hello."

I jumped at the table, then looked up to find the double doors open again as Georgina entered the library.

She hadn't been at breakfast, though I assumed she and Frederick were at home. She looked as perfectly pressed as she had yesterday, from her blown-out brown hair to her coordinated white pantsuit and the heirloom jewelry glinting from her ears and fingers.

"Hello, um, ma'am—"

"Your Grace," she corrected me with a snip in her tone. "I am still a duchess, even though my husband has passed. The correct address is Your Grace, the same as the current duke ought to be addressed."

Her comment was pointed. Clearly, she had heard me calling Xavier by his first name and did not think it was appropriate. Or perhaps it was just me who wasn't appropriate.

I bobbed again nervously.

"And for goodness' sake, you don't have to curtsy. I'm not the queen, you know."

I found myself wanting to bob again but restrained myself. "My apologies, Your Grace. I'm still learning the appropriate nomenclature and customs."

To be honest, I'd thought I was fairly familiar with them from all my reading. Clearly, I was not.

I glanced at an ornate clock, noting it was nearly time for lunch. Good lord, I'd spent nearly the entire morning in here. Well, it would be easy to make my excuse to leave, at least...

"That clock," Georgina said, following my gaze. "It's working again."

I blinked. "It wasn't before?"

Her brown eyes shot back to me. "You don't know its story?"

I didn't know what to say. It was like dinner all over again, where conversations were constantly had about things I was expected to know but obviously couldn't, given the fact that I had never actually been to Corbray Hall before that morning.

"There is a legend around that clock," she said. "They say a witch tied its chime to the health of the Duke of Kendal a very long time ago. Now, when the duke passes, the clock is stopped and broken. And when his son takes up the title and the seat of the family, he fixes it—or has it fixed, really—and returns it to its rightful place." She eyed me suspiciously. "That wall has been empty for nearly five years. Did you know that?"

Again I blinked. "I—no, I did not, Your Grace."

Georgina sniffed. "Yes. It was broken when my husband passed away. And they tried to give it to Xavier. But he wouldn't take it. Now it's back, just yesterday. And working again."

We both stared at the clock for a long time, and suddenly, I realized I recognized its carved edges and inlaid gold. It was the clock that Xavier had pointed out at his apartment just a few days earlier. The clock his uncle had sent to him, apparently—a bid to return as the duke he was.

And now it was here. Working.

Had Xavier made a decision about his future here that I wasn't aware of?

I wasn't sure how to react to the story. It was the first I'd heard of this tradition, but more than that, it seemed like she was blaming me for something. It was a good thing, if Xavier wanted to take up his inheritance, right? Regardless of how I felt, it couldn't change the fact an estate like this needed an owner. The people who had written the journals I'd read were passionate about their family's lineage. They were passionate about everything Kendal symbolized: prosperity. Propriety. Endurance.

A clock, as it were, seemed a fitting token.

A clock that Xavier had returned.

"So, you like...books, do you?" Georgina peered around as if just seeing the library for the first time.

"Oh! Yes," I said, grateful for something else to think about. "Xavier offered me the key to the library. I used to study English literature, you see, and he thought I might—"

"Dusty things. So very dirty. I always thought we should store them elsewhere. This would make a lovely sitting room." She nodded toward the door, where Gibson was entering with a tray of what looked like lunch. "On days like this, I prefer to take lunch in here to enjoy the gardens. It's absolutely wasted otherwise."

I frowned. "Aren't there already several sitting rooms?" My tour of Corbray Hall had been brief, but I recalled at least two we'd visited throughout dinner last night and another I'd passed on my way in here.

Georgina snorted. "I meant a private sitting room. Not one to be shared in tours, of all things." She turned to the butler after he had set up her lunch on a small table near the French doors. "Gibson, have you the papers? I'd like to take a look."

"Yes, ma'am." Gibson reached under his arm and procured a stack of the day's newspapers for Georgina.

She took them but made no move to sit down or dismiss the butler, who hovered near the library entrance, clearly waiting for her instruction. He did not, I noticed, ask if I needed anything. As far as he was concerned, I wasn't even here.

"Nothing, nothing, nothing," Georgina commented as she flipped through the broadsheets. "Ridiculous republicans, more royal gossip —oh, look, dear, there's something about you. Again."

Her annoyance wasn't exactly subtle, but I ignored it again to accept a few pages from a paper called the *Daily Mail*. Sofia and I weren't front page news—not like American celebrities or the party politics. But in a country that followed gossip about its royals like the weather, the combination of a handsome duke-turned-chef-turned-father was apparently catnip to local readers.

"Why are they so interested in us?" I wondered as I perused the paparazzi pictures taken of Sofia and me a few weeks ago when Xavier had accompanied us to London Bridge.

"Why, indeed?" Georgina murmured as if—but obviously not—to herself as she looked through the other dailies. "Oh, look, here's another."

She tossed the paper at me so hard I could barely catch it. This one was a smaller publication called *The Reporter*, which appeared to be a regional paper that covered most of Northern England—not national, but not completely small town either. This one included an interview along with the headline.

Is she even his?

The Duke of Kendal's so-called "daughter" and her mother were spotted arriving in Kendal yesterday on the afternoon train, following the duke's arrival earlier that morning. Dressed down in jeans and trainers, the American and her daughter were picked up by a member of the duke's staff and transported to Corbray Hall directly from the station.

Fellow passengers reported that the duke's daughter, reportedly named Sofia, and her mother spent the train ride pointing out simple sights along the way like cows and sheep. They were reportedly amazed by the most common livestock.

"They were friendly enough," said a man from Liverpool who was next to them on the train. "But the little girl was loud and very American. What's more, when someone else asked her mother about the rumors the girl isn't actually the duke's daughter, she didn't say a word. I thought it was very suspicious."

The duke's representatives had no comment either when *The Reporter* reached out for a response. Is it possible the duke doesn't actually have a daughter, just an American trying to get her hands on the wealthiest estate in England outside the crown?

I slapped the paper on the table harder than I probably should have. Georgina looked up from hers, and a triumphant smile flashed across her aquiline features before she fixed it back in its dour position.

"Something the matter?" she asked.

"I—"

"Ces?"

Before I could answer, the doors opened again, and this time Xavier entered, clearly looking for me. I was more than a little satisfied by the expression of disappointment and outright contempt when he caught sight of Georgina. Clearly, he had hoped to find me in here alone.

Georgina, however, didn't seem to notice.

"Hello, darling," she greeted Xavier. "Your 'friend' and I have been reading through the news."

"Look at this," I told him, handing him the paper.

He glanced at the headline and batted it away before placing a kiss atop my head. "Ces, I told you. Don't pay attention to the tabloids. It's all rubbish."

"It's rubbish that's libeling our kid and me," I told him. "Again. Xavi, they think we're only here for your money. They actually suggested that Sofia isn't even yours—just a child I brought to make you think you owe me something!"

The idea was so infuriating it made me want to scream.

Georgina, however, looked like the cat who had just located the motherlode of cream.

Xavier was obviously stressed after his morning surveying farms, his Oxford shirt wrinkled down the front, shoes tipped in dirt, and the knees of his jeans showing signs of dust. He obviously didn't want to be talking about this right now.

"Ces," he tried again. "Just let it go. It doesn't matter."

"I wouldn't say that, darling," Georgina put in as she unfolded another newspaper.

Xavier rubbed his face, then turned to his stepmother. "And why is that, Georgie?"

She grimaced at the name. I fought the urge to laugh.

"Well," she continued. "I don't have to tell you how important this Season is for Frederick."

Xavier huffed. "Georgina, I don't care whether or not Frederick makes a good impression on some stuffy peers or an heiress."

"You should if you want Freddy to become the new steward once he finishes with university, as you suggested last night," Georgina put in. "Running an estate like Kendal—and the others belonging to your title, I might add—is much like running a large corporation. You need the respect of your community, your peers, to do it well. Henry refused to take part in socializing, and you've seen the state of the books."

"That's because of his strokes, the doctors said," Xavier argued. "Not because he didn't go to a bunch of ridiculous parties."

"Nonsense." Georgina slapped her paper onto the little table, but it was the only sign of her frustration. "You own an empire of restaurants, darling. Don't you need the cooperation of influential people to make them a success? Kendal doesn't exist as an island any more than the Parker Group does. Connections are everything. You know they are."

Xavier opened his mouth to argue, but it was obvious he couldn't. Even I could imagine how much he depended on style influencers, restaurant critics, food suppliers, investors, and so much more for the Parker Group to be a success.

So maybe Georgina was right. Maybe the aristocracy functioned in a similar way.

Which meant, I realized with a sinking feeling as I glanced again at the headlines, that if Sofia and I were perceived as a scandal, we could also be Kendal's downfall before Xavier even had a chance to save it.

"Sofia's my daughter," Xavier said. "Not a social liability."

Relief washed over me like a cool ocean wave. *Take that, you bitch.*

"Of course she is," Georgina concurred. "No one is doubting that. No one of importance. Yet."

Well, someone was, I almost pointed out.

"So what are you suggesting?" Xavier asked irritably. "I'm not sending Francesca or Sofia back to New York, if that's what you're thinking."

"Of course not," Georgina purred. "Wouldn't dream of it. I was only considering the future, really. The Season has started, and Frederick, well..." She tipped her head as if she was just coming up with the idea. "Imogene did suggest last night that you attend a few of the local events, perhaps the Garden Party next week. At the very least, the Ortham Ball might continue to put you in good graces with the viscount and his sort, not to mention what the Troop's Cup might offer. Everyone will be there."

Xavier gaped. "With everything there is to do around here, you want me to dress up like a penguin and sip tea and play polo with a bunch of stuffed shirts? With Henry only so ill and things a mess here?"

Georgina only offered a sweet smile and pushed a paper bearing yet another salacious article his way. "The estate needs these connections, darling. It's not about tea, it's about money. You'll go, satisfy people's interest in you, make Frederick's introductions, and secure your family's continued success before you trot back to London to live your life, just as you please. Don't you think that's what Henry would want rather than us sitting over here mooning over him? Don't you think he would wish for you to preserve his life's work?"

Xavier eyed the papers, then me, then looked back at Georgina. "I—" He sighed. "I suppose."

My eyes widened. Really?

Xavier avoided my gaze.

"Good. It's settled, then. I'll have my assistant send our responses." Georgina practically gleamed at the idea, then eyed me carefully. "And you, my dear, may want to stay in here. Or better yet, in London. Terribly boring, these things. No place for an American."

"No," Xavier cut in fiercely. "If I have to go to these things, Ces comes with me. That's all."

I found myself standing up proudly, eager to be tugged next to him, to take my place beside Xavier, as he said he just wanted. His hand curled around my shoulder, and I found the urge to stick out my chest like a puffed-up pigeon.

Take that, lady. You're not getting rid of this American so fast.

My sisters would be proud.

Apparently, even Georgina knew when not to push the current

Duke of Kendal on his will. Once again, she looked me up and down, as if trying to determine exactly how to pull a particularly large weed in her beloved garden.

"Well, then," she said at last. "We'll just have to make do, won't we?"

SIXTEEN

"**P**osture, miss."

Two weeks later, I was standing as tall as my five feet, three inches would stretch atop a small platform while a prickly stylist stabbed me with pins and fitted me with a new wardrobe. It took her most of the week, but when Georgina realized that Xavier would not be dissuaded from bringing me with him to every event he attended as part of the Season, she insisted that he pay for new clothes. And to my surprise, he agreed, even going so far as to suggest that we hire a personal stylist to orchestrate it all. That stylist, apparently, was also Georgina's.

Odd, really. Though Xavier had a taste for some of the finer things in life, I'd never had the impression he cared much about what I wore. He'd always liked me however I came, whether that was in oddly-printed pajama pants or a vintage dress.

Now, however, I stood in the room filled with pastel-colored frocks and too many hatboxes to count, and my only company was this stolid, somewhat rude woman. Regina didn't seem to want to be there any more than I did, but she was getting paid enough that she was willing to put up with me.

"This is the last one, right?" I asked.

Regina looked down a snub nose and exhaled through the pins trapped between her thin lips. "Yes, miss."

"Good. I was hoping to get in a bit more research today."

Heartily tired of this entire process, I swished back and forth in the salmon-pink, floor-length confection that could politely be described as cupcake-esque and was designated for the Ortham Ball tomorrow night—the first major event I would be attending on Xavier's arm. It was basically a mountain of ruffles, one I couldn't escape easily to get back to my beloved library.

For the last week, I'd been spending most of my mornings working through the family journals, then used the afternoons to take Sofia somewhere around the countryside before dinner. We would see Xavier briefly for an hour or so before Sofia went to bed, and he would generally work longer before toppling into bed beside me—if he made it there at all.

Things were...working. I supposed. I had a bit more purpose, as I'd requested, and Xavier made a point to be affectionate whenever we were around. The problem was, that didn't happen often. And no amount of library treasures and farm visits could change that.

I tried to remind myself that he hadn't invited us here on vacation but to join him in his actual life. He couldn't help the issues arising in his family any more than I could. But that didn't change the fact that September was coming, and I was due back for the school year in a matter of weeks. I had no idea what was going to happen between us, nor did I feel like this was the time to broach the subject. Was he expecting me to stay indefinitely? Did he think I was going back to New York? Either way, where would Sofia and I stay? What would we do?

To be honest, I wasn't even sure I wanted to stay in England past August—not if it meant living in a museum and dealing with his family's snooty behavior. At the same time, it was difficult to imagine going back to my old life and spending half my time reviewing fractions and filling glue containers for a living. Teaching was fine. It had always been fine. But it had never given me the sliver of excitement I had felt digging into the library over the last week. I honestly wasn't sure I could go back now and make do. Whether he liked it or not, Xavier had opened up a whole new world for me here. I just didn't know how I'd traverse it in the weeks and months to come.

And then there was my sister's voice—which one, I wasn't sure, as they all had the same thoughts about marriage—niggling at me, asking again and again: "Has he popped the question, yet?" Given all the stress Xavier was enduring, I was still trying not to think too hard about the M-word, despite the fact that my sisters brought it up every time we spoke. Although, sheesh, sitting here in a blush-pink gown wasn't exactly helping things.

I pushed all the thoughts out of my mind. Next week. Next week, I could bring up these concerns. Right now, I needed to focus on figuring out how to be a duke's girlfriend in a world that *really* did not want me to belong to him.

The door opened as Regina was placing another pin, and Sofia skipped in, followed by Miriam, her new nanny. Well, "nanny" was putting it generously. Miriam was actually just a local girl I'd met in the village and had chosen over the three sterner, Trunchbull-ish type women Georgina had procured alongside Elsie's recommendations. She had zero child-rearing experience, but she reminded me of my sisters, which would only make Sofia more comfortable with her. Not to mention me.

"Mama, where are you?" Sofia demanded, then stopped abruptly when she caught sight of me. "Whoa, Mommy. That's a big dress."

I looked down at all the layers. I did sort of look like I was being eaten by a sea anemone. Definitely not something I'd have chosen, but since I wasn't paying for it, I couldn't really say much.

"It's Jenny Packham," Regina informed us. "It's *de rigueur*, and absolutely appropriate for a society ball."

Sofia, Miriam, and I all blinked as if we should know who she was talking about.

"Well, it's really fluffy." Sofia dropped her doll on the floor and came over to investigate, pulling out some of the layers as if to see where they ended and I began. She did not find the answer.

"The silk, miss," drolled Regina as she stuck me with another pin near my shoulder blade. "Please. It's very delicate."

"Sofia, babe, give Mama some space," I said.

"But I can't find your legs! You look like a shower puff!"

"I know, peanut. It's all right, all right. I promise they are still there. Have you been having fun with Miriam?"

"Oh, we had ourselves a grand time," Miriam chimed in her thick Northern accent. "Saw the new foals, and Colin, the stable manager, even let us feed some, didn't he, Miss Sofia?"

"Yep. Colin likes My Little Pony too," Sofia tittered, still enamored by the delicate folds of the dress, which she only touched before checking covertly that Regina wasn't watching her.

The Ortham Ball was a charity event the Douglases put on every year at their house outside of London. It was a private event included in the very public London Season, but unlike the public events, this one was invite-only rather than something anyone could purchase tickets for. And that meant it was one of the places Georgina wanted Xavier—and by association, Frederick—to do the "important connection-making"—she was so keen about these days.

It also meant I needed a new dress.

"Let's go show Daddy," Sofia said, already reaching out for my hand and pulling me off the platform.

"But we still have to fit a few more pins, miss," said Regina stiffly.

"We'll be right back," I told her and Miriam.

Miriam smiled.

The stylist sniffed.

Then Sofia yanked me out the door.

I might still have felt uneasy in Corbray Hall, but Sofia had taken to the place like a duck to water. To her, the estate was simply an enormous playground, and after she had met a few of the kitchen maids' children feeding ducks, I barely saw her beyond mealtimes and the little day trips we took some afternoons.

"No, it's this way, Mama," she said, tugging me down a different corridor toward Xavier's office after I'd made another wrong turn.

"Slow down!" I laughed, holding up my skirts. "I have to be careful in this, bean. Can't tear things the day before the party."

"Pretty party," Sofia cackled to herself before stopping at Xavier's office. She frowned. "What's that sound?"

I paused, then heard the thumps of a deep bass vibrating through the thick wood doors, accentuated every so often by a hard thwack of...something.

I furrowed my brow, listening harder. Sofia, however, wasn't inclined to wait. She threw most of her tiny body's weight into opening the door, and immediately, we were assaulted by the harsh, unforgiving sounds of extremely heavy metal.

"Ouch, my ears!" Sofia cried, clapping her hands over said parts.

I covered them with my own, frowning into the room. The thwacking sound was louder now and clearly wasn't part of the music. The problem was, I wasn't sure what was causing it, if it was intentional, or if I needed to get Sofia out of here.

She, however, didn't wait for me to decide.

"Daddy?" Sofia gasped as she peeked inside the doors.

In one corner, the sedate leather chairs had been replaced by a heavy bag hanging from the otherwise ornately carved ceiling. Foamed floors had been installed on top of the sleek hardwoods underneath, along with a set of hand weights against the wall.

Xavier stood in front of the setup, shirtless in a pair of black trousers that weren't exactly designed for exercise but had molded perfectly to his sweaty body. His tattoo was on full display, completely at odds with the posh surroundings, the wild black dragonesque creature slithering all over the shining muscles of his left arm, shoulder, and side, teasing up the neck currently corded with muscle. He looked a far cry from the sophisticated chef, the dashing duke, or even the playful Arsenal fan we generally knew him as. Right now, he looked like a warrior. An extremely crazed warrior capable of a lot of violence.

"Fucking FUCK!" Xavier howled as he landed a complex combination of punches that sent the bag swinging violently through the air.

"Sofia." I pushed my daughter out of the room and removed her hands from her head.

Her bright blue eyes shone curiously, but not without a bit of fear. I didn't blame her. I'd never seen her dad like this, and it was likely a lot more intimidating as a little girl.

"Go find Miriam, babe," I told her. " I'm going to talk to Daddy and calm him down."

With a swift nod, she took off down the hall, running as fast as her little legs could take her. I turned back into the room, wincing against the harsh music, and closed the door behind me.

"Xavier?" I asked.

He continued beating the bag, bouncing on his feet to the harsh music, which was howling nearly as loudly as he was.

"XAVIER!" I shouted as forcefully as I could.

Still no answer. Frantically, I looked around for the source of the music. Eventually, I located a speaker in the corner, which was probably attached to his phone or computer. I picked up my skirts and headed toward it, only able to relax a bit once the screaming vocalist and thrashing guitar were silenced.

"Oi!" Xavier turned around, face contorted with annoyance, until he located me standing next to the speaker. Then the irritation turned to mild repugnance. "What the fuck are you wearing?"

I smarted, although I kind of wanted to smile, too. It had been a while since I'd heard his typically foul language. I sort of missed it.

"A dress," I told him.

His brow crinkled. "Why?"

"For the Ortham Ball tomorrow. Sofia wanted me to show you..." I fluttered my hand in the direction she had run off.

Xavier just continued to stare at me with an expression of abject horror.

"You look like a Victoria sponge cake," he stated bluntly. Then, catching my expression, "Nice, of course. I didn't mean you didn't. But it's just very...very, ah, sweet."

"Don't bother," I told him. "But honestly, what's wrong with sweet? I think you said I was sweet. I thought you liked it."

I was trying for flirtatious—after all, it hadn't escaped me that, along with time with Sofia and me, Xavier's stressful schedule had also been biting into our intimacy together. Normally, going for a week without sex wouldn't have bothered me. After all, I'd gone five years at one point.

But Xavier and I had only just gotten back together a few months ago now. It didn't seem like the fire should go out quite yet. I missed my insatiable chef. Especially when I was staring at the sweat dripping down his ripped body. Damn.

Xavier just chuckled and wiped a bit of sweat from his glistening brow. "You are, babe. You are. But you're sweet with an edge. What happened to your hair? And your earrings? These look like something Georgina would wear. Or maybe her mother."

"She lent them to me."

I lightly touched the updo Regina had tried out for tomorrow and fingered the wreaths of diamonds at my ears. They were pretty, yes, but admittedly mumsy. When Georgina offered them, I didn't have the heart to say no. I was still trying to get the woman to address me by name.

"Well, they look awful. Take them off." He looked me over. "Actually, take it all off."

"And what? Walk down the halls naked?" I joked.

Xavier didn't seem to think it was a horrible idea. I just snorted, though my face flushed a little at the idea. Especially if he took it off me.

Lord, I was becoming easy.

"What about that red dress you brought from home? The one you wore to the Chie opening?" He bit his lower lip mischievously. "I liked that one."

"Red is not appropriate for a society ball," I said, though I was only quoting Regina, who had said the same thing to me when I'd suggested it. "Also, apparently this thing is black tie. The red dress only comes past my knees."

"Pity."

He crossed the room and took a bit of silk between his fingers. Then tugged some more, forcing me to come nearer or tear the fabric. "Nope, I can't take it."

"You're not supposed to touch me right now, you know," I said, batting at his hands.

"I'm paying for it," Xavier said, hands working a bit more now to pull up the layers of silk. His eyes shuttered briefly when he found skin, skating palms up my thighs until he located my ass and grabbed. Hard. "I can do whatever I want to it. Including rip the damn thing to shreds."

"You'll mess me up," I told him, though I wasn't particularly concerned about the dress anymore.

"Fine by me."

"What are you saying, you prefer me messy, Your Grace?"

Xavier smirked. "When I do the messing, especially."

I sighed with utter contentment as he picked me up and carried me back toward his desk, where he set me on the top and sat down in the large chair behind it, for all his shirtlessness, looking very much like the aristocrat he was, surveying his belongings. Which, at that moment, was me.

"God, you're beautiful," he said softly as his thumbs stroked my inner thighs.

I wanted to lean back and let him explore higher. But something about the way he was looking at me bothered me. With desire, yes, but it was mixed with melancholy I hadn't seen before.

"What was with the headbanging session?" I asked, noting another drop of sweat currently rolling down the curve of his tattoo. It was very distracting, alongside the inward movement of his hands.

"Hmm?" Xavier wasn't particularly interested in talking as he spread my legs wider and pushed the ruffles above my knees.

"The music? And pounding the crap out of that heavy bag over there. When did you have that put in, anyway?"

"Last night. I have one in my London office too. It's useful when I need to let off some steam."

The hands fully pushed the silk layers onto the table, shoving some aside with an audible tear. Well, I supposed I was out of Regina's good graces, if she'd ever let me in.

I wanted to ask why he needed to let off steam. Why something was bothering him to the point he needed to punch his hands bruised and listen to banshees on acid to tame whatever beast was raging inside him.

But Xavier didn't elaborate as he leaned forward, intent clear as he gazed between my legs. Instead, I captured his face and forced him to look at me.

He was so beautiful. It was easy to forget. His body was so large that sometimes his size masked the fact that many of his features were deceptively delicate. The sharp cheekbones beneath my stroking thumbs, the porcelain quality of his skin, the blue of his eyes that in this light glimmered like translucent Murano glass.

"Xavi," I said. "Please, talk to me."

He opened that full mouth, and for a moment, I thought he might name the beast that was thrashing inside him. Give it some shape and form. Allow me to help him vanquish it.

I so wanted to try. After all, princes (or in this case, a very upset duke) didn't have to do all the saving. Sometimes a man needs to be rescued as much as any damsel.

Instead, he shook off my hands and tugged me to the edge of the desk.

"Kiss me," he ordered.

Skin pebbling with the thrill of his touch, I couldn't help but obey.

It started off soft but almost immediately turned into something much more insistent. Xavi might have been positioned below me, but his arms had me pinned to the desk, and his lips were glued to mine through some kind of magic I couldn't comprehend.

"God," he croaked after a few minutes. "Will you—"

I swallowed. There it was. The start of the question part of my heart was aching to hear. I fought down the words. I didn't want to force him. I wanted to hear him ask me of his own accord.

"I just—" He kissed me again, like he was seeking the answer without finishing his request. "Francesca, will you—"

Just before he could, there was a swift knock on the door, which opened abruptly. I swallowed a litany of curse words as I pushed my dress back to my knees.

"Kip? Oh! And Francesca, hello."

We both twisted around to find Imogene entering the room, clearly shocked to find me sitting on the desk in front of a very shirt-less Xavier.

Perhaps I should have felt ashamed, but I really couldn't. Not with her. Not with my own boyfriend in his own office behind closed freaking doors.

Hadn't she ever heard of knocking?

"Hello, Imogene!" I said in a sharp voice that sounded like it was trying way too hard to be nonchalant.

I tried to close my knees, but the hands on my thighs were iron. Then one slipped between them while the other pulled my ruffles back over his arm.

I whipped around to find Xavier biting his lower lip while he slipped a hand farther to brush against the edges of my underwear. And to my complete shock, one finger breached the fabric and slid into me completely. The devil himself smirked up at me. His hand disappeared under my skirts, where his thumb located my clit and started to circle.

"What are you doing?" I mouthed.

Xavier's smirk deepened before he looked around me to speak to Imogene. "Did you need something? Ces here just came in at the end of my workout."

"Er, yes." A glance over my shoulder told me that Imogene was trying very hard not to look at the effects of the workout, but even her polished manners couldn't prevent her gaze from sliding over my man's muscles. "Right. Mummy sent me over to have you check the seating order for tomorrow night. I have you and Franny next to the Murray-Harts and Sir John de Lesseps. Will that do?"

"I think so," Xavier said amiably as a second finger joined the first. "And it's Francesca."

I gasped through my satisfaction. Generally, I was the one who had to correct her.

"Of course, of course," Imogene seemed to stumble. "Francesca, are you all right?"

"Yes, I'm fine," I said over my shoulder in a voice slightly higher pitched than normal. "Xavi is just helping me, uh, stretch my ankle. I rolled it coming down the stairs to show him my dress."

Xavier chortled but continued what he was doing. Inside me, the fingers curled, a silent admonishment—or perhaps congratulations—for the lie. Xavier's thumb located my clit and flattened against it, pressing and rubbing in a slow, clockwise direction.

I bit my lip. His gaze zeroed in, and he shook his head infinitesimally with an arched brow. It drove him crazy when I did that.

I grinned.

"Vixen," he mouthed.

"Rake," I mouthed back.

That smirk turned to an outright grin as his fingers continued their relentless work.

Imogene continued to rattle on about seating arrangements at the party, or hors d'oeuvres, which Xavier alternately agreed with or asked for small changes. I honestly couldn't tell you what they were talking about. I was too entranced by the movements of his thumb and the subtle thrusts of his fingers, too focused on trying desperately not to give into the tension building all over my body.

It was no good. He pressed harder on my clit, and the knowledge that he was doing this to me, on top of his desk, in front of this woman in particular, proved my undoing. I came right there on the desk, choking down a scream while Xavier gripped my ankle in his other hand and continued to talk pleasantries about cocktails and guest lists.

"Right, then," Imogene said. "I'm off. Fran—cesca," she caught herself before misnaming me yet again. "I hope your ankle is better for tomorrow. Shame if you can't dance."

"I—uh-huh, yes," I half-gasped, unable even to turn around for fear she would see exactly what was happening written all over my face.

"She'll be fine," Xavier told her as he stood. The hand between my legs stayed where it was, but his erection pressed into my thigh, hidden behind my skirts from Imogene's view. "See you tomorrow."

The minute the door closed, however, his composure evaporated. In a single harsh movement, Xavier practically ripped open his pants and shoved into me with a movement violent with blind, animal need.

"Fuck," he hissed as he seated himself deep. "You naughty, naughty girl, teasing me like that. You little minx."

"I d-don't know what you're talking about," I stuttered, barely able to form words as he started pounding into me. "Th-that was all you. T-total rogue. Do what-tever you want, whenever y-you want."

"And don't you fucking forget it."

He thrust mercilessly, finding a rhythm that had my heels knocking against his desk drawers and a moan erupting from my chest that was louder than any music he'd been playing earlier.

Then he paused, took my chin firmly with one hand, and forced me to look at him.

"Wear red tomorrow," he ordered before delivering a long, flaming-hot kiss that left me breathless. "For me."

He thrust one final time with a groan, and we both shattered together, falling back onto the centuries-old desk, covered in sweat and desire.

His tongue ran over my shoulder, licking up my own mild glow until he found my face again and kissed me, softer this time.

"Please," he whispered as he worshiped my mouth. "I want to see you in red."

Of course, I couldn't say no. Not while he was dousing me in kisses and laying me flat on the desk for round two.

Maybe that was really the problem. When it came to Xavier, I had a hard time refusing him anything.

PART 3

THE GENTLEMAN

INTERLUDE II

ELEVEN YEARS EARLIER

Xavier

"I told you, I'm not fucking going back."

"Watch your mouth, boy, or I'll watch it for you."

"I'd like to see you try, gnarly old git," I retorted, turning to pick up the dough I had been weaving into a plait.

Gavin, the village baker, had given me a bit of his starter last month, and I'd finally trained it in the kitchen to the point where I thought I could get a decent rise. I'd wanted to try a plaited sourdough for a while. Even if Gavin swore up and down it wouldn't work in the cool Lakeland humidity. I thought that Corbray Hall had enough elevation that it just might make the difference.

Before I could make it through a third weave, a cast iron pan clanged into the wall above my head.

I bent down, narrowly missing the second one before it banged into the brick over my shoulder.

"Evelyn won't be happy that you're ruining her prized skillets," I remarked as if he had only dropped one on the ground.

"My cook's concerns are the least of my list of worries. My son's blatant and complete disrespect is at the top."

"Well, good for you, Your Grace, getting your priorities in order at last," I said, feigning nonchalance over the anger simmering. The anger that was always simmering. Like a pot ready to boil over if he turned up the heat a bit too much.

"You will go back to university, Xavier. Do you have any idea what kind of favors I had to call in to ensure you a spot at St. Andrew's, after what happened at Christ Church? They say the prince of Denmark shall never have the same nose again."

"That's really too bad, since no one asked you to do it," I told him as I pulled another thread of dough across the plait. "I already told you, I'm not going. Not to St. Andrew's or Cambridge or any other of these posh schools you want to force me into. I want to learn to cook properly. And I don't need your help to do it. I've already been accepted to the London Culinary Institute, as it happens. And under the name Sato too. Without your fucking favors."

I continued plaiting as if he wasn't fuming on the other side of the counter. Rupert watched until it looked like a vein at the top of his forehead might burst.

"Ungrateful little bastard," he snarled. "That's what you are. If I hadn't—"

"Hadn't what?" I snapped. "If you hadn't what? Shagged the cook?"

"Your mother and I met at university first, as you well know—"

"Got her pregnant?" I went on. "Eloped in an impulsive wedding? Or maybe it was abandoning your family for fifteen years until you suddenly grew a conscience, eh? My God, if only you hadn't done that, we wouldn't be here at all, would we?"

"My son will *not* be no better than a kitchen boy, and that is final!"

Seething and swollen with anger, Rupert Parker opened and closed his mouth like a blowfish. Blowfish could be poisonous. They were delicacies in Japan, but if you didn't remove certain parts, they could also be deadly. A delicious game of Russian Roulette.

Sort of like fighting with my dad. Five out of six times, he kept his cool. Get that last bullet, though, and you got a cast iron pot thrown at your head. Or maybe a priceless heirloom, depending on which room of the house we were in.

Apparently, I was looking to play.

He watched me for a few more minutes with those annoyingly blue eyes of his. The ones I inherited. The ones I fucking hated.

"I've really tried, you know," he muttered, more to himself than to me. "The polo. Took you to Scotland. Sent you to the finest schools, did everything to help you learn to be a part of society. You can't tell me I didn't."

"Yes, you have tried," I said, picking up the edges of my plait once more. "Tried to shove a square fucking peg in a round hole, Rupert. But some things just don't fit."

He stared at me for a long time, then shook his head. "He really can't tell me I haven't tried."

Great. Now I was being talked about like I wasn't even fucking there.

"You call this trying?" I demanded. "Forcing me into your life and throwing tantrums when I don't fit?"

"You ungrateful—"

"Wretch. Brat. Bastard. I know, I know. Don't bother, because I've heard them all. Just more reasons I've no desire to be the Duke of fucking Kendal. And let's be honest, you wouldn't know real effort, real hardship if it bit you in the arse."

Rupert stood up hard enough that his stool went toppling to the stone floor and left the room with a bang of the door against the stopper.

"Don't let it hit you on the way out," I called and went back to my plaiting.

"Don't let what hit me?"

I looked up to find Henry coming in. I jumped at first, thinking it was Rupert again, back for another round. They looked alike from afar, nearly as tall as one another. As tall as me. But where Dad had steely blue eyes and an expression to match. Henry's was softer, somehow. Not kind, per se. No one in the Parker family was ever really kind. But at least he didn't throw pans at me. Maybe a jibe or two, but that was it.

"You can't imagine this is really about whether or not you want to make bread, of all things." Henry looked at the plaited dough as if it might jump out and attack him. "It's about your future. About his future, really."

"Oh?" I said, finishing off the plait and tucking the ends under the loaf before scooping the whole thing up and gently setting it into a proofing basket. "Please tell me why my desire to cook has anything to do with his future. Dad can be a self-righteous twat, whether or not I'm working in a kitchen."

"Well, for one, he'd miss you," Henry said. He bent down to grab the stool Dad had knocked to the floor and set it upright for himself.

"Go on, tell me another," I said. "I'm the thorn in his side. Have been since I was born. He just couldn't ignore me anymore after Mum died. Even worse, that I turned out to be his actual heir."

Lord, that had been a prize fight. I'd been the one throwing things that night, once I'd learned that not only was I the next Duke of Kendal, but that titles weren't really something you could refuse. I was what I was. Like it or not.

I turned around and started washing my hands in the sink. Sourdough really did turn to cement when it was left to dry, and it was like glue when wet. Horror to work with, but I was determined to master it no matter what. Plus, one of the few perks about Corbray Hall was the proper bread oven, lined with bricks and fully fired. Most industrial bakeries didn't have as much. It was too good not to learn.

"Be that as it may," Henry said once he'd sat down on the stool. "If you do leave again and become a chef—aside from what it will look like for the Duke of Kendal's son to be a common cook, on top of needing to get that thing on your arm—"

I grinned. I had particularly liked Dad's reaction when he caught sight of the tattoo I'd brought home from America. Up and down my left arm, a little bit up the neck and over the wrist, so it couldn't be hidden with the best of collars, the longest of sleeves. A serpent designed to recall Kiyohime, the woman who turned into a serpent demon in order to kill the man who betrayed her. Mum told me a lot of Japanese folktales when I was a kid, but that was one of her favorites. It never occurred to me to wonder why until I'd come to live with Rupert Parker.

"If you left," Henry continued, "it would also mean you wouldn't stay here and marry Lady Imogene. As you are meant to."

I paused, hands still under the half-boiling water. "You want to say that again, Uncle? Who's getting married to Imogene Douglas?"

Uncle Henry sighed, like he was speaking to someone particularly slow. "It's been in the works since you were first brought here. It's the obvious choice, boy. The estates adjoin, and we've known the family for generations. Imogene will inherit Ortham and her parents' income, if not her father's title. Their estate will become a part of Kendal and still remain part of a different, greater title that can maintain everything. It all works out."

"Why not Lucy?" I asked. "She's the eldest."

"Xavier, please," Henry replied. "Lucy will not live beyond thirty, if she is lucky. We all know it. That future is not one to be planned for."

"You don't know that."

I turned off the faucet and wiped my hands on my pants. Henry sighed irritably, then yanked a dishtowel from a rack behind him and threw it at me with a bit more force than necessary.

"Imogene?" I asked disbelievingly as I finished drying off. "That's what this is all about? He wants me to marry Imogene Douglas?" The idea made me laugh outright. "She's, what, fourteen?"

"Fifteen," Henry replied calmly.

"Jailbait, that's what," I countered. "I'd rather just marry Lucy, if I had to do it at all. Which I don't. But at least we're actually friends."

"Don't be a fool, boy. For one, Lucy can't have children."

"And how would you know that, you old lech?" I leered at him.

Henry would know the ins and outs of a prospective girl's reproductive system, though. He knew more about this place and everyone in it than anyone who'd ever lived here, I'd wager. He probably had her lady parts tested too. Counted the eggs and everything.

"Her parents told me," he replied, impervious as ever to my jokes. "We've discussed the match a great deal. They are very supportive, even with their prospective son-in-law's...unusual proclivities."

I recoiled. The idea of these imperialistic old geezers sitting around talking about my and Imogene's future like it was a game of chess made me physically ill. And I didn't even like the girl.

"It's a no," I told him. "And I mean absolutely not. I might have to take Dad's title or die, but I'm not getting forced down the aisle. Lucy's my mate, but Imogene is..." I made a face. "Well, she's annoying."

"She is still young."

"Exactly. Every time I'm over there, she chases me around like some kind of puppy."

"Well, she is very young. But it bodes well that she likes you, I should think."

"It bodes nothing, Uncle. I'm not interested. I'm also not even twenty-one yet."

"Exactly. She's coming out this year," Henry said. "In a few more, she'll start university. Look, boy. No one is saying you must marry the girl now. Sow your oats, as they say. Do what young men do. But when all's said and done, you must keep your future in mind. And while apparently that does not include a degree from Britain's finest institutions—"

I snorted. Yeah, I didn't fancy getting kicked out of another university. Three was enough.

"It should include doing what is needed to be a true Duke of

Kendal," he concluded. "And eventually, that will mean getting married and carrying on the line. I realize they question you now, boy, but should you marry the Douglas girl, you wouldn't hear a word about it ever again. Be the heir, establish an heir. Have your fun discreetly. You understand?"

I opened my mouth to joke again, to tell him he'd lost the plot completely. But Henry was looking at me in that way he sometimes did. Like he thought he knew me better than I knew myself. Like he knew that deep down, there was a part of me that wanted to be accepted by my father and his people and be more than Rupert Parker's funny-looking boy who fought and swore too much. He knew it, even if I wasn't willing to admit it.

I knew one more thing, though. That, out of the few people left in this world who actually cared about me, Henry was the only one who could tell me the real, honest truth of things, whether I liked it or not.

That didn't mean I was ever going to marry Imogene Douglas, though.

Before I could say as much, the kitchen doors burst open, and my father reentered the room, red-faced and ready for another argument.

I clenched the towel, prepared for battle.

Instead, he surprised me with an olive branch.

"All right," Rupert said, "you can go to bloody culinary school. I'll even pay for it. On one condition."

I glanced at Henry. He shrugged, clearly as curious as I was about what was happening.

"Oh?" I asked. "And what's that?"

"That you, when you're finished, you come back here and follow the plan."

Henry looked at me again as if to say "I told you so."

I just snorted. He might have imagined that future, but there was no way I was ever marrying Imogene Douglas. Just like there was no law that said the Duke of Kendal had to reside in Kendal.

"Fat chance, that one," I told him. "Once I leave Kendal again, I'm never coming back. I don't fancy having another pan thrown at my head or any more of this matchmaking business you and Uncle have been cooking up. No fucking thanks."

Henry sighed as his brother turned his murderous gaze on to him. But Rupert barely managed to hold in his anger before he turned back to me. The dealing wasn't done.

"And if you and your smart mouth had a place of your own?" he asked.

I looked up, this time genuinely surprised. "What, you mean a flat in town?" I shrugged. "I can get that on my own. I still have Mum's, you know."

"I mean a restaurant," he said, as if I should have known. "A shabby little pub to do with what you like. So long as you stay here and finish learning the things you ought to."

I peered at him, wondering what other motive was behind this. There was a time, years ago, when Rupert tried to make nice with me. After he realized I was legitimate, he did try a little, like he said. Taught me to play polo, for fuck's sake. Well, that part I liked.

None of the rest took. Especially when it was so obvious he'd had to. His wife and stepson were hardly around. And so he was left with one option: a black sheep for his only heir and legacy.

I glanced at Henry to see what he thought. His face didn't move, but his thin shoulders rose and fell, as if to say, "Why not?"

I turned back to my father. "All I have to do is live in Kendal? And you'll stop haranguing me about uni and everything else? You'll let me do what I want? You'll let me cook?"

I wanted to hear him say it.

Rupert's face contorted with struggle, but at last, he sighed, wiped his forehead with the back of his hand, and nodded.

"Yes," he said through his slightly crooked teeth. "Come back and stay, and you can cook. But you *will* become a duke."

SEVENTEEN

Francesca

Ortham House, where the eponymous Ortham Ball was being held, wasn't exactly a house. More like another tiny castle, which seemed to be a pattern with the few remaining "houses" still belonging to the upper aristocracy in England. Despite the fact that, as Xavier had explained, the tenant system of land ownership had given way to corporate investments long ago, the remaining families still in position to nab estates seemed to grab them like Monopoly properties. The Parkers had obviously been part of that exclusive club following the Depression and war years, and they had assisted the Douglases as well in their own portfolio management. I was starting to understand why the two families were so deeply entwined —they'd been scratching each other's backs for generations.

Situated about twenty minutes outside of London, Ortham House would have been an easy enough commute from Xavier's apartment, but on Georgina's advice, Xavier agreed that we should stay at his family's own stately home near Hampstead Heath.

"But isn't your Mayfair apartment closer to Chiswick?" I had wondered, checking Google Maps as we were on our way to the flat earlier that evening.

I insisted on getting ready there with my own things after weeks of making do with a weekend bag in Kendal, plus the assorted pieces accumulated through Regina. Xavier agreed because he needed to take care of some Parker Group business in town before the party.

"It is, but Georgina had a point," he had responded as he checked his phone for messages. "These people won't look for the Duke of Kendal in Mayfair—they'll call Parkvale. The entire point of attending this circus is to help the family."

I didn't bother to mention the fact that said "family" seemed more interested in what Xavier could do for them than Xavier himself. It was what he wanted, and I was determined to support him.

And so it was that Miriam took Sofia to Parkvale while Xavier dropped me off in Mayfair, from where I'd be driven on my own to meet him at the ball when it started.

At the time, the prospect of arriving to a society event on my own hadn't really bothered me.

Now that I was here, however, nervous didn't even cover it.

"Frankie?"

I looked up to find that Ben, Xavier's driver, was standing outside my open door, hand extended to help me out of the Rover. He smiled kindly—one of the few staff members who did on a regular basis (Elsie and Jagger were the others). It was hard to believe I'd been intimidated by him or anyone else in Xavier's employ when I'd first arrived here. Then again, compared to the Parkers, Xavier's people were utter salt-of-the-earth types, even agreeing to use my given name instead of "miss," as if to emphasize my young and very unmarried status.

I took Ben's hand and allowed him to escort me to the curb before I brushed off my dress and checked that I had my shawl and clutch. People were streaming into the large Victorian house, which was framed by vine hydrangeas growing up the brick exterior and dangling over the large white columns that marked its entrance. Bright lights gleamed inside, from where a chorus of posh voices, laughter, and music emanated into the night air.

"Enjoy," Ben said, then got into the car and drove off, leaving me to be swept up in the line of glamorous attendees making their way into the house.

The door was blocked by a woman in a sleek silver dress holding a clipboard next to two large security guards. Some things never changed, I thought as I approached. Exclusivity in England looked the same as in New York. Same snooty doorkeepers on power trips everywhere you went.

"Good evening," I said with a smile. It felt like the polite thing to do.

The woman looked me over with one of those stares that felt like it was undressing you, and not in a good way. "Your name, please."

Okay, so I wasn't dripping in diamonds and didn't have on a freaking tiara. But that didn't make me chopped liver.

"Um, yes," I told her. "I should be. I'm here with Xavier Parker—er, the Duke of Kendal and his family."

"Your *name*," she repeated without looking up again.

I swallowed, then glanced behind me at the other attendees, who were starting to look impatient. "Sorry. Francesca Zola."

The hostess flipped through a few pages. "Sorry, not on the list."

I frowned. "Well, if the duke is inside, perhaps you could let him know I'm—"

"I'm afraid that's impossible." She looked around me brusquely at the couple behind. "Ah, Lord Moreley. Lady Moreley. Pleasure to have you this evening."

I wanted to cry as I was unceremoniously pushed back down the steps in favor of actual peers. I pulled out my phone to call Xavier, though I doubted he would hear anything inside the party. It went straight to voicemail anyway. Great, his phone was off, and I was stranded outside, no better than a stray dog looking for scraps. A gender-swapped version of *Lady and the Tramp*.

"Frankie?"

I whirled around to find the last person I ever thought I'd see in London staring at me like I was, well, the last person he thought he would see.

Adam Klein, art teacher at P.S. 058...but definitely not the Adam I knew.

"Adam?" I gaped.

Gone were the paint-stained jeans, driver's cap, and tortoiseshell glasses that marked him as one of the Brooklyn hipster class. In their place was an elegant black tuxedo, contacts, and chestnut-brown hair that had been tamed and slicked back. He looked like he had walked out of the society pages. Or maybe a Bond movie.

He said something to the people he was with, then came to join me on the steps. "Holy shit, Frankie, yeah. What are you doing here?"

"What am I—what are you doing here? In London? At a ball, of all things?" I couldn't help grinning. It was just so good to hear an American voice at a place like this. Even better that it was someone I knew, even if it was the guy with whom I'd had a sort of disastrous date last spring.

Adam just shrugged. "My dad still works at the embassy here. Diplomat, remember? And we have some cousins in the area who were coming tonight, so they got us an invitation." He rolled his eyes conspiratorially. "Honestly, it's a bunch of stuffed shirts, but the food is usually good. What the heck are you doing here, though?"

"Xavier," I said simply. "His family was also invited." I looked toward the building, as if I might see him through the shaded windows. "They're close friends with the Douglases, apparently."

"Oh...so you're still with him, huh?"

I didn't like the surprise in his voice. "Well, I wouldn't be in London if I weren't."

"I just thought you might have..."

He trailed off, and there was an awkward pause.

Adam just looked around. "So, where is he, then? Shouldn't he be escorting you inside? The security at these things is usually pretty tight, you know."

"I noticed." I flailed a hand holding my cell phone. "Xavier had some business before, so we had to come separately. Now I can't reach him, though, and for some reason, my name isn't on the list. I don't even know if Xavier's in there, but now I'm officially late."

I checked my watch, then looked around for the Rover, wondering if I could catch Ben in time to drive me to Parkvale, where I could trade this dress for a movie night with Sofia. Unfortunately, the car was nowhere to be seen.

"Don't worry about it," Adam said, offering his hand. "You can come in with me. We'll find him."

I eyed the hand, slightly wary. The last time I'd interacted with Adam, Xavier hadn't exactly been friendly. Adam had tried to kiss me, much to my dismay, and hadn't really taken no as an answer. He'd apologized, and then we'd run into each other a few more times at work and even, oddly, at Xavier's last restaurant opening. Things were friendly. But I doubted that Xavier would appreciate me walking in like I was Adam's date and not his.

Adam's brown eyes blinked kindly, as if none of the previous awkwardness between us had ever occurred.

I glanced back at the doorwoman. What were my choices here? Ben had driven off, I didn't have his number, Xavier wasn't answering his phone, and there was no way I could afford an Uber to take me all the way back to Parkvale.

"All right," I said and allowed Adam to weave his fingers with mine. "Thank you."

"No problem. And Frankie?"

"Yes?"

Adam's brown eyes glowed warmly. "If he doesn't tell you tonight...that dress...wow."

I blushed. Less than two hours ago, I'd eschewed Regina's cupcake-pink monstrosity in favor of a dress and some costume jewelry I'd found last minute at Topshop that afternoon. It wasn't exactly couture, but it was the best I could do on short notice without Xavier's unlimited budget. More importantly, I felt like me in it rather than some kid playing dress up.

I blushed, relieved to know my efforts weren't a complete failure. "Oh. Thank you."

"No," Adam said eagerly. "Thank you."

IT WASN'T the kind of ball you'd expect to see in an Austen adaptation, but it wasn't that far off either. Ortham House was appropriately decadent, a nineteenth-century neoclassical manor dripping with ridged columns, bright white millwork, and crystal chandeliers in every room. All the men were dressed in full tuxedos, the women wore floor-length gowns, and a quartet was playing lively covers of pop music in the corner while caterers flitted about the rooms with trays of champagne and hors d'oeuvres.

As Adam led me into the ballroom with my hand tucked into the crook of his elbow, it was obvious that people noticed. Not just me, but him too. They were looking at both of us. Together.

"Adam," I whispered.

"Yeah?"

"You're not just a teacher, are you?"

He chuckled and patted my hand. "Tonight, I'm just your friend, like I always was. Nothing more."

"I still think people are noticing you."

"They're noticing you, Frankie." He swiped a couple glasses of champagne from a server passing by and handed one to me. "For one, they probably saw the paper this morning."

I paused, flute to my lips. Dread burrowed into my stomach. "What was in the paper?"

Adam looked uneasy. "Shit, you didn't see?" Fumbling a bit, he pulled his phone out of his jacket pocket, then did a quick search before handing it to me. "It's, um, why I thought maybe you were here alone."

There it was. Right across the top of the *Daily Mail*'s local gossip page:

'Frankie's no duchess. Trust me, I raised her.'

'The truth is, Frankie is the coldest of her sisters,' said Guadalupe as she dabbed away tears with a tissue. 'I'm not saying I've never made mistakes. Everyone has. But she won't even let her own daughter meet her abuela. She thinks family is a joke and refuses to even meet my eye when we speak. It's been like that her entire life, the entire time I raised her. I really think something must be wrong with her.'

I gawked at the article, scrolling down to the end. It was a hit piece, an exclusive interview with the *Mail* about me, Sofia, and Xavier...given by none other than Guadalupe Ortiz.

"This is—this is my mother." I shuddered and squeezed my eyes shut.

Seeming to notice that I couldn't read anymore, Adam patted me weakly on the shoulder. "I know. I'm sorry. Seems like when people get any kind of fame or fortune, they show their true colors. Are you close?"

"No," I said emphatically. "We are not close at all. Adam, I barely know her! She walked out on me and my siblings when I was practically a baby. She's an addict—a drunk who would do anything for a bit of cash. Oh my God, Adam, how could they print this without doing a basic amount of fact checking? I mean, how did they even find her?"

Adam shrugged. "That's the UK tabloids for you. They get a scent of something interesting, they're like bloodhounds."

"But it's not true!" I practically exploded, drawing curious, disapproving stares around us. I lowered my voice, though it was no less frantic. "Oh my God, but all these people have read this. Did you think that Xavier broke up with me because of this?" I shook my head. "They all think I'm this horrible person who has been tricking Xavier and jilting my mother and—Adam, these are lies!"

I couldn't tell if he believed me or not. His expression was one I'd seen on people's faces my whole life. Anytime my mother showed up out of nowhere to claim me or my sisters, usually stinking of bourbon with her hair unwashed and stains littering her clothes. When we would refuse to go to her, she'd scream at us from the sidewalk. And before our teachers, coaches, and babysitters understood the relationship, it was always the same look on their faces: pity. Pity and doubt.

"I swear it," I said again, quieter now. "Adam, we don't have a relationship. These are lies."

"All right, all right," he said, pulling his phone out of my grasp and tucking it away. "Frankie, I believe you. I do. Come on, have another drink."

I did as he suggested but couldn't help noticing the gazes still flickering my way from around the room.

"They're still looking at me." My face was flushed. "They're thinking about that story."

"None of these people care about the *Mail*. I told you, they're looking at that dress," Adam corrected me.

"I'd have to agree."

At the sound of Xavier's deep voice, I swung around so fast I nearly spilled champagne all over my chest. Which, I noticed, my handsome duke was now eyeing with an expression between blunt appreciation and possessive irritation.

Okay, so it wasn't exactly a conservative piece of clothing. You find a floor-length red gown under two hundred dollars, that is. While the skirt did, in fact, cover every inch of my lower body, it also had a generous slit up one leg and clung to my legs and backside in a way that didn't leave a whole lot of my shape to the imagination. The bodice was even more revealing, reaching only halfway up my back and wrapping around the front, where two thin straps led to a V-neckline that draped down to the bottom of my sternum.

Honestly, it showed about as much as an average bikini top. And fine, on a well-endowed woman, it would probably have been completely inappropriate. Indecent, even. But I was small, and everything was covered up just fine. I thought I looked pretty good, especially with the wreath of cubic zirconias around my neck and the long strings of them dangling from my ears. Not diamonds. But they still sparkled almost as bright.

"Francesca," Xavier said without a word to Adam. "Shall we dance?"

His hand extended toward me, a slip of tattoo extending beyond his wrist, and didn't waver. It wasn't really a request.

I nodded to Adam. "Thanks again."

He was watching Xavier. "Any time. And I do mean any time."

Xavier bared his teeth in a very good imitation of a panther but said nothing more as he led me to the dance floor, where more than a few couples were enjoying a casual waltz. Mentally, I thanked Nonna for making us all learn basic dance steps when we were little. At nine, it hadn't seemed practical to be learning the waltz with my grandmother instead of the latest NSYNC choreography, but right now, I was utterly grateful for the lessons.

"You wore red." Xavier nodded a greeting toward an elderly man a few partners away.

"I did," I replied, a bit icily. I was still reeling from the article, but I hadn't forgotten about being stranded outside. "You were supposed to meet me on the curb."

"I got tied up." The hand at my waist tightened. "You look unbelievable."

"Not like a sponge cake anymore?"

"Definitely not. Still something I'd like to devour, though."

That familiar excitement zipped through me, but for once, I didn't respond the way he obviously wanted. Instead, I focused on matching his steps, which were much larger than mine.

He tipped his head toward Adam, who had settled on the periphery of the room, watching us over the rim of his glass while he chatted with another attendee. "What's he doing here?"

I shrugged. "Here with his family, he said."

"Tosser. He touches you again, he's a dead man."

I sighed. "Why do you have to be like that?"

Xavier looked down at me, honestly shocked. "You forgetting what happened when you let him take you out? He's a twat who doesn't know when to stop. And this time, I'm your man, not the babysitter. It's my right to fuck up someone who doesn't know the limit."

I sighed heavily but smiled under the looks we were attracting—obvious curiosity regarding the prodigal duke amongst them. Xavier didn't seem to care what any of these people thought of him, but I certainly did.

"He didn't do anything but escort me inside," I said through my teeth. "And you're lucky he did, by the way, because they wouldn't have let me in otherwise. And then you would be in for a nice fight with *me* when you got home."

"You in the mood for a fight, babe?"

Something glinted in his blue eyes, like he wanted me to say yes.

I almost did. I almost threw his arms off me right there and told him not to touch me again unless he wanted to be the dead man in the room. I could see it play out perfectly, a game of cat and mouse in this room full of glittering people. I would hurry through the crowd, maybe out to a shadowed part of the garden. He'd chase me out there, just like all rakes do. We'd snarl at each other in the dark, until eventually, it was too much, and then I'd compromise my reputation completely by allowing him to ravish me amongst the hydrangea bushes.

Or something like that.

Xavier tipped his chin, clearly waiting for whatever remark I had for him. "Which novel is in your head now, babe?" He leaned down so his lips brushed the top of my ear. "By the look on your face, I hope it's a dirty one."

I shivered. But in the end, found I didn't particularly like being teased. Not right now. Not here. And not by the only person who supposedly wanted me here.

As the music ended, I stepped out of his arms as gracefully as I could. "I'm thirsty. I think I'll track down some punch, or whatever they're serving, that isn't alcohol."

Xavier eyed me a long while, like he was waiting for something.

For what, I didn't know.

"Right," he said finally. "There's food through those doors over there. I've got to talk to some people anyway. Find me when you're ready to go."

And with that, we both allowed the next round of music to play us off the dance floor. In entirely different directions.

EIGHTEEN

I didn't tell him when I was ready to go. Either time.

The first was minutes after we had last spoken, and I just didn't want to be that girl.

The second was because I was drunkety-drunk drunk, and I'll admit, a complete mess.

As promised, I found the punch, then proceeded to anger-drink several more glasses of champagne and tell at least five verifiable noblemen to sod off in my best Queen's English when I caught them staring at my décolletage. They did not find it amusing.

I kept spotting Xavier lurking about the party, almost always with his hand on Frederick's shoulder, doing his duty and introducing his stepbrother to the right people. I was drunk, but not to the point that I wanted to ruin the real reason they were here. It was when I spotted Xavier woefully accepting Imogene's offered hand and escorting her to the dance floor that I was really and truly done.

I borrowed fifty pounds from Adam in exchange for my London phone number and got a car to Parkvale. By the time I arrived, I found myself even angrier than before. And still completely three sheets to the wind.

"May I help you?" asked the man who opened the arched front doors. Like Gibson, he was also dressed in a starched black suit. A livery, was it? Did butlers wear livery, or was that just footmen?

I was honestly too wasted to remember.

"Step aside, Jeeves," I ordered. "I've had a hell of a night, and I need a giant vat of wine and a bath, if you don't mind."

"Pardon, miss!" The butler blocked my entrance to the house. "We are not in the business of allowing vagrants on the premises. I must ask you to leave."

"Fat chance," I snarled as I tried to shove my way around him.

Screw this guy. Screw all these people. I had absolutely no tolerance for this world right now, and that included this pompous penguin.

Then something occurred to me. "This is Parkvale, isn't it?"

It would be just my luck that on top of everything else, I'd have ended up at the wrong freaking house.

"Bledsoe, it's all right."

The butler and I both turned to find Elsie clipping down the hall, clad in her usual attire of a wool skirt and knit cardigan, even in the balmy August evening.

"For heaven's sake, Bledsoe, that's Lady Sofia's mother, Miss Francesca," she scolded him. "Let her through!"

"Gotcha, Jeeves," I cut at him as I ducked under his braced arm. "I do belong here, after all."

The butler sniffed and closed the door behind me with a harder click than was strictly necessary.

"My, my, aren't we in a state?" Elsie took my arm and guided me down the hall. "Aren't you home a bit early? I wasn't expecting you until later." She glanced over my shoulder, as if the front door might open again. "And where is the boy?"

"The boy?" I repeated. "The boy is too busy kissing every arse in England and dancing with Great Britain Barbie to bother with the mother of his child. If Sofia's even his, that is. Who knows these days, am I right?"

My words slurred together, but even beneath my drunken haze, I was embarrassed. Embarrassed by my own behavior, but also for being that stupid girlfriend, the needy one who requires her boyfriend's attention all the stupid time.

I wasn't this girl. I was a mother. A good sister, half-decent teacher, all-around respectable gal. I was a reasonably self-sufficient human being who had never once needed a man to make her feel worthwhile.

And yet here I was, bitching and moaning because my boyfriend didn't dance with me at the party.

What a wreck.

"Oh, darling, of course she's his. Everyone knows it. After all, she's the spitting image, isn't she?"

God, I was tired of hearing that.

"I dunno," I slurred as I was guided into a sitting room with a large fire crackling between several enormous built-in bookshelves, all filled with what was probably another priceless library. "Haven't you heard, Els? I'm a liar, prob'ly just out for his money. Pullin' it over him with a secret baby. The papers all say so." I snorted loudly. "Maybe we should just get a DNA test and be done with it, amiright?"

Elsie settled me into one of the chairs near the fire, then waved a hand at the butler, who was lurking in the doorway like a disapproving bat. "Tea, Bledsoe."

"But, ma'am, I shouldn't think it right to leave you alone with...her."

"At once," Elsie snapped.

Bledsoe nodded and left.

"So long, Jeeves," I called as I collapsed into one of the over-stuffed chairs. "Elsie, where's Sofia? I want to say good night."

"Oh, Little Miss has been asleep for hours. Went out like a light, if I do say so. You'll see her in the morning." Elsie took her own seat across from me. "Now, why don't you tell me what happened that

sent you home alone without your escort, eh? I know I taught him
better than that."

But I just shook my head. "He had more important things to
attend to than a sad American in a cheap dress." I pulled at the mate-
rial. "I bought it for him, you know. Spent a whole two hundred
dollars. That's a lot for me."

I was sulking. Hard. I knew I shouldn't be so upset. These were
small things, and Xavier was under so much stress. Was it so bad to
expect me to experience the party on my own?

No, Lea's voice echoed within me. Or maybe it was Kate's. Or
Marie or Joni's. Honestly, they were all blending together tonight.

*He asked you to come. Said he needed you there. And then he
freaking abandoned you with those snobs.*

I sniffed. Somehow, thinking like that didn't make me feel
outraged anymore. It just made me feel sad and lonely.

"Oh, sweet girl," Elsie said calmly. "I'm certain Xavier cares more
for you and Sofia than he does about anyone—or anything—else in
the world."

I shrugged like a sullen teenager. "Sure. That's why he went off
and danced with Imogene, right?"

Elsie shook her head, almost like she couldn't believe it. "Just you
wait, boy," she muttered under her breath.

"I can't really blame him, Elsie. He saw me talking to this man
from back home. A man he really doesn't like. I got mad at him for
being rude, and so we barely spoke all night. I get it. He wasn't there
for me. He was there for his family. I had no right to ruin it all."

Elsie watched me for a long time. Her brow furrowed a bit until
she seemed to come to a decision.

"You can't see this, my girl, but he's changed since you and Miss
Sofia came into his life," she said. "Something in him died when his
dear mother—bless her soul, you know that Masumi was one of my
very best friends. I tried to help her son, but he was very hard, you
know, for a long time. But when he found you and the little girl, he

came back to life again. It's just now...I think he's figuring out what to do with that life, if that makes any sense."

"Sort of feels like he knows exactly what he wants to do with his life," I mumbled. "It's us he doesn't know what to do with. Not here. Not there. Not in a box. Not with a fox." I chortled to my Dr. Seuss imitation but waved a hand around our opulent setting, figuring Elsie would understand who exactly I meant.

She just sighed. "Ah, well. Things become a bit more complex when you throw the Parkers into the mix. For so long, he wasn't even welcome in these halls, you know. And then suddenly, the duke wanted him after all. It was quite a turn."

"Because he turned out to be his heir, right?" I chimed in. At least I knew some of the story.

"That's what they said," she agreed.

I perked up, sensing something more. "But?"

Elsie shrugged. "But nothing. I just always wondered if there was more to it than just carrying on a line. Maybe I'm just a romantic, but I always thought maybe the duke secretly loved Masumi. She was so lovely. Maybe he was forced to let her go by his family and the boy along with her. Keeping them close would have been too hard, perhaps. He didn't become the Duke of Kendal until Xavier was maybe fifteen, sixteen? And by then, of course, it was too late for him to bring Masumi home to him where she belonged. But he took in Xavier, who reminded him of what he'd lost. They reminded each other, I think. So together, they never fit."

I thought about that for a moment, long enough for Bledsoe to wheel in a cart containing tea. Elsie shooed him away and poured out for both of us while I ruminated.

"Elsie," I said seriously. "I think you might like romance novels even more than I do."

She looked up from the pot with a gleam in her eye. "Well, why not? There's enough sour in life without a bit of sweet from time to time."

We sat there for several minutes, sipping tea together while I considered all she'd said. It was quite a romantic story, the way she told it. Much more than the one Xavier had told me. In his view, he was only the product of a tawdry affair, not a doomed love.

Star-crossed lovers certainly added...something to it all.

But maybe that's what was wrong, fundamentally. Was there a part of Xavier that was trying to make good with the family he'd never wronged?

Or was Sofia's and my presence just a reminder of what he'd lost? Or maybe what I'd cost him?

Elsie finished her tea, then got up and stretched. "I've got to get home, my dear. You'll be all right?"

I nodded, significantly sobered. "I'm sure Bledsoe can show me my room."

"Of course he can. And a word, treat the butlers like dogs. If you try to be friends, they'll never respect you. Command them and they'll follow you like thieves."

I chuckled and accepted a kiss to the cheek. "Good night, Elsie. Thank you. I'm sorry to be such a disaster."

"Nothing to it, lovey. Sweet dreams to you and the boy."

She left, but I remained by the fire a while longer, pondering not just what she'd said but also the rest of this odd life we'd taken on by coming here.

Three houses in less than two months.

More chandeliers than I could shake a stick at.

In essence, Sofia and I had become squatters in very expensive flophouses. My head was reeling from all the change, and I couldn't believe it was good for Sofia, happy though she was to be near her father. What little of him she saw these days. Even less when we left in a few more weeks. Or so I assumed.

"Wanker," I snapped at a portrait of Xavier hanging across the room.

I hadn't noticed it before now. At Corbray Hall, there had been no portraits of the current duke to join his ancestors. Here, at last, was one, as stern as ever, Xavier in a full suit, hair shorter than I'd ever seen it, tattoos erased from his hand and neck.

It wasn't a Xavier I'd ever known. Yet I wondered if he was becoming something more like this man every day.

Just as I was getting ready to leave, my phone buzzed in my purse. I pulled it out to discover a FaceTime request from Matthew. I checked the time. It was only about ten o'clock here. Just five back home.

I accepted the call and held my phone out. "Hey."

Matthew's face appeared on the screen along with Nina de Vries, his girlfriend—wait, no, his fiancée. I kept forgetting they were technically engaged, despite the fact that Nina was still trying to get out of her marriage to a truly horrible man. Supposedly, that was happening sometime soon.

My heart twisted as I caught a few glimpses of home behind them—the ugly brick fireplace, a TV playing what looked like a baseball game, and a bit of the black-and-white photo of the Brooklyn Bridge hung on one of the walls. I happened to know that Nina had a beautiful apartment on the Upper East Side, so it warmed my heart to know she was happy to spend time with Matthew in his own natural spaces. Happy, yeah. And a bit jealous.

Nina waved at me. "Hi, Frankie! So good to see you. Wow, you look beautiful!"

I smiled, unsure of what to say. I wasn't used to Nina greeting me with this kind of enthusiasm. Clearly, they were both excited about something.

"Where you been, sis?" Matthew wondered.

I looked down at my dress, then back to them. "Oh, uh, Xavier's family had an event tonight. I, um, wasn't feeling well, so I came back to the house early."

"Bummer," Matthew said.

I waited for him to pry the way only my family could. The way he normally would, back when he wasn't so taken up by another woman in his life. Or maybe just when he wasn't this happy.

Mentally, I chided myself for wanting otherwise.

"Well, we wanted you to be the first to know," he said.

I tipped my head. "First to know what?"

"We're getting married," Matthew said. "Me and duchess—I mean, Nina, here."

"Well, I knew that, you goon," I told him. "Unless you forgot that big bomb you dropped on everyone last spring. You about gave Lea a heart attack when she saw Nonna's ring on Nina's finger. It still looks nice, by the way."

Beside him, Nina chuckled. "Who could forget that?"

She gazed at my brother with such unadorned adoration, that jealous twinge in my stomach turned into an outright stab. For all our doubts about the woman, she really did care for him. And what's more, she didn't bother to hide it. There was no doubt on her face, no closed expression. Nothing but pure, unadulterated love.

After brushing a light kiss over her forehead, Matthew turned to me. "I just meant we've set a date. October."

My mouth dropped. "What? That's in less than two months. Why so soon?"

"Nina's divorce was finalized last week, thanks to a few smart judges. I know it's fast, but we don't want to wait. We have been for too long. So we're going to have a ceremony in Italy, actually. This church we found when we were there in January. You'll love it, Frankie, for real. I can't wait to show you. Olivia's going to be Nina's bridesmaid, so obviously we'll need Sof to be the flower girl. What do you say?"

I swallowed. Matthew was babbling, and my brother didn't really babble. It was because he wasn't just sharing news.

We'd never really talked about it, but Matthew knew as well as I did that his getting married would be more than just a party for Sofia and me. It would affect every part of our lives.

Immediately, questions bubbled up in my mind, and not the

"what does her dress look like?" sort. Where were the two of them planning to live? I wasn't under any illusion that a Park Avenue princess like that would want to relocate to a shabby row house in Brooklyn, nor would she want to share a thousand square feet with her new husband's sister and her four-year-old. But what did that mean for Sofia and me? Would Matthew want to sell the house? Did we have to move out? Find a roommate? Or, God above, move back in with Nonna?

"There's more." Matthew pulled me out of my spiral.

I inhaled deeply. More? What else was about to happen?

"The wedding's not until October, like I said," he was saying with a cheeky grin at Nina. "It's the first date we could get at the church. But, before then...well, next month, actually...we're moving."

"Uptown?" I guessed. That answered one question, I supposed.

"In a way. Boston."

I nearly dropped my phone.

"Nina wants to go back to school, and she only has a few more semesters to complete at Wellesley. That's where she originally started a degree in art history, but she had to drop out when she had Olivia. You know how it goes."

Something in my chest cracked. I did know. I hated that I knew. Matthew's lady friend—shit, his fiancée—and I had next to nothing in common except the fact that we both understood how having a child could singularly and totally change your entire life plans.

Except in her case, she could go back to school whenever she liked. She could pick out a new apartment or house or freaking mansion like she was choosing nail polish, pop her kid into the best school in the country, marry the man of her dreams, and not worry a thing about food, electricity, utilities, or rent.

That was the difference millions of dollars made, right?

I kind of hated her for it.

Or maybe it was just that I hated myself for having none of that at all without depending on someone else. For a while, Matthew had provided me with a safety net. And now it was being ripped out from under me.

What about Xavier?

Kate's voice in my head sounded a tone of reason.

What about Xavier? My absent boyfriend? Baby daddy? Duke friend? We loved each other, yes, but I still didn't know what to call him. Tonight, the way I was feeling, I didn't even know what I meant to him anymore.

He said Sofia would never want, and I believed that, but was I supposed to come crawling to him every time I needed help with a phone bill or preschool tuition? Was I supposed to continue chipping away at my sense of dignity and self-reliance until there was nothing left at all?

I could never seem to get out of this situation. I could never seem to stop depending on the whims of others to support me.

I hated it so, so much.

"Con-congratulations to you both," I said hurriedly, already feeling the hot rush of tears threatening. I looked away, not wanting them to see my expression.

"Thanks, Frankie. But I also wanted to tell you—"

"We'll talk soon," I interrupted him, swallowing back sobs that already threatened. "Tomorrow, I'll have Sofia call so you can tell her yourself. Love you! Congrats to you and Nina."

"But Frankie—"

"Love you, bye," I rushed and ended the call before he could answer. I swiped at my face, where tears were already streaking downward.

One month. That's all I had. One month to figure out my life before Matthew left New York and gave up on me for good.

They were getting married. And yes, it was a rush, but what I heard in my brother's voice was something more than just a crazy whim. It was the same thing he'd had every time he'd talked about Nina and their future. Love. Conviction. He knew what he wanted with her. He'd always known what he wanted from the second he saw her in that damn bar over a year ago. One look, and he'd seen their entire future and had pursued it endlessly until every sizeable obstacle was out of their path.

I was happy for them. I really was.

But I was terrified, too. More than that. At that moment, envy stabbed me with such violent thrusts, I genuinely thought it might tear me apart.

NINETEEN

Bang.

The sunlight streaming through the drapes was at just the right angle to feel like a bullet to the brain. I rolled over in the plush covers of my third-floor bedroom at Parkvale, only to wince as the pressure in my head pierced the other side.

Ow. Yeah.

My head was throbbing.

"Jesus," I muttered as I rolled onto my other side, away from the firing range. "Frankie, you freaking lush. How much did you drink?"

"I lost count after your third champagne."

Xavier's deep voice perked me up, but only just. I stared at the wall, at the ornate white wainscoting that bordered blue silk wallpaper. The question wasn't whether he was correct. It was whether I was imagining his voice, too.

My conscience had a funny way of sounding like everyone else but me.

I rolled back over, scooting out of the sun's glare, then opened one eye to find the man himself sitting on a velvet-upholstered chair next to the bed, knees wide while he balanced a bouquet of lovely pink roses on them.

"She lives," Xavier said softly with a wry smile. He held out the flowers, ragged stems wrapped with a flour sack and a ribbon.

I took the flowers shyly, holding the sheet to my chest when I realized I was wearing nothing more than my underwear. Apparently, I'd just stripped down and hopped right into bed last night without a care about who might find me.

"Thank you," I said as I pressed the roses to my face.

They were fragrant and sweet—the perfect thing to chase away a hangover. I wondered if he had picked them directly from the garden himself. The idea warmed me, even if it was unlikely.

"Did you ever come to bed?" I wondered, noticing that he was still wearing his tuxedo pants and white shirt from last night.

The top three buttons were undone, revealing a bit more of his tattoo than usual, and his shirttails were out and wrinkled. His feet were bare, and the ends of his bowtie were loose on either side of his collar, where a bit of his tattoo said hello. Dark circles ringed his eyes, and his hair was a bit mussed. Regardless, he still looked as edible as ever. Maybe more than when he was polished and put together.

Xavier shook his head. "I didn't sleep," he admitted. "The ball lasted until nearly four in the morning, and Frederick and I stayed later trying to get the Earl of Ketchley to invest in a wind farm. I heard you found your way here at a reasonable time, though, even if you were quite...animated...with the staff."

I cringed, remembering some of my comments to the butler. And to Elsie, for that matter. Not my finest hour. I had been the very definition of an Ugly American.

"I'll tell Jeeves—I mean, Benson?—I'm sorry," I said. "God, I really was awful."

"Bledsoe," Xavier corrected me gently. "And don't worry about it. I've called him worse. We pay him very well to put up with us." He shrugged, turning to look out the window. "When I got home, I just sat in the other room until I thought you'd have slept enough. Smaller house. Nosier staff. Thought it best to avoid gossip."

I laid back on the pillows, rotating the bouquet in my hands. "Since when did you start caring about gossip?"

He glanced at a pile of papers, obviously thinking about the headlines. They were the ones I picked out. "Since when did you?"

"Since they started printing lies about our daughter." And me, though I couldn't quite bring myself to say so.

Xavier shrugged. "I told you, they've been doing that about me since I was a child, too. But I don't like them printing rubbish about you and Sof either. Or maybe it's just that I see how much it affects you, and I don't like that."

I frowned. "Then why don't you do anything about it?"

His brow furrowed with confusion. "What do you mean?"

"I mean, I tell you about it, and you don't seem bothered. You say you've experienced it all before and to pay it no mind, like it doesn't affect me that people all over this country believe I'm a liar and a thief and a terrible mother."

Xavier scowled at the papers. "What do you want me to do, Ces? Chase down the reporters who print it and threaten them with their lives?"

"I want you to care as much about your family as you do about a chef messing up your soup or threatening some guy who likes me!" I tossed the flowers onto the bedspread and sat up fully. I was the one who had been a mess last night, but now he looked awful contrite. "Why do you do that?" I pressed. "Lose your temper that way? Especially at the ones like the chef who are just doing their jobs? It's like there's an on-off switch with you. You either don't care at all, or you treat people like scum."

Xavier looked up, blue eyes nearly the color of the sky outside my window. "Why did you last night? I don't think I've ever seen you be rude to anyone, but poor Bledsoe took the brunt, didn't he?"

I swallowed sheepishly. "I said I was sorry. I was drunk, for one."

"Come on, Ces. It was more than that."

I considered. "Fine. I was mad. Really mad. At you, mostly. But also at...I don't know. All the people who treat me like I'm nothing. The news-papers. The hostess last night. Imogene and your stepmother. All those people who have watched me down their patrician noses, waiting for me to mess up for the last several weeks, maybe the whole time I've been here. Bledsoe was just the really snobby cherry on that particular sundae."

Xavier nodded. "Well, then you've some idea of how I've felt my entire life." He blinked. "Really, really mad."

"Not right now," I pointed out. "Now you're sitting there like once again, none of it matters."

"That's where you're wrong." He shook his head, then shoved a hand through silky, bedraggled hair. "I'm always angry, Ces. Most days, I spend my time trying to shove it down. And the only way to do that is to numb myself. Act like I don't care."

"Even with me?" I wondered. "Even with us?"

"No." Xavier looked up, expression softened. "That's how I knew, you know," he said quietly. "With you, with Sof, the world is just... quieter somehow. With you, I feel so much more than anger. With the two of you, I only felt peace."

"Until now," I finished for him. "When that world is shoving its way in."

He examined me for a long moment, then got up and moved to sit next to me on the bed. "Only if we let it, babe."

I allowed him to gather me into his broad chest and stroke my hair like a child. It felt good. But like everything else he'd been offering of late, it felt like a tease.

And it wasn't enough.

Tell him, I thought to myself. Tell him what you want. Tell him not to dance with Imogene. Tell him you need him to stand up for you. Tell him that you can be there for him, support him, love him no matter what. But tell him that you need all of that, too.

I wanted to say so. I really did.

Instead, I changed the subject.

"My brother's getting married," I said.

"To the de Vries girl, right?"

I nodded. "October. In Italy."

"Good for him. She's a catch. You'll enjoy Italy too. Especially the food. You've family there, right?"

"Some distant cousins, yeah," I murmured.

He hadn't, I noticed, said *we*.

"It's fast, I know," I continued on, mostly to ignore my own perceived awkwardness. "But they love each other. My brother especially. Matthew loves Nina more than anyone. I've never seen him like this before over a girl. So fierce with her. He would do anything for her."

I waited for Xavier to say something. I didn't know what. Maybe I wanted him to tell me he understood. That he felt the same about me and Sofia. That he thought about doing the same thing with us, whisking me away to a chapel and making us the real family he knew we should be.

Again, I wondered why I was so eager to march down the aisle. Xavier and I had only been together officially for, what, a few months?

The idea, though, wouldn't let go.

Maybe it was because things were different when you had a child together. Maybe it was because I'd believed him when he said he wanted to be together for good. Maybe I'd let myself jump too far when he said he wanted to leap together.

Whatever we were doing, though...that wasn't leaping. I felt like I was falling from a cliff alone.

"They're moving to Boston," I told him. "At the end of the month."

"Oh?" Xavier asked as he fingered the edge of the sheet around my back. "What's going to happen to his house? Will they sell it?"

I shook my head against him. "I don't know yet. I don't know what Sofia and I are going to do. But we have to decide soon."

He seemed to think about that for a long time. "It'll be all right, Ces. You'll figure it out."

I waited for something more. For him to take the opening. Tell us to stay here, tell me he'd come back to New York with us, tell me something that suggested his investment in our future past the end of August.

"Well, send him my congratulations. Like I said, she's a catch."

I sat back up to look at him. "You sound like those people out there talking about you."

Xavier snorted. "What do you mean?"

"Do you have any idea how many women I heard talking to their daughters about how to 'land' you last night? I realize the Season isn't strictly about matchmaking anymore, but there were an awful lot of mamas there trying to make their daughters a duchess."

Xavier just started laughing. "Never. And I only meant, good for them both. Your brother seems like a nice bloke, even if he did punch me in the eye."

"Well, you dishonored his sister," I pointed out. "He was duty-bound to sock you."

"What would he do if he knew I was dishonoring his sister on a nightly basis?" Xavier offered his trademark shark grin.

But it didn't do what he wanted.

"Stop," I said as he nuzzled into my neck, inhaling deeply.

"Never. Been waiting since last night, and I didn't even get to peel that dress off you. God, you smell good."

He was joking. I knew he was joking and relished in his touch as much as he clearly did mine. But the allure of the joke was fading, and I was too shy to say it. Just like I was too shy to ask him all the things I really wanted to ask. Things like, have you thought about honoring me and your daughter instead of dishonoring me all the time? Would you ever want to run away to Italy or France or even Japan, if that's what you want, to do something crazy like elope?

Would you actually want me to be your wife? And Sofia to be your real daughter, not just the accident everyone thinks she is?

But when I opened my mouth to speak at last, Xavier only captured it with his, delivering his patented kiss that knocked nearly every thought out of my head as he rolled me onto my back.

Nearly.

"Xavi, I said stop," I said, pushing him off me completely.

He backed off with a groan, though he couldn't stop his gaze from slipping down to where my nipples, evident through the thin sheets, were making it very clear that even if my brain wanted to stop, my body definitely did not.

Traitor.

"Xavi," I said sharply, then snapped in front of his face. "Up here, please."

He rolled his eyes but did readjust his gaze eventually. "Fine. What?"

"You can't keep doing this."

"Doing what? Worshiping my girlfriend? Come on, Ces, it's the only good thing going for us right now."

"What, sex? That's all? Xavier, I am not a consolation prize. Or a security blanket."

He recoiled. "I never said you were! But it's better than these sad-sack, everything's wrong conversations, don't you think?"

My mouth dropped. "Are you serious right now?"

Xavier shrugged, sitting back onto his heels on the mattress. I yanked the sheets farther up my chest and sat back against the pillows, eager to get as far away from him as possible.

"These are real issues," I told him. "Real shit we are dealing with right now. These things affect my life. Sofia's life. In a matter of weeks, too. And you couldn't care less."

"That's because on top of your 'real issues,' I've got a boatload of my own, Francesca," he shot back as he got off the bed. As if he, too, wanted space between us. Well, that was fine with me. "In case you missed it, my uncle is practically on death's door. I've got a thousand-year family legacy to protect that suddenly means more than it ever has in my life. I've got family members circling the whole thing like vultures, and on top of that, I've got a daughter to get to know. I don't have time for stupid gossip and your brother's wedding and all your fucking insecurities! I just don't!"

By the time he was done with his tirade, I would have thrown just about anything in the room at him to get him to stop. At last, the truth was out. I didn't have to suspect anymore that Sofia and I were at the bottom of his list of priorities. He'd just spelled it out for me, clear as day.

"Your Grace?"

The butler's quiet knock sounded on the other side of my bedroom. Xavier moved to open it, then looked at me.

"Don't. Open. The door," I gritted through my teeth. "We are still talking."

Xavier glared at me for a long minute. Then he turned and twisted the knob.

Bledsoe popped in, took one look at me in the bed, and averted his gaze completely. "Mrs. Crew wished me to remind that you are due at the polo pitch in approximately ninety minutes, Your Grace. Benjamin has the car waiting in the front drive."

"Thanks, Bledsoe. I'll meet him out front." Xavier closed the door, then turned back to me. "Look—"

"Don't," I said sharply, staring down at the sheets. I absolutely would *not* cry right now.

He opened and closed his mouth several times, followed by a similar action with his fists. He looked like he wanted his heavy bag in the room but would have to settle for a pillow.

"I've got to go," he said carefully. "The earl is going to be at this event too, and Frederick is actually all right talking polo. There will be members of the royal family there. We can't miss it."

"Of course you can't," I told him, my lower lip trembling. "I wouldn't expect anything less."

At this point, I really didn't.

"I'll send Ben back for you and Sof," Xavier said. "The match is at noon. She'll like the ponies."

At that, I finally looked up. "You can't possibly think we are coming to watch you ride a horse and hit a ball with a stick after the shit you just said to me."

He stood there for a long time, then served me with a gaze that just about broke my heart, twisted as it was with confusion, love, pain, and yes, anger. And the anger, as he promised, was always there.

"You're the only ones I want there," he said quietly. "Do with that as you like."

Without waiting for an answer, he left.

I just buried my face in my hands and sobbed.

TWENTY

I wasn't going to go. I mean, I really wasn't going to go.

The second Xavier left the room, all I wanted to do was pack up whatever random things had been brought to Parkvale, go back to Mayfair for as much of our other stuff as I could find, then get a couple of one-way tickets home to New York for Sofia and me and forget this summer of experimentation ever happened.

When I had finished crying, I yanked on a T-shirt and stormed into Xavier's bedroom to tell him, too, only to find that he had already left. But what I saw on the nightstand stopped my emotions cold.

A small two-by-three picture, framed in unassuming silver, sat at the bedside table along with a book of classic Japanese poetry, a culinary magazine, and a notepad with my name scrawled across the top, under which he had written and crossed out three separate poems.

*How desolate my former life;
Those dismal years, era yet
I chanced to see thee face to face*

Just as I would beckon you, my love,
Heedless of stinging rumours...

With rudder lost, how can they reach
The port for which they long?

I picked it up and brushed my finger over each unfinished stanza that appeared to be copied from the book. It wouldn't have been the first time he had used this sort of poetry to apologize. It was like he realized his own language wasn't working, so he was trying to speak to me in mine.

I put down the poems and picked up the picture. In it was a photo I'd never seen before—a picture of me and Sofia, asleep together in her bed at Mayfair, when the afternoon sun was shining down on us. He must have snapped it sometime after we'd first arrived. I'd obviously fallen asleep while putting her down for a nap, and something about it had touched Xavier to the point where he'd felt the need to capture it and keep it close while he himself slept.

"Damn," I whispered as I put the frame back on the table. "Oh, damn."

More than anything I had seen in weeks, this collection exemplified Xavier. A reminder that even if he didn't show it, he kept the things most important to him near and dear.

And that did, apparently, include Sofia and me.

I sighed then. I had to get ready for a polo match. And, apparently, a mea culpa.

UNLIKE THE ORTHAM BALL, the Troop's Polo Cup was a public event, so Elsie had made sure as soon as Xavier was invited to play that Sofia and I had tickets to get in along with Miriam. There would be no snooty hostesses to embarrass me at the gate. Nor would anyone look down at me for my inappropriate clothing. And I'd have company in the form of Elsie and Jagger, much to my relief.

"It's hardly the Royal Ascot," Elsie had told me. "But you must dress up a bit and wear a hat. And have some fun!"

I followed her advice, making use of one of the conservative outfits supplied to me by Regina. Today's rendition of "Frankie Attempts Society" consisted of a sleeveless brown frock with cream polka dots, coordinating cream pumps, lacy kid gloves, and a matching wide-brimmed straw hat that would shade my face in the sun. Sofia, too, was dressed in a little blue sailor dress and patent-leather Mary Janes. We'd even gotten an outfit for Miriam so she wouldn't feel out of place.

The polo cup, however, was more than an event. It was a spectacle. The crème de la crème of English society were all here to see and be seen by everyone else who'd procured a ticket—if the hats hadn't told me, nothing else would.

Elsie shepherded Sofia, Miriam, and me onto the grounds, which contained a clubhouse, stables, restaurants, and several pitches corralled by a ring of white fences. On the far end, I could see the players warming up atop their horses (which everyone called ponies, for some reason), swinging the mallets around as if they wished they were lances for jousting, or perhaps swords, instead. Xavier was easy to spot in his red and white polo shirt, sitting at least a head above most of the other men on the field.

The Troop's Polo Club was apparently one of the most prestigious clubs in the UK. It was sponsored directly by the crown and where many members of the royal family had learned their sport—so I was informed by at least three different people as we walked in. Royal sighting was at least as important as watching the actual game.

"Why was Xavier asked to play?" I asked Elsie as we found seats on one of the bleachers set up around the main pitch. "This seems like a professional sort of thing, or at least something where the players need to be very proficient."

"It's not professional, no," she said. "More something you watch for fun, simply because it's a chance to see the Royals, for a lot of the spectators. But Xavier is quite good. His father taught him to play, and he took it up at Eton, which, of course, practices here. It was the only thing he and Rupert Parker really had in common, actually."

We watched him for a few minutes, practicing with some of the other players and occasionally flashing the broad smile I rarely saw anymore. Once, he even appeared to laugh. When he did that, he really was charisma incarnate. A born leader. I could understand why these people were attracted to him like flies. From what I could see, that kind of natural charisma was rare in any class. For a duke to have it and command of one of the largest fortunes in the country? He was the catch every mother in the country wanted for their daughter and what every man wished he could be.

"He doesn't play much now," Elsie said, catching my gaze, "but the family always kept its membership at Troop's. When the team discovered Xavier was available, naturally, they asked him if he could step in. Look, dearie, there's Daddy."

She pointed out Xavier to Sofia, who briefly looked up from the coloring book she was working on, then dove back into making sure Elsa's dress was pink instead of blue.

Considering the prestige that obviously went into membership at Troop's, I had a feeling the invitation had more to do with the sort of networking Xavier was trying to accomplish with these fellow equestrians (and they with him) than any sort of legitimate skill he might have.

That was until I saw him play.

I knew nothing about polo, but even I could see Xavier had some talent. He was obviously at ease on the horse, and it was a treat to watch the way the muscles moved in his thighs as he squeezed the saddle or the way his biceps and back rippled whenever he struck the ball with his mallet.

I could have watched him for hours.

"Did I miss anything?"

We all sidled over when Jagger appeared dressed neatly in slacks and a sports jacket that had to be hot on this August day. It was reasonably cool out here under the trees but still warm enough to make everyone glow a bit.

"Hello, love," he said, leaning over to deliver a kiss to my cheek before taking a seat on Elsie's other side. "You look a treat. Oh, God, she's here?"

We all followed his gaze to the far end of the pitch, where Imogene Douglas was stepping onto the grass. She looked tall and willowy in a pale blue summer dress, her blonde hair dangling down her back, tied back on one side with a fascinator that barely passed as a hat but complemented a pair of large white sunglasses. She was as bright as I was dark, tall and chic while I was homely and small. Kid gloves or not, I simply couldn't compete.

"I bet she doesn't get hangovers," I mumbled to myself. My head wasn't pounding so badly as this morning, but sunglasses were still a necessity.

"Well, of course, she's here," Elsie chided Jagger. "The Douglases are members too, aren't they? Frederick played for Eton, same as the boy. They never miss the Troop's Cup. Now, don't be salty because she turned you down years ago."

"Aw, you had a thing for Imogene?" I teased Jagger lightly. "What happened, didn't quite add up to a Cinderella story for you, Jag?"

He did not seem to find it funny. "Never did. Past tense." He shrugged. "It was ages ago, but it wouldn't have worked anyway. Hard to have a relationship with someone who's in love with your best mate—oof, Els, what the fu—"

Sofia jerked up with her foxlike hearing for profanity.

"Christ, Els," Jagger gasped, doubled over upon receiving a hard elbow from Elsie. "What was that for?"

"For not thinking before you speak," she said primly. "There are children present."

"It's all right," I said, although Jagger's statement had sent butter-flies whizzing around my belly. He only had one best friend, right? "I assume you mean Xavi. I didn't know he and Imogene were ever involved."

For some reason, that almost hurt more than discovering he was a duke.

"It was a little crush," Elsie assured me. "On her part, not his. Lasted only a second or two, after her sister died."

"If by a second you mean twelve bloody years," Jagger joked, even as he dodged another smack from Elsie. "Come on, she's bound to know. She was up there in Kendal with them." He looked at me knowingly. "Rupert and Henry wanted them to get married, so Xavier promised Lucy he would to spite them and make sure Lucy inherited her share even though she was sick."

I nodded. That didn't sound so bad. Typical Xavier, if I was being honest. And it was so long ago, I likely didn't have to be concerned.

"Imogene, though, never gave up," Jagger continued, checking to make sure Sofia was focused on her coloring. "She pops into the restaurants sometimes, looking for us. Waits for hours for him to show up. I don't mind telling you, she wasn't very happy when he stayed in New York all that time for you and Sofia." He leaned back to look at me. "You telling me you didn't notice the way she follows him around? Calls him 'Kip?' Drapes herself all over him like he's a piece of furniture?"

He was trying to make light of it, like Imogene was no more intimidating than a silly schoolgirl with a crush on a football player. I continued to smile like nothing about that bothered me, but the effect was starting to become painful.

"So...did anything ever happen?" I couldn't help but wonder.

"Never," Elsie assured me with a dirty look Jagger's way. "Their families have always been close, and she's fond of him. But there's nothing more to it than that. This one's only got a grudge because she threw him over."

"I'm no one's second choice," Jagger said evenly. "And when a girl uses me to get to my mate, you could say it's a deal breaker."

After receiving another death glare from Elsie, he didn't offer any more details. But I didn't need them anyway. I was too busy watching Imogene lean over the fencing as Xavier rode up and greeted her. They did nothing more than chat, but there was something in the way Imogene was laughing, the way she tittered like a bird whenever he spoke, or how she tossed her head back, giving him a view down the front of her dress. Elegant, always. Never suspect. But it reminded me very much of the cheerleaders in high school who would flirt with the football players during practice. Pressing their limits just because they could. And because they wanted to show them other things under the bleachers later.

"You see?" Elsie said, following my gaze as Xavier rejoined his team on the pitch. "Just family friends."

"Yes," I said as I watched Imogene's gaze, which hadn't moved from Xavier, no matter how far he rode. "Yes, I see."

IT WAS an exciting match to watch, particularly with Jagger in my ear, explaining the game as they went. Xavier was rotated in and out depending on the stamina of the other players, but he was clearly an asset to the team, playing what Jagger called the Number Two position.

Other than in the kitchen, I wasn't sure I'd ever seen him so at ease. Despite his proclamations that he hated the aristocracy and everything about that part of his life, Xavier seemed to fit right in here, even smiling when the crowd cheered at a particularly good play.

But by the end of the second period—or, as Elsie informed me, a chukker—I couldn't watch him any longer. Miriam had long since taken Sofia to peek at the ponies, and I decided now was a good time to find some refreshment and stretch my legs too. While many in the stands tottered out onto the field to replace the divots with their shoes (apparently a longstanding tradition), I made my way toward a tent where drinks were being served and got in line behind two women about my age who seemed to have already had a few, if the volume of their conversation was any indication.

"The Prince of Wales seemed out of order, don't you think?" said the one on the right, who was wearing a large hat with roughly half an ostrich affixed to the crown.

Her friend, a curly-haired brunette outfitted in a bright pink dress and matching hat, clicked her tongue. "He's only mad because the duke showed up and stole his thunder. Gorgeous as ever, though, isn't he? Did you see those thighs?"

"And his chest. And that tattoo...golly. And he swore he'd never come back. Lucky us."

"They all say that. And they all do in the end."

The two of them tittered as they stepped up behind the rest of the line.

Maybe it wasn't Xavier, I told myself as they chatted. There were plenty of other dukes in England. Maybe not so many that two flighty socialites would be interested in. Maybe not so many that would be termed gorgeous. With muscular thighs and shoulders for days and a tattoo that made nice English girls blush.

No, there had to be others.

"She's here, you know. Did you see her?" asked Pink Dress.

"No, but I'm dying to have a look after what Imogene said. Total barbarian, apparently."

It could be another Imogene too, I tried to convince myself.

Yeah, who was I kidding?

They took another step but continued to gossip just as loudly. I kept my head pointed down and my face as still as possible, too ashamed to listen but too embarrassed to move away.

"Not that it matters," Ostrich Feathers continued. "You don't really think he's going to end up with an American, do you? Now that he's back, I can't imagine it."

"Well, they do have a child together, even if it is rather unorthodox. And he did bring her all the way here. For the Season, no less. That's got to mean something."

Ostrich Feathers just gave a rather unladylike snort. "Please, obviously, the child is a trap. They say she's not even his, and until there's a DNA test, I wouldn't trust a thing."

"Oh, come on, Beth. Didn't you see her picture in the papers? She looks just like him. Even you must admit that."

Ostrich Feathers—or Beth, apparently—stood her ground. "At this age, they all look alike. She could be anyone's. Not that it matters. He didn't marry her then, and the girl can't inherit anyway, even if she is his daughter. Yes, I'd like an Aperol spritz, please."

"Pimm's for me," added Pink Dress to the bartender.

Ostrich Feathers turned to her while the bartender mixed their drinks. "So, really, there's no point, and if the American thinks there's a real future for them, she's a fool. He'll get it out of his system and find someone who's good for him. Imogene will be first in line, of course, but who's to say it couldn't be any of us?" She shrugged. "After all, why would he go through the motions now for a sad little girl who can't inherit and her brutish American mother?"

"Probably because she's fantastic, and any man would be lucky to have her."

The women, shocked, whirled around, followed by me, and found another American right next to me—close enough to hear every word the women were saying. And close enough to know I'd been listening.

Adam Klein smiled through his glasses, though the rest of him was looking as dapper as he had at the ball in a bright white suit and red tie.

He was the absolutely wrong person to show up right now.

His presence would make Xavier absolutely furious.

And at that moment, I had never been so happy to see anyone in my life.

TWENTY-ONE

"Adam?" I gasped. "What are you—how did you—"

It shouldn't have been a surprise, really. If he was here visiting his family and was getting roped into these events, just like I was, it made as much sense that he would attend something like the Troop's Cup as the Ortham Ball.

He was fully dressed the part of an English gentleman in a pristine white shirt and light gray suit, along with a jaunty straw fedora perched on his head. His knowing smile told me he understood how dashing it all was. As did the two women's expressions when they caught who was stepping in.

"Frankie," he said as he leaned in to press a kiss to my astonished cheek.

Then he turned to the women, who were staring with mouths so wide I honestly thought flies might buzz right in.

"Americans aren't all brutish. I should know." Adam nodded at them as a curt hello. "Beth. Chelsea." Then he turned back to me. "Francesca, may I introduce these two busybodies I've known since childhood, Lady Elizabeth Ruckston and Miss Chelsea White.

Ladies, this is Francesca Zola, lately from America. I believe you're familiar."

The women stumbled overtly, their expressions feigning kindness, though their eyes furiously ping-ponged back and forth between Adam and me.

"Nice to meet you," I said, extending a hand, which they each clutched as lightly as they possibly could. "For a barbarian, I mean."

"Likewise," murmured Beth, the one with the ostrich hat. "Er —must go."

"Indeed," agreed Chelsea. "Don't want to miss the rest of the match."

"Nor the duke's thighs," I agreed.

The two socialites goggled at Adam and me for a few moments before rushing away to avoid any kind of confrontation. Adam stood by while I approached the bartender.

"Er—sparkling water, I guess?" I'd had enough to drink last night, and I wasn't interested in making a fool of myself again. Well, no more than I already had even being here.

"Make it a Pimm's," Adam put in, setting a few twenty-pound notes on the bar top. "Two."

"Oh, that's really not necessary," I told him. "Also, if anything, I owe you some money. Hold on, I'll get it."

"No, I insist," he said. "You can buy me dinner back home sometime. Pimm's is sort of tradition at these things, and honestly one of the few perks, unless you're that into watching a bunch of grown men riding ponies and waving sticks around."

I giggled a bit at that characterization as I accepted the drink from the bartender. "Thanks." As we walked away, I clinked my glass to his. "Cheers. When in Rome, right?"

"Exactly." He grinned.

"So, you never played at Eton, then?"

Adam seemed to visibly shudder. "Ah, no. I was too busy doing things like studying and reading. Novels, mostly."

I perked. "What are your favorites?"

Adam tipped his head back and forth. "Fitzgerald is my jam. I'm a pretty big *Gatsby* fan, like everyone. But *Tender is the Night* is also great."

"I can see that about you. You are sort of a Nick."

Adam looked wounded. "Nick? Seriously? The guy has no guts. I'd rather be Gatsby. I'd want to be the guy who gets the girl."

I smiled. "I don't know. I think being shy and underrated isn't so bad in the end."

I took a drink of my Pimm's, looking around. This was all right, so long as it didn't catch Xavier's eye. It was just nice having a real conversation with someone that was actually about something I enjoyed. "So, what about art?" I wondered, realizing I still didn't know that much about Adam. "When did you decide to become an art teacher?"

"Well, that's usually what happens when you're not talented enough to make it on your own," Adam joked. "Kidding, I guess. The truth is, I tried to go to art school after college, but found myself more attracted to what the teachers were doing than my own work. I'm not much of an artist—really a better mimic. But I thought I'd make a pretty good teacher. And so, here I am."

"Here you are," I said appreciatively, then held up my glass to clink with him once more. "Here's to the teaching life."

Adam grinned again, then looked over my shoulder, his attention caught by something. "Mum, Dad," he called, waving a hand at a prim-looking couple in deep conversation with a lady in a bright blue summer suit who looked familiar from the back. The man turned and waved at Adam, but the woman continued speaking, deep in conversation, to the point where I couldn't see her face. Neither could be bothered to join us.

Apparently, word was out about the harlot in the polka dots.

"Mum?" I asked. I'd never heard an American use the word.

"Well, that's what they say in England," he said good-naturedly. "I don't think she'd really like Mom."

I blinked, missing something. "Your mother is English?"

Adam nodded. "Yeah, she's from Hampshire. Dad's the American, and so am I." He winked, and I found it oddly charming.

I chuckled. I didn't know why I found it so funny for Adam to say that. Maybe because the way he said it was so distinctly American himself, threaded with a cultural disdain for titles and aristocracy and things like that.

Honestly, I hadn't known I'd even felt that way until I was here.

We walked a bit farther into the tent, away from the line of people, but toward a quieter section that was blocked off a bit from the noise of the crowd. The game had started again, but if I was being honest, I had no interest in watching. Not after what I'd just heard in the drinks line. I knew if I went out there now, I'd be obsessed with how many other women were currently making plans on how best to run into Xavier with every goal he scored. Meanwhile, I'd also be conscious of just how many of them had figured out who I was and were watching me too.

"What?" I asked when I caught Adam staring.

"Nothing," he said. "You just...you look so different."

"Well, so do you. It's called not wearing stained elementary school teacher hand-me-downs, don't you think?"

It was a joke, of course, but Adam shook his head. "I didn't mean that. I've seen you gussied up before. This is different, though. You look like one of them."

He cocked his head and continued to scan me up and down, well past the point where I felt comfortable.

I looked down at the polka dots and touched the brim of my hat with a gloved hand. "Er. I don't feel it."

"I didn't mean it in a bad way. Just surprised, that's all. Never thought of you as the hat and gloves type."

I wasn't sure what to make of it. Did I really look so odd in what was essentially a nice summer dress and a big hat? Apparently so.

"Xavier's stepmother—" I started.

"The Duchess Georgina, you mean?" Adam interrupted.

I frowned. Did he know her too? "Yeah."

Adam chuckled as if at his own private joke. "She's a character, that's for sure."

"I didn't realize you knew the Parkers so well," I said. "I thought you and Xavier just ran into each other at Eton. You barely seemed to remember each other in New York."

He stiffened slightly, like he'd been caught in a lie. "Ah, well, I don't. Not really. Mum knows her. They grew up together, so I see her around whenever I visit family here. Plus, don't forget that Xavier and I never really saw eye to eye. We pretty much avoided each other like the plague in grade school."

"A bit more than just a diplomat's son, then?" I prodded.

Adam finally looked a little bit sheepish. "Maybe a little, yeah. But it's not really who I am. This suit is just a costume. Probably like that dress."

There was an awkward pause until I realized he was staring again. Did I look that strange?

"I was just saying that Georgina thought I needed a stylist," I admitted. "Xavier wanted me to come to these things with him, and she didn't think I owned anything appropriate. She was probably right. All I can afford on a teacher's salary is Target and the Goodwill."

Adam shrugged. "So you got some new clothes. Nothing wrong with that. The red dress worked out pretty well for you."

I chuckled. "The red dress was mine. She was pretty mad about the Ortham Ball, apparently. I got a big lecture on it this morning. They had this giant pink thing picked out for me that made me look like cotton candy. I changed it last minute."

Adam grinned. "Well, I wasn't disappointed. Gutsy move, though. Francesca Zola, Yankee rebel. Never knew you had it in you."

I shrugged. "Xavi asked me to wear red, so I did."

At Xavier's name, Adam's smile vanished. "Look, don't take this the wrong way, but do you do everything he tells you?"

I balked. "No."

It was a weak response. Far too defensive.

"Really?" Adam pressed. "So you wanted to come to a polo match and listen to people making fun of you behind your back?"

I opened my mouth to say that was not why I had come. That I was genuinely curious about English society and always had been. That I'd wanted to support the man I loved.

But our fight this morning kept flashing in my mind's eye.

"That was amazing back there," I said instead, doing my best to change the subject. "With those women. I'm still trying to figure out how to put that type in their place."

"It's easy," Adam said. "You just have to answer their snobby questions like they are real ones."

"Well, thank you for standing up for me. I just—it's so odd, having all these people know my name, assuming so much about me. It seems like it's been that way all summer."

I pressed a toe into the silky green grass, finding myself longing for concrete. For the first time since coming here, I yearned for New York. I missed the dirty sidewalks and the thronged subways. All the places I could sink into a crowd and not be noticed.

I missed being a nobody.

"We Yanks have to stick together," Adam joked. "Besides, it's true. I've said it before, and I'll say it again. Any man would be lucky to have you. Even if he doesn't know it."

"That's very kind."

"So, does he at least know that?"

I didn't answer, hoping Adam would let it go. But when I looked up from my now-finished cocktail to find him watching and waiting for my answer, I just sighed.

"It's...complicated," I admitted.

"Maybe because you know the truth?"

I smarted. I could talk about my relationship, but why should anyone else. "Oh, and what would that be?"

Adam tipped his head, then gently took my empty glass, and handed it to a passing waiter before continuing. "Look, I've known

Xavier Parker for a really long time. Maybe we've never been close—"

"You acted like you barely knew each other last spring," I pointed out.

"But I've still known him," Adam continued like I hadn't said a word. "The guy I went to high school with didn't think about anyone but himself. And from where I stand, not much has changed."

I didn't reply. Given Xavier's and my argument earlier, I was having a hard time arguing with his points. But that didn't mean I wanted to hear them.

"The guy was selfish, rude, and frankly an asshole," Adam said emphatically before tossing back the rest of his drink as if to punctuate his sentence.

"He was damaged," I said. "Show me a sixteen-year-old boy who just lost his mother, was yanked from his home, and shoved into a stuffy boarding school who wouldn't be kind of an asshole."

Adam just shrugged. "And has he changed? Can you honestly say he thinks of you and Sofia before he thinks of himself?"

Lord, it was like talking to one of my sisters. Except this guy didn't really know Xavier. And as friendly as he was earlier, he didn't know me either.

"What are you doing right now?" I snapped, maybe a bit more than was strictly necessary. "Honestly? What is the point of this whole conversation?"

At first, Adam tried to adopt that calm, placid expression I was starting to recognize as his "Butter up Frankie" face. But when he glanced at me, something seemed to tell him it wasn't going to work. The mask fell, and his brown eyes met mine straight on.

"All right, you want truth?" he said frankly. "Here's some truth. That guy out there doesn't give a crap about you or your daughter."

"And you do?" I set my hands on my hips. "We work a few classrooms down from each other. We went on one date. You don't know a thing about any of us."

Adam rolled his eyes. "I know more than you think. For instance,

I know he should have stood up for you in front of those two peacocks in there, not me. Just like I know he should have escorted you around the Ortham Ball, introducing you to the people in this world instead of letting you manage it on your own and drink too much."

"He has to ride today," I argued, albeit weakly. "He's here to network. I can take care of myself."

Adam just scoffed. "Please, spare me, Frankie. If that's really what you think, you're dimmer than I thought."

I scowled. "Excuse me?"

"You think it's easier to conduct business on horseback than mingling in a crowd full of rich, drunk people?" He gestured around toward the very men and women I imagined Xavier probably needed to be speaking to on Frederick's behalf. On his own behalf.

I followed his gesture. Now that I looked around, it was obvious that certain people were doing more than just watching polo and gossiping. Across the tent, I caught sight of Frederick standing in a circle with his mother and several middle-aged men in expensive-looking suits. More than one of them pulled out a business card to give to Xavier's stepbrother. Others pulled out their phones and took someone's number. Notes were taken. Handshakes were exchanged. The same thing was happening all around the tent and in the stands too. And Xavier wasn't a part of any of it.

Adam pulled me closer to speak directly into my ear. "Here's another secret, Frankie. The Duke of Kendal is one of the richest men in the UK, second only to the crown and a very few older, richer aristocrats. He's not here to network, honey. He doesn't have to. They've been waiting years for the youngest duke in a generation to return to their little club. And they aren't going to let him go just because he's got a new American girlfriend. If anything, they're going to make it as hard as possible for you to stay. And they'll make your departure feel like his idea." He released my arm, as if he'd just accomplished something particularly satisfying. "He's not here to network, honey. He's here to have his ego stroked. And he doesn't need you to do it."

I brought a gloved hand to my lips, as if I could taste the poison of his words. Suddenly, I could see it so clearly. The hunger in all these people's eyes whenever they talked about Xavier. The utter disdain they had for me ran so much further than the fact that I was from another country.

I was infringing on territory they saw as theirs. The fact was that as soon as his parents' marriage certificate was found, he was no longer the bastard son of Rupert Parker, a social outcast with funny eyes and too-black hair, but the true heir to the Duke of Kendal. He gained membership into one of the most exclusive clubs in the world. And you could only exit one way: death.

"But he loves me."

My voice was small, like I was a child struggling to figure out why my mother kept leaving us. Trying to understand why she said, again and again, she would come back, but never did. Refusing to see the truth for what it was: that she just didn't care.

"Does he?" Adam wondered. "Ask yourself this: are these the actions of a man who even knows what love is?"

It was like a pipeline to my innermost doubts. After all, hadn't he told me that the very night we saw each other for the first time in five years?

I think we're all lying when we say it.

Maybe fooling ourselves a bit.

Whether we want to admit it or not, there's always something another person can do to ruin things.

I suddenly felt like I was choking. I was an idiot. Such a fool to think that he could change, really change, in just a few months. Xavier had told me from the beginning he didn't believe he could ever really love someone. He thought that love was only real between a parent and a child.

Which meant that, sure, he had that with Sofia. I saw it every day when he looked at her and talked to her.

But that didn't mean he loved me.

Not truly.

Not all the way.

"Frankie?"

I looked up to find Adam watching me with real concern. He reached out and touched my shoulder, chilled fingers lingering there a moment too long.

"There's one more thing I know," he said, just loud enough to be heard over the bustle of the crowd. "I know if you gave me a chance, I could make you happy, Frankie. That's all I need. One little chance."

And then, before I could stop him, his lips were on mine.

They were warm, yes. And familiar. Sort of like a rubber hot water bottle, the kind that Nonna used to put at the end of our bed in the winter instead of turning up the heat.

I didn't like them as a kid, and I didn't like it now. Just like the last time Adam tried this, I felt absolutely...nothing.

He broke away, eyes bright, clearly expecting to see some kind of thrill reflected in mine.

Instead, I just started to shake as I set a hand on his chest and pushed him forcefully away.

"Oh my God," I said. "Adam, what are you doing?"

"Yes," said a voice that had rumbled through my dreams for five full years. "That's just what I'd like to know."

TWENTY-TWO

Just like always, that deep voice made me shiver with anticipation. This time, though, it was flavored with fear.

Clearly just off the pitch, Xavier was wearing Troop's red and white polo shirt, white second-skin pants that left little of his powerful body to the imagination, and riding boots that made him look like he was on his way to a Regency duel. He might have cut a dashing figure if it weren't for the look of outright murder in his bright blue eyes.

He didn't look like the kind, passionate man I'd fallen for again over the course of several months, but the one who'd strode into my life last December with the intent to overturn everything without a care for the cost to others.

He didn't look like the man I loved. He looked like the man I hated.

"You motherfucker," Xavier growled, prowling toward us like a red-striped tiger. Without his helmet, his black hair had fallen into his face, just grazing the tops of his knife-sharpened cheekbones. "You slimy little *fuck*. What did I say would happen if you touched her again?"

"Xavi, don't," I said quietly, already noticing the way several people were peering over their cocktails at us.

"Please," Adam retorted. "You've always expected everyone to be terrified of these tantrums you throw when things don't go your way. But not everyone is scared of the big bad Xavier Parker."

"If people are scared of me," Xavier said as he grabbed Adam's collar and jerked him up so they were nose to nose, "it's because I give them a good fucking reason to be."

By the time he was finished talking, the entire tent had gone quiet. Whispers floated through the air, and I had a feeling there were more than a few cell phones filming.

"Xavier." Georgina's voice echoed across the tent in a hushed tone with clear disappointment.

"Xavi," I said in a low tone between my teeth. "You need to stop."

"Why?" he asked without taking his eyes from Adam's irritatingly stubborn face. "Why the fuck should I?"

"Because otherwise, you're going to sabotage every goal you had in coming here," I said in a low voice that hopefully only he could hear. "And besides." I took a deep breath. "You know, this is really between you and me. So let's go talk. Somewhere without an audience."

Xavier took three long breaths. I knew because I counted, watching the rise and fall of his chest until the last one was expelled. Then, at last, he dropped Adam to the ground and turned to me, that blue fire blazing in his eyes.

"Fine," he said before turning to Adam. "This isn't over, though. You touch her, you're dead. And you'll pay for that fucking kiss."

Then he grabbed my hand and towed me out of the tent after him.

"XAVI, slow down! Xavi, oh my God, *stop!*"

We were all the way behind one of several sets of stables before I managed to prise Xavier's hand from around my wrist. Bits of mud were splattered around my ankles. I didn't even want to think about what Regina's pristine cream shoes looked like.

When I broke free, Xavier finally whirled around, sending a spray of dirt out behind his boots along with tufts of grass.

"What the fuck were you doing with him?" he demanded. "I'm gone for five fucking minutes, and then I find you snogging that stale scone in the middle of my fucking polo match. I know you're starved for attention, but for fuck's sake, Ces, are you trying to get me arrested?"

Under normal circumstances, I might have laughed. There was no way he would know that kissing Adam had roughly the same appeal to me as a day-old pastry.

But it didn't matter now. I was too mad.

"You're kidding, right?" I asked. "Five minutes? We had a horrid fight this morning, the Ortham ball was a disaster, but I came here anyway because *you* said you needed us. Me and Sof. You know, your daughter?"

"That's completely unfair," Xavier cut in. "Sofia's not the one with the problems here. It's you."

"You're damn right, it's me!" I yelped. "Why did you even want me here? To ignore me all over again? I honestly don't know why you want me to attend any of these things with you, considering the second we arrive, I'm freaking invisible."

He looked at me like I was speaking gibberish. "What do you want me to do? Ask you to research wind farms? Slap you onto the back of my pony?"

"Maybe you don't have to play at all!" I shot back. "No one forced you to do the club a favor. Just like no one forced you to ride up to the fence to flirt with Imogene like she was a medieval lady giving a knight a favor."

Xavier's jaw dropped. "You're joking, right? You're fucking joking. *Imogene?*"

"No, apparently the joke is on me," I snapped. "Because to my surprise, I got to come listen to a million socialites scheme about how best to get you down the aisle and leave me in the dirt. Super fun! *So* glad I made time to watch my boyfriend flirt with his neighbor and listen to rich people shit talk me and my kid for the millionth time. It's been *great*."

I shook my head, willing away the tears that were rising to the surface. I didn't want to be this girl. I didn't want to be so clingy my partner couldn't do things for himself or spend time away from me, so jealous I couldn't even handle other women speaking to him. Xavier couldn't help what other people were saying any more than he could help the fact that his neighbor had a crush on him.

I took a deep breath. I needed to calm the hell down.

"Xavi, for the record, Adam kissed *me*," I tried again. "And I did *not* kiss him back. I believe my response was to push him off and demand to know what he was doing."

Wrong move. Xavier's eyes flamed all over again, and he turned around, like he was looking for Adam.

"Hey!" I cried out. "I'm right here. It's me you want right now, isn't it? Or is that just not the case anymore?"

That got his attention.

Slowly, he turned back around, chest heaving under his attempts to control himself. "How could you even say that?"

My lower lip trembled. I would not cry. I would not cry. I would. Not. Cry.

"Have you been listening to me at all?" I choked, pulling at my neckline. "This place. These people. These stupid dresses—"

"No one is forcing you to change," Xavier put in.

"Oh, really? That wasn't your stepmother you agreed with when she said basically everything about me was unacceptable for the Season. For *these* people, whom you've had more to say to over the past few weeks than your own daughter and me!"

"That was all for *you!*" Xavier shouted. "All the clothes, it was all to help you! If you didn't want any of it, you could have just said!

And I hated that pink dress. I practically tore the fucking thing off, didn't I?"

"I think we both know what you wanted there," I retorted. "And if it had more to do with what was under the dress than in it. And look at me now! I look like I'm cosplaying Julia Roberts in *Pretty Woman*, Xavi. I look like a freaking cartoon! But what did you say when you saw this dress in my closet? That I would finally 'fit right in.' Isn't that right?"

"Apparently more than fit in," Xavier returned through his teeth. "Half the bloody field was interested in what was up your skirt, and your 'friend' was about two steps from finding out!"

"Oh my God, he was *not*!" I shouted. "But honestly, if he was, it would serve you right."

"What is *that* supposed to mean?"

"Oh, I don't know. I guess that's what happens when you dress a girl up like a doll and then treat her like one, left at a table while you play with your other toys!"

I gestured toward the stables and the horses, toward the clubhouse where the mallets and other polo equipment were kept, and toward the tent on the other side of the stables.

"I didn't come all the way across the big blue ocean to be abandoned, Xavi. But since you decided to do just that, maybe I should make the best of it."

"By kissing the first idiot who pays you any attention?" he seethed.

"If that's what it takes."

My words dropped like bombs between us. But Xavier seemed to be done yelling too. He just stared at me, blue eyes flashing, the muscle in his jaw ticking like a bomb itself, waiting to detonate.

"You want a kiss?" he asked in a dangerously low voice as he took one step toward me, then another. "I'll give you a fucking kiss."

Then his mouth was on mine. And once again, there was no love in that touch, just straight-up lust and power. It was a direct attack. Well, that was fine. As it happened, I was in the mood to fight.

"Asshole," I snarled between desperate, biting kisses, full of teeth and tongue, and bruising takes.

A second later, I was shoved against the barn's wall.

"Trollop."

"Fucking *bastard*."

"Whore."

"Fuck you."

"You already have," he snarled as his hands found their way under my skirt so he could lift me up against the wall. "And in a second, you will again."

It took him all of two seconds to undo his pants and sheath himself within me. I would have screamed, but his mouth had already covered mine, swallowing my cries, suffocating them and anything I might have to say with his lips, with his entire body.

"These lips are *mine*," Xavier huffed as he began to pump into me. "This body is *mine*, do you hear?"

"Fuck—you—" I could barely get the words out even as I was clawing at his shoulders, trying to pull him ever closer. I wanted to do more than just be at his mercy. But he wasn't giving me the chance.

He drove forward, setting a harsh rhythm that had me careening toward climax faster than I ever had in my life. By some sick logic, it was as if all the tension in our fight had coiled us like springs, ready to release at any moment.

"Xavi," I hissed as his teeth found my neck, like an animal pinning me down. "Xavi—I'm close!"

Two, three more thrusts, and I was almost there. No tender touch between my legs, no adoring, no *savoring* as he had always loved to do. Or so I'd thought. This wasn't savoring at all. It was quick, purely animal. This was revenge. And by God, if I wasn't enjoying it on some sick level.

"*No*," he said, then shoved into me one last time before every muscle he had tensed completely, smashed me against the wall while he came hard, my body still aching beneath him for the release I'd never get.

"Ahhh!" I cried, arms flailing, legs kicking, dying for what he wouldn't grant. I yanked at his hair, scratched at his shoulder, rocking my hips into him while he pulsed within me, the rest of him stone. "You brute," I panted. "You complete and total *bastard*."

When Xavier pulled back, the beast in him had vanished. But what was left broke my heart. He looked down at our bodies, still joined, and sighed heavily, then gently pulled away and set my feet back to the earth. My legs were wobbly, though the rest of me was still tensed, dying for the orgasm he'd so blatantly withheld. As he handed me a handkerchief to clean myself up, his expression was full of sorrow. And regret.

"Ces, I—"

"D-don't," I said. God, the tears were still threatening.

Sex with Xavi—still the only man I'd ever been with—had only ever been a joy. Had only ever made me feel cherished. But here, behind this barn, away from where some of the most glamorous people in England were carousing and drinking, I was only another thing to him, no different than a mallet or a skillet. Something to use. And then be done with.

I balled up the handkerchief and chucked it behind a bush, eager to be done with it as I put the rest of myself together. The last thing I needed was to walk back into that crowd with my dress tucked into my underwear. If I made it back at all.

Sounds from the party grew from the other side of the stables. Or maybe that was just the roaring in my head. Still, I couldn't help but wonder if people were listening.

"Frankie, are you all right?"

I swore under my breath at the sound of Adam's voice. Xavier, having put himself back together already, turned on his heel, hands balled into fists.

I stepped in front of him, praying my hair, so carefully tamed by Georgina this morning, didn't look like a rat's nest. "Adam, this is really not the time."

Adam approached, though his eyes were on Xavier, not me. Lord, the man really had a death wish. "I think it is."

"Mate, you'd better listen to her. For your own fucking good." A muscle in Xavier's jaw started ticking dangerously while his fists clenched by his side. His eyes were so dark a blue, they were practically black.

"One, I think we both know I am definitely not your 'mate.' And two, I think this is a perfect time for me to step in. This beautiful lady is crying, seemingly because of you, and I've never been one to walk away from a woman who needs my help."

"Adam, please," I started again, even as I swiped the evidence off my face. "This really doesn't concern you."

"I think it does," Adam interrupted, placing a hand on my shoulder.

"Get your *fucking* hand off her!"

Before I could stop any of it, Xavier's fist thrust between us, finding purchase with Adam's face and sending the man sprawling into the green while the force of their collision threw me back against the barn all over again.

"What the hell!" Adam shouted, clutching his nose, where a torrent of blood was spreading down his face to join the dirt already smeared over his suit. "You just bwoke my fugking dose!"

"I'll break more than that if you don't stay the fuck away from my woman!" Xavier snapped, stepping over his body like a predator attending its prey.

"Your woman?" Somehow, I managed to find my voice as I stepped between them and shoved Xavier hard in the chest. "After what you just did, you have the audacity to call me *your fucking woman?* Well, I have news for you, buddy. I am not at your beck and call. I am not your cheap plaything or something you can just pick up whenever you feel like. *I DO NOT BELONG TO YOU!*"

We stood there for what seemed like hours, staring at each other over Adam's moaning, bleeding carcass.

"Adam?"

"Mr. Klein?"

"Good lord, what's happened?"

Several voices joined us, but I paid them no mind. For the first time in weeks, I had Xavier's undivided attention, and I wasn't about to lose it now.

"Is that so?" Xavier asked, voice low enough that only I could hear it.

I swallowed, conscious of all the eyes watching us.

But it wasn't them that forced me to hold my ground. It was the one set of eyes that wasn't watching. Little blue ones, just above a button nose, belonging to someone who called me "Mama." The one person I could never afford to see me like this, but who was far too close anyway.

"I—yes," I said, tilting my chin up. Stiff upper lip indeed. "Yes, it is."

His glance darted between me and Adam, who was now being helped up by some of the club's staff. When it landed back on me, he seemed to have come to a decision.

"Then I think," Xavier said at last, "perhaps you should go."

"I—" I tried to tell him I wasn't going anywhere. I tried to say maybe he should leave. He was the one throwing punches, the one acting like a Neanderthal.

But through the trees, I caught sight of more than one long nose pointed our way and several pairs of snooty-eyed expressions veiled only through the leaves. None of them were directed at him. They were all looking at me.

The American. Dirty Yank. Mistress or girlfriend or sidepiece, or whatever the papers were calling me.

One thing was clear: I didn't belong to him. But I didn't belong here, either.

"All right," I said softly. "I'll just...go back to the house. Enjoy—" I gulped back a sob. I wasn't going to give our audience the benefit. "Enjoy the rest of the party."

"Francesca—"

I didn't wait to hear him finish his sentence. Instead, I turned and left, conscious of all the eyes watching me leave. Watching and thinking, yes, it was for the best.

TWENTY-THREE

"Come home."

This time, I wasn't imagining one of my sister's voices. Kate was very, very real, looking imperious and bespectacled through my iPad while I shoveled a spoonful of rice pudding into my mouth—comfort food I'd picked up at Sainsbury's.

After the disastrous fight at the polo club, I'd found my way back to Mayfair, an arduous process without a car, as I had stubbornly refused *not* to find Xavier's driver. Sofia was safely in the hands of Miriam and Elsie, and it was better anyway that she be sequestered from all the drama. In the end, though, it took me nearly two and a half hours consisting of a mile-and-a-half walk to the nearest bus station, from there to a train station, then another train, and finally a taxi back to Xavier's apartment, where I had practically fallen into the bathtub to soak my troubles away and rethink my entire life.

My iPad was set on the caddy spanning the tub, and Kate was chatting with me while she priced new clothing items at her shop.

I stuck the spoon into the pudding and sank further into the bubbles. "Don't tempt me."

"I'm not tempting. I'm telling. Come. Home."

I sighed. "It's not that easy."

"What's not easy? You've made a Herculean effort to make it work with this man. You flew across an *ocean* for him, left your entire support system, and he does what? Works like crazy, gets swept up with the rich family that treats you like garbage, and then beats up the one person who was nice to you?" She shrugged. "Screw him, babe. You deserve better."

"But he's Sofia's father," I put in weakly. "The whole point was for them to have a chance together. What am I supposed to do? Stand in the way of that all over again?"

"No, but you're not supposed to sacrifice your entire self to make it happen either," Kate said. She finished hanging a blouse on a rack next to her, then turned back to the camera to give me her full attention. "You've been doing that your whole damn life, Frankie. Me and you were always the peacemakers, weren't we? We took the shitty bedroom in the attic so Lea and the babies could have the good ones. You taught third grade instead of going to grad school so you could be more available for your kid. Hell, you've been sleeping at the top of the stairs for the last three years so Sofia could have her own space. When are you going to do what's best for you?"

"How about when I don't have a child to raise?" I snapped back a little too harshly. "Putting myself first isn't a luxury I generally have."

"Would Xavier say the same thing?" she asked pointedly.

I shoved another bite of rice pudding into my mouth. It tasted like sawdust, though. "It's not the same thing. He's just learning how to be a parent."

Kate just gave me her patented "Come the fuck on, Frankie" stare.

"Sure he is," she said finally. "But maybe consider what you're modeling for Sofia, too. All you're doing is showing her that love means forgetting yourself. She's going to fall in love one day too, and she'll end up accepting less than she's worth because she watched her mom do it every single day."

Her words felt like slaps across both my cheeks with each

pointed syllable. What's worse was that I knew she was right. I just didn't know when things had become so complicated. When had decisions about what was best for Sofia become so utterly and morally gray?

Kate sighed as she folded a couple of ascots. "What I mean is, you're a woman and a mom here, Frankie. You know what it means to self-sacrifice to the point of losing ourselves. Just about any woman does."

"You didn't," I argued. "You took your piece of Daddy's life insurance and bought your shop. You've been doing your own thing for years."

Was I a little jealous? Yes. But mostly, I'd always been stupidly proud of my big sister for making her way in the world on her own damn terms.

"Sure," she agreed. "I chose the less traveled path, or whatever."

"'I took the one less traveled by, and that has made all the difference,'" I quoted. "Robert Frost. Good man."

"See, that. *That* is what I'm talking about. Has Xavier made any time for that? I know he's done the *Beauty and the Beast* thing and showed you a couple of cool libraries, but I'm talking about your future, Frankie. He has every ability to give you the opportunities you lost when Sofia came around. You could go back to school, stick your nose in those damn books as much as you want, actually *be* a professor instead of just acting like one all the time. Has he even talked to you about any of those dreams?"

I opened my mouth to argue with her but found I couldn't. Xavier tried to do something. Make us happy, I supposed. But the future? We'd barely spoken about it.

The truth was, I wasn't sure Xavier knew how to support someone that way. He'd never received it himself, except maybe from Elsie and Jagger, and they worked for him. I honestly thought he believed throwing money at things would solve those problems. Like if he provided enough, the future would just happen.

But that wasn't how real life worked.

Instead of answering Kate, I sank below the bubbles, soaking my head and moving out of view for a moment or two before resurfacing.

"My other question," she said as if I hadn't gone anywhere, "is why he hasn't done anything about the press."

I grimaced. "What can he do, really?"

I sounded like him. I sounded weak. Maybe that's because I was.

"Well, there are these things people send. They're called responses. It's called Xavier sending a note or a text or a doing a fucking interview as a semi-public figure. It's called him saying once and for all that Sofia *is* his daughter, and you *are* his girlfriend, and that he loves you both very much and considers you family whether or not things happened out of order. See? It's one sentence."

I opened my mouth, but nothing came out. The truth bombs kept hitting pay dirt, the way she laid it out like that so simply. Kate was always the most direct in the family. Everyone thought it was Lea, but that's just because Lea was the loudest. Kate was the fairest. She just called a spade a spade and left it at that.

"And then there's *Mami*," Kate said with such utter loathing, it caught me by surprise.

"Easy there, tiger," I said. "You sound like Matthew."

She just made a face. "For once, I agree with the stubborn ass. She's gone too far this time. Even Lea thinks so."

"Lea knows?"

I'd only sent the story to Kate, not wanting to disturb everyone with it. It was in a London paper, unlikely to get picked up in New York. I hadn't given it to Lea because she'd been working so hard to repair her relationship with Mom, and I didn't want to get in the way of that.

"Well, I was at Sunday dinner when you sent it, babe. So everyone knows now."

I buried my face in my hands. This was excruciating. It was bad enough that all of England thought I was a lousy mother and free-loader. Now my own family had to read those stories printed about us. They wouldn't believe any of them, of course. But they'd be embarrassed.

"What did Lea say?" I wondered.

Kate made a face. "It wasn't good. You know Lea doesn't like being proven wrong. Considering all the time she'd put into Mami over the last year...yeah, you could see that face was just about dead to her."

I cringed. "Ouch. I feel bad. I didn't set out to ruin their relationship all over again."

"Pssh. Babe, you didn't ruin shit. No one asked our mom to run her big mouth to the tabloids about something she knows *nothing* about."

I shrugged. Something about all of this didn't feel right. It was a throwaway line, but I did wonder to myself who *did* find our mother, who was nothing more than a convenience store clerk in the Bronx. Who offered her an interview? What did they give her that made her think it would be acceptable to throw her daughter under the bus?

"Anyway," Kate said. "It's just one more thing Xavier could have helped with. It's not like Mr. Moneybags couldn't have requested a gag order or something."

"Libel laws are different in England," I said. "The press has a lot more freedom."

Or at least, that's what I'd been told when I'd brought it up to Xavier and his family members. They'd made it sound like there was nothing I could do.

I sighed. "I don't want to talk about it anymore."

"Fair enough. You can deal with her when you get home. Meanwhile, did you hear? Marie is going to Paris. And Joni was in the hospital this week."

"*What?*" I covered my mouth in surprise. "Okay, back way, *way* up. Start with Marie."

"That's the good news! Apparently, the main cook at that fancy house she works in announced an early retirement or something, so the family is fast-tracking Marie and sending her to study at the

Cordon Bleu for a year. Marie's gonna get Frenchified. She's leaving next month."

My heart squeezed with excitement for my little sister. Marie was the other wallflower in the family—maybe even shier than me. Constantly overshadowed by lively, flirtatious, and very beautiful Joni, who was less than a year younger than her, Marie had sort of sunk into her apparent homeliness at a very young age and never really bloomed.

The funny thing was that Marie wasn't *not* pretty, nor was she uninteresting either. She was good at her job—that I knew, having enjoyed the fruits of her labors at home when she cooked for us. She was quietly perceptive when she wasn't busy picking on Joni, and she had habit of noticing things that no one else did about the world around her.

But Marie was also painfully she. She had few friends, spent most of her time in the kitchen, and barely went out. I'd never heard of my little sister having a bit of romance in her life, so living in the city of love for a year would be good for her. Great, even.

I hoped it would go better for her there than it had for me in London. But then again, she had a real purpose in going. Therein lay the difference.

"What happened to Joni?" I pressed.

Kate shrugged as she folded a sweater. "Dance injury, I think. Honestly, she didn't want to talk about it. I think she's embarrassed. But Lea says she basically holed up in her room at Nonna's and wouldn't come out for a week. She won't eat or anything. Totally depressed."

"ACL tear?" I wondered. "Floating kneecap?" That was the extent of my knowledge when it came to possible knee injuries.

"All I know is she came home with a giant knee brace and has to have surgery. The doctor says her professional dance career might be over."

"Oh, God." I clasped a hand to over my mouth in disbelief.

If Marie was the wallflower, Joni was born to perform. Always the center of attention, the baby in the family had struggled in school, to hold down jobs, really do anything other than dance. Dance was her life. Dance was her only real passion.

If Joni couldn't dance, I didn't want to think about what would become of her.

"Lord, and she just got a break, too," I murmured. When I was about to leave, Joni announced she was going to be an understudy in *Chicago*. It was her first real Broadway show, something she'd wanted since she was maybe five.

"I know," Kate agreed. "She just got moved up to the main cast too, when another dancer broke her foot. Heartbreaking. Joni's a brat sometimes, but no one deserves to have their dreams ripped out from under them like that."

"Wow. Yeah."

Guilt clenched my gut as I thought about my family. There was so much change afoot. Matthew leaving. Marie leaving. Joni healing.

And I was here, missing them all more than ever.

It felt strange to be hearing about this so distantly, knowing all this change was happening without my help. More than strange. It felt wrong.

Kate checked her watch, then looked back at the screen. "I have to get going, babe. I got a client coming in for a fitting in about ten minutes."

"Is this the big shot client from Silicon Valley you were telling me about?" I teased. "Is he cute?"

"Not my type," Kate said shortly. "But I have to get his stuff out for him. I'll call you tomorrow, okay?"

"Sure."

"And Frankie?" she said just before I ended the call.

"Hmm?"

"Don't let him bully you around."

I didn't have to ask whom she meant.

"Love you," I told her.

"Right back at you, babe."

I MOPED around the apartment for a while as the sun was starting to set over Hyde Park, and although I knew that Sofia was happy being spoiled by Elsie, she'd need her parents back.

The problem was, I wasn't sure I could go back to Parkvale. Not after what happened.

I sighed. Kate was right. It was time to throw in the towel on this British adventure. Xavier and I might have loved each other once, but it was becoming more evident that we did not work in the long term. If being with him meant playing second fiddle to judgy aristocrats and his never-ending schedule of work and old boys' events, I was always going to be trailing after him, feeling like a used shoe. One that was kicked around whenever I wanted something more.

I couldn't do it. And clearly, he couldn't either.

And the more I thought about it, the angrier I got.

Suddenly, I found myself checking for flights back to New York from Heathrow. There was one tomorrow that we could make, maybe even sneak away while he was at some godforsaken garden party. I found our suitcases stored in a closet in one of the many rooms of the flat Xavier barely used, then pulled them out and started tossing whatever I had left in the apartment into them. My clothes were fragmented all over this damn country—some in Cumbria, some in Parkvale. Well, whatever I missed, I could easily replace. Same as Sofia.

Once I'd made the decision, I turned into a tornado, not caring for folding or sorting, just chucking books, clothes, anything I could find that was ours into the bags. I was more afraid of losing my nerve than anything else. I knew if I stopped, I might not start again.

But then, when I was opening and closing drawers, trying to remember all the random places I'd put things, I found something that stopped me in my tracks.

It was another picture. This one was even smaller than the last I'd found and not even framed, just resting simply in the drawer on top of a spare handkerchief and next to a few loose cords. It was a photo of just me that Xavier must have taken, again when I was asleep. My eyes were closed, and I had a sort of half-smile on my face like I was lost in some sweet dream.

I flipped it over to find a date scrawled on the top.

Francesca, June 28
Home at last.

He'd taken it on our first night here. Right after he'd made love to me, after the onsen, after he'd promised me everything.

I think I'll always long for you, Ces. Even when you're right here.

I stopped, sweater in hand, but I was fully frozen.

Oh, God. What was I doing?

"No," I said, dropping the sweater on the bed and shutting the drawer harder than I probably needed. I looked back at the suitcases, both of them nearly full by now. "Oh, *no.*"

I moved in a frenzy, running back to them and starting to yank things out even faster than I threw them in. I wasn't doing this. I wasn't going to give up on the love of my life. It had only been a few weeks since his life was turned upside down. I owed him more than that.

Really, I owed him everything.

And so my thoughts ran until there was a knock at the door, startling me so much that I shrieked and threw handfuls of clothing into the air. They fell around me like oversized confetti as I turned to view my intruder.

Xavier stood in the doorway, looking quite a bit worse for wear. In addition to the rumpled hair and dirt smudged across his handsome features, his red and white shirt now bore more than a few bloodstains. There was a hole in his right knee, and he had a large cut above his left brow. He'd been brawling—that much was obvious, and by the smell of cheap liquor wafting off his big body, I doubted it had been with any more polo spectators.

Honestly, though, I would have hated to see the other guy.

He wasn't looking at me, however. His eyes were glued to the open suitcase on the bed and the stacks of clothing next to it. His gaze drifted over the room, down to the garments scattered across the floor, then found my bare feet and drew slowly up my body.

And then, at last, he spoke in a gravelly voice, though no less toe curlingly delicious, particularly since that South London edge was out stronger than I'd ever heard it.

"What...the fuck...are you doing?"

TWENTY-FOUR

For a moment, the last four weeks disappeared. We'd never gone to Kendal, never gotten involved with his horrible family, never gotten to this point at all.

I could have almost pretended that I was fresh from New York, unpacking, and blissfully ready to start the summer. I could have pretended that Sofia was exploring her bedroom for the first time. Or that maybe a few weeks had passed, and we had finally slipped into a lovely rhythm—breakfast on the terrace before Xavier left for work and Sofia and I went sightseeing, then returning at the end of the day to find Xavier cooking us a delicious dinner while drinking wine and listening to an Arsenal match. We'd play a game or maybe read some books before putting Sofia to bed, and then there was the two of us, often in this room, savoring each other for a few more hours before we went to sleep and started all over again.

My heart yearned for those days. For a few scant weeks, we had really felt like a family, hadn't we? Or at least on the verge of being one. I would have appreciated them for what they were had I known they would be over so soon.

Xavier slowly took in the scene: the suitcases on the bed, the clothes half in, half out. And then he trailed back to me once more.

"Ces. What's going on?"

My heart ached.

"Xavi—" I started.

"You're leaving?" His deep voice cracked with pain, hoarse like he'd been yelling for hours.

"I..." I shook my head. I couldn't lie. "I was thinking about it."

"Thinking about it with suitcases." He shook his head, causing that errant lock to flop forward.

I fought the urge to march over there and tuck it back.

"Christ, were you even going to tell me?" he asked. "Or were you just planning to disappear again with our daughter?"

"Would it even matter?" I mumbled to myself as I folded a white blouse.

"Pardon?"

I looked up, suddenly full of anger all over again. "I *said*, would it even matter?"

His eyes narrowed. "And that means..."

"It means you've spent all of five minutes with me or Sofia over the last several weeks. I honestly doubt that if we left, it would make much of a difference to you."

He worried his jaw for several minutes, hands flexing in and out of fists. But to my surprise, he didn't shout. Not yet.

"Where have you been?" he asked instead. "I've been trying to call you for hours. I went back to Parkvale, but Elsie said you'd asked her and Miriam to take care of Sofia while you ran some errands. Were you just going to leave her there forever?"

"Obviously not," I returned. "I would have come there eventually. I just—"

"Just decided to leave?" His gaze floated again over the clothes strewn about the bed. "Because, what, we've been having a bit of difficulty?"

"It's been more than a bit of difficulty, Xavi."

"True. It's been a fucking lot for me, actually, between my uncle going missing and having multiple strokes, then taking over my family's business and estate at a moment's notice. What a joke that I might expect a *bit* of support from my girlfriend, eh? Rather than watching her fuck around with other men and then see it reported in the bloody paper?"

He threw the newspaper he was carrying down onto the bed with a smack against my shoes, where it rolled open, showing a picture of me at the Ortham Ball, clearly visible in my red dress, talking to Adam with a smile on my face.

I barely glanced. His words had already set me off.

"Oh, *now* you're interested in the headlines," I said. "Not when they were printing lies about Sofia and me. Not when my own mother gave an interview about how horrible I am. No, when it's *your* pride that's hurt that you finally give a shit, right?"

"I care about all of it!" he insisted.

"What a load of garbage," I retorted. "You've been treating us like accessories in your life when we should be front and center. Especially your daughter! I didn't bring her here so she could get to know a freaking nanny better than her dad, Xavier!"

My head hurt from having this argument for what felt like the millionth time. What didn't he understand here?

"Fucking hell!" he finally exploded. "What more do you want from me?"

His roar shook the delicate crystals dangling from the chandelier above us.

I fought not to cower.

"I brought you to London. Bought you all them fancy clothes and what. Took you to the best restaurants, gave Sofia the fucking world. But it's not enough, is it? It's NEVER FUCKING ENOUGH!"

By the time he was finished, I was already on the move. Something in me clicked, something deep down. The part of me that was still that scared little girl listening to her parents rage after a bender or when her grandfather used old-school discipline a *little* too harshly. She woke up and was screaming for help.

I couldn't do it. I couldn't be here.

"Where are you going?" Xavier demanded.

"Out. I need some space."

I dodged around him and strode out of the bedroom, down the hall, and back into the kitchen, where I swiped my keys off the counter, then made for the elevator. Sofia was with Elsie. There was no reason for me to stay here—with this. I could wait him out. I could.

But Xavier was quicker.

He stepped in front of me, blocking my way to the elevator. For a moment, it was like playing chicken with a linebacker. If I hadn't been so upset, I might have laughed.

I darted around him, but he caught my arm. "Why the fuck are you running again?"

"Because of this!" I shouted finally, whirling around and wrenching my arm free.

I was done. *Done.* He wanted a fight? Well, now he was going to fucking get it.

"Because of *you!*" I continued. "Because of your neglect, your jealousy, your fucking temper! Xavi, I cannot do this anymore, tiptoeing around, worried that if I step wrong, or someone looks at me wrong, or I say the wrong thing, I'm going to get belittled, ignored, screamed at or worse! I am not a vending machine you can stick money into and get what you want. I am a fucking PERSON, XAVI!"

"Worse?" he parroted, looking genuinely confused. "What do you mean, worse? You can't possibly think I'd ever really hurt you or Sofia?"

I gulped. I didn't think that.

Did I?

"I've seen you threaten violence more times than I can count," I told him. "And it's been like this since the beginning. The night we met again, Xavi—*the night we met*—you were at my front door screaming like a madman because you had convinced yourself I had a man in my house. I've watched you practically strangle an employee, and today you actually assaulted someone for checking on me." I shook my head. There were too many red flags to count. "As for you and me...can you really say what you did to me today was out of *love?*"

His mouth fell open, but nothing came out. It was as if he couldn't argue with the facts.

Then another thought appeared to cross his mind. "Maybe not," he admitted. "Maybe not that time. But can you honestly say a part of you didn't enjoy it?"

Shock was replaced with something else—something knowing. Calculating. And as his gaze dropped down my body, I knew exactly what it was.

"Absolutely not." I immediately ducked around him and sped to the other side of the kitchen counter.

A rakish half-smile spread across Xavier's face. "Don't run away from me, Francesca. It'll only make it worse."

I hated myself for being even the slightest bit confused. A part of me wanted to obey, wanted to go to him, let him soothe our anger and troubles with his deft touch. He could take his frustration out on my body and help me learn to do the same.

But another part of me, a bigger part, hated him for even trying.

"Stop it," I told him. "Seriously."

"I don't know about that," he said as he prowled into the kitchen.

I moved to the other side of the counter. He blocked that passage. I tried the other way. He was still too quick.

I was trapped.

"Stop bullying me!" I shrieked.

And at that, Xavier stood up straight, looking for all the world like he'd just stuck his fingers in an electrical outlet. "You think I bully you?"

"I think you bully everyone," I said bitterly.

"I don't—"

"You *do*," I interrupted. "I'm a third-grade teacher, Xavi. You don't think I know a bully when I see one?"

I shook my head with realization. As soon as the words came out, I realized I'd known this all along but had shoved it under the carpet, time and time again.

"Bullies are kids who hurt people because someone hurt them," I told him as I splayed my fingers across the counter. "Someone taught them long ago that their feelings didn't matter, so they don't know how to access them. They shove them deep down, sometimes to the point where they don't even know they have them anymore. But they're still hurt. They're scared. And the only way they know how to feel better is to hurt someone else in return."

Xavier continued to stare at me like he was punch-drunk. "And you think I *hurt* to feel better?"

I shrugged. "Sometimes. I think you dominate me. Especially with sex. At the polo club. Behind your restaurant."

"I thought you liked it when I took you like that."

I chewed on my lip, trying to understand as much as he was. "I like knowing you can't wait to have me."

Satisfaction settled over his carved features, but I went on before he could say anything.

"Those times weren't about me, though," I continued. "They were about control. They were about asserting yourself when I presented a challenge. You felt vulnerable. Angry, yes, but mostly vulnerable. And fu-fucking me makes you feel strong. Doesn't it?"

He swallowed thickly, conviction erased. "I—I don't know what to say."

Finally, he backed away from the counters, leaving me ample space to slip out. I did, but paused near the end, looking back at him. His shoulders were hunched, and he was clearly processing what I'd said in a way that was quite painful.

"Xavi," I said.

He looked up.

"Please consider it," I told him. "For your sake, but also Sofia's. Kids who grow up seeing that, Xavi...it's what they expect for themselves."

It was as if I'd delivered the final blow to knock him out. He sank to a stool at the counter, head in hands.

"All right, then," he murmured. "I guess I should let you...go."

Heart breaking, I took that as my leave to return to the bedroom to pack...or figure out what else I could do.

Because really, what was I saying?

That I wanted a life without Xavier Parker in it?

That I wanted Sofia to live without her daddy too?

I hadn't taken ten steps before turning around once more, feeling more confused than ever but knowing one thing for sure. I didn't want things to end like this.

"Xavi," I called as I walked back into the living room. "Xavi, wait."

I didn't need to say anything. He had gotten up only to move to the couch, where he had collapsed on the white leather, head in his hands, while his cell phone sat on the table in front of him.

A message was still visible on the front as I approached.

> Georgina: We're needed in Kendal. Henry's had another stroke. In a coma. Doctor says he may not have long.

"Oh," I breathed. "Oh *no*."

I stood beside him, not knowing if he even wanted me there or not. His big shoulders were hunched, but it wasn't until I touched one that I realized he was shaking too. He flinched, but then a second later, flung his arms around my waist and buried his face into my hip. He breathed deeply, like I was a direct source of oxygen.

I stroked his hair. I couldn't help it.

"Please, Ces," he whispered into me. "Please don't go. You're all I've got left. You and Sofia. I can't—I can't lose you too."

Perhaps I should have said no. Our fights, these hardships—they didn't just disappear because he was sad and needed me.

But at that moment, I realized something else.

I'd never seen Xavier Sato Parker this vulnerable.

Which is also why I knew I couldn't just walk away.

PART 4

THE HEIR

INTERLUDE III

FIVE YEARS EARLIER

Xavier

"I tell you, boy, you *will come home!*"

Henry Parker's voice thundered on the other end of the line, to the point where I had to hold my phone away from my head so as not to break my eardrums.

"You promised, Xavier," he was saying when I brought it back. "And now, after all I've done to—"

"All *you've* done?" I interrupted. "What have you done? It's my idiot father who shoved all this on me. Shoved *you* on me. I didn't want it. I would have been fine being his bastard the rest of my life if he preferred it."

"YOU ARE NOT RUPERT PARKER'S BASTARD!"

I held the phone away once more until Henry was done shouting, then tentatively brought it back, nursing my beer bottle as I did.

"All right," I said. "Calm down, Hal."

"Say it, then," he ordered. "I want to know you understand."

I gritted my teeth. Why was it so hard to say something that, by all accounts, should have been a relief? "Fine. I'm not a bastard."

It was like I could hear his shoulder relax through the phone's speaker.

"Good," Henry said. "Now that that's cleared up, you need to come home. You've a duty here. You learned to cook, as we promised, and then you went off to Japan too. Now, you can't just keep flitting about the earth like a migrating bird, Xavier. You must come back and take your place at Kendal."

"Why?" I shot back. "So the old geezer can keep me around as a punching bag? I'll wait until he's croaked, thanks."

"You don't have to live at Corbray Hall. What will do it? Perhaps another restaurant? There's a pub in town—"

"I want more than a pub, Henry," I said. "I want an empire. I can't build that in the middle of the fucking Lake District."

He mumbled something on the other side of the line that was unintelligible.

"What's that?" I asked.

"I *said* it's the first time you've truly sounded like a Parker."

I opened my mouth to argue, but it was like he'd struck me dumb. How was I supposed to respond to that?

"And what about Lucy?" he asked.

That really was jabbing below the belt. "Henry, that's unfair."

"She's your best friend, isn't she? And you promised to marry her, if only to save her dignity. Well, her father informs me that she is very ill indeed. If you won't come back for your own family, perhaps you'll come back for her. Don't you at least owe her that?"

"What I owe Lucy is between me and Lucy," I snapped. "And if you're smart, you'll leave it at that."

I ended the call and stomped back and forth, up and down the sidewalk outside the bar. Why did the arsehole always feel like he could order me around like that? My own dad didn't seem to care where I was until I was right in front of him, and then all he knew how to do was yell. Henry, on the other hand, was like the world's worst nanny. Managing my every move. Well, I was twenty-fucking-seven now. I didn't need him doing that anymore. If I ever did.

The bistro in Kendal had been a success, hadn't it? Ranked one of the top new restaurants in Cumbria, and within five years, had given me enough seed money to start two new places in London and Bath before I saved enough for this trip to scope out the scene across the Atlantic with Jagger.

Three weeks here, and I found I liked America. Specifically, I liked New York. It wasn't like at home, where the second I got off a plane or popped into a club, I was hounded by paparazzi like I was the Duke of fucking Cambridge himself.

It had been like that since word got out that the Duke of Kendal had a half-Japanese love child who turned out to be his sole heir. For more than seven years now, the papers couldn't get enough. It was good for business—the free publicity had made all my ventures a near-overnight success. But the rest of it could jump into the Channel for all I cared.

Here, I was a nobody. Not Masumi Sato's troublemaker, nor the errant son of the Duke of Kendal. I was just Xavier, a really tall chef with an arm full of tats the girls seemed to like. A lot.

I turned on my heel to re-enter the bar where Jagger was holding court with a bunch of students from the nearby university. Columbia, I thought it was. We were on the Upper West Side. So, a bunch of smart birds, but still young enough that they thought Jagger was sophisticated.

Before I went in, though, guilt struck a chord in my chest as I recalled Henry's parting shot.

Lucy.

Lucy sick. Really sick. Again.

"Fuck," I muttered and pulled out my phone.

She answered on the fourth ring. "I was sleeping, you know."

I checked my watch. "You were not."

"Was too. It's one in the morning."

"And you never sleep before two. You and Henry, night owls, both of you."

Lucy chuckled. "Well, you have me there. But I was nose deep in a very good book."

"One of your dirty ones?"

"What others are there?"

I chuckled. Had to love that about Luce. On the outside, she was as prim as they came, but underneath, her mind was as foul as any bloke's.

"Has Henry been guilting you into coming back to this bore of a town again? You won't, will you?"

I toed my trainer into the sidewalk. "He tried. Says you're sick again. What's going on?"

There was a long sigh on the other end of the mobile. "It's nothing, really. Mummy is up in arms because I fainted at Imogene's graduation. I told her it was because it was so dreadfully boring, but she took me to the hospital anyway. I'm home now. Over exhaustion, per usual."

"You sure?" I asked. "You'd tell me if it was more?"

"Probably not, but that's how it goes. I shan't have you ruining your life for me. You're supposed to be living it for both of us now, remember?"

I smirked. I hated thinking of Lucy trapped up there, locked in a room while her parents pretended she didn't exist. Lord and Lady Ortham were never the kindest people, but they put up for me mostly because they still thought one day I'd end up with their younger daughter and bring their family's properties together with Kendal.

I wouldn't have done it for Imogene. Absolutely not.

But Lucy? I'd do just about anything for my friend if it would make her well again.

"Don't worry, Luce," I told her. "Four weeks here, and I'll have the new place scoped out. Then I'm coming back to London and moving to a new flat in Mayfair. Has an elevator and everything. I've got a room picked out for you, too."

"And a bathroom too? You know how I feel about sharing with

one of your 'women.'" She said the last word like "cockroach" would be more fitting.

I just chuckled. "You'll have a whole wing to yourself."

"Well, it's settled them. You stay in New York and take care of your business," she said. "Go chase girls. I'm fine, *really*. Henry is just making excuses to get you to come home, like he always does."

I swallowed. She sounded all right. But it was always hard to tell with her.

"I..."

I trailed off as two girls approached the bar behind me. Students most likely. Cute, in that street-wise way girls in New York tended to be. One was blonde and tall—not my type in the slightest. But the other was probably the most gorgeous woman I'd ever seen. Short, small enough that I probably could have scooped her up and put her in my pocket, with a soft sinuous shape that would bring any man to his knees. Her hips swayed in a pair of painted-on jeans, and she wore a red top that slid over her curves like oil and cut off just above the navel. Her body was a map begging a man straight home.

She tossed her dark hair over her shoulder and smiled at me as she and her friend checked IDs with the doorman.

"Let's see," the doorman droned as he looked, clearly taking his time so he could flirt with the two of them. "Emily Bradford. You're good. And Francesca Zola." He looked up at the dark-haired bird and grinned. "You twenty-one, sweetheart?"

Her blush was visible even under the dim street lighting. Something in my gut pulled as she toyed with her hair, revealing an elegant stretch of neck calling for my lips.

"Fuck me," I whispered.

"What was that?" Lucy asked.

"Have fun," the doorman told the girls.

Just before entering, the dark-haired one winked at me, and it was like flipping a switch to an electrical current deep inside me. Not my cock, exactly, although that was wide awake too. But something else was flickering too. I didn't understand it. But it felt fucking amazing.

"Ah, Luce?"

"It's a girl, isn't it? I stopped talking at least two minutes ago, and you've just been breathing heavily like one of Mummy's greyhounds."

I swallowed. "Er—sorry."

"Go, Xavier," Lucy said with a laugh. "Live. Please. But only if you promise to tell me everything later."

I grinned, even though she wasn't there to see it. Lucy always knew how to get me to smile, even if no one else could. "You got it, babe."

"But Xavier?"

"Mmm?"

I was distracted again, watching through the bar's window as the girl in the red shirt ordered a beer at the counter. I liked the way her big earrings dangled down near her chin when she laughed. Fuck, I liked just about everything I saw.

"Try not to break her heart, will you?"

I laughed at that, a great bark that echoed around the street. "I don't know about that one, Luce. Who's to say she won't break mine?"

TWENTY-FIVE

"**I** miss home, Mama."

Xavier and Elsie had once again left by helicopter yesterday evening but had bid us to join them in the morning along with the nanny via Range Rover, driven by Ben. It was still a long ride, but I supposed better than the train.

Miriam sat up front, flirting with Ben while he navigated deeper into the Northern English countryside. Sofia, however, didn't seem to be entertained by any of it. Not the sheep she could spot out the windows. Not the games on her new iPad. My little girl simply slumped with her head leaning on my arm, sighing every so often while she threaded her little fingers through Tyrone's rainbow tail, which was getting threadbare these days.

I stroked her curling black hair away from her face. "You mean the flat?"

Sofia shook her head and sat up. "No, I mean our house. I miss *Zio* and Nonna and my aunties and even those hooligan cousins."

I blinked, holding back a smile. For one of the first times, Sofia was able to pronounce "hooligan" without any impediment around the *l*. Sometime over the summer, my little girl had grown up a little bit more.

I couldn't help feeling like I'd missed it.

"I know, baby," I told her honestly. "I miss home, too."

"When are we going back?"

I shrugged, wanting to be able to give her something definite, despite the fact that a four-year-old wouldn't really understand the difference between one week and ten, and that dates might as well have been a foreign language.

"I don't know, sweetheart," I said. "But we'll have to figure something out before school starts."

Sofia nodded as if that sufficed. "I want to show Zio my drawings of the big Ferris wheel," she said, and then continued to babble about the other drawings and knick-knacks from the summer she wanted to bring back with her.

I avoided the truth—that I honestly wasn't sure if we had a home to go back to. My baby girl didn't know yet that her beloved uncle was leaving and that we might have to leave that house too, even if it was to go back to the Bronx to live with Nonna. Granted, I didn't think Matthew would pull the rug out from under us right away, but he did say he was leaving in September. Which meant we needed to get home sooner rather than later to figure out these answers. Whatever they might be.

As I stared out the window toward the still-foreign land around me, I couldn't help feeling like we were traveling in the wrong direction.

WE ARRIVED in Kendal just past two, and Sofia was swept off immediately to the nursery for a snack. I dropped the things I'd brought to Parkvale in the bedroom I'd been assigned last time, then crept down the corridor where Xavier's office doors stood open. I peeked inside and found him hunched over another mess of papers, shoulders hunched, hair falling forward from his brow. He looked exhausted. And very sad.

"Um, hi," I ventured quietly.

Xavier started, then stood when he saw me. He had changed out of his rugby clothes into more comfortable jeans and a T-shirt. But he hadn't shaved or even brushed a comb through his hair, which made me wonder if he'd even eaten or slept at all. He moved like he wanted to come to me, but then stopped himself and remained behind the desk.

"Hi," he said softly. Then, with a shy smile, "I'm glad you've come."

I nodded. "Of-of course." I wanted to add so much more. Things like "I'm here for you" or "I need you" or "We're a family, right?"

But I couldn't. Not when I didn't know if he felt those things too. Not if I didn't know for sure if they were true.

"How is he?" I ventured as I slid into the office, though I kept one of the leather club chairs and the desk between us. "Your uncle."

I assumed Henry was still with the living—if anything, because there wasn't that veil of mourning I distinctly remembered from when *Nonno* died. That kind of sadness touches everything.

"He's..." Xavier sighed. "Still with us. But I'm told it won't be long. A hospice nurse arrived this morning."

I frowned. "So there's no possibility of any recovery?"

Xavier shook his head. "No. The stroke was too severe. Too much damage to his brain, they say. He's not brain dead yet, but it's advancing. And when he is, they'll remove the ventilator, and that will be that. He had an advance decision written up years ago. It was very clear about a case like this."

I swallowed. "I'm—I'm so sorry, Xavi."

Those big shoulders gave a heavy shrug. I'm sure he'd been hearing that all day.

"Could I...would it be all right if I sat with him a bit?" I wondered. "Only if no one else is there, of course. I don't want to impose on your time with him."

I remembered *Nonno* in the end. As uncomfortable as it had made me, just a kid at eleven or so, I could see the joy that flickered in his eyes when his grandchildren visited him. Often, the old and frail receive the least amount of love in this world. I didn't know Henry Parker. But he deserved what little compassion I could offer in his final days.

Xavier looked up in clear surprise, warmth flickering in those blues. It was my favorite expression of his, but possibly his saddest. It told me exactly how infrequently he had encountered true kindness.

"Of course. He liked—*likes* you," he corrected himself quickly. "Come on, I'll take you."

"No, it's all right," I said. "You're busy. And I remember where it is."

Xavier looked wounded, like he wasn't sure what to make of that response. To be honest, I didn't know what to make of any of this. After last night, everything was up in the air. We'd shouted at each other for an hour, and I'd genuinely thought we were through, only for him to break down in my lap until he finally got up the nerve to call for a car to take us to Parkvale. From there, things had gone quickly—him to a helicopter, me to bed.

And now we were here, with a mountain of things left unsaid between us. And no place and time to start going through them all.

"Oh, Kip! There you are!"

We both turned to find Imogene entering the office with the grace of a tree nymph, tall and willowy in a sage green jumpsuit and pearl necklace. She passed me as if I weren't there, easily breaching the invisible barrier I'd constructed between Xavier and me so she could wrap her arms around his shoulders and pull him into a tight embrace.

"We came as soon as we heard," she told him, rubbing his arms. "Mummy and Papa are downstairs comforting Georgina, but you poor thing. How are you? You always were a brick."

She pulled back, keeping her hands resting on his forearms. His hands remained at her waist until he caught my expression. Only then did they drop, like he was touching a hot coal.

"We're all right," he said stiffly. "Just...waiting."

Imogene nodded as if she understood completely. Then she glanced at his desk and sighed. "Well, I see you already saw the papers."

I looked where she was pointing and realized Xavier hadn't been wrestling with business documents at all, but with piles of newspapers, all bearing photos of him and Adam at the polo match. And another of Adam trying to kiss me. I craned my neck to see it better and was relieved to find that my expression was obviously *not* interested in said kiss. Small mercies.

But no wonder Xavier had looked so upset when I walked in.

"Absolute nightmare, I imagine. Adam is always getting himself into trouble, of course."

I frowned. How did Imogene know Adam? Was he that frequent a visitor to these sorts of events?

"Seems that way," Xavier mumbled, reaching behind him to shove the papers out of sight.

"And the press is brutal," Imogene rattled on. "Completely unfair." She looked sharply at me. "We really can't be too careful, *I* think."

I said nothing. Honestly, I didn't think it was any of her business.

"You know the *Mirror* never gets their facts straight," Xavier said, clearly not in the mood.

I waited for him to say more. I waited for him to tell her none of the papers knew what they were talking about, that they had had it out for Sofia and me from the beginning and had wanted to stir up trouble from the start.

But he didn't, and as Imogene babbled on about this piece of gossip and that, Xavier remained silent, barely noticing me where I stood.

Just as he barely noticed when I left.

HENRY PARKER'S room was quiet when I entered but for the occasional beeping of the monitors next to the bed. It was an odd mix of modern and traditional, these ugly, life-saving machines in the middle of such old grandeur.

The man in it, however, looked completely different.

He was still thin, of course, though the long limbs beneath the thin blankets spoke to the fact that he had once been a much larger man. One side of his face, however, had fallen completely slack, his eyes were shut, and it was obvious that his chest was only moving because of the tube that had been inserted through his mouth.

I wasn't sure if there was a person alive in there. But Xavier had said the doctors didn't think he was brain dead. Yet.

So perhaps a visit didn't mean nothing.

"Hello," I said, despite knowing he would not respond at all. "I'm —it's Frankie. Francesca. Er, Xavier's friend. Sofia's mother." I sighed. "I don't really know what to call myself, if you want to know the truth. Girlfriend never sounded right—like we're in high school and just starting out, despite the fact that we already have a four-year-old. But what's the next step from there, you know? Fiancée? Partner? Wife?" I shook my head. "Whatever. Just Frankie is fine."

I patted the hand that lay still on the bed. It didn't move, but I was surprised to find it was still warm.

"Don't exert yourself," I joked. "Really, not on my behalf." Then I sighed again. The jokes were done. "Sorry. I'm just uncomfortable. I've never talked to a comatose man before. And definitely not one who is uncle to the man I love, and I'm pretty sure the only person in the world he cares about besides his own kid."

In response, the machine beside him beeped. Outside, the birds were chirping, and a finch hopped along the windowsill. I hoped he could hear them. I hoped Henry Parker could take every sweet thing shining through the glass with him, wherever he was.

"Well, I don't know if you've heard, but things between Xavier and me are kind of weird right now," I said. "So this might be the last time you see me. Er, well, you know what I mean. I'm sure Sofia will come back. After all, she's your grand-niece, right? Or something like that. And she'll want to visit the sheep again. She likes sheep a lot."

I paused again, stroking the man's hand, unsure of what else to say. I didn't even know how I felt either. I was so confused.

"For what it's worth, I really do love your nephew," I said softly. "More than maybe I've ever loved anyone, except my own daughter. I don't think he understands that, but it's true. And I—" I fell forward, rubbing my face. "The thing is, I don't care if he's a duke or anything. Honestly, I think I might like him better if he weren't. The pressure of this place, this world, it just kills him. But I don't know if he sees that either."

I swiped sudden tears from the corners of my eyes. Lord, this was getting personal, wasn't it?

"But I think he's chasing something," I continued in a creaky voice. "Your approval, maybe. Or his dad's, even if he's dead. I know what that's like. My dad died when I was little. I barely knew him, but I still think that if you weren't enough for your parents when they were alive, you'll never be enough when they're dead. But Xavier's enough on his own. He really is. And maybe if he figured that out, all the other stuff would go away. His temper, the secrets, the fighting." I sighed. "Maybe he'd smile more than frown. Maybe he'd actually let someone love him back."

I pulled my hand into my lap. God, I wished that were true. If it was, maybe I could stay. Maybe I could help Xavier heal in a way he didn't even realize he could.

"Anyway, thanks for talking," I told Henry Parker. "And if you do wake up, please watch out for your nephew. He loves you. Just like I love him."

I sighed, then touched my lips and pressed my fingers to the back of the man's hand as a kiss. After, I stood and found Xavier watching me from the doorway with a heartbreaking tenderness in those big blue eyes.

"Er—hello," I said, tugging nervously on my skirt.

"Hey, Ces," he greeted me softly as he entered the room.

"How—how long have you been there?" Had he heard my entire confession? If so, what was he thinking?

"Just a few moments. Long enough to hear that you still love me." He glanced at his uncle. "See, I told you, Hal, you don't have a chance with this one."

It wasn't, I noted, exactly the same admonishment he'd given him before. Not "she's mine," but more "don't even try."

I wasn't sure what to think of it.

"I was glad to hear it," Xavier told me softly. Then, before I could answer, "Do you mind leaving us for a bit? I've some things to say to him myself."

I nodded and stepped aside so he could have his time.

"And, Ces?" He grabbed my hand before I was out of reach.

Electricity jolted through me, warming my face.

"Yes?"

"Don't go far," Xavier said. "Please. I've some things to say to you, too."

TWENTY-SIX

I waited for a minute or two outside the door but then felt like an unconscionable lurker, so I decided now was a good time to take a walk in the gardens while Xavier said his peace with Henry. I let the butler know where I was going in case Xavier tried to find me, then went outside in search of Sofia, who had undoubtedly dragged Miriam up to the stable to feed the horses and the sheep. I ended up getting lost within a maze of topiaries and carefully pruned hedges that made me feel like I was in a Lewis Carroll novel. Good lord, where was I supposed to go now?

"'That depends a good deal on where you want to get to,'" I murmured with a smile to myself, quoting the Cheshire cat as I sank down on a bench. "Where is that, though?"

"Need some help?"

I turned to find Frederick rounding a corner.

"Oh," I said. "Maybe. I came out looking for Sofia."

"I believe I saw her towing Miriam in the direction of the pastures," Frederick said with a small smile. "Looking for sheep. Then they planned to come back to hunt for gnomes in the garden."

I nodded. "Sounds like her. I'll just wait here, then."

"May I join you?"

Surprised, I moved over on my bench so Frederick could take a seat. We sat there for a bit, taking in the view of the gardens before he spoke all at once.

"For what it's worth," he said. "I think you're good for him. My brother, I mean."

I perked. I hadn't heard Frederick talk about Xavier before, though being this much younger than him, it made sense he would think of him more like a brother than simply "step" brother.

I found myself wondering if there was more to it than that. If I were a young boy with a rebellious heir for a sibling, I'd probably look up to him. Actually, thinking of Matthew, I knew what that was like completely.

"I have an older brother too," I told him.

Frederick looked down at me curiously. "Do you? What's he like?"

I smiled. "Matthew? He's..." I tipped my head. "He's kind of like Xavier, actually. Not as big, and his temper isn't *quite* as bad. But he's smart and kind of broody. Doesn't smile enough. Really loyal to his family. Like, would do anything for us." I rubbed my palms on my knees, suddenly aching for my family. "He took care of Sofia and me for years. Let us live with him when we didn't really have anywhere else to go."

Frederick, I realized, was an uncommonly good listener. His body language turned to me slightly, yet completely, and he watched me until I was finished speaking before he looked away. There was no judgment in his light gray eyes, and it occurred to me I assumed he was just like his mother when, in fact, he'd barely said anything at all around her.

"Why didn't you tell Xavier?" Frederick asked after a moment's thought. "About Sofia, I mean. I can't believe he would abandon you. He would have supported you, too, I'm sure of it."

"Would he?" I frowned, looking back at the house.

I had thought so briefly, but now I wasn't so sure. Xavier would have given us money. But I wasn't sure he understood how to really take care of another person. It required so much more than money could buy.

"It's what he did with Imogene's sister, before she died, and they weren't even involved like that," he said.

I bit my lip. I didn't want to think about Imogene right now. Sometimes I wondered if she resembled Lucy more than people said. I wondered if that was why Xavier never seemed to rebuke her completely.

Frederick was quiet for a bit longer, picking a daisy from a weed growing at the base of the bench and fiddling with it a bit before speaking again.

"I was only six when Xavier came to Kendal," he told me. "The duke had just married my mother, you see. But then he had that accident, and it was obvious he couldn't have any more children. Mother even left him for a bit, and we went back to live with my grandparents. There was talk of another divorce, but it was just a separation in the end. I suspect Mother liked being a duchess too much to end it completely."

I bit back a snort, despite Frederick's wry tone. That seemed very true to Georgina's character.

"Then Xavier's mother died, and so he came to Kendal until he could start at Eton."

I blinked. "That must have been...interesting."

I could only imagine what Xavier had been like after losing his mother, and then coming here with the understanding that he was a mere illegitimate offspring—with no right to any of the grandeur that surrounded him. He would have been so sad. But probably very angry.

"I was young," Frederick said. "But I do remember, there was this one night Xavier found me crying in the library. I don't know why." He gave a crooked kind of smile that told me, even at six, this was embarrassing. "Young gentlemen are not supposed to cry."

"I think that's what men of all ages learn pretty early on," I said. "Gentlemen or not. Complete malarkey."

"Yes. Well. Xavier found me, but instead of leaving, he smiled and told me to wait there. Then he dragged a duvet and some pillows in from the bedroom beside the library—they were Mother's." Frederick chuckled at the memory. "I couldn't believe it. Mother would have boxed my ears for even entering her chamber, but Xavier didn't care a fig what anyone thought. He draped the duvet and the pillows over the Chesterfield in the library and built a fort for the two of us. And then snuck down to the kitchen and brought up some ham and cheese. We had a proper picnic, right there on the floor while he read to me from *Wind in the Willows*."

"I'll bet he enjoyed that too," I said. "More than you think. Even at sixteen, boys like to play more than they let on."

Frederick only shrugged. "Perhaps. But you know, I was the one smiling about it, not him." He gave me a long look that seemed much older than twenty-two. "Since you've been here, I've seen my brother smile more than all the time I'd known him. It's clear to me that you make him happy. Even if we do not."

I opened my mouth to respond but found I didn't know what to say.

Did I make Xavier happy?

All we seemed to do lately was fight.

"Thank you for telling me, I—Adam?"

Frederick turned, and we both watched as the last person I expected to see came walking down the path into the gardens: Adam Klein, looking for all the world like he knew his way perfectly around the maze of hedges and flowers. Like be belonged here. Like he thought it was all his.

"Frankie," he greeted me, albeit not particularly fondly. "You're...here."

He sneered, but the action made him wince. His entire face was black and blue from the effects of yesterday's brawl. He wasn't wearing a brace, but it did look as though he rather needed one.

"I am," I said. "And so are you. *Why* are you here?"

"Not to get another broken nose," he supplied helpfully as he came to stand in front of us, prompting Frederick and me to join him.

"You couldn't have possibly thought coming to Kendal was an intelligent move," Frederick said in a droll voice. "Not after what happened at Troop's. We've all seen the papers."

Adam sniffed, then winced again. "It's what family does, isn't it?"

I gaped at both of them. "Family?"

Frederick turned to me, already looking bored. "Adam is a cousin to both me and Xavier."

"Not so distant, really. After all, our fathers are related. "

My eyes were bugging out of my head. "Wait, what? You and Xavier are related?"

Adam just scoffed. "Please. I share barely any DNA with that overbearing gorilla. We are related primarily by marriage."

"If you're going to intrude, you should do it accurately," Frederick put in. "After all, we do all three of us share a common ancestor in the tenth Duke of Kendal. He is why you are here, after all." He turned to me as an aside. "The English gentry is a very small world."

I blinked. "I'm confused. You're related...but you're not?"

"We all three have the same fourth great grandfather," Frederick explained. "The tenth Duke of Kendal had two sons. One line continued down to Xavier. The other continued through our grandfather, a lower baron who was stripped of his title. And then to our fathers, who had none."

I turned to Adam. "I thought your name was Klein, not Parker."

"It is Klein. Mum was widowed young and remarried my father when I was a baby. She gave me his name."

"You already know my mother is divorced," Frederick supplied. "But yes, my father's name was also Parker. It made the transfer seamless, I suppose."

I turned back to Adam. "You weren't going to tell me this?"

He just studied his nails. "It's a distant connection. Xavier and I barely knew each other, like we said. There didn't seem any point."

"So...what, does that make you, a...?"

"It's makes me a nothing," Adam said, not quite able to mask the bitterness. "Which is what happens when your lying grandsire has his title stripped by the throne, and then your mother runs off with a Jewish diplomat. Try as I might, I could never fit in with them. Not that they'd ever want me. It's just one more claim they have to get rid of."

"Claim?" I repeated dazedly, glancing between the two of them. "Claim to what?"

"Neither of us has a claim to anything," Frederick insisted, more to Adam than to me. "Much less to the dukedom of Kendal."

"Tell your mother that," Adam said. "She and Mum haven't stopped searching for alternative records for a decade."

Frederick didn't reply.

"What is he talking about?" I wondered, tired of feeling out of the loop.

"The fact is that until ten years ago, we both thought one of us might have a claim to being the next Duke of Kendal. Until that stupid marriage certificate was found." Adam spat on the ground. "I'll never forget the day I realized I was going to remain a fucking elementary school teacher for the rest of my life. It was the same day I realized I was never going to stop working to overturn the whole damn thing."

"Arrogant as always," Frederick returned as he picked another daisy. "There's no point."

"Oh, please. Like Auntie thinks any differently. She's been trying for years to get Parliament to strip the title on the basis of a godless marriage." Adam snorted. "A Buddhist temple marriage? Rupert Parker? Pictures or it didn't happen, so they say."

"But it did happen." I found my voice at last. "Henry went to Japan and got it from Masumi's family. It's why Rupert Parker had to acknowledge him as his son."

"Convenient, isn't it?" Adam put in.

"They would have verified it," I said. Or maybe just assumed.

"Parliament wouldn't have just signed off on his inheritance. Would they?"

"Would they?" Adam parroted with the low tone of conspiracy.

All signs of the friendly compatriot from yesterday had vanished. All that was left was a bitter, mocking little man.

"Or maybe they just wanted to have a quick and easy line of succession rather than digging through the weeds of Debrett's and hashing it all out in the Lords." The look on Frederick's face made it clear how likely he thought that was. "I don't know how you thought you were going to accomplish that in America."

"It's called biding my time, you complacent moron," Adam spat. "I just had to watch and wait for things to sort themselves out.

Frederick shrugged. "So what if it did? The estate would still remain with Henry, the second son, would it not?"

"Only if Rupert left a will," Adam said. "Which he did not."

"And now that Henry is just about gone, we're not wasting the opportunity to set things right. Anyway, Kendal is one of the oldest Dukedoms in England. The queen wouldn't have wanted it to die out. Nor would she want one of the oldest fortunes in the world to go to the wrong man."

"That's what this is about, isn't it?" I finally found my voice. "You don't really care about the title. You care about the money."

Adam's eyes rolled. "Well, of course I care about the money, Frankie. Who wouldn't care about a net worth of eight billion dollars?"

My jaw dropped. I'd known Xavier was rich, that his family was one of the wealthiest in England. But I hadn't known it rivaled the GDP of a small nation.

"It's a moot point, regardless of what you, Mother, and Aunt Caroline think," Frederick replied, turning to me. "Xavier Parker is the Duke of Kendal and will be until his death. And so it will die with him unless he has a legitimate son of his own."

"Rupert didn't think Xavier would inherit," Adam claimed. "He knew it would be you or me, especially since he couldn't have any more children himself. And since he was a freaking anti-Semite on top of everything else, he married Georgina to give you a greater claim when the time came. You know and I know. It was Henry that changed the plan. It was always Henry's doing. And I'm going to find the evidence if it's the last thing I do."

TWENTY-SEVEN

I left the garden as soon as I could in search of Xavier, but he was nowhere to be found. He was no longer with his uncle. The office was empty, his bedroom too. He wasn't exactly prone to using any of the sitting rooms, drawing rooms, or the library on the estate, but I checked all of them regardless. Nothing.

What I wanted to say, I wasn't exactly sure. Mostly, I was full of questions.

Why hadn't he told me that he and Adam were somehow related? Did that have anything to do with the animosity that so obviously burned between them, even in New York, when they'd pretended to barely know each other in front of me? Why the lies? Why the deception?

More than that, however, I wanted to know if Xavier was aware of the plan to...what? I honestly wasn't sure of the word here. Dethrone him? No, he wasn't royalty. De-duke, then. Did he know that several members of his own family were actively working to undermine his authority and inheritance? What was he doing about it?

Or maybe, that was the reason he had stayed away all these years anyway?

I honestly didn't know. But I needed to find out. More than that, I needed to know how I fit into all of it myself.

"Gibson!" I called when I spotted the butler laying out silverware in the dining room. "Do you know where Xavier is?"

There were nine places in all—three for us, another for Elsie, and likely two for Frederick and Georgina. I assumed Imogene had gone home, but was Adam staying? Was it for his mother? Her husband too? No doubt, it would be the world's most awkward dinner.

"His Grace chose not to partake of dinner today," said the butler with a wrinkled nose, answering my silent question. "He wished to prepare it himself instead."

It was clear by the way he said it that he could not be more mortified by the idea of a duke doing his own cooking. But all I could think was *of course*. Xavier was stressed. And what was more therapeutic for him than food? What brought him more peace than that?

"Thanks, Gibson," I said, then turned on my heel before stopping almost immediately. "Er, could you point me toward the kitchen? I don't know where it is."

I swore the butler rolled his eyes. It was hard to tell since that was basically his perennial expression.

"Of course, miss," he said, setting down the last salad fork. "Follow me."

THERE WERE ACTUALLY two kitchens at Corbray Hall, a fact that shouldn't have surprised me. A smaller, modern one had been constructed about twenty years ago just below the family's main living quarters, outfitted with the few things a duke might need to make himself a midnight cup of tea or something like that. One glance told me that not only was Xavier not there, but he also never used it. The cupboards were stocked with all types of diet foods, nonfat milk in the fridge, and bits and pieces of highly processed snacks I'd never known Xavier, the ultimate food snob, to eat. This was clearly Georgina's domain.

Gibson then led me to a cavernous space in the bowels of the estate, which was really more like three kitchens in one, though I doubted it was used that way unless they were hosting a truly enormous gathering.

Multiple Wolf stoves and ovens lay around the periphery of the kitchen, while an island the size of Ireland covered with soapstone sat in the middle. My daughter was sitting atop that, hands in a bowl of something she was mixing with her father.

"Thanks, Gibson," I murmured to the butler, who hurried off as if to avoid sullying his eyes at the sight of the duke up to his elbows in flour.

Xavier stood next to Sofia, kneading a lump of dough firmly into the soapstone.

"Don't want to overdo it," he told her as he worked. "You want the dough light and fluffy, but the gluten still needs to activate."

"Got it," Sofia announced as she mixed her "dough" in her bowl with a spatula. From where I stood, it looked more like flour and maybe salt or sugar mixed together. "Light and fluffy. Like a puppy dog."

"That's it. Now, see what I'm doing here? I'm pulling it apart to look for the window pane. Once the dough stretches enough to see through it but not break, you know it's ready. Just a bit more."

I leaned against the doorway, watching them interact. I hadn't seen Xavier this calm in weeks, his voice taking on an almost meditative quality as he narrated his actions. Sofia didn't really seem to take in much, but she mimicked him every so often as she mixed her own concoction. They were both clearly enjoying each other's company and the act of being in the kitchen together. Somehow, in the depths of this overwrought palace, they'd found a corner to call their own. A place to feel at home together.

My heart ached with the desire to join them. Oh, I wanted to be a part of this. I wanted it so badly I could taste it.

But was it even possible anymore?

"What are you making?" I asked, startling them both to the point Sofia's spatula went flying, and Xavier huffed loudly, causing a cloud of flour to rise into his face.

"Mama!" Sofia crowed. "You scared us!"

"Sorry," I said as I walked into the kitchen and joined them on the other side of the island. I didn't mean to sneak up on you."

"Sofia rescued me from the office," Xavier mumbled as he went back to kneading his dough. "She was hungry after her nap, so I brought her down here. That all right with you?"

The slight sharpness in his tone had me on alert again.

"Of course it is. But Gibson is setting out things for dinner too. And isn't there a cook on staff?" I looked around for said cook. I wasn't expecting that Gibson was coming back down to prepare everything himself.

"Everything's done and in the warmer," Xavier said, not looking up. "I can make my own and finish everyone else's myself."

"Oh, do you really have to—"

"I've got it, Ces." He looked up then, blue eyes straight as arrows on the other side of the counter.

"We're making man goo, Mama," Sofia said proudly as she held up her bowl of something that roughly resembled sand.

"It's *manju*," Xavier corrected, more to me than her.

"It's a dessert," Sofia added. "Like a cake. Or a cookie. Dad, which is it?"

Xavier just shrugged as he slapped the dough down on the counter, then used a pastry cutter to split it into smaller pieces. "It's *wagashi*," he answered. "Sort of like a cake, I guess. With red bean paste inside."

"Is this your creation?" I ventured, hopefully. Xavier's concoctions were always really good.

"The dough is," he said shortly. "The rest is traditional. Like my mum made it." He offered a smile to Sofia. "Your gran, Sof. You would have liked her."

He went to work, flattening each piece into a rough round. Sofia abandoned her mixture and crawled across the counter to watch him work with me. I opened an arm to help her snuggle against my side, uncaring of her floured mess rubbing onto my clothes. Her little warm body simply felt nice. I hadn't known how much I needed a hug right then, even from my little girl.

We watched as Xavier dropped scoops of a dark paste into the center of each flattened piece he'd cut, then efficiently wrapped the dough around it and sealed it at the bottom. When he was finished, he had a dozen neat buns laid out on a piece of parchment, which he placed into a large bamboo steamer, then popped over a pot of water I hadn't even known was boiling until that moment.

"All right." Xavier turned back around and started the process of cleaning up. "Ten minutes and we'll have a nice treat to ruin dinner."

I smiled at his joke, but he didn't appear to see it, focused as he was.

I picked up Sofia and set her on the floor. "Pea, why don't you run upstairs and ask Miriam or Elsie if they can help you get dinner in the nursery. I'll bring you up some *manju* when they are ready."

Sofia, already bored with the idea of cleaning up, nodded, then scampered off in search of the nanny.

I turned back to Xavier, who looked at me warily as he wiped down the counter.

"I thought you were going to wait for me," he said mildly.

"I did," I told him. "But I didn't want to hound you, so I went to the gardens to wait. And that's where I ran into Frederick. And, ah, Adam."

Xavier paused but didn't look entirely unsurprised. "Did you?"

I sighed. "Were you ever going to tell me he's your cousin?"

"That meddling fucking twat is *not* my cousin," Xavier said fervently. "We are in no way related."

"That's not what Debrett's says," I countered. "Nor Frederick."

"I don't give a fuck what Debrett's or anyone else says."

"Big shock," I replied, already weary of the sarcasm. "But you might, considering he wants to overthrow your entire life along with your stepmother."

I proceeded to relay what I'd learned in the garden. It only occurred to me at the end that Adam hadn't even tried to stop me when I left, that Xavier might not be particularly surprised to hear any of it. Indeed, he was watching me speak with an expression that more closely resembled pity than surprise.

"Is that the real reason you've been here?" I asked. "It wasn't about your uncle at all, was it? It was about protecting your estate. Protecting your title."

"It had everything to do with Henry," he said. "I never lied to you. But Georgina has spent most of the last three months sniffing around in places she shouldn't. Why do you think she suddenly enjoys the library so much? She wasn't allowed to raid the office anymore." He shook his head. "I don't know what she thinks she's going to find. My parents were married. End of. It's time to move on."

He didn't sound very happy about it.

"Why don't you just let them have it, if they want it so badly and you don't?" I demanded. "You have your own successful business, and you and I both know this was never where you really wanted to be. If they want the title so much, why not just give it to them?"

"Because it's not something I can bloody give, is it?" he exploded. "You can't just give a title away if you don't want it, Ces. That's not how it works."

"There isn't some way to abdicate or something?"

I was floundering. Obviously, I didn't know about British law and how it governed things like this, but Xavier couldn't be the only duke in the history of England who didn't want to be a duke.

"Not really," he said wearily. "It's not something I can choose. The title could lay in abeyance until I pass, but it would essentially mean throwing out centuries of work my family has done to maintain their standing. Am I supposed to be the one to end the legacy of Kendal?"

Yes, I wanted to say. If it made him so miserable, then he absolutely should. Clearly, the only person on this estate who cared about him at all was at death's door. He didn't owe anyone else a thing.

But before I could say as much, Xavier continued talking.

"Look," he snapped. "It's clear this life is not what you want. I thought maybe you could live with it, being the lady of the manor. Maybe even a duchess one day."

My heart squeezed when he said it. It was the first time he'd even acknowledged such a future was on the table, only to rip it away.

"You like those bloody stories enough, maybe you'd want to live in one for a bit," he continued bitterly. "Maybe even enjoy it. But now that you've learned it's not all parties and dresses and what, it's obviously not for you. I can't blame you for that."

My mouth dropped. "I can't believe you just said that. That is *not* what my problem is here."

"Oh, no? You hate the press, the gossip, my scheming relations. You're lonely and sad, but I haven't the time to give you enough. None of that will change, Ces. It's part of the package."

"You were busy with your restaurants too," I countered. "I didn't say anything then. You said yourself, you're *different* here, Xavi. I don't understand why we can't just, I don't know, teach Frederick to manage the estate like you wanted and go back to the way things were."

"Because Frederick is not the Duke of fucking Kendal! I am!" The words themselves seemed to shake his whole body with fury. "I can't change what I am, Ces. I know you want me to. Just like I spent years trying to ignore it. But the fact is, I am Rupert Parker's son, and the more I run from it, the worse things get." Xavier shook his head, shoulders sagging in defeat. "I'm the Duke of Kendal, and there's nothing to be done about it. I'm sorry."

And on that note, he turned, yanked the buns off the boiling pot, tossed the steamer onto the island with a clatter, and left the kitchen.

"Xavier, wait," I called, but he sped up the stairs two at a time, leaving me alone in the basement with a basket of buns growing cold.

I took off the top and stared at the buns for a long minute, then back up the stairs.

"Oh, no, you don't," I told his invisible form. "We're finishing this discussion this time."

TWENTY-EIGHT

Xavier had already disappeared by the time I made my way back up to the main floor of Corbray Hall. Stupid long legs. Honestly, I wondered sometimes if the man was half giraffe, he was so tall.

I immediately headed for his office on the second floor, only to run smack into Georgina.

"I—oh, Georgi—I mean, Your Grace," I corrected myself, albeit through my teeth.

I knew the title was official, but for some reason, addressing Georgina as a duchess didn't feel much different than calling Sofia a princess just because she was wearing a tiara and a sparkly dress.

"Francesca," she said through a thin half-smile as she fluffed her hair. She was dressed as elegantly as ever in a pair of cream trousers with a navy blouse and tasteful pearl and diamond earrings dangling from her ears.

"Excuse me," I said, in a hurry to find Xavier and make things right.

But her voice called me to a stop.

"It won't work, you know."

Ignore her, I told myself. You can just ignore her. You don't *have* to engage.

Unfortunately, good manners won over better judgment.

I turned at the landing a few steps above her. "I'm sorry? What won't work?"

That haughty smile reappeared, this time showing a bit more teeth. "You and my stepson. It'll never work."

I frowned, took a step downward, then another, so we were nearly eye to eye. Everyone in this place was taller than me, so I needed the extra height.

"I'm not sure that's really any of your business," I ventured.

"Not my business? Darling, please." She waved a manicured hand. "*All* of this is my business. This is my legacy. And if you really think I'm going to allow a pikey little Yank with a bastard brat to become the next Duchess of Kendal, you really haven't learned a thing on this adventure of yours, have you?"

My mouth fell open. "I—"

"Look at you," she continued, gesturing up and down my body. "We've done our best to help, but you're still a hopeless mess. Dressed in rags, hair like a dirty black mop, horrid posture, manners like a caveman."

I straightened at her comments. "Now wait a—"

"And don't get me started on your dancing, my girl," she said. "Best leave that to the ones who grew up learning it." She cocked her head and took a step up so we stood on the same stair, giving her at least six inches on me. "You know, I never realized it before, but you really are quite tiny, aren't you? Beside the duke, you practically disappear. Or at least look more like his child than a partner ever should."

It was like she had a dashboard of buttons that she could push to link directly to every one of my insecurities. Button one, height. Button two, class. And so on.

But I had one card left to play.

"I'm still not sure why you care so much who Xavier ends up

with," I said much more confidently than I felt. "After all, it's common knowledge you've been trying to overturn the entail for years, haven't you?"

She looked at first like she very much wanted to slap me. But then, it was as if a wave of calm swept across her genteel features, leaving behind that typical mask of supercilious knowing.

"I see my son has been chatting," she replied as she examined the tip of one French nail. "Bad habit he's formed since starting university."

"Don't think Xavier doesn't know," I warned her, more than ready to knock the woman off her high horse.

"Oh, of course he knows."

Okay, maybe not.

"Why do you think we've never got on?" she continued. "He fits in here only slightly better than you do, and that marriage certificate is almost certainly a farce. I'll prove it one day, I'm sure of it. But until then, I won't have my son's sullied by the likes of you."

I sneered. "Because you're so much more knowledgeable than the queen or all of Parliament, for that matter?"

"When it comes to my late husband, I rather surmise I am," she said. "And Rupert would have no more married his cook than Xavier will marry a schoolteacher." She bent down so her steely gray eyes were directly in line with mine. "The fact remains that you are merely a dalliance. A passing fancy, which, if Xavier's recent temperament is any indication, has long grown stale. And whether he stays the Duke of Kendal or my son takes the title, one thing is true. *You*, my dear, will never be a duchess."

"You—you don't know that," I said, though my voice was already quivering. After all, hadn't Xavier just said the same thing in his own way?

"Please," she said serenely. "You have a child together. If he was going to ask for your hand, it would have happened long ago."

Georgina straightened and continued down the stairs while I just stood there numbly, trying to relocate my legs. When she reached the bottom, she turned once more and looked me up and down, like she could see the doubt seeping through my pores.

She hadn't heard our arguments, I told myself. She hadn't seen anything. It was all in my head, and meanwhile, I knew Xavier and I could at least try to make things work if that was what we both wanted.

We had to. We were a family.

Or at least, we could be.

"The writing's on the wall," she called. "It's only a matter of time. Best cut him loose and move on before he does it for you."

I STOOD FROZEN on the stairs, clutching the carved banister for what seemed like an hour before I finally managed to tamp down the tears and stop myself from running after Georgina. Tearing apart her perfect coif and finding whatever shred of self-esteem I had left.

But what she thought ultimately didn't matter.

It didn't matter if the Dowager Duchess of Kendal didn't believe I had what it took to stand in her admittedly perfect shoes.

It didn't matter if she thought I was nothing more than an uncouth American who belonged in a barn more than a country manor.

I sniffed. Shows what she knew anyway, if that were true. I was born and raised in New York freaking City. This entire manor was closer to a barn than the house where I'd grown up.

Anyway, the only person's thoughts that mattered were Xavier's.

And I hadn't given up on us yet.

I jogged up the rest of the stairs, then, with more self-assurance than I'd had since arriving at Kendal, navigated the maze of corridors with their contemptuous portraits and priceless antiques until I had found my way back to Xavier's office.

Where I heard another prim, collected voice speaking to him inside, audible only through the crack in the slightly open door.

"Honestly, Kip. I'm worried about you. We all are. I've never seen you this unhappy, and you really don't deserve it."

I froze in place at the sound of Imogene's saccharine voice floating through the door. I wanted to go in. But the thought of facing her after I'd just dealt with Georgina left me cold.

I turned to leave. But stopped when I heard Xavier's response.

"Maybe I don't deserve happiness."

I swallowed. Normally, if someone said something like that so overtly, I'd accuse them of fishing for compliments. I'd suspect that they were just self-deprecating to get others to rain praise.

But I knew Xavier. He was more prone to keeping things bottled up to explode than stating how he felt, for attention or otherwise. The fact that he was saying this at all broke my heart even more.

"You can't be so hard on yourself," Imogene told him. "It's not your fault if she doesn't appreciate Kendal."

"Isn't it?"

I winced. I could just imagine him sitting there, shoving his hands into his dark hair and rubbing his temples the way he did when he was stressed. Sometimes he let me rub them for him. We would sit on the bed together, me leaning against the headboard, him laying back on my chest, my legs wrapped about his waist. I loved the warm, solid feel of his body pressing mine into the mattress and the way his head would rest on my chest while I worked. And then, most rewardingly, the heavy sigh of relaxation when my fingers coaxed his worries away, enough where, just before he fell asleep, he would turn over and reward me with a sweet, drowsy kiss.

I never imagined I would be the reason he needed that kind of release, though.

There was some shuffling in the room, and I heard footsteps on the herringbone wood floors. Light taps of a woman's heels as she paced.

"Kip, no one respects your sense of adventure more than I do, truly," Imogene said. "You opened up your life to someone whom, let's be honest, you hardly know. You took a great big leap with her. But it's not your fault, darling, if she couldn't leap so far. It isn't."

There was a loud, unintelligible grumble, but no argument.

"She is unhappy," Xavier gave in at last. "I just can't seem to get it right."

"I know this isn't what you want to hear, but perhaps you need to. Francesca, lovely as she is, may simply be one of those people who *can't* be happy, no matter what the circumstances. I wish it weren't true, but there it is."

"No," I whimpered to myself, then bit my comments back.

Tell her she's wrong, I wanted to screech. Tell her that's not me. Tell her that while we have so many challenges, we can absolutely be happy. Perfectly, beautifully, blissfully in love, in fact. We've had it before, and we can have it again!

Or maybe I was just trying to convince myself.

"Did you hear something?" Imogene wondered.

I sucked in a deep breath and backed away from the door, on instinct plastering myself against the wainscoting when the door opened and I saw Imogene's head poke out.

She looked down the opposite direction and halfway toward me before backing into the office again without another glance.

I exhaled, though I wasn't exactly sure why. Why shouldn't she see me?

Why was *I* feeling like the intruder here?

I listened to the sound of her shoes clipping again across the floor.

"There's nothing out there," Imogene said. "Nothing at all."

Xavier didn't respond.

"As I was saying, though, look at everything you've offered her," Imogene continued as if nothing had interrupted them. "The clothes, the houses, your entire life. Not to mention the fact that you, Kip, really are a catch. Horridly handsome—don't give me that look, you *are*—and impossibly charming when you want to be."

I practically bared my teeth. This *bitch*.

In the back of my mind, I could easily picture all my sisters' faces at those comments. Joni was probably removing her earrings, Kate her glasses while all four of them readied themselves to pounce.

God, I wished they were here.

"This life is one most women would salivate after," Imogene said. "And you've offered it after knowing her for what, six months?"

"Five years," Xavier corrected her testily, showing for the first time a bit of annoyance. "A little more now, actually."

I smirked. Take that, you snooty cow.

"Right, of course," Imogene corrected herself. "Except..."

"Except what?"

"Except, well, it hasn't *really* been five years, has it? You had a brief fling with the girl—and I'm not judging, Kip, really, I'm not. We've all had our larks, haven't we? Only, that means that most of that time since, you didn't know each other at all, did you? Meanwhile, she goes and has a child without saying a word. Putting aside how dreadful that really was, she also made things so much harder for herself than they needed to be. Now, I ask you, does that sound like someone who *wants* to be happy?"

Say no, I begged silently. Say you understood why I did it. Say we've evolved so much from that first revelation, that we mean more to each other and can get through anything together.

"I just don't know anymore." Xavier's voice was weary, as tired as my own heart felt. "I love her. I do. But everyone I love dies, eventually, don't they? My mother, Lucy, Father. Now Henry."

I clutched my chest. Oh God, that couldn't be how he really felt, could it? I hadn't ever considered that the amount of death and loss Xavier had experienced would have affected him that way, but now it made sense.

He gripped us so tightly it hurt.

Maybe it was because he was afraid of losing us.

"Maybe being with me is killing her too," he said. "Maybe you're right, in a way. She doesn't belong here."

I silently hiccupped back a sob. No! He had to know it had nothing to do with him!

"Kip, listen to me," Imogene told him. "If she can't see what's good about you and be happy with it by now, she never will. And you deserve to be with someone who appreciates you for how wonderful you truly are. Someone who is strong enough to take on this life, with all its challenges."

He snorted. "And who might that be, eh?"

"You really don't know?"

My eyes flew open. *No*, she was *not*. It was clear that the time for eavesdropping was over. And the time for action was now.

I flipped around and opened the door, prepared to tell this stupid, conniving wench that if she wanted to see an unhappy version of Francesca Zola, she was about to get it right in her perfectly straight nose.

But as soon as I entered the room, I stopped in my tracks.

And watched with horror as Imogene tenderly cupped Xavier's dejected face.

Shuddered as she leaned down through a waterfall of her perfect golden hair.

Quaked as she set her glossy pink lips to his.

And felt my heart split into ten thousand pieces as he remained still and let her.

I backed away from the door with a stumble that was swallowed by the thick rug protecting the floor of the hallway. Moving purely by instinct, I ran back the way I'd come, getting lost approximately four times before finally locating the main stairs, taking them two at a time without really knowing where I was headed.

Sofia. I needed to find Sofia. Needed to ground myself in her sweet, sweaty scent and unicorn chatter. Remember my true raison d'être in this world, no matter what happened here.

And after that...shit, what was I supposed to do?

Ideas were flying through my mind when I rounded a corner toward the main entrance and once again ran straight into Georgina.

"What the devil—" she sputtered. "Oh, it's *you*."

"Georgina," I said. I was finished with the titles. I was finished with everything about this place, including her. If she would help me with just one thing.

Though she started at the use of her given name, she seemed to sense my desperation. "Yes?"

"I—" I swallowed. "I want to go home." I glanced up the stairs, terrified for a moment that Xavier might see me and stop me from doing what I now knew was right. "I just—I want to go home. As soon as humanly possible. Can you—would you help me?"

She cocked her head, looking up the stairs where I had come from and back down at me. Then a distinctly evil smile that made my blood run cold spread across her face.

"Yes, of course," she said quietly, almost so low no one else who might have listened could hear. "You find your darling little girl. I'll have Gibson pull the car around and take you to the heliport. Ten minutes, and you'll be on your way. The rest of your things will be sent home shortly. Will that suffice?"

Still sniffing back encroaching tears, I nodded. "Y-yes. And you'll tell no one else where we've gone?"

Her smile only broadened, making her resemble a very beautiful, satisfied crocodile.

"Wouldn't dream of it, my dear," she said. "Now, off you go."

TWENTY-NINE

It's shocking how quickly you can get from one place to another when you have legitimate cash to do it. Especially when you have the wicked witch of Northwest England paying your way.

Georgina might not have been quite as rich as Xavier, but she certainly had the money and connections to whisk Sofia and me back to New York within the span of relatively few hours. It was a bit odd to realize that the woman hated me enough to spend tens of thousands of dollars to make sure I left the country, but at that point, it served my needs.

Sofia and I were shuttled via helicopter to an airfield in Liverpool, and from there onto a private plane that took us straight to Teterboro, all with promises that the rest of our things would be shipped to us at the earliest convenience.

I didn't even care. I had my essentials—the rest could hang.

And so, after sleeping on the bed in the back of the plane, we were in New York by sunrise, blissfully unaware of Xavier's reaction to our sudden absence, or any of the other ramifications of leaving. I looked down at Sofia, who was snuggled into my side on the 144 bus to Port Authority, quietly singing a song about starfish to Tyrone.

She'd asked me only once where we were going as we got on the helicopter, then why as we boarded the plane to New York. I'd told her that Daddy was dealing with a lot with his uncle so sick, so he sent us home ahead of him. That he loved her more than anything and would meet us here when he could.

And like the innocent she was, she believed me.

I hated myself for that.

I spotted the New York City skyline just before our bus dipped into the Lincoln Tunnel and breathed a sigh of relief.

We were back to normal. Back to crappy public transit, dirty sidewalks, and cheap hot dogs. Georgian buildings and green lawns had been replaced by no-nonsense tenement housing and endless subway tunnels.

But we were home. I had never been so happy to see it in my life.

"FRANKIE, you can't hide from the guy forever. For one, Sofia's his kid too, and he deserves to see her. He deserves to know where she is. Not to mention, you don't want to be charged with kidnapping, you get me?"

It wasn't until nearly seven o'clock that evening, after Matthew had come home from being out with Nina and I'd finally allowed Sofia to fall asleep (the poor kid was exhausted, being on London time) that my brother and I finally talked about what happened and what had suddenly brought me home.

I sat at our faded Formica counter while Matthew opened a bottle of wine, poured us a couple of glasses, and proceeded to dispense advice threaded with legal action the way only a former prosecutor could.

I took a sip. "This is good. What is it?"

"Barolo. Nina's favorite."

"Ah." I put the wine down.

"Don't be like that. She bought some for the house, but it's to share with everyone. Go ahead and enjoy it."

I took another sip, but it didn't taste the same, knowing it was another gift from another rich person that we couldn't have possibly afforded on our own. "You know, if I learned anything this summer, it's handouts from rich people just don't work for me. I'm not fancy like you, Matthew. I'm not caviar and designer clothes and opening night at the opera. I'm grilled cheese and sweatpants and my favorite book on a rainy night. Simple."

Matthew didn't respond, just watched me with that particular look I imagined he implemented a lot when he was in court, cross-examining criminals. It said, clear as day, "Don't bullshit a bullshitter."

Whatever.

I sighed and reached for the wine again. I supposed I could deal with it. "Don't worry. I texted him when we landed. He knows where we are and knows we're safe. I told him I'd be willing to talk tomorrow." I checked my watch. "Well, tomorrow for him, since right now it's about one in the morning over there."

"Good. Because you know if he didn't hear from you at all, he'd be breaking down your front door."

I looked up. "You mean our front door? Or have you vacated too without telling me? So long, sweetheart, is that right? Hello, Boston."

Matthew heaved a long sigh.

"I wish you could be happy for us," he said while he turned his glass in circles, the only sign that he was the slightest bit nervous. "I don't have a job in New York anymore, and Nina wants to finish her degree up there. It's a fresh start for both of us. And we really need it, Frankie."

I couldn't deny him that, though the idea of living in a world without Matthew made my stomach tie into a series of ship-worthy knots. Sure, Sofia and I hadn't noticed his absence in our lives this summer, but what about now? I knew that once I got up the nerve to talk to Xavier, he would provide at least a modicum of child support, probably enough to pay whatever rent I ended up needing. But what would happen if things didn't pan out? Where would we live? How would we survive without Sofia's *zio* to keep us afloat?

What would *I* do without my big brother's sage advice on nights like these?

It was time for me to figure things out on my own. I just wasn't sure I could do it.

"Anyway, I did mean yours." Matthew gave me a knowing look, then rounded the counter and sat down on the other stool next to me. "The front door, that is. It can't have escaped your notice that the only things I packed are in suitcases."

I shrugged. I had noticed several bags already stacked near the front door and had chosen to believe they were empty.

"I thought that was just because Nina doesn't like your second-hand crap. She's pretty fancy." I held up the wine as if to demonstrate.

Matthew chuckled. "She doesn't. But also, I thought it should stay here."

I nodded. "I'm sure someone will buy the place furnished."

"Only if you want to sell it," he said. "Since now, the house belongs to you."

I jerked my head up. "What?"

He slid a nondescript piece of white paper across the counter bearing the title "Quitclaim Deed" in bold letters across the top. I turned it and scanned the legal language, picking up my name, then Matthew's, then the address of a local law firm.

"Nina paid off the mortgage," Matthew told me. "Not to mention, well, setting me up with enough funds that I could buy the house ten times over if I wanted. I know you just said you don't want handouts from rich people, but do me a favor and take this one, all right? For my peace of mind, if nothing else."

It was obvious by the way his shoulders lifted that he wasn't altogether comfortable with the arrangement. I personally thought it reasonable that Nina support Matthew, at least for a while, anyway.

She was rich as high heaven, and his involvement with her had cost him his job and livelihood in the city he loved. The very least she could do was make sure his bank account didn't suffer.

This, though...

"But the Red Hook house belongs to *you*, Mattie," I blurted out. "You bought it. You fixed it up. You poured your heart and soul into this place, and—"

"And it's *your* home," he cut in. "Way more than it was ever mine, Frankie. Yours and Sofia's. You've been here all the time while I was either at the office or spending half my nights in beds I had no business sleeping in. You know it's the truth."

I swallowed. My brother was selling himself short. That was also nothing new. Just like I knew he wouldn't let me argue with it either.

"I don't need it anymore," he continued with a pat on my hand. "I got something better coming for me. Nina already owns a house in Boston—a real nice one too, in a good neighborhood, close to her daughter's school. I got a family now too, Frankie. And you deserve better than the upstairs landing. Just sign the fuckin' paper."

I stared at the deed, which might as well have been made of porcelain, for how precious it seemed. "I—"

"Sign it, Frankie. I don't want to leave without knowing you and Sofia are taken care of."

"Pete," I said instead.

Matthew frowned at the paper, then at me. "Pete? Something about the basement tenant got your interest?"

I just shook my head. "No, I—what does he pay again in rent? I forget."

Matthew frowned. "Ah, it's up to fifteen hundred a month right now, with a ten percent yearly hike to match taxes. You'll get that money if you want to keep him, but I figured you and Sof might want the extra space—"

But I found myself shaking my head vigorously. "No, I just wanted to know so we could match it. I could afford that. I could pay you and Nina rent. Or maybe a mortgage, if you insist."

Matthew's frown deepened. "Frankie, honestly. We don't need it."

"I told you, I'm done with handouts," I said more viciously than I intended. "Mattie, this is so generous. More than I could ever express. But I think...I think it's time for me to do something on my own. So if you want to sell me the house, fifteen hundred at a time, I'll agree to that. But that's all."

His mouth opened like he wanted to argue, and I prepared myself for a cross-examination.

But instead, his shoulders slumped in defeat.

"All right," he said, withdrawing the paper. "I'll draw up the new agreement. Rent to buy. But the whole thing is always on the table if you need it. Don't forget."

"I won't," I said. "I love you, big brother."

His green eyes, which matched my own, shone across the yellow counter. "Right back at you, kid."

———

LATE THAT NIGHT, I crept into bed on the landing for what would be one of the final times, gazing around this tiny patch of my house. Down the hall, I could hear Matthew murmuring on the phone to Nina, whispering sweet nothings that made my whole body hum with envy and sorrow.

For a few brief seconds, I'd had that. Or at least I thought I had.

I pulled out my phone and turned it on. And, of course, there was a train of messages from the man I had fled just a day earlier, which I had absolutely refused to read other than to send him the one I'd told Matthew about.

> Xavier: Georgina told us you went back to London. Why didn't you tell me you wanted to go?

> Xavier: Did you make it back all right? The train should have arrived ages ago.

> Xavier: Jagger stopped by the house. Said there was no sign of you or Sof. Where the fuck are you???

> Xavier: Georgina just mentioned a pap saw you at Liverpool. What the fuck is going on????

> Francesca: Hey, we just got off a flight to New York. I know it was sudden, but it was really time to leave. We are safe at home in Brooklyn. I will call when I can.

> Xavier: You're in New York?!!

> Xavier: What the FUCK

> Xavier: Call me now, Francesca. I mean it.

> Xavier: Ces, please. We need to talk.

> Xavier: Ces, I'm sorry. I'm sorry for all of it. But you can't just run off like this. I thought you were done running.

They didn't end there. There were at least ten other messages sent throughout the night, alternating between spewing profanity-laced frustrations and shocked questions. But by the end, somewhere around two in the morning London time, he had apparently given up the fight. Just an hour ago, there was one final text, neither an admonishment nor a question.

> Xavier: Ces, please. I'm dying here.

I wiped my eyes. Fuck (and I almost never say that). But really, *fuck*. What was I supposed to do now?

Face the music, I supposed.

I pulled up Xavier's number and pressed the dial button. It was probably four in the morning in London, but the last text was sent at two. I had a feeling he would pick up anyway. And if we didn't have this conversation now, I probably wouldn't sleep either.

He answered on the first ring.

"Ces?"

He wasn't angry. There was no shouting. Just his deep voice, groggy, but not asleep. Sad. And desperate.

"Hey," I peeped. "I—yeah, it's me."

"Ces...I..." There was a long sigh. "I'm glad you called. I'm glad you're safe."

I twisted my blanket over my knees, then pushed it off, suddenly hot. "So, you're not...you're not mad?"

Xavier paused for a long time. "I was. I don't know, maybe I still am. But honestly, I understand why you left. Took me about twenty-four hours to get here, but I understand."

I tied a corner of the blanket into a knot. "You do?"

Did he realize I had seen him? Did he know I was perfectly aware of what was going on between him and Imogene?

"Yeah," Xavier said. "I do."

"Oh."

Lord, I was exhausted, but suddenly, all the anger and betrayal I'd felt upon seeing them together came flooding back. I wanted to yell. I wanted to scream, jump, punch a hole in the wall next to me. Suddenly, the entire trip seemed for naught, since I wanted to rush right back across the ocean and slap him across the face for humiliating me the way he did.

"I'm sorry for it," he said. "But it's the way it had to be. I'm sorry if I ruined things in the end."

My mouth opened and closed so many times I might've thought my teeth were chattering. In the end, though, I didn't know what to say. He had done what he'd done. And I had already made my choice to leave. It didn't really matter how either of us felt anymore, did it?

"I miss you, Ces. You and Sof. I'll always miss you."

I was silent for a long time. What the hell was the point of saying something like that *now*? "Well, maybe you should have thought of that before..."

I couldn't quite say it. Before you kissed Imogene. Before you made out with that stupid blonde Amazon. Before you crushed my heart in half.

No, it didn't matter.

Xavier just huffed on the other side of the phone. "I have more regrets than I can count. I promise you that."

"Okay," I said stiffly.

"But it was time for you to go back," he continued. "I can accept reality. I can accept that I'm not good for you anymore. Maybe I never was."

"Xavi—"

"No," he cut me off gently. "It's the truth. Look, I know we had something special once. And for what it's worth, I want you to know that I did love you all those years ago. Just like I love you now. But we aren't those people anymore. I'm not the man I was at twenty-seven, and you're not the girl I met in that bar. You don't fit into this life. Not because you're not good enough for it, but because it's not good enough for you. Or Sofia."

I could practically see him shaking his head as he talked. I was glad he couldn't see me. See the way tears were already running down my cheeks in currents. See the way my lip was trembling, my pulse quickening, face reddened with fury and frustration and sorrow all at once.

"I'm only going to break your heart, Ces. I break my own fucking heart every day, and I don't even try. I don't want to hurt you and Sofia more than I already have. So it's best you're gone."

I covered the receiver and hiccupped back a chest-deep sob. My throat ached, both with the need to scream and wail. I couldn't do either. Not with my brother and Sofia around to hear. This was my life, and always had been, and that, if anything, was the real difference between Xavier and me. I didn't have the luxury of flying into rages and screaming when things didn't go my way. I couldn't act on impulse whenever I wanted, whether that meant sleeping with random men or kissing women in my office.

I had to just sit with it. Feel it all deep in my bones. Let it all rattle and rage until eventually, like the current in a river, it too would pass.

If it didn't break me first.

"Can I ask one thing?" Xavier wondered.

I drove my nails into my knee. "What's that?"

"I have to stay here until Henry passes. Take care of the estate and keep things in line. But once that's gone, I'd like to come back to New York and see Sofia. Would that be all right?"

I softened. I was angry at Xavier. So, so angry. But he was Sofia's father—that too would never change.

"You're still her dad, Xavi," I said quietly. "Of course you can see her. Whenever you want."

"Good." His voice was soft too. "Thanks."

We sat on the phone together for a long time, not hanging up, but also not sure of what else to say. I had a world of questions and thoughts inside my mind, but none would come out. And yet, I didn't quite want to say goodbye either.

I had a feeling that would be goodbye to more than just a call. It would be goodbye for us. For good.

"All right?" Xavier asked sometime later.

I swallowed, tears starting to well again. "I—yeah."

"What is it?" he wondered. "It's all right. You can tell me."

I sucked in a breath. I had a thousand things I wanted to say. I wanted to tell him this was wrong. That I still loved him and always would, even if he cheated on me, even if he smashed my heart every day for a year. I also wanted to tell him he really was a bastard for letting us go so easily. That we were worth fighting for, Sofia and me, that fighting for the future was what families did, no matter how hard it got.

In the end, I decided to just say the final thought that entered my mind and seemed to linger. "I don't want this to end."

It was the most honest thing I could think of.

Xavier was quiet for a bit more, breathing heavily, to the point where I wondered if he was crying too.

But eventually, he answered. "Me too, Ces. Me too."

I swallowed, and it felt like my chest threatened to split in half. "I—Xavi?"

"Yeah?"

He sounded almost hopeful. Like I might take everything back. Like I might ask for another plane ticket, beg him to let me stay, plead for him to love me all over again.

He would say yes if I did. I really believed that.

But those were all just fantasies. This was our reality. This heartbreak. This goodbye.

And Sofia and I deserved someone who would fight for us of his own accord, not just because we begged for it.

"Take care of yourself," I murmured.

"Yeah, Ces. You too."

"Let me know when you want to see Sofia. I'll make sure we're around."

"All right. Thanks. And we can talk later this week. Figure out money for Sof, all that. I owe you a lot from years past."

I nodded, though he couldn't see me. "Right, yeah. Okay."

"Good night, Francesca."

I squeezed my eyes shut. God, this hurt so badly. "Good night, Xavier."

After the call ended, I stared at my phone for a long time.

In the end, I got up and did something I hadn't done in years.

One night, when Sofia was maybe six months, and we were still living in Nonna's attic, my little girl wouldn't stop crying. Nonna was on a trip somewhere with her friends, and my siblings all had work, thus leaving me alone at the house in Belmont with no one but a sick baby for several days. In addition to that, I was having a hard time breastfeeding and hadn't slept in days. I had never felt lonelier—or angrier—in my entire life.

People think postpartum depression is just sadness, but sometimes, especially when you're alone and trapped, it comes out as rage, plain and simple.

Sometime around two in the morning, I realized that if I didn't give myself space to break *something*, I was liable to do much worse.

So after Sofia nodded off at last, I took the baby monitor and marched out to the garage, mostly intending to scream my lungs out until my throat was sore. Instead, I spotted an open box of dishes—ugly flowered ones that I recognized as belonging to my parents when Daddy was alive and Mom was still halfway a mother.

Without thinking, I grabbed one off the top and hurled it onto the garage floor as hard as I could.

At the sound of ceramic splintering on the concrete slab, something inside me was set free. I grabbed another and did the same thing. And another. And another.

I worked through seven plates total until the warring ocean of feelings inside me had calmed to a mere pond. And then I took a deep breath and cleaned up the mess, then went back inside and curled up beside my baby to sleep until morning.

After hanging up with Xavier, a similarly vast ocean rocked inside me with a brewing storm.

I crept out of my bed and tiptoed down the stairs, careful not to wake Matthew or Sofia. This house's garage was mostly packed with things Matthew was taking with him to Boston, but when I got down there, I found the same box I had brought with me when Sofia and I had moved in, piled in the back on a few other things I'd never had the space to unpack from Nonna's.

There they were, the rest of the Mami's flowered plates.

Just the sight of them reminded me of her horrible article. Which reminded me of every other horrible thing anyone had said to me over the course of the summer.

The crying started immediately, emerging in choked, painful sobs that clogged the back of my throat. Memories of the rest of the summer flooded through my mind. Xavier's blue eyes blinking at me at the airport. His tender kisses that turned fiercely passionate in a second. Every touch. Every argument. Every betrayal.

Tears streamed down my face as I smashed plate after plate onto the ground.

Smash! That was one for kissing Imogene.

Smash! Another for my mother's betrayal.

Smash! Smash! Two for Xavier's temper tantrums.

Smash! Another for making me still miss him.

By the time I was finished, the box was empty. And now, so was my heart.

But I was back to being one thing again—Frankie Zola.

Third grade teacher and friendly neighbor.

Reasonably kind sister and beloved granddaughter.

And above all, one thing that would never change, no matter how many horrible words, thoughts, or deeds were thrown at me.

Sofia's mama. A really damn good mother.

EPILOGUE

ONE MONTH LATER

Xavier

Henry was dead. Had been for four whole days.

He held on a bit longer than the doctors thought he would, but a week ago, he was pronounced brain dead. And after that, once the ventilators were detached, he died peacefully in his room at Corbray Hall.

Now I sat in the office, waiting for the lawyers to come and clear up the remains of Henry's will, but also trying to determine who would be a useful steward if and when I decided to leave. I never wanted to play the duke, but here I was, having left Jagger to run the Parker Group while I was up to my neck in portfolio analyses and tenant bills and the infinite other small businesses that kept the estate and the Parker net worth running.

I hated it. And now it had become my life.

I stared up at the burnished walnut walls, outfitted with fancy woodwork, some kind of tartan wallpaper, and mini portraits of every duke there had been in the estate's history, all looking at me down their long English noses. My heavy bag hung still in the corner, unused for several weeks.

It was odd. Generally, I needed an outlet for my anger, but since Francesca left, it was as though she'd taken it with her. Anger and love for me seemed to walk a thin line. Both were based in passion, I supposed. And everything I'd felt passionate about had either died or gone back to New York.

God, I hated this room. Every time I was in it, someone died or was about to die, or wanted to die (if they were me, anyway).

It was here I'd first learned that Lucy had passed, informed by Father, with a smirk on his face. Like he knew it meant the inevitable, that I'd crack and marry Imogene Douglas and carry on the Parker line just as he wanted.

Then, years later, when Henry told me Rupert was gone, and I'd packed up and left for good, intent on never returning at all.

And again, when the nurse crept in to inform me that it was time for Henry to go.

Dead, dead, dead.

There was a knock on the door, and I perked up, ready to put on a slightly less miserable face for the lawyers.

Instead, Imogene Douglas walked in.

I frowned. "Imogene. I wasn't expecting you."

She shrugged and shut the door behind her. "I know. It's just, I was about to leave for London, you see. The summer's over, and I've got that job at Sotheby's, if you remember."

I shook my head. I didn't remember. But then again, I hadn't seen the girl in nearly a month, and at that time, it had been balls-awkward when she'd tried to kiss me, and I'd nearly chucked her across the room.

Daughters of viscounts do not care for rejection. I learned that fact with a very hard slap across the cheek.

"I know it's been uneasy between us," Imogene said. "But I wanted to check on you after hearing about Henry. We haven't seen you since—"

"You don't have to say anything," I told her. "It's in the past."

"Yes, but—"

"Imogene," I cut her off.

"I *know*," she said, rounding the desk to come sit on it next to me. "I'm not going to talk about the event. From before. I wanted to make sure you're all right before I go." She glanced at my computer screen and clearly caught the title in the email. "Is that from her? After all this time? Good lord, she really does not deserve you, does she?"

"*Imogene.*"

Something in my voice must have scared her because she got up immediately and went to sit in one of the club chairs on the other side of the desk.

I sighed. "Look, it's simple. You tried to kiss me, I pushed you off, and that was that. Forgotten. Done. But my business with Francesca is between me and her alone. Now, I'll thank you not to say another word about the mother of my child, all right?"

Imogene swallowed visibly. She really was a pretty girl. Nice enough, too. I could admit that, at least. But not at all my type, which was a small basket of curves that spoke frankly with a faint Bronx accent.

Imogene would make some bloke happy enough one day. It just wouldn't ever be me.

"Oh—okay, yes. All right." She stood. "If there's anything I can do—"

"I'll let you know," I told her. "The service will be in two weeks, in case you want to come."

She nodded. "Yes, of course. I'm sure Mummy and Papa will let me know the details. Xavier, I'm so very sorry for your loss."

I nodded. "I appreciate it."

And I did. But it wasn't her kind wishes or words or anything else I wanted right now. It was the woman who was currently five thousand miles away and wanted nothing to do with me anymore.

My God, what I wouldn't give to see her sweet smile right now.

To feel those deft fingers on my temples, neck, and shoulder. To feel her lush curves under my own touch.

Francesca really was more than a beauty. She was a refuge. And I'd burned down the whole thing.

Imogene left, and I stared at the email for a long time.

It was the first I'd heard from her in a long time. We sent texts here and there, usually just updates about Sofia or, on my part, requests to FaceTime my daughter. She was growing so bloody much. Could already pronounce her *r*'s and *l*'s perfectly. I was missing it all.

From my perspective, then, an email was more than just a check-in. It could only mean one thing: something bad.

"Man up, Sato," I told myself. "It's just a fucking letter."

Still, I waited. Until, finally, I couldn't take it anymore and opened the email...to find nothing.

No note. No "Dear Xavier" or any kind of signature. There was only an attachment, which I quickly downloaded and opened to reveal a photograph of a handwritten letter.

Messy and drafted on a wrinkled sheet of lined yellow paper, it looked like it had been crinkled up and tossed more than once before she'd finally got the nerve to take the picture and send it herself.

Very strange. Not that I didn't like looking at Francesca's elegant handwriting that looked somewhere between script and print. But it wasn't exactly a normal way to communicate.

I squinted, then expanded the screen so I could read the words properly.

Xavi—

Elsie called this morning to let us know about Henry. Please accept our deepest condolences from me and Sofia. She misses you very much but understands this is a terrible time. I did not have the privilege of knowing the man well myself, but I know you cared for him, and so he must have had a lot of something good to merit that.

I am so, so sorry for your loss.

I'm also sorry to have to complicate your life even more right now. But unfortunately, this can't wait. Because I refuse to repeat the same mistakes. You deserved better then, and you deserve better now.

You were right. I'm not the same girl you met five years ago. I can't be. It's why I left London. It's why I came home to New York. It's why I wouldn't stay to fight. It's also why I won't run from the truth anymore, even when it's hard.

So, here goes. The truth. Do with it what you like. Or nothing at all. I honestly don't expect anything, but you need to know, from the beginning, this time.

Xavi, I'm pregnant.

~~If you want, you can~~

~~I don't expect anything, but~~

~~Next time you're in New York,~~

Nope, that's it. I'm pregnant. I'm keeping it because if there is one thing in the world I know I can be, it's a good mom. At least this time, I have a bit of practice.

And yes, of course, the baby is yours. It could have only ever been yours.

All my love,
—Frankie Francesca Ces

TO BE CONTINUED
in LAST COMES FATE, coming June 2023)

ACKNOWLEDGMENTS

Holy smokes. Okay. So I know this book was supposed to come out, oh, Fall 2022, and many, *many* of you have been waiting patiently for it since then. And the only thing I can say is THANK YOU so much to all the readers who have been following Frankie and Xavier's story since then. I promise the next book will be out this summer, possibly earlier—it's already well under way! I hope you loved their next chapter as much as I did.

I also must give credit to the alpha and beta readers whose cheerleading never ceases to bring a smile to my face: Patricia, Dawn, More credit due to Michaela, who gives me choice phrases like "Christ on a Bike" and made sure my London tourist advice was sound, alongside checking the ins and outs of English society. You are priceless.

I must also thank my absolutely essential publication team: Danielle Leigh, my assistant, an absolute gem in less than lovely world; Dani Sanchez and crew at Wildfire Marketing, who always reminded me of just how many people were asking for this book; Emily Hainsworth, my lovely editor whose comments I live to review; and Marla Esposito, whose proofreading skills are top notch.

And most of all, to my family—Mr. French and our kids—whose support is essential to this life, and friends, specifically Jane, Laura, and Vivian, whose advice on all things bookish and otherwise I could never do without. I treasure you all.

xo,

Nic

www.ingramcontent.com/pod-product-compliance
Lightning Source LLC
Chambersburg PA
CBHW020312260626
47156CB00016B/2107